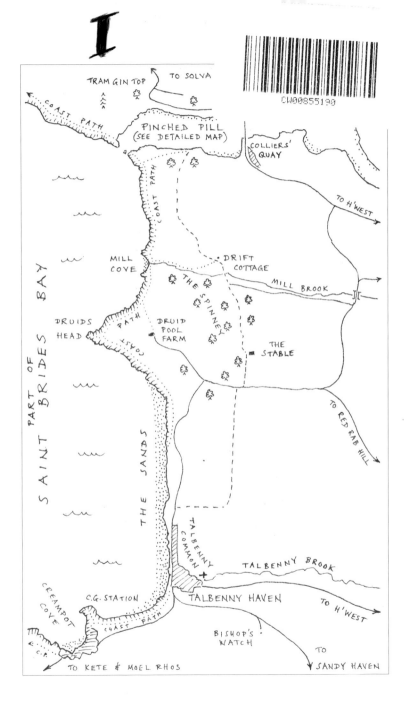

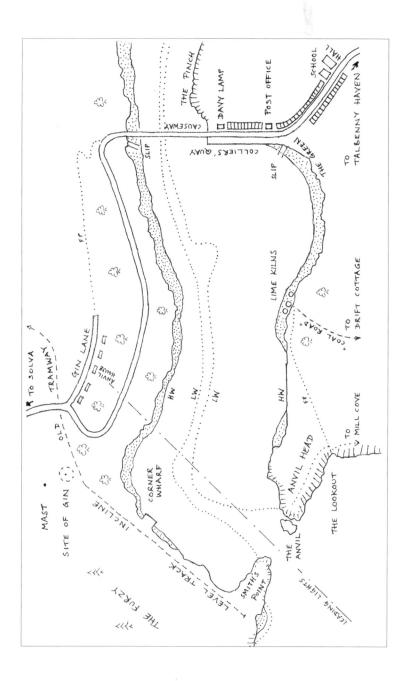

# *A Summer Break*

## *A Novel*

### *by*

## *Christopher Jessop*

**Springboard Press**

*This book is dedicated to people everywhere
who are having to stay in hospital,
and would rather be somewhere else:
may the Spirit of Story hasten your recovery!*

Published in 2014 by
Springboard Press
1 West End Marloes via Haverfordwest Pembrokeshire
West Wales
SA62 3BE
United Kingdom

**www.asummerbreak.co.uk**

ISBN 978 0 9928774 0 8

A CIP record for this title is available from The British Library.

Typeset in Perpetua 11 on 13pt

Printed and bound in Wales at

Gomer Press, Llandysul, Ceredigion

*Acknowledgements*

I would like to thank everyone who provided encouragement while I was writing this book; I am thoroughly indebted to the members of my "Tasting Panel" who read the manuscript and/or scrutinised the illustrations and whose comments – and corrections! – proved invaluable. Deserving of special mention are Sophy Cullington, and Penny and Amelia Bird.

My thanks, also, to everyone at Gomer Press for being so helpful.

This section would not be complete without my acknowledging the Pembrokeshire coast itself – constantly inspiring through the seasons, whatever the weather, by day or night.

*A Summer Break*

Drift Cottage, Norchard Mill Lane, via Talbenny Haven,
PEMBROKESHIRE
West Wales

Dear Reader

The events described here took place a long time ago, in 1980: I was a young girl, then.

When I was unexpectedly whisked away to Pembrokeshire that July, my mother had to stay in our home town because she had promised to flat-sit for someone. In any case, she'd planned for a daughterless fortnight: here was her long-awaited opportunity to try writing an adventure story.

As soon as that Welsh holiday began Aunty Jill, with whom I was staying, started sending daily postcards to Mummy – not just so she could be sure I was all right, but also because Jilly hoped that knowing what sort of things I was getting up to might inspire this would-be author; and, importantly, getting my news would assure friends left behind that they weren't forgotten.

I loved Pembrokeshire immediately: it seemed to free me, and everything was new. Once I had met Tracker and the other horses, the really exciting times began; from then on Jilly had to take great care over her reports, or Mummy might think I was behaving recklessly. I truly wasn't, ever; nevertheless, I did get into situations which were very tricky for me and my fellow adventurers.

The fact is, no human can survive without taking risks – and excitement and danger often go hand in hand. What's important after an escapade is to understand what made it perilous; thus you learn how to anticipate possible problems before you next do something similar. And there's this: only when you, or someone dear to you, has survived a close scrape can you truly realise just how precious and precarious Life is. That's also how most folk learn to not value possessions above people; however, having lost my Daddy when I was small, in 1980 that was an essential truth I already knew.

I must say this, though, lest you worry that this book – and its cover – set a bad example to young readers: it is true to its time. In 1980, people generally thought far less about safety than we do now: it was common to roar off in a car, never bothering to "belt up"; also, many folks went boating without taking lifejackets or even saying when they should be expected back. So, similarly, with horses and bicycles: we just got on them dressed as we were and headed off – and thus, I must admit, ran serious risk of suffering injuries, especially head injuries. A particular incident, which this story relates, taught me my lesson; I still shiver to think how differently that morning might have turned out.

I ask you, therefore, to please remember while you read that, as the saying has it–

### That was then; this is now.

One last thing...

You will understand that for the sake of privacy every name in this book is fictitious, and places have been deliberately disguised. May your imagination, thus freed, discover a unique and therefore such a special Pembrokeshire within these pages.

Sophy Solva

# CHAPTER 1

Sophy woke up so excited: the summer holidays were starting that very morning.

And she was ready for her first trip abroad: her packed suitcase stood beside the bedroom door. Inside it she'd written her Leamington Spa home address in felt pen – ending in WARWICKSHIRE, ANGLETERRE so there should be no confusion.

It was her mother, Carol Fossway, who'd stencilled S FOSSWAY on the suitcase lid: being a widow, she had to do everything Sophy couldn't manage. Her husband Keith had died three years previously; since then Carol had moved from the house Sophy had been born in to a flat near the town centre. Which was easier to manage, but neither mother nor daughter found life without Keith Fossway easy: both had loved him dearly, and would never stop missing him as long as they lived.

A quiet flat, in a quiet street. Too quiet, sometimes, making Sophy turn on her radio: pop music on Radio One if she was drawing, or painting, or playing with Lego or Meccano; usually classical music if she was reading. Or writing: she had a grandmother in Australia whom she didn't know well; nevertheless, Mummy insisted she pen occasional airmail letters.

What the flat needed, Sophy knew, was a cat. Some of her friends had cats; cats were much better than dogs because they didn't bark or yap or… And if they liked you (Sophy had such a knack for making cats like her) they could be very affectionate. Unfortunately, everyone who lived in those flats had to obey certain rules, including– NO PETS.

As well as cats, Sophy loved horses. Beginning riding lessons aged six, she'd gone pony mad: consuming pony stories by the ton, cutting pictures from magazines to stick on her bedroom walls.

Alas, regular lessons had had to stop when Daddy died. Making the aftermath of his death extra sad, because she had made good friends at the stables with the other girl riders and the grown-ups there. And she'd shown a flair for riding – not by being daring or competitive, but by developing a good understanding with every pony she'd ridden. She'd talked to them; they'd known exactly how to behave: great things had been expected from an older Sophy Fossway.

Happily, the girl's relationship with horses hadn't ended there: she was treated to a few half days of riding every holiday, and the previous summer she'd gone for a week's pony trekking in the Forest of Dean.

The perfect base, that campsite had been, beside the Wye: river swims first thing and again before supper; all rides along woodland tracks, well away from traffic. Although Sophy had got on well with most girls that week, she hadn't made special friends; however, she had fallen in love – with a strong little black pony called Romper, who'd been so empathic. She'd sent him a card at Christmas; back from the kind-hearted holiday people had come a photo of him in his box, showing her card stapled to the door.

Half past ten in the morning: in eighteen hours Sophy would be departing with her best friend Hannah Southam and her family: down to Portsmouth for an English Channel ferry to Saint-Malo, then another long drive to Brittany, the tip of north-west France, and a cottage close to the sea.

The journey, Hannah had warned, would be tiring and boring; however, tingles inside Sophy said that, because everything would be new to her, it should prove exciting: driving on the wrong side and breathing foreign air were such novel concepts!

And, being pretty good at French in school – as far as she'd got – Sophy was enthralled by the prospect of trying to speak it, in France, with French people. She had even memorised the continental road signs shown in Daddy's road atlas: this knowledge could be useful *en route*.

In fact Sophy was pretty good at most subjects; she liked her girls' school, and worked hard there.

Sophy thought she felt fine about going on holiday without Mummy.

She sometimes stayed overnight at the Southam's; happily, she was fond of Hannah's brother Bruce, who was much younger. Indeed, being an only child she loved doing the big sisterish things: bathing him, reading bedtime stories, hearing his (hilarious) prayers. Even, when Hannah's parents had been very busy (both taught at the University), getting him up and giving him breakfast.

Carol Fossway would cope by keeping busy, flat-sitting for the Fenny-Comptons.

That retirement development on the far side of Leamington was deadly from a child's perspective: it was a long walk from anywhere interesting, and any sort of exuberance (singing indoors, running in corridors, playing on lawns) was forbidden. The ideal hermitage, therefore: here Carol, utterly undistracted, would be attempting to write a children's adventure story – something she'd always wanted to do.

Yes, she'd be taking leave from work; but she had time off owing and the threat was, "use it or lose it". Meanwhile the Fenny-Comptons, owning rather choice antiques and oil paintings, so valued peace of mind that they would be remunerating her generously – *and* free food for the fortnight was being delivered to the door by eversogrand Ffyldes!

To help pass the time, Sophy was making Mummy a coffee–

Somehow unlikeable, the way the telephone rang.

'Hello, Mrs Southam.' Formality with Hannah's mum, because she was pretty jolly rich: Sophy wasn't supposed to know, but the Southams didn't expect any contribution to the cost of the holiday.

Was Mrs S reminding Mum about the very early start tomorrow?

It didn't sound like it: 'Mrs Southam, Sophy will understand. Give Hannah our best wishes, won't you? Do you think a visit…? No, not so groggy. Meanwhile, if there's anything I can…? We'll be praying for her, and thinking of little Bruce, too… Of course; goodbye!'

'Mummy…?'

Hugged, 'Hannah's broken her leg, I'm afraid: she slipped, giving Bruce a shower.'

'She won't die, will she?' Life without Hannah… It wouldn't be life.

'No, darling, I promise! But she's in such pain we, um, can't visit her in hospital until…'

No French holiday.

No point, though, in screaming, 'IT'S SO UNFAIR!!!' As she'd done uncontrollably over Daddy; it hadn't helped, nor had the door-kicking or toy-smashing. 'Poor, *poor* Hannah! And Bruce!'

'You good, brave girl.' And Mummy's best sort of huggy kiss.

To her room, there to quietly cry. For Hannah; for poor bewildered Brucie; for the lost holiday.

There was nothing redeeming that Good Old Mummy could say: instead of a foreign holiday with her best friend, the child now faced two weeks' incarceration in what she'd jokingly described two days previously as a warm mausoleum.

*Excitement kept Sophy awake very late last night; perhaps she'll cry herself to sleep.*

How Carol Fossway missed dear Keith: he, stoically sharing the difficulty, would have made coping easier – and straight away "put on his thinking cap". Also, whenever he'd said, 'Worse things happen at sea', he'd known what he was talking about.

In her bedroom, to his Merchant Navy uniform portrait, 'Help me, please, darling, if you can.'

A very quiet lunch.

At tea-and-biscuit time, the doorbell's trill: 'Aunty Jill, AT LAST!'

Plus a wicker basket whose tabby-shadowed interior said 'Miaow!'

Even before kisses, 'That's surely not Mogulus?'

'Au contraire, ma chère, he's pretty sure he *is* Mogulus.'

'Mi-AOW!'

Here came Carol: 'Then come in and close the door, so we can let the poor creature out!'

Sophy *loved* Mogulus.

Friendly and humorous, he remembered her straight away every time they visited; and whenever AJ 'phoned, there was his background accompaniment of purrs and mews – convincing the girl that the cat thought as frequently and fondly of her as she did of him.

But he wasn't AJ's cat.

Mogulus was only Jill's name for him: he belonged to her Cambridge-shire neighbours. However, much preferring her company (proof of good taste), he regularly sparked panics of two types in her house: 'Please-get-out-I'm-in-a-hurry!' and 'Am-I-sure-I-haven't-locked him-in?'

Here he was, though, eighty miles from home and cool as a cucumber about it.

Jill Ribblesdale and Carol Cropredy had met on their first day at university. Lancashire farmer's daughter reading Computer Science and only child of Home County teachers there to study English, they had clicked together like Lego.

Joining the same societies, they were soon taking turns to choose films, buy band tickets, decide on art exhibitions. At the first year's end they'd hitched to Cornwall and found jobs in the same hotel, sharing a poky room; for their second and third years they'd rented a flat.

Jill, still single, well paid by an industrial consultancy company, lived near Cambridge in a comfortable modern house and drove plush company cars—

Not any more.

Carol Fossway exploded, 'WHAT?'

'That's my Morris Minor traveller outside; I call it Bumble. No more job, ergo no company car.'

'Mummy, AJ did say she had Special News, when she 'phoned about calling in today.'

Mischievously grinned, 'And there's more yet; but first puis-je have encore une tasse de thé, s'il vous plaît? Bumble isn't quick, alors Puss et moi have been on the road a good long while.'

'Maow!' he concurred, from Sophy's encuddlement. Who asked, 'AJ, why keep using French?'

'Parce que it's jolly good practice pour les vacances. Which reminds me…' Jill peered into her bag and pulled out a sleek one-piece swimming costume in fashionable turquoise: 'Sorry it isn't wrapped, but I've been so rushed. I *loved* the colour the moment I saw it; Mum told me what size. May you have such a sunny summer break, ma belle, that you wear it every day!'

…

'Sophy, are those tears…?'

Still just young enough for AJ's lap and poshly-perfumed cuddling, 'The very worst sort of summer break, eh, sweetheart? I feel awful, dropping in to announce my good fortune.'

Carol frowned, 'But you've just lost your job!'

Jill winked, 'If that's what I said, it's not what I meant: my job lost me.'

The coin took time to drop: 'You *resigned?*'

'It's a heckish long story, Carol.'

Puss plonked onto Mum, Sophy sprang kettlewards: 'How long? Another pot of tea long?'

'MAOW!'

Jill nodded, 'He's right: if you want the works, it's please-may-we-stay-the-night long, actually.'

Sophy must hug Jill round the neck: 'You and Mogulus couldn't, could you?'

'We can – if Mum lets me buy fish and chips to save her cooking.' *Plus some decent vino from the off-licence.* After sharing which, Carol might approve Jill's idea about an alternative holiday for her everso disappointed daughter.


## CHAPTER 2

Jill had kept in touch with her primary school teacher, Miss Gwinear.

Sent to that village in England's northern hills by unfathomable bureaucracy, this bluestocking from Wales had felt obliged to stay at the edge of its society; typically for a lady teacher then, she'd never married. She had taught with a fair firmness; a keen walker and gardener, she'd loved to crocodile her charges out of that clatterlatch lobby: wellingtoned and dufflecoated, bare armed and gymshoed, as suited the season. And these outdoor-playing children, many with family ties to the land, had been surprised – to hear the hidden stories of quite commonplace plants or creatures, by learning the newly-discovered reasons behind natural occurrences.

So much that community had owed to this slim, sparkly-eyed lady, she for whom the village library had frequently requested hefty volumes from Central County, the only local subscriber to certain learnèd journals. Unsurprisingly it wasn't only the Ribblesdale's girl who'd sent Christmas cards, and made a point of calling round from time to time.

Always "Miss Gwinear"; always "Young Jill". Through grammar school, with advice about GCE revision, then choosing A-level subjects (mutual regret that Art must be dropped); on returns home from uni, when Miss G had clearly envied the gallery visits but, surprisingly, also wanted to know lots about Jill's coursework and had enthused about the potential of 'these new machines'.

On retiring, Miss Gwinear had moved away. It had been the tradition of her era, but she would have gone, anyway: a cottage in West Wales, neglected but dear to her heart, wanted for occupation. Many in the village were deeply saddened; only Jill Ribblesdale, come home specially, had said at that party, 'Au revoir, Miss Gwinear.'

Cornish by ancestry, minerals in the blood, Miss Gwinear's great-grandparents had moved to Pembrokeshire, the furthest west county in Wales, early in Victoria's reign.

Great-grandfather had managed a mine hard by Saint Brides Bay, its anthracite highly praised by maltsers and nurserymen. Alas neither investment nor Celtic ingenuity could compensate for faulting and thin seams; once steam power began making fuel from deeper, more abundant deposits in Carmarthenshire easier to win and cheaper to deliver, the writing was on the wall.

The mine having closed, Grandfather Gwinear had farmed in a small way. Apprenticed to a millwright, from water and steam power his son had progressed to internal combustion engines during the Great War; moving to the county town, Haverfordwest, his skills were soon in great demand. Eventually running his own garage he had died heartbroken in 1947: both sons had been lost at sea in '42. His ten-years-younger wife hadn't joined him in Parson's Garden until 1965.

The sole heir, Miss Gwinear had sold the house, investing its proceeds wisely. Thus in 1970, aged sixty and very fit, she could afford to retire 'if you're prepared to live frugally,' her Kirkby Lonsdale accountant had cautioned. She'd replied, 'Do you think I was ever paid much?'

Before making announcements she'd journeyed to Pembrokeshire and had a builder survey her grandparents' cottage, untenanted some fifteen years. A reasonable sum would make it "drier and brighter, only slightly bigger, and still pretty basic." This had chimed perfectly: small, well-lit, and unsophisticated had been her lot in North Lancashire.

In 1968, graduating with first class honours had guaranteed Jill Ribblesdale a good job.

The Cambridge firm had promised her variety; she'd shown aptitude for on-site troubleshooting at factories, process plants... After applying her diagnoses, companies' computers had often delivered better performances than originally promised. Very quickly given a car and an expenses credit card, Jill soon had a well-stamped passport. Tackling ever tougher assignments, she'd earned pay rises and bonuses – but had never been in the office often enough to manage or train others. Had she ever time to reflect, therefore, she might have seen how lonely this line of work would always be: bearing huge responsibility, always operating alone, it had similarities with being a ship's pilot.

She'd bought a handsome house near Cambridge; not to would have been madness. But she could be away for weeks; and, as for visiting Lancashire or seeing Carol... At least she'd attended the wedding and, crucially, satisfied herself that handsome Keith Fossway deserved to be her best friend's husband.

May 1974: a rare day off, catching up in the garden "assisted" by Mogulus – thus she'd nicknamed her neighbour's boisterous kitten...

From its first ring the telephone had sounded implacable; to annoyed Jill's amazement the acrobatic tabby's miaows had seemed to mean, 'Answer it!'

An apologetic Julia, her boss's secretary: 'Oil refinery... Milford Haven, I'm afraid.'

No niceties from him: somebody else's control system; the owners had lost faith. 'They're not processing anywhere near enough oil; daily that's costing blipping thousands! I know tomorrow's Friday, but you must set off first thing. Their demand is, you work 'til it's fixed; they'll pay bonuses if you're quick.'

Nonchalantly, 'Just make sure Julia books a quiet hotel with good room service. And when I finish there, I'm not rushing back: that's a day's drive away.' Instantly Jill had determined that she would visit Miss Gwinear: Milford Haven was in Pembrokeshire. Ringing off, she'd soliloquised, 'It will be so good to see her again.'

'Maow!'

Jill had jumped, quite unaware that he'd come in: 'Have you been listening?'

'Prrp!', rubbing around her legs.

'Well,' she'd stroked, 'you were right and I was wrong: that was a call worth taking.'

Quickly she'd proved the computer itself to be operating faultlessly; however, chauvinistic oilmen taking much convincing re temperatures and pressures not properly transmitting to it, not until the Sunday's dawn had that red-eyed Crisis Team departed a smooth-running process unit.

Early on the Monday Jill had returned to an again hissing and rumbly oil works, chimneys belching like Bolton cotton mills as the place strained, flarestacks flaming hugely orange, to catch back up. A report telexed to her office, she'd headed for Haverfordwest to buy a local map, and a monster box of crystallised ginger (her ex-teacher's weakness).

Locating Drift Cottage had been difficult; Jill hadn't minded, for the pleasure of finding Miss Gwinear even fitter looking, really brown, and – this, the huge surprise – tending that prolific garden barefoot, in a short sleeved man's shirt and ragged-cut shorts.

Never a suit-wearing sort of consultant, after an elated reunion over Proper Coffee, Jill was back into oil-scented jeans and "bovver boots" for veg tending while catching up with her old teacher – who, though content with retirement, was getting worried about what Man was doing to the planet.

And, her own solitary existence having been obligatory, Miss Gwinear hadn't liked this "girl" paying for her success by having little social life, nor even taking all her leave entitlement. Mind, it was understandable that holidays involving much travel didn't appeal; also, Jill being Jill, soon after returning to the family farm (now managed by cousin Tom), she'd be asking, 'What jobs are there?'

Jill had fallen in love with Drift Cottage: it was in a lovely setting; the place felt right, spiritually; 'And,' she'd laughed, 'it has no 'phone.' After lunch she slept until, 'Sea's still pretty cool, but you'll be glad you swam!'

It had been, and she had been; she'd ended up staying the night. Over supper she had learned about tar from ships coming in on the beaches, hence Miss G's coolness towards the oil industry; on the other hand Jill's voluntary work, helping a bird charity with computer analysis of migration reports...

There'd been much talk of the wildlife thereabouts – and then, the neighbours and other locals; for here was a community the lady had no reason *not* to get involved with. Her grandparents having been well regarded, nearly everyone was pleased to again have Drift Cottage occupied by a Gwinear, and being well cared for.

After a rare night of profound sleep, Jill had left next morning promising, 'I will be back.'

Thereafter she had visited two or three times a year, always staying at least a couple of nights, and ever learning more about environmental issues, as they were now being called; thus she came to be much more circumspect about what went on at the places where she worked.

Badgered by guess who, the Ribblesdale girl had tried a specialist holiday offering oil painting tuition; her interest in art rekindled, she'd enrolled for figure drawing evening classes, thus meeting members of a local art society. An excellent impressionist portrait of Mogulus, entitled *My Neighbour*, had sold in a flash at the private view of their next show!

Meanwhile Jill's attitude to work had changed: though given increasingly swanky cars, she'd felt less and less like jumping aboard to zoom off and sort problems out, despite the financial rewards.

Eventually she'd started pondering an academic career move: how about someone experienced in making computers do what industry wanted teaching *applied* computer science at Cambridge...?

But one rainy evening in February 1980 when a (now rather portlier) Mogulus had invited himself round for some exquisite Telemann on her new hi-fi, the telephone had rung. A crackly Pembrokeshire accent: the husband of one of Miss Gwinear's friends...

Mile after guilty mile, driving to the funeral: she'd not visited for eighteen months.

A full church: friendships aplenty Miss Gwinear had made – or re-established – in ten years at Drift Cottage; and how uplifting, those early, early daffodils! Proudly Jill Ribblesdale had stood beside that coffin, its greensharp wreath woven with ancient sentiments; in an accent unfamiliar to those ancient stones, such gratitude she had shown to her early guide.

Who, on retiring, had stopped talking of Jesus Our Friend as teachers of little ones should; she had no longer, either, worshipped on Sundays "Regular as t'Milk Train", as the saying at home had been. Told during each stay at Drift Cottage that 'Doing Outdoes Praying', Jill had agreed; however Miss Gwinear had to have recently communicated with the vicar at length, for he'd well described the lady.

But why his talk of work left undone? Having in 1970 made Drift Cottage a much pleasanter home without compromising its character, Miss G had since transformed its garden marvellously.

On the service ending, thirst had flowed people away through wearily squeaking Georgian gates, over the slate slab spanning the stream, urnwards into the village alongside its sea-seeking descent.

But the vicar had stayed Jill in that churchyard corner. While a robin had busied about the grave's heaped soil he had complimented her oration; then, perceptively, 'You're amongst many, Jill, in wishing there'd been a chance for farewells; do be cheered that Miss Gwinear didn't die lonely.'

'Not found by the postman, then?'

'Yes; but the stable's little dog was there, and Martin was sure it had been with her all the while. Though my Head Office decrees that animals have no souls, many are highly sensitive, hmm?'

Allowing herself a quiet chuckle, 'Miss G would definitely have agreed.'

'Spend some time here quietly, now; when you're ready, Alice Williams is waiting by the porch.'

'Oh, good! I do want to talk to her.'

'You'll accept her offer of a bed tonight? Because, I tell you, she'd blockade your BMW if you tried heading home today – and you're so obviously tired, I'd be standing beside her.'

'Thank you. And, about just now: you've made me…'

'Less unhappy?'

Yes.

Her death had rendered Miss Gwinear's close friend Alice Williams distraught; husband Hector had telephoned Jill first with the news, and later the arrangements.

Now the lady could smile again: 'From the heart you spoke, girl: nobody would have doubted.' Then, peering within the young woman's eyes, 'To clear the air: you're upset, I reckon, about not having come down for a while; but recently hadn't Miss Gwinear stopped asking when you'd visit?'

Jill had flinched, 'How did you know?'

'Because she went the same to us all, locally. They dried up, those postcards saying, "Do drop in soon!" or, "If you're going to town…". And, you'll see, she pretty much stopped gardening.'

Astonished, Jill had been.

'Quite so; which leads one to conclude…'

'That there'd been a sign – a warning?'

'Her father died in his sixties, nor did Grandfather G make old bones, I'm thinking she had a turn, and instinctively knew what it presaged. I picture her first being resentful; then, there might have come gratitude for being given a warning: let's hope, hmm?'

'So Miss Gwinear abandoned gardening to give something else priority? Gosh, that whatever-it-was must have been important! Mrs Williams, have you any idea–?'

'Let's talk more later; I'm delighted you're staying the night, by the way.' Pointing past the lych, 'It's time you were at the Talbenny Arms, being the nearest Miss Gwinear had to next of kin.'

'B–'

'That's how she spoke of you, m'dear.'

Jill hadn't known. She frowned, 'Um, did *everyone* call her Miss Gwinear, as I did?'

'She asked us all to, even those who'd known her since toddling age. So proud, she was, to be a Gwinear; also, the name Millie had aged badly: feeble spinsters in Ealing comedies, hmm?'

'Sadly true, because Millicent Gwinear has the loveliest ring.'

'It literally does; and so appropriate, for a girl with metal-mining ancestors! Anyway, "Miss Gwinear, Retired Teacher" commanded great respect in Pembrokeshire and further afield; although, when she signed protest letters "M. Gwinear," most editors assumed that was a man writing.'

'Protesting about what?'

But here was the hotel: tea or sherry; sandwiches and cake; hands to shake; again and again, 'We'd hear so much about you, Jill: your letters were very important.'

Gradually the noise had lessened; one by one hovering bachelors and polite children were beckoned by the WI matrons so that homebound pockets could receive napkined sandwiches or foil-folded cake.

Alice Williams had finally ushered over a charcoal-suited black-tied brown-briefcased white-haired gold-spectacled gentleman: 'Mr Prendergast.'

With crispest Cambrian diction, 'Miss Gwinear's solicitor', then a nearly Prussian almost-bow; 'The hotel manager's office has been placed at our disposal.'

A wax-sealed envelope, addressed in copperplate script: 'Miss Ribblesdale, I'm glad you aren't rushing away, because you should read this carefully; as for taking it in, it's good that you're staying with Alice and Hector Williams, tonight.' Bowing again, 'I'll be outside, in case of questions.'

*My dearest Jill*

*How can I look forward to your receiving this letter? By hoping that it will encourage you.*

*Recent pains warned me unmistakeably: no huge surprise, considering Father's weak heart.*

*The doctors suggested something; had it failed, my remaining life would have been miserable. So Nature knows best: far better snuffed straight from blazing like Daddy than lingering, a feebly guttering candlestump.*

*It's disappointing, having little time left; but now every day delights. What's more, my final memories should be of Drift Cottage – or, if I'm very lucky, Mill Cove.*

*Dear Drift Cottage: it's yours; and my possessions, save odds and ends going to friends. Having neither nephews nor nieces, I can't see anyone contesting: any relatives left are so distant, we've never met. You may do with the property as you wish, of course; however, while your life's busy and you've that lovely house in East Anglia, please don't act hastily.*

*Jill, I was very fond of you as a pupil: it delighted me, your keeping in touch during the Grammar years, then all through university. So many letters, dear girl! All so eagerly received.*

*Even after graduating, you still thought of me as your teacher; it was your initial visit to Drift Cottage which triggered the change. By then you had learned much for yourself: that made you more than my equal. Thereafter you taught me, which experience I deeply enjoyed. Your clearing that hurdle, Jill, allowed us to become much closer; leaving you Drift Cottage is my thank-you for that precious friendship.*

*It surprised you, how I changed after coming home. Firstly, regarding behaviour, I was only reverting: having two brothers, I grew up a tomboy – only reluctantly answering to Mother's "Millie", much preferring Father's "Gwyn". Then, there came my revelation: the unpleasant truths about what we're doing to this planet.*

*The Dear Earth! Such fortune, being sent to your beautiful part of Lancashire; again I was lucky, leaving before they pushed that detestable motorway through the Lune gorge. Saddening, then, to return to this precious coast and find shores filthed by plastic rubbish, and oil tanker tar.*

*The pollution at first depressed me: nothing could be done, I was told. The County Council ignored my Mill Cove reports: they don't even class it as a beach, never mind a "Leisure Shore" (hateful term!). But, inspired by a Woman's Hour* special called **Taking The Initiative**, I decided to clean it single-handed; and, should the binmen refuse to take what I collected, I was resolved to somehow get it dumped on the steps of County Hall!

The next day some well-dressed ladies out walking discovered me in my oldest clothes, gathering tar balls; amazingly one immediately improvised driftwood tongs, and asked for a fertiliser bag...

Thus I met dear Alice; I'll explain later why she's my Noble Conspirator – and, also, why I've not disclosed that fact before, nor details of our conspiracy.

Jill, please keep Drift Cottage at least a year before entertaining thoughts of selling or even renting it. Come down whenever possible, always calling on Alice so you get to know her better – and the Madocs, for one couldn't wish for better neighbours.

Or – why not let the Cambridge house? (From beyond the grave, unlimited cheek without fear of rebuke!) It's not too mad an idea: you've shown such potential, you should try painting full time.

People like your pictures so much, would that strategy be very risky? After all, you've worked so hard for them, your firm might grant a sabbatical. If not, (cheeky me, again!) suppose that you resigned, gave painting a serious go, then decided it wasn't for you: surely you'd easily find another job – perhaps an even better one, who knows? As they say, better to have tried and failed...

Consider the satisfaction from your balancing the scales of Fate: as the door of opportunities closes on me, it opens to you. Therein an Enlightenment elegance, I submit – and Enlightenment is the motive of the Jill I've always known.

Why should you try painting?

Both of us in our work have strived to make things better. However...

Hating to seem grumbly, I never mentioned this – but when in my later years younger teachers promoted newer, supposedly better methods, I struggled to agree.

I never punished gratuitously; but children aren't just like young animals – they <u>are</u> young animals! As a farmer's daughter, you knew that kittens and puppies needed cuffing or shutting in after misbehaving. Children in certain moods weren't to be reasoned with; bad behaviour couldn't be tolerated: youngsters spoiling things for their classmates, exposing themselves to danger, indeed. Also, occasional smackings or detentions gave everybody else the soundest of reasons for not crossing the line!

*Although pressure from the "modernists" was growing when I retired, I went feeling great sadness, assuming that my opportunities for making things better were over. But when, soon after arriving, I decided with Alice that something must be done about marine pollution, we realised that to improve every beach huge changes were needed: therein, a cause no less pressing than children's education.*

*We started to clean beaches; also, to question why they got filthy: thus began a frustrating yet fascinating journey. Of course crude washed ashore because tankers discharged it; but why jettison stuff so valuable that it caused wars? We and other concerned people wrote to oil companies, then shipping lines, then politicians...*

*And I realised: though no longer teaching children, in trying to clean up the planet they would inherit I was working as hard as ever on their behalves. Furthermore, considering their views about how I had been teaching, I might in the eyes of other adults be doing more good for children as an "environmental protestor" than I ever had before!*

*Why did I play down this environmental work when you visited?*

*Lest I compromised you: many folk think that to care for this planet is to be unswervably anti-industry. That's untrue; although I do hold that consideration of not just what an industry makes but the processes it uses and the pollution it creates can change one's mind about whether a product is a Good Thing. The point is, government departments and companies probably have files on Alice and me; so, if they could have proved I was "raising issues" with you...*

*Anyway, Jill, I didn't want you to feel bad about what you were doing, or whom you were working for; but now I'll put my cards on the table – in the hope you won't think me cowardly, seeing as you can't answer back.*

*Having learned much, I have sometimes bitten my tongue when you've enthused about your achievements. Of course I've always been pleased, dare I say proud, of how you've improved things for your industrial clients; nevertheless sometimes I wanted to shout, 'BUT WHAT'S IT ALL FOR?'*

*Anyway, you've recently had similar thoughts: as you said, all very well improving the efficiency of plastic bag making, but our roadsides prove that Man can't be trusted with the blasted things!*

*This from an ex-teacher might surprise you but, ultimately, Nature matters more than people.*

*Why?*

*A question to answer a question: what would humans do without a healthy planet to live on? And, of course, you've spotted the paradox: even for someone who insists they don't give a fig about Nature, it takes scant intelligence to realise that caring for the Earth is enlightened self-interest, because the Earth is all we've got.*

*So — how to make people care for the Earth, especially pro-Establishment sorts who are deaf to what they consider airy-fairy messages about "loving the forests"?*

*Art might provide the answer.*

*You've never tried abstraction, or anything in the modern vein: your trees are identifiable; your landscapes portray real places; your water either lies still, or moves, as it should. Truly your art holds a mirror up to Nature; thus, it should have wide appeal: people love being reminded how beautiful the world is.*

*By painting you might achieve a lot: a well-displayed picture influences many more people than just the individual who buys it. Thousands might see your works in an exhibition; if, in time, prints are made of your paintings, they can become very well known — and, literally, can educate the masses.*

*For the meanwhile you might do more good by painting instead of consulting: it will surely be some time before Industry starts seeking good brains like yours to help cure its smoking chimneys and its dead rivers — and Commerce its dirty ships. So while Big Business overcomes its inertia, why not be furnishing th e world with well-messaged Ribblesdale canvases?*

*Thinking of opportunities and appropriate moments...*

*You would have said, had you met anyone special: without accusations of selfishness, therefore, you may steer any course. Indeed, Jill, your not having met anyone evinces three good reasons for taking the plunge.*

*Firstly, your current job and "lifestyle" aren't inductive vis-à-vis meeting interesting people. Secondly, you are a lovely girl and I'm sure you <u>will</u> meet someone one day; pragmatically, why not get painting out of your system, if it thus transpires, while fully at liberty? Thirdly, working as an artist might improve your chances of meeting a suitable man...*

*Or woman, indeed: that's how some girls are, and love is love. (As I've <u>always</u> known, and accepted, if you were wondering).*

*Whichever, I pray you do find someone — and that, whatever the circumstances, you'll be blessed with children to raise; for I'm sure that you'd prove as good, as lovingly practical in your approach to that challenge, as your own dear mother was.*

*Drift Cottage will welcome you, Jill. I was always happy here as a child, and as a grown woman visiting my grandparents: unlike the Haverfordwest house, it never felt stuffy. And so contented I have been throughout my retirement – especially when you've came to stay and said how happy both house and setting made you. But do sell it if you're <u>sure</u> it can't fit in with your plans, and thus give someone else the chance to love it.*

*In the meantime...*

*Lest you anticipate finding it too quiet here (except for when the "fly boys" come over – can't imagine ever preventing that pollution!), herewith some thoughts.*

*Never having driven, I loved our excursions: to Saint David's, to Kete with its sailing, to beautiful Moel-Rhos Sands – what inspiration along that coast, too! Over to Skomer to see those precious puffins and the other seabirds; less ambitiously, just for meals at traditional inns. Spring, summer, and autumn, if you've spare time there's plenty to do (always taking a sketchbook, of course); and, despite appearances, there's never nothing happening in Pembrokeshire in winter: historians, natural history enthusiasts, amateur dramatists, environmentalists indeed... Many groups hold winter meetings – some staging events, others planning for next year.*

*While I'm not a television person – and you don't often watch – you bringing your super radio down made me realise what I've been missing; so stupid, when friends who have good aerials receive concert broadcasts with marvellous clarity. Plentiful culture, beamed in from Prescelly; Irish broadcasts there to be picked up, too, they say!*

*A very different tack, now: animal companionship. On the pretext of saying hello, naughty Taggle will come scrounging biscuits; you don't like dogs much, though. So – could you borrow your neighbours' cat for a try-out? If a reasonable traveller, he could enjoy a seaside holiday; being amenable, he'd soon settle in, giving you a good idea if a feline studio assistant would make for a happier dauber (me and my assumptions, again!). As for my friendly birds... Even if he can't be trusted (Tinkerbelle collar required?), we both know – down to discipline, again! – that kittens can be trained.*

*Enough of my planning your life, Jill; before signing off, though, there is something spiritual, and quite serious, to explain*

*About my attending church recently and befriending the vicar: bluntly, I want to lie with my ancestors, his graveyard's nearly full, and a non-worshipping*

Gwinear mightn't be admitted. Shameful, yes; but more pacific than claiming a Celtic blood-entitlement to be interred there and, dismissing the diktats of some jumped-up modern creed a mere two millennia old, causing a Druidic confrontation!

Yes, I could have had my ashes scattered at Mill Cove, except the County Crematorium is utterly soulless. So tedious a drive there, too, wasting petrol and time. And, anyway, I've a suspicion...

The pagan Celts revered flowing water: springs were sacred.

Not coincidentally, many Pembrokeshire churches are close to water sources – never a primary Christian consideration. Furthermore, some feature Roman gravestones re-used as foundation blocks: the Christians appropriated Roman temple sites; the old stones came in handy.

And the Romans...?

Talbenny Haven church, hard by that prolific spring: surely a place holy since prehistory – revered, maybe, by the first folk arriving after the ice retreated? I believe it was a people well preceding the Celts who initially enclosed the issue to exclude animals and create a formal shrine.

Eventually the Romano-British took its holiness over, you might say: Caesar's invaders cunningly did that at Bath, tacking names they knew onto those of the natives' incumbent deities.

Thus Saint David's disciples did little different, claiming that to be Holy Ground – knowing that their new religion would stand scant chance of succeeding, if it challenged ancestral beliefs by proposing anywhere else as a better place from which to seek assistance from their novel Almighty.

The best news: I'll be buried alongside my Cornish antecedents – resting in a place forever considered by local people the correct, the best for that longest of sleeps.

Only visit if you want to, Jill, never because you feel you must: I hope to become a spirit, if I'm to exist at all afterwards. Wandering freely, but unobtrusively, thus able to follow your progress wherever Fate takes you.

What will you do? I do hope spirits can't divine the future; how horrid, knowing what will happen for all the rest of time. The curse of immortality indeed: I'd far rather have to wait and see.

The time I've spent thinking about you, my love! I hope to follow the progress *of a truly happy Jill Ribblesdale; if leaving you Drift Cottage allows you to live a life more fulfilled, I shall be the merriest of spirits drifting from that spring which, excellent omen, always chuckles so contentedly.*

*About fulfilment: I am extremely glad to have been a teacher at your village's school; I so wanted to do good for my country, feeling such an obligation because both brothers gave their all in the war. Nevertheless it could have fulfilled me more, doing something else – writing, perhaps. Might possibly have enriched very many lives, had I been any good...*

*But on reflection, only since retiring have I realised which subject an author ought to concentrate on – whether tackled head on, or alluded to: this beautiful planet, and what we are so sinfully doing to it. Ah, well; perhaps after I've found my feet in the next life I might put in to come back as an "eco-scribbler", some time hence!*

*An awfully big adventure, indeed.*

*May Drift Cottage make you happy, Jill – whether you keep it or sell it.*

*Re-iterating what I said to you, what I said to every pupil leaving my Primary classroom for the last time – whether they were listening, or not...*

*DO WHAT YOU THINK IS BEST – AND DO IT THE BEST YOU CAN.*

*With all my love, dearest Jill*                    **Millicent Gwinear**

*P.S. (Heavens, the number of drafts I've done, and <u>still</u> I leave something out!). This is a terribly selfish request – but then again it isn't, for I don't ask it just on my behalf.*

*I doubt many Gwinears are left in the world; should you have children, my dear, might you give one the middle name Gwinear? And, when they're old enough, explain to them why? You never know – it might bring them Cornish luck!*

*P.P.S. I've just remembered: the cat who cheers you up is called Mogulus. Good old Tabberius Mogulus Maximus. Well, please don't decide <u>anything</u> without consulting him: I'm convinced he has wisdom – even if he can, as you put it, act the twit at times!*

# Chapter 3

They cleaned the screen; then for the oil, tyres, radiator, screenwash, battery, brake fluid...

'Mum doesn't always do all this.'

'But such a precious cargo she carries: you! Everyone should take an engine driver's care with their passengers' lives; ergo they must guard themselves against harm, too. In fact, even selfish people should want other road users to keep safe: nobody can predict who'll suffer in an accident. However, what some folk think is safe, dawdling on main roads, isn't.'

'Because people act recklessly, trying to overtake?'

'Exactly!'

There'd clearly be much brainy talking this holiday; *But let's have lots of activity, too!* Going outside beat the pants off being indoors, *And gardening's much more rewarding than housework.*

Basketed, Mogulus went aboard. Then wellies; and walking boots; a winter jumper, too: you can't tell with seaside summers. Against prolonged rain, Sophy's holiday homework.

'Darling, I'm sure you'll be helpful; you know you're going as a friend, not a guest.' Hugging, capturing that fine hair's sweetness, 'Enjoy yourself!'

Sophy hoped Mummy couldn't sense her second thoughts; always, those, even before the loveliest of happenings.

From the car, 'Prraow!'

The girl beamed, 'Now it's official: we three will have fun.'


Time for Jill's have-we-forgotten-anything ritual.

Carol's arm was round her ever-taller daughter's waist as they surveyed the well-packed Morris: 'About not calling Jill "Aunty" any more: thinking of her now as an older friend should work, seeing how you two have clicked this time. Thus – this is so important, darling – you mustn't bottle anything up. If you feel ill, worried, unsure for *any* reason, say so. Never be embarrassed: Jill remembers being a girl, and knows that at your age uncertainties can take you over uncontrollably – a bit like blushing, hmm?'

True; but wasn't it reassuring, her putting the point so well? 'Righto, Mum! Anything else?'

'As the adult, Jill's responsible for you; but she's also our special friend, and this is a brave move she's making: please look out for her, hmm?'

'Understood.' Because Sophy watched over her mother. She kissed, 'Good luck, Mummy; I won't tell you to work hard. Rather, will you promise to not frazzle yourself, trying to write **War and Peace** in a fortnight? Take time off for walks, and other things.'

Jill rejoined them, brandishing her toothbrush: a good omen. 'By the way, Carol, we know it's to be a children's story—'

Sophy's old-fashioned expression.

'Begging your pardons, a story that children should enjoy...'

That was better.

'...Any thoughts, yet, regarding the plot?'

'Actually, although I'd scribbled some scenarios, none of them really lit my fire. But, on waking this morning...'

Jill and Sophy chimed, '*Well?*'

'A girl finds herself, complete surprise, setting off for Pembrokeshire adventures.'

Sophy bubbled, 'My story!' Then frowned, 'How do you know I'll have any?'

A Blackbeard finger under her daughter's chin: 'Because adventures is what coasts is all about!'

Another frown: 'But how can you predict what—?'

'Adventures,' Jill exploded, 'must be like surprise fireworks: when, without warning, one starts fizzing, nobody knows what to expect – but it might be a massive bangflinger!'

Round as her daughter's, Carol's eyes: 'Good stuff, Jill! Should *you* be trying writing, too?'

'Happenstance,' the friend scoffed. 'Stubbed my toe on a wordnugget, that's all.'

Seatbelts, buckled. Ignition on, petrol clickling into the carburettor. Jill leaning across: 'Carol darling, a missing message mustn't vex you: sometimes, a mouse eats the letters.'

Sophy boggled, 'Really?'

'Miaow!'

Setting the choke, 'Is somebody saying the little darlings won't dare raid my letterbox again?'

'Mauow!'

Whirring the starter, 'Puss, we'll hold you to that!'

Hannah's dad's Jag fired up like a jet, VOOOFF! Stumbling from slumber one pot at a time, Bumble settled to a sewing machine tick-rhythm. Jill showed Sophy the oil pressure and amps climbing: 'Always check 'em, sweetheart!'

'Safe journey, both!' ... 'Miaow!' ... 'Sorry, Mogulus: you, too!' ... ''Bye, Mummy!': a wavelet, ending with fingertips touched. ... 'A bientôt!', letting the clutch out...

And away, exhaust bugling fruitily as Jill whoopsclonged first into second.

She must know straight away: 'AJ, *do* mice destroy your post?'

Jill grinned, 'A corner's nibbled, occasionally... Actually, the saying's a jokey Pembrokeshire way of admitting you've overlooked a bill, or haven't written back to someone. However it's not unknown,' she nudged across, 'for folks from away to swallow the story whole.'

Sophy sniggered: country people hoodwinking townies wasn't so different from schoolchildren redherringing an unpopular teacher.

'Miss Gwinear often trotted it out to confound officious outsiders; but her not answering most post wasn't down to laziness or oversight: too preoccupied with campaigns, she was.'

The girl was intrigued: what had so engaged this quirky-sounding old lady? Then, 'AJ, how can mice get at letters you *send*?'

'Martin The Post isn't obliged to; but, agree where you'll leave them, and he'll collect stamped letters when he comes delivering.'

'So if he didn't call for a few days, your missives might become mouse mattresses.'

Jill laughed, 'Spot on! And aren't those good words your mum might do with using?'

'AJ? Will my, um, exploits really be interesting enough for Mum's story?'

'Think, now: aren't the great-to-read-about scrapes which story children get into pretty hairy?'

'Like the night expedition in **Swallows and Amazons**?'

'Exactly: nobody knew where they were; nary a lifejacket: your mum would have had kittens!'

'Maow!'

'So you're saying that whatever things I get up to in Pembrokeshire, even if they feel exciting at the time, those story ingredients will need spicing up to make a decent meal for a hungry bookworm?'

Eyes fixing the approaching roundabout, 'Exactement! And to turn your exploits into a rare old yarn, Madame Fossway must apply her excellent imagination to invent loads of *extra* episodes.'

It *was* excellent: when Sophy had been younger and life had had more time, great stories had been spun along car journeys, during after-bath dryings, towards the flagging ends of walks.

'Anyway, writing the beginning to set the scene will take some time; meanwhile, we'll regularly transmit action reports back to Leamington HQ, for The Author to embellish out of all blooming recognition.'

'Brilliant!' Such contributions would reassure Mummy that they were right behind her project; and, visiting poor Hannah – often, Mum had promised – she could tell of Sophy's Welsh doings.

'And as we mustn't,' Jill must nudge again, 'hand Carol Fossway, famous-author-to-be, her Prize Winning Novel on a plate, we'll only forward bare bones, leaving her to do the fleshing out.'

'That's essential, or the result might be too much like a report she'd compile for work.'

'Fellow expeditionists, we have a plan!'

'Prraow!'

'Mind, my love, militarily speaking we need a Plan B. Here's the scenario: you're that busy adventuring, our situation reports fall behind; The Author signals asking why. How to reply?'

'Um, "Sometimes, a mouse eats the letters"?'

'MAOW!'

No: better not use that excuse. And, in fact, neither would condone any deception: consciences giving them no choice, they'd have to keep sending news home, come what may.

An excellent view of the road ahead, and the Morris's cruising speed allowed contemplation of passing countryside, even distant scenes.

Compared with the back of Hannah's dad's mileroaring Jaguar, superlative: nearer to being a lorry driver's mate, this was.

Lifting a plywood flap on the dashboard, 'The one thing I would have really missed from the BMW; as I'd paid for it myself, I kept it – and made this lid, so Burglar Bill shouldn't see.'

A very good stereo radio which played cassette tapes.

'Choose something, sweetheart.'

Hating to squint at tiny titles, a grab: 'Mozart piano concertos?'

'Lovely!'

Beelining the nearest motorway junction, with yellow nudging red revs Mr Southam would have, "LIFT OFF!", blasted straight for the outside lane, ignoring horns and flashes. Jill, heading for Stratford on Avon, said that they'd avoid main routes where possible: she hated their pressurised impatience. But the same speed limit applied on B roads so, if the way was clear, 'Let's put on steam!' – always sensibly, though: loaded, Bumble didn't corner brilliantly.

On adverse gradients progress was... Stately, the friends agreed.

Pilot Jill had listed the route; Navigator Sophy checked progress. It helped pass the time; also, 'You'll be pathfinding us round any hold-up before other folk can work out where they are!'

Through the Vale of Evesham's market gardens; now west, appropriately Elgared, past Worcestershire's orchard pears and plums. Then Herefordshire: red soil, russet barns and oast houses, ruddy beef cattle. Ranked hop poles, too, their plants not yet tanging the air beery with frothy flowers. And rows of trees, busy filling bullety malachite apples with sharp juice; which, sun-sweetened in ambering August, crushing Autumn's presses would seethingly extract against cider's thirst.

The radio's Morning Story as they wheeled into the Marches, here broad barley and wheat valleys whose air was history-hazed; then, at a river bridge, The Beginning of Wales.

Now deep valleys began, castle-defended between abbeyed Black Mountain and bleak Beacon ridges. These latter edged the northern extent of southerly industries: mining and metals which, chimneying the sunrays brown, had long since fumed those high tops treeless.

No choice of route, they must now join the smoky spattery cattle lorries and hill-dragging caravans. This busy trunk road, linking Westminster to Fishguard, farm to market, Gloucester's ice cream factory to Cardigan Bay cafés, coal merchant to pensioner, brewery to tavern cellar, shepherd and panting collie to flock, suburban street to campsite.

Luckily in tedious traffic here came *Just a Minute* – as and when Sophy's dextrous tuning could unhide its signal amongst those farmhoused hills. Although the youngster did wonder, was Kenneth Williams sometimes genuinely rude, and not pretending, for all of Britain's amusement?

Brecon refuelled Bumble through a petrol crane swung out from the street side: 'Pity you're too young to remember steam locos: this reminds me of watching them watering.' That county town's portly policemen sported silver-embellished helmets; Jill's image of attracted lightning blowing off constabulary pants and boots detonated a fit of passenger's titters.

At army trucked Sennybridge Jill sent purse and girl for cod and chips: 'Supposedly the best for umpteen miles.' All the way to Trecastle Mogulus's nose approved noisily while Sophy lapped them warm in the rug; by a once-magnificent coaching inn Bumble peeled off...

And climbed and climbed and climbed, finally finding a hushing edge of heather-islanded spruces, with lumber stacked beside. Jill's handbrake-ratcheting declared, 'LUNCH!'

Three souls, alone.

A buzzard-soared moor; peaty air, enhancing the meal's indeed deliciousness. After, skirt-tucked Sophy paddled the tea-coloured stream; poor Puss must promenade undignified by a dog lead.

Foil-wrapped apple slices, hot from Bumble's exhaust manifold, then Thermos coffee: 'Whatever happens later, we've had a square meal, hmm?' Showing her Mate the atlas, 'We've quiet back roads right through to Carmarthen – via Carreg Cennen Castle, if you like.'

Sophy *did* like: stony, tangible History on a blue-distanced scramble-up-to-it crag. Didn't like, must hesitate down to, the horrid dungeon cave; but, silent far below, escarpment-shed water winked silvery.

After, long strides down to Cream Teas and, 'My very first Welshcake!', warm from floury griddling.

They passed signposts to little Bethlehem whose post office travellers busied in December, keen to have Christmas cards uniquely inked. More castles along the Towy valley; an old railway route, too, level crossings still gated after twenty years. As if those ivied halts and peeling signalboxes believed that nostalgia's tank engines could somehow return…

Ah, but omnipotent Merlin would, for certain, waking when needed from legendary slumber up there – or was it up *there?* – beneath that perspicacious ridge.

A folly tickled them; Sophy loving the name, Golden Grove received Jill's crinkle-lipped agreement; eventually they met the Swansea traffic, and a hugely busier road.


To describe Haverfordwest, "pretty" wasn't optimum; nevertheless many workworn buildings were pleasingly proportioned.

Certainly its well-wagoned railway station, and its depots, merchants' yards, and Regional Dealerships told you that, from far around, here was where people headed to get things – up to and including redyellow combine harvesters. To get things done, too: there were workshops, vans proud to be SPECIALISTS IN…, tall townhouses with brass plates beside bellpulls.

This river was the C-l-e-d-d-a-u; you pronounced it, approximately, "Cleth-eye". Crossing a handsome bridge, 'We're beginning the end of our journey: welcome to West Pembrokeshire!'

The landscape didn't suddenly change; it did become easier, though, to appreciate small lush fields and modest woods, because the road to Saint David's was much quieter than the A40 they'd been back on since Carmarthen. The atlas showed Sophy why: that spate of cars and lorries was rushing to Fishguard Harbour and the FERRY (V) across Saint George's Channel to Rosslare in the Irish Republic.

*No point in thinking about the ship I should be on – so I shan't.*

The sun was low, but Sophy wouldn't feel tired: her window tasted air so fresh; *and* that was an interestingly patterned sky. Also, cottages hereabouts intrigued, so different from Warwickshire's; indeed, would Breton houses have looked more unusual to her eyes? With whitewashed low stone walls and crouching chimneys, they were roofed with tiny slates; always small, mostly square, the windows which peered back at you.

Bumble winked to turn West, and the scenery swallowed them: between high banks, little more seen than tarmac leading to the next bend – plenty of them! – and ever-reddening mackerel clouds. And this lane was *narrow*: Jill had to shush beside sheafy grasses – they seed-showered Sophy's seat! – for an approaching car.

A farmyard; a startled collie to brake for: it bounced about, bark-biting headlamp beams, until wearily collared by a slippered lady.

As Bumble humptibumped a bridge, poor Mogulus grumbling, Jill patted Sophy's knee. 'Almost there: that's our brook we're crossing.' Afterwards crawling, she wheelhauled onto the narrowest track Sophy had ever travelled. Even taller banks brushed both sides at once; how little used was a route whose middle grew such lush grass, the car's underside squashed rustlingly along?

Suddenly, a safari's worth of flying things: tiny sparklers, monster moths, crazified barrel-bodied beetles out-droning the engine – and flitterjinking, looping, suppering bats.

Jill snapped off the headlamps, 'Whoops, sorry!' Now their grey-green craft navigated a mist-scented green-grey gloom, meandering indignantly spinking blackbirds.

Two fields southwards, an impressive roof outline; then ahead and to the left, a rising sky-wall of trees into which corvine silhouettes kept papercindering down. 'The spinney!', Jill sighed. Entering its jackdaw-racketed silence they came to a gate; on stiffjointy legs Sophy yawned over. After Bumble had eased through she called, 'I'll follow!': the cottage couldn't be far.

Stealthily through the green coolth… This was a bridge over that same brook, surely: sideless timber beams, swirl-ripples mirroring that raspberry sky; a damp darkness of soft flutters, nothing frantic: no car now, incomprehensibly flaring the air yellow.

Woodland tapered into brighter gloaming; beside where a field gate ended the track, Bumble was ticking cool. Between apple trees came happy mews, then a milk-whiskered Mogulus.

Hawthorn trailed tendrils of dusk-dulcing honeysuckle; she tiptoed, then stooped, to scent flowers rich and pale. The path curved…

Once a pair of dwellings, Drift Cottage's cream-painted frontage had four white windows in cornflower surrounds, and two blue doors;

chimneys at each gable end balanced the central stack. It wasn't so squashed-looking as some places they'd passed, and that roof was steeper than most.

'Aha!' From the western end wall one glass pane peeped... *A spidery loft, or a proper attic?* The latter, she hoped: that looked a lovely window for gazing from. No to distant views, though, because of the hedgy surroundings; but, appreciating privacy, *I don't mind.*

Mogulus-urged, she went right round the back: there was the kitchen which Miss Gwinear had added. Jill, emerging with mugs on a tray, motioned Sophy to its patio.

'So quiet here!' Save for sated Pussy's rumbling.

Sandwiches gone, 'A walkabout, taking our tea?' One without Mogulus: he'd already gone off on Jungle Patrol.

'Not much of a garden, I'm afraid.'

'AJ, it's *huge*!' The flat's courtyard was tiddly.

'I meant that Miss Gwinear let this place go well before... Beforehand. So far, I've just had it scythed; unfortunately everything was that tangled, most flowers got scalped in the process. Hence nothing but green and trees, without looking carefully.'

'But don't the glades make perfect disappearing places?' *I wish I could hide outside at home!*

Jill nodded, 'A pattern of privacies, the poet might say.'

'Prettily put! Anyway, AJ, won't here have to stay simple, because you'll be so busy painting?'

'Aye, but I mu'n't do nothing: there are Miss Gwinear's fruit trees to care for.'

'Lucky you, growing your own apples.'

'And pears, and damsons, and greengages, and plums.'

'WOW!'

'Blackcurrant bushes somewhere, too.'

'I *adore* blackcurrants! Oh, good old Miss G!'

'And her grandparents.'

Quietly, 'Amen.' Then, firmly, 'Roses apart, growing fruit beats the pants off having flowers.'

Jill chuckled, 'A chip off the Keith Fossway block, and no mistake!'

Proud nods: 'If you can't eat it, don't grow it! But,' the girl conceded,

'Mummy's flower garden helped her a lot, afterwards: while I was off school, she loved our tending it together.'

'I'm so lucky with all the wild blooms, here: early in spring daffs and primroses seem to explode from every sunny bank; and, Sophy, the scent…!'

'AJ, is that water gurgling?'

'There's a stream, just beyond that hedge.'

'Your very own – how fantastic!'

'It drains the drift mine which gave this cottage its name.'

Flummoxation: 'It isn't called Drift Cottage because…?'

'That's what everyone assumes, as it's just a short half mile to the shore. Drifts, by the way, aren't vertical shafts; they're bored sideways, like railway tunnels.' Jill pointed, 'Long ago, the one *there* produced anthracite: high quality coal.'

'It sounds a really interest–'

'Sophy Fossway, *under no circumstances* shall you go looking: from time to time Miss Gwinear heard a rumble, meaning that another section of mine roof had collapsed.'

'Hugged with huge sincerity, 'I *promise* to not be tempted.'

'GOOD! Now that stream feeds into the Mill Brook, but I haven't yet discovered how. Maybe one day, when my Garden of Many Glades is complete…'

Foreman-like arm-folding: 'Soonest started, soonest finished: Mum said I must pull my weight.'

As the girl sank her tea refill, 'Properly arrived, now? Soul caught up with your body?'

'That *is* how it feels, AJ! And for you?'

'Yes, thanks; but, when I was travelling, my two parts hardly met each other. And wasn't your Aunty Jill a ruddy fool, seldom taking all her holidays?'

'Hmm. …Um, may I look for the stream, now?'

Four feet wide; maybe a foot deep? Gin clear water, but its stone-lined channel was a colour between yellow ochre and burnt orange: 'Amazing!'

On the far bank, a quaint thatched structure. Bouncing the plank bridge, Sophy went to peer…

Jill, returning with towels, 'Primitive facilities, didn't I warn?'

Yes; but Sophy had already used Tŷ Bach ("The Little House"), Jill's stone-built outside loo – and truthfully commented, 'Millions pleasanter than the School Camp toilets.'

The Shower Hut, this was: just foot-pumped stream water, sprayed from a watering can rose. Jill beckoned; then, stepping inside after Sophy, 'One pumping while t'other washes is much the easiest way.'

Feeling 'scrupulously clean', Miss Fossway finally crossed the threshold.

Knowing Jill's good taste, pleasing décor was a cert; but, even this late in the evening, 'AJ, it's *so bright!*'

The artist walked the girl around: 'Miss Gwinear stipulated a skylight for the kitchen; I was immediately struck by how well it worked. Now the dining room has two units, *voilà*, because it'll double as my studio; and, to save on electric light in the study…'

In what had been the east cottage, a bookshelved and desked den; through it, you reached Jill's bedroom. To the dining room's right, a low-ceilinged parlour, rugs and comfy chairs, where a woodburning stove presided: 'Here's The Snug; and it truly is, when that's lit! The attic above, by the way, is your bedroom.'

'Oh, wow! How d'you reach it?' She'd seen no stairs.

Back in the dining room, 'Unlatch that cupboard door.'

A pine staircase, where the old hallway of the west cottage had been. It turned left, climbed straight, then twisted right…

White ceiling slopes, timbered sturdily. That one western window; on the chimney's other side, a built-in bed with roll-under lockers. Left of the stairhead, curtains hid a hanging rail; opposite was a washbasin.

Jill called, 'The taps'll work when we're fully plumbed; it does already drain, so you can take a jug up.'

'Just like olden days.' Stepping back down, 'AJ, it's perfectly sweet.'

'Aye; noisy on wild nights, mind, being in the roof – and, with respect, there's Warwickshire windy and Pembrokeshire windy; but maybe you'll get accustomed. Anyway it's The Snug for cosiest sleeps, every time, if that stove's been lit.'

'Even in summer?'

'Sometimes, sweetheart, here's like the Pennines: all four seasons in a day. And with other weather moods, you might want brightening up more than warming up; whatever, one should always try to be amused by the Pembrokeshire climate, even when it's a study in cussedness.'

Sophy yawned, 'More contrary than a crosspatch cat, eh?'

Straight off, Jill pointed: 'Tŷ Bach, first; next, cocoa; after, teeth; then, I think you can guess!'

Kneeling before the open window, featherily falling air felt her freshened skin lovely.

In that bird-murmured blue-grey gloom, beyond the spinney did a horse whinny? And was that faraway slow breathing sound the sea…? *I'll pray, get into bed, then listen some more.*

Instantly asleep.


# Chapter 4

A slate-shuddering, tummy-jellifying roar.

Animal instinct buried Sophy deep in her bed: *What just exploded? Not Drift Cottage, thank goodness. So – has the old mine collapsed?*

The sensations diminished; she emerged. *Certainly not an atom bomb.* According to a TV documentary she shouldn't have watched, even indoors with eyes closed the flash could blind you.

*Halleluiah!* For there was AJ, humming along to Handel on Radio 3. Also, birds were belting out songs. *A thunderclap, perhaps?* She only saw cloudless blue, but maybe—

Another explosion-or-whatever – *Sweeping over, like a wave!* She sprang to the window.

Not a nuclear bomb; but perhaps a nuclear bomber, streaking away unbelievably low.

While registering a raked tail and sharky wings, her senses fixated the two stabbing cones of blue flame: The Voice of Fire it was, shaking these floorboards and pummelling her torso.

Austrian, Jill guessed; emphatically Art Nouveau. Its technique was so bold, the artist suspected that Sophy's nightdress was an early century original. And quite feasibly: Carol had always had the canniest eye for secondhand gems.

Emphasising Sophy's willowy frame, from the hem parallel viridian stripes climbed either side of the back panel. They splayed at hip level and then interwove, culminating in stylised golden tulips: embroidered across the shoulders, these perfectly complemented that tumbling hair.

For a fast-growing girl, its spring theme was so apt; *At the very least, I must draw Sophy wearing it*. And, if she'd pose in it for a painting...

Aircraft now inaudible, the girl turned: 'Oh, hello, AJ!'

'Were you shocked? I meant to warn you last night, but you were already away with the fairies.'

'Where do they come from?'

Inappropriate, a tease re fairy origins. 'The Americans operate our local airbase; low level exercises seem compulsory for visiting 'planes. But I do wonder if spinney-pruning is a game of dare the high-ups don't know about.'

*Which puts Drift Cottage at risk!* 'What sort were those?

'F-111 bombers: Vietnam War era. Nothing noisier!'

'I wondered, were we being atom bombed?'

'Oh, *sweetheart!*'

Sophy hugged back, 'Only until I heard you humming downstairs; then I felt disappointed.'

'*What?*'

The girl giggled, 'I meant that, being exploded awake, I couldn't remember my dreams. I like working out their meanings at breakfast-time – only Mum often grumbles that there isn't time.'

Stroking hair, 'Assuming your weird and wonderful recollections don't get exploded in future, as *we* needn't rush breakfast, you can sift through them with me.'

'So 'planes don't come over like that all the time?'

'Sweetheart, no. We civilians shouldn't be in the know, but those F-111s leave tomorrow.'

'Thank goodness: their blue flames are so noisy, they're shaky.'

'Not subtle, afterburners. The usual patrol 'planes and choppers aren't anywhere near as bad; they don't buzz us, either.'

'Big helicopters can be jolly rackety.'

'I happily tolerate the regular flying: yes, the American men hunt Russian subs, but they also give every assistance when the RAF helos carry out sea rescues – or airlift folks to hospital, if snow closes our roads.'

A pacified Sophy pointed, 'Russian submarines, out there?'

'British territorial waters apart, anyone may go anywhere in the sea; I think the Marine Patrol 'planes go beyond the continental shelf, where Ivan has plenty fathoms to skulk in.'

'I wish he didn't do that.'

'The non-volunteer Russky sailors would probably be with you; life aboard can't be much fun.'

'I thought people only got conscripted during wars.'

'Here, yes; behind the Iron Curtain…? But, heavens: such serious conversation, Miss Fossway!'

'Thinking in new directions gives me a lovely feeling, because Daddy encouraged it.'

Jill waited… 'For breakfast, boiled eggs and buttery brown bread?'

'Brilliant choice! So – what to wear, AJ?'

'For a bit of exploration, shorts: you'll get some sun on those lovely legs.' And Jill turned–

'AJ, thanks so much for inviting me; I hope I'll fit in.'

'Sweetheart, you already do: your walking the last bit home yesterday confirmed it.'


Over a stile; off across the neighbouring meadow, climbing out of the Mill Brook's valley.

The bright breeze exciting her heart, 'May I run about?'

'The hay's been taken; you'll do no harm.'

Away Sophy sailed with arms wide, letting her legs decide where; Jill's camera clicked.

The sky above the spinney opened; girl now looping figures of eight around artist, they together composed a nonsense poem: with every crossing, words added.

The second field, and a far blue ridge appearing in the north-east: the Prescelly Hills, which folk insisted were special – and not just because of proven links with Stonehenge. You couldn't see much else, though: these hedges weren't like those edging Midlands fields. Here, land was enclosed by broad banks, grass-profuse and wildflowered; on top, sky-scratching thorns and sinewy gorse.

Still no sight of the sea: 'Oh, Grr!' Although, tantalisingly, shossles sometimes sounded, and that westerly azure sky surely stretched a briny horizon. But, 'Ah, well!', for today was lovely.

The third meadow draped a ridge; then they were gated into a bosky steep descent, agreeably hummed by bees. And, 'I think I can see water!'


Pinched Pill was a small sea inlet. A part-wooded valley gave shelter; the kinked mouth weakened approaching waves because it faced south, not straight into Saint Brides Bay. On the pill's south side clustered the hundredish cottages of Colliers' Quay.

'Picturesque!' But disadvantage Sophy, still aching for a *proper* sea view.

The hamlet's shoreside buildings stood on The Pinch, a rock outcrop: projecting far into the waterway, it had dictated the limit of navigation in olden days. The coast road originally forded the pill here, but since 1830 vehicles had crossed on a squat stone causeway with stooped arches; nevertheless some travellers still halted at the inn, The Davy Lamp, to "wait for the ferry".

In Colliers' Quay Post Office they bought milk, food basics, blank postcards, and stamps.

Holidaymakers thronged a nearby patch of sandy shore; Sophy wondered, why not walk to another beachlet? Some weren't far; all were quieter and cleaner.

Jill murmured, 'Not so handy for the shop or the pub.'

'Hmm.' Their shapes suggested that many sunbathers regularly broke from basking to visit both.

Colliers' Quay: the name told its history well. Jill described coastal sailing ships – built flat-bottomed for sitting out low tides – delivering limestone for kilns, or pit prop timbers, then loading coal from the nearby mines, 'ours included'. Today's backwater (tourists' cars excepted) had one hundred years earlier been a hive-like hub.

'Did carts bring the coal?'

'From other workings,' Jill nodded; 'but that drop we came down is so steep, trains of ponies with pannier baskets brought anthracite from our drift. Hard work, but preferable to hauling tub wagons underground, I'm sure. The ponies' return loads couldn't have been that heavy, because of the slope; mind, they'd have *hated* carrying lime: even a slight dusting can be horribly irritating.'

'Poor things!'

'Compassion, please, too, for girls and boys your age who worked underground.'

After coffee, 'AJ, when can I see the sea…?'

Crunching crabshells, along the pill's southern shore; though wooden boats drawn above the tideline by antiquated windlasses looked unlikely to ever sail again, they and those contraptions could yet prove utile as picture subjects.

Sophy's 'miniature castles' were derelict lime kilns. Fiercely hearted with tight-tamped coal, these had converted limestone, which is calcium carbonate, into calcium oxide, known as quicklime. Builders had used this straight from "burning" to mix mortar; slaked into calcium hydroxide by adding water, it had sweetened the land for better potato and barley crops.

Industry, then; now silence, save for the creek's garrulous small gulls.

A footpath climbing obliquely was soon furnishing views far beyond the causeway: at the pill's head was a reed-edged lagoon which curved out of sight to the south-east, behind The Pinch. Dry yet awhile as the tide hadn't long turned, wading birds dotted its rivulet-creased mud.

Looking down on the kilns Sophy imagined stone stacked and smoke emanating, and had all those old boats in fine early century fettle readying for the tide; she also pictured large vessels, masts tree-tall, beached beside the causeway. Wagons descended the main street heaped with precious coal, while horses strained different loads the other way; trains of basketed ponies hoof-clinked quaywards, nodding wearily. No humans sun-idled down there, back then: all worked, some cursing the heat. Hammer and saw of ship repairs carried upwards; dull gunpowder booms echoed down valley: miners, enlarging one of the adits. In the adjacent field, people hoed – and over there you could forget the fast ruthlessness of tractor attachments; instead, bending backs picked and dug while other folk followed, tidying up. Going barefoot, some children were planting whatever went in next; others had jobs bird scaring, or leading horses while–

'Whoa, sweetheart!'

The girl jumped: how long had she been soliloquizing? 'Um, Mum recently read me some Daphne du Maurier passages, describing Cornwall in the old days; jolly inspiring, they were.'

'Well,' Jill knapsack-fumbled, 'you've proved that here's the *perfect* viewpoint for a painting recreating the past. Maybe a diptych – a triptych, even: two or three pictures which, hung side by side, create a panorama. Oh, clever you, and good old D.D.M! I bet that was ***The Loving Spirit***.'

'And bits of ***Frenchman's Creek***; both are on my must-read list, now.'

'Of course.' Pointing up the path, 'You needn't wait while I do a sketch: The Lookout isn't far.'

So Sophy scampered…

'THE SEA!'

The southern sweep of Saint Brides Bay and, by furthering your eyes beyond that headland – that island, perhaps – you could even see, onyx expanse, the Atlantic Ocean.

For how many hundreds of years – how many thousands – had people been climbing to this spot? Certainly soldiers had stood watches here in the last war: over there, ivy invaded a concrete pillbox. As for those much older bramble-humped walls – *Something to do with cannons?*

Yes.

Hating tall car parks, even bridge parapets, why could Sophy calmly contemplate from one hundred unguarded feet small swell flourishing over shattered rocks? *Funny things, human brains.*

Indolently bobbing, here came a boat: the one cap-and-fag bloke's slow oarsplat, the other's trailed line jigging glintily–

A catch! And, cigarette ear-wedged, urgent coiling-in.

Two fishes, brilliant in deep-peering viridian lightshafts: swerving, twisting…

Dead. So vicious, their gunwale-whacking before that gill-bloody toss onto the bottom boards: 'Poor things!' However, *I bet they'll be delicious.*

*Isn't it reasonable, asking AJ how much longer?* So, off that bottom-warming pillbox roof and—

After leaving Jill she'd never glanced back, and here she'd only stared seaward…

On the valley's other side the coast road climbed northward through unkempt woodland; some way above it the land shelved, and spaced along this natural terrace were five properties. Weathered stone facades, lichened roofs, unostentatiously *right*: Georgian villas, readily recognised by a Leamington girl.

Viewing the pill entrance and the bay beyond, they must enjoy full sun; the land's continuing rise afforded shelter from north winds. The middle house, optimally proportioned, was already Sophy's favourite; in its garden, no ordinary flagpole but a ship's mast: how appropriate! 'I'd have cannons, too,' she murmured. Indeed, back when pretty much everybody was The Enemy, and piracy ubiquitous, *Private firepower could've come in damned handy!*

A battered rusty blue quarry lorry rattled the causeway; as it began racketing up, she ear-monitored its progress… And, actually, could glimpse its roof – and smoke – through gaps in the oak canopy. Eventually reaching the top, as it graunched up a Blang! gear, Sophy noticed close by another mast, one far stouter. And so prominent: from it you'd see out to a horizon far more distant than The Lookout's… had you the climbing courage.

'That's interesting!' Scrutiny suggested a tree-hidden way descending diagonally from the mast to… *There's a wharf!*

Overshadowed by age-contorted oaks, bitter chocolate seaweed camouflaging its stonework; huddled where the northern shore crooked toward open water.

Jill puffed up, 'Anything special to report?'

'Men catching fish. And…,' Sophy pointed.

'Ah, those lovely villas.'

'Number Middle's my favourite.' Then, blurted blushingly, 'Not that Drift Cottage—'

'We all harbour fantasies about pretty houses – even pretty harbourside houses, hmm? Harmless fun, provided you realise nowhere is perfect.'

'Those gardens: *they* can't keep secrets.'

'And the villas must take everything southerlies chuck at 'em. So we aren't moving, after all…?'

Big grin plus shaking head: *Good old AJ!* So lovely, to be getting on so well so soon.

'…That mast? Tram Gin Top, the place is called; "Gin" as in "Horse Engine": they walked round a circular track, harnessed to a rope winder via wooden arms. Coming from a coal pit over *there*, full tram chaldrons were braked down to the wharf; the empties got gin-hauled back up. …No, not counterbalanced like North Wales slate inclines. …Hmm, you're right: we should explore it all one day.'

The right-hand path leaving The Lookout sloped them out along the shoulder of land which bulwarked Pinched Pill against Atlantic swells. So dangerous their great waves became close inshore, as they reared and then broke: along the brown-grey cliffs which stretched southwards, driftwood had been storm-lodged in amazingly high nooks.

Directly below the point's end spread a stone reef, just dry at half tide: 'The Anvil,' Jill said. 'It's fissured; really big waves so compress the air, spray bursts right up over here, BOOM! When The Anvil rings, tradition says The Devil's working his forge, of course.'

'Ominous.'

'Hmm; although you could say there's a primæval sort of equilibrium. The bay's no place for crabpot men when it does ring; but waves crashing so violently dissipate their energy: the pill remains relatively calm for the crab-potting boats. Mind, I've never heard it: you need a particular swell, and the tide behaving a certain way, for the phenomenon.'

'Heckishly worth coming for, should it happen.'

'And as I could sketch safely from that wharf, you've found me another cracking subject.'

That dinghy bluffed homeward now, mackerel shimmering all about the kill-man's boots; their slender craft slipping easily, two canoeists set off up the coast.

A squash-swig, then they headed south.

# CHAPTER 5

Climbing, their view kept widening…

At the cliff's summit, such a far horizon – with a snottyfunneled supertanker, slothing Saint George's Channel southbound. Inshore the canoeists, though now red specks, still scintillated sun-wettened paddles.

Inland, the airbase sprawled concrete; outside their huge hangars, warplanes dwarfed military vehicles: 'So much murderous metal,' Sophy scowled. Consolingly she could also see heat-purpled Prescelly's every undulation.

Determined to discover the Mill Brook's destination, the girl humphed when wind-quiffed blackthorn started edging them inland. There was novelty in walking thus tunnelled; but how thereabouts did land meet sea? She hurried ahead, seeking a spying place.

On her left, a meadow gate flashed by; then, right side, what was that…? Gymshoe-gritting to a halt, she backed and then peered: where did it lead, that barely discernible stoop-down dissolving into green gloom? Statue-still, Sophy strained to outhear a wren's silvery persistence.

From below, the shossles of earlier; and, apparently beneath her, water's chucklesome soliloquy, but muffled: *The Mill Brook's in a culvert!*

Jill grinned, 'You don't disappoint Miss Gwinear's spirit: well found! Now, after you…'

Once the stream came levelling and mud hazarded, the artist must duck willows; but here her trousers won: those young bare legs ahead must warily pass stinger after stinger.

Mill Cove.

Tiddly, some might sneer; but that fine sand was atoll white, and sheltering headlands tempered the air tropical: Sophy jigged, 'Our very own beach!' A privilege Mum and she had never enjoyed.

'Thus, do as you will; but *pianissimo*, please.'

Understood: they must ever guard this secret gift of wise Nature – who'd made Mill Cove invisible from above, and devised a discouraging descent.

Back from exploring, she flopped.

Pointing pencils with a bosunish knife, 'Why the sigh?'

'No swimmers, AJ.'

'That's my fault: I didn't think we'd walk so far. But, ahum, d'you actually *need* them...?'

Sunbathing thus was *serene*!

Heat-spoilt Sophy cat-stretched; then she sat up, eye-shielding: 'Is the swimming safe? I can see patterns in the water.'

'Sweetheart, it's blissful; but well observed. A rock reef crosses the cove; the tide hasn't long covered it, hence those smooth patches: they're caused by water upwelling. The reef protects you from coastwise currents; sunshine warms the lagoon it encloses.'

'Could I climb on to it, and dive?'

'You know to always check the depth; alors, bien sûr!' Kicking shoes off, 'In you go; I'll swim later.' Stripping to a navy blue bikini.

Getting a perplexed look.

'Sweetheart, I didn't trick you into not bringing swimmers: as did Miss Gwinear, I normally wear a cotton bikini underneath so that, wherever I go, I'm always ready to swim, or sunbathe at lunchtime, or, QED, work like this. Good idea?'

A thumbs-up.

'Alors, La Belle Sophy a besoin d'un bikini. D'accord?'

This glass-clear Welsh sea was, indeed, warmer than she'd expected.

Duckdiving her way out to the reef, Sophy thrilled to glide above sand shining so Carribeanly; and how kind that allover water-flow felt! She found a good scramble-up, waved, then sprang out...

She *adored* swooping so smoothly down: an entry to new feelings, this. Time and again she must clamber, limber, and spear back in – must explore underneath, more and more.

Jill snatched sketches; but how to motion-capture that shimmering youthful gold?

Shivers hinting after much sea-play, Sophy shallowed herself: lukewarm, here, for lolling shell scrutiny, backsplashed by sunripples – until a sketch book flapped shut and paper bags appeared...

After lunch, both in. Jill breast-stroked; the seal-keen girl dived and *dived*: 'The more ably you manœuvre, the more elegantly too,' the engineer-artist assured.

'If only *we* lived near this beach! Whenever it's nice and a lesson's boring, I'll think of you down here, AJ. And I *know* you work very hard at your art, but…'

'Yes: I am Lucky Jill. But remember: just weeks back *I* was longing for Mill Cove; and you know you've to go through school and college, same as Mum and me. But afterwards, Sophy, the right job could take you straight to the sea – or *to* sea, hmm?'

An otter-sleeked head nodded.

'But, as I sympathise, whenever I'm here I'll send Leamington my blessings. And maybe if Sophy's kind to this cove, its spirits will send her their love as well.'

'That's a deal!'

Sharing squash afterwards, she frowned, 'About a bikini…?'

'It's all about confidence, sweetheart. First wearing one in my garden, then at places like this, you'll get to love the freer feeling; soon you won't worry where more people are around.' *Much harder to first try a two-piece after you've started developing more noticeably.*

'Okay!' *That did make sense; also, AJ earlier called me "La Belle Sophy"!*

Sun-floating goldenly alone, ears sea-whispered: like the gull gliding far above, entirely Nature's creature.

Towelling herself, Sophy saw a big canvas bag conjured out for driftwood; dressed fast, she shingled over to join in.

'Free fuel,' Jill grinned, 'and beautifully dry.'

Pretty hefty, stuffed full! As carrying the bag side-by-side was out, AJ posted a branch through the handles: 'We'll sling it like a shot tiger.'

Setting off, Sophy giggled 'Poor Pussy!' She'd henceforth bring her knapsack, too: firewood could fill any spare space.

Jill mused, *And this girl fretted about not fitting in!*

On regaining the Coast Path, 'Still energy left? Then it's off,' Jill pointed, 'towards Druids Head.'

That name! Immediately Sophy crammed long-ago crags with beardy bards, auguring for woaded warriors re outwitting foes, and advising golden-tressèd maidens about their admirers – or vice versa…

Alas, Jill was now climbing a stile to head inland.

Leaving her 'grievously deflated', the girl alleged.

'I only said "towards"; anyway, Druids Head is a far longer walk, best enjoyed tigerless.'

After the driveway of Druid Pool Farm, proper tarmac; this road, Sophy realised, ran along the Mill Brook valley's other ridge. Stunted ash thicketing either side, when Jill at a junction indicated 'Talbenny Haven's thataway!', Sophy had to take her word. A half mile on, a wideish pebbly lane branching away southwards was fingerposted as a bridleway; Jill said, 'That's how the horses get down to The Sands.'

*Whose horses? Which sands?*

After five minutes, a north-side lane was their turning. It eventually opened into a stable yard: from stalls, nosy ponies observed the pair's arrival. Burden left outside the OFFICE, Jill led Sophy through an archway and past barns to a farmhouse. This, though Georgian-windowed, looked genuinely castleish: turrety chimneys corbelled from walls easily three feet thick – hence the previous evening's impressive silhouette.

In her undiluted Pembrokeshire accent, did Sophy hear Devonian undertones? Thoughtful-eyed Mrs Madoc, founder of this stable: still regularly a' saddle, though walking somewhat stiffly. Her married daughter Anna Broadway had taken over the business a while back; but, she now almost full term with her first pregnancy, again mother and daughter were jointly managing operations. 'It's quite challenging: one stable girl's down with 'flu, *and* we've the County Show very shortly to–'

Tight formation, four jets scorched over.

To Sophy's amazement, not one whinny of concern.

Having "noisy neighbours", Mrs Madoc explained, advantaged this stable: 'If your mounts are difficult to spook, beginners gain confidence fast; and half the battle's won in show jumping, given a horse which isn't easily distracted. Anyway we never complain, because some servicemen and women come riding.'

More Sophyboggling: flinging a thunder-machine around the morning skies, intent on blowing Russkies to smithereens; then, after lunch, a trot on a chestnut cob.

A Land-Rover drew up; its kind-looking driver couldn't greet them before that green vehicle had disgorged a scruff who looked pure trouble.

A terrier: Taggle, short for Raggle Taggle. Apparently he didn't always make trouble; however, if there was any about, he had to get involved. But he was utterly loyal, accompanying Anna or the stable girls whenever they took groups out. Mrs Madoc nodded down, 'His name's doubly appropriate: he'll *always* tag along. Tremendous stamina.'

'RALF!'

'I'll say,' Mr Madoc sighed. The same Welsh-and-West-Country accent: 'Sticks with 'em on surf gallops; even tries keeping up if they swim the horses. But that's terriers for you: taking on anything, waves included, no matter how big.'

Gleaming with imagined sea-exhilaration, 'Mrs Madoc, would that be at Colliers' Quay?'

'No, Sophy: they aren't good riding roads in that direction; anyway, bait digging leaves pits and soft spots all over the bed of the pill.'

And no vet could cure a horse with a broken leg.

'And,' Mr Madoc lit his pipe, 'because – of the pub – there's often – broken glass.'

Jill pointed the way they'd come: 'The Sands are really long: they stretch from the far side of Druids Head right to Talbenny Haven.'

Blue-clouded with satisfaction, 'A spring tide, indeed, will walk you dry-footed round below the coastguard station and into Creampot Cove.'

'Sounds lovely!'

Jill warned, 'Very different from where you've been today!'

More smoke: 'Lovely, but busy: you see, it's a beach folk can drive to.'

Mrs enlarged, 'The horses exercise early, when there aren't the bods about.' Adding, to test, 'Which doesn't suit stayabeds, of course...'

Sophy positively glittered, 'Who wouldn't get up early for the chance to gallop by the sea? A-And as for the horses – don't they absolutely *love* it? If I were a horse...'

Pensive clouds: *The girl thinks like a horse: she's a natural rider!*

Jill said, 'As the Madocs have lots to do, sweetheart, and I'm having visions of a teapot…'

Handshaking, Sophy hoped the stable girl would recover soon; Jill offered, 'Mrs Madoc, do send word if help's needed.' At which, Sophy nodded her earnestest.

As they left the yard Sophy huffed, 'So *snooty*, some ponies! Carrying firewood makes us look like beggars, I suppose.'

Jill, firmly, 'Attitudes learned from certain riders, I reckon.' As the girl must soon be back here, she should know that some properly uppity little madams attended this stable.

Thus perfectly described, a pacing Sophy reflected, three of last year's supposed pony chums: Jocelyn Flake, Anna-Barbara Fforde, and India Taverner. But thanks to the girl she'd clicked with, Penny Bird, they hadn't got the better of her; 'And how they tried to!'

'Then bless that girl Penny, and good for you!'

Pooh Bear would have loved the spinney's disordered trees and un-coppiced clumps; entering its bird-loud cloisters, again Sophy tasted such sweet air. This was a living architecture of flexing limbs, springy branches, and myriad twigshivers: sun-splashes danced on bark, sky patches kept changing shape, rustling foliage had a sappy, dynamic acoustic. 'So beautiful!'

'Useful, too, like everything natural.' Jill was allowed to haul home storm-downed branches; apparently the hazels cropped nuts reliably.

'And it protects Drift Cottage from southwesterlies…?'

'Aye: Gwinears down the years have blessed it often.'

They discussed, then, that other gift of trees: Nature's alchemy, the making of oxygen.

Jill spotted him first: 'Here's somebody who'd tell you he's beautiful *and* useful, could he talk.'

'Mogulus, dear priceless Moggilulius: you love us so much, you came to escort us home!'

'Mee-OWW!' *Where the HECK have you been all this time?*

Useful, certainly: not one, nor two, but three mice, neatly mortuaried on Jill's back doorstep.

'*They* won't be eating any letters!'

Pouring tea, 'Sophy, about us exploiting Nature: its genius is in how each separate organism flourishes through being a long-term partner in the scheme, in the end giving as much as it takes.'

'But we behave rather differently, don't we?'

'Ever more of us, ever more so.'

The stone-built woodshed had been a donkey stable; its loft had stored hay.

Sophy thought Jill already had oodles of fuel, but wood is much bulkier than coal. 'Also,' her friend pointed, 'today's winnings, dry enough to use immediately, go on *that* pile; sea-wet stuff stays outside until rain washes the salt off, then it's stacked *there* – and drying takes months, sweetheart.'

They showered their salt away; afterwards, sun still warm and breeze kind, drying-off Sophy rinsed Jill's briny towel. Pegging it, she smelt supper starting and– *I'm HUNGRY!*

Fried bacon, egg and potatoes, plus fresh tomatoes and tinned peas: gone in minutes. After bread-polishing their plates, apples. 'That was brill, Jill!', the girl giggled while by her feet Puss crunched rinds and eggy edges. 'Kettle on for washing up?'

'Thanks; then off to read in bed? I'll come soon to show you today's drawings.'

Sun-glowed face, pillow-scattered hair: si jolie! And spark out.

Not going-to-church religious, Jill Ribblesdale prayed in her own way for Sophy and Carol.

She let Mogulus walk her round the garden, sipping wine and inhaling scents...

*Sophy needs a father.* But, Carol and Keith having been so right for each other, a very special fellow it would be whom her friend could take to now: 'Different in character, of course; but as loyal. A generous listener, or it'd *never* work.'

'Miaow!'

And Sophy, as well as taking to him, would have to accept his loving her mother; ideally, indeed, she should want it.

'Hmm...' Sophy being so like Carol, a good preliminary test, that could be, for any chap: how well would he get on with the daughter? 'And, Pussy, talking of tests, could he possibly cope with All – The – Questions?'

'Mioo!'

## Chapter 6

Breakfast was proceeding calmly...

Mogulus scrabbling for the attic steps growlious with hiss and tail fluffed huge, Taggle arrived at the kitchen's threshold barking officiously. He got cuffed silent, when she caught up, by a girl of eighteenish, open-faced but distinctly off colour.

'Sorry to bother,' Bronwen wearied against the door frame, 'but Anna's feeling at odds, so Mrs Madoc's taking her to Surgery. Mr M's away with the tractor, so Sabrina and I really have our work cut out. Could you 'phone-sit, Jill, 'til we've the first class started?'

Already table clearing, 'That's fine, Bronny: we'll see you soon.'

'Horribly boring for you, I'm afraid, Sophy.' Bronny shrugged, 'Bring a book, perhaps?'

Coming to feel the older girl's forehead, 'NO! Surely there's muck to shovel, feed and water and straw to sort out, and tack to fetch? I've done all those before – and you're still pretty poorly.'

The not-denying-it Swansea girl sighed, 'You really want...?'

Jill ruffled Sophy's hair: 'Keen as mustard!' She'd explained the day before how country-dwellers should look out for each other: 'The Gwinears and Madocs were good neighbours; I hope to be well thought of, in time.' Now, here was pleasing proof that those words had sunk in.

They had; but also Sophy knew that stable work could be rewarding. Horses showed gratitude for being groomed; indeed, some remembered kindness: the next time you rode them, they were more companionable. In this situation that latter fact wasn't relevant, of course; nor that on the trekking holiday volunteers had found keener ponies assigned to them: *No chance of me getting a ride today, at such a busy place.*

Endless, the tasks seemed, but Sophy didn't mind: she loved that feeling of friends all working hard – including Jill who, whenever not taking calls, was dashily sketching from the office doorway.

Uppity indeed, certain pupils. Always spoke their minds, gave not a fig who overheard. Descending spotlessly jodhpured from Range Rovers, in overtailored jackets they waited, chatting: let that lesser, junior creature lend a grubby hand. Fourteen and older, these were upcoming County Girls – and being County *mattered*. Hence because hers was an ordinary Pembrokeshire family, they only respected Sabrina reluctantly: being handsome, and such a skilled horsewoman, marrying well could make her socially acceptable.

For Bronny, redemption was unfeasible. Firstly, everyone from further west hated Swansea people because they were "so above themselves"; secondly (and rather contradictorily) she had been raised in a council flat. Thus the snooties' addressing of her had ever been at best uncaring, and today it was downright rude: someone must be blamed for this delay, and what right had working-class types to be ill?

Sophy was aware of being observed by her "superiors"; fortunately, they knew nothing of her background. But the young madams could fault her size, cause of her struggling with heavy things; also her taking time, because of learning the ropes: 'Slow Flea!' was soon being cattily hissed.

Which pleased her: being partly blamed for the class's lateness meant Bronny wasn't a lone target; also, that snidery did at least acknowledge that Sophy was doing her bit to get things ready.

At last the class was under way, with feline Sabrina in charge on agile Slipstream: such a distinctive spirit in both, Sophy could tell.

Slog over, she and Bronny could relax in the office with Jill, Taggle, and cocoa.

But, 'Won't be a mo!' Because Sophy must *en route* dodge into the Tack Room to view the roster board, where whoever had fettled a horse chalked their initials beside its name: it would be satisfying to see that morning's column completed. However – and she hadn't noticed this before – below the alphabetical list (*ASTRAL* to *WHICHWAY*), and then the spare rows, was another name… which wasn't signed off.

Catastrophe for Bronny's dunked ginger nut as the girl exploded in, 'TRACKER'S MISSING!'

# CHAPTER 7

He wasn't.

Tracker had his own field: setting off towards Jill's, you branched right down a curved track.

'Which I wondered about, yesterday,' said Sophy. 'A shame, our going straight past.'

The artist noted, 'He mightn't have come to say hello, if you had gone looking.'

Bronny table-tapped, 'Tracker's super inquisitive, 'n' tack-sharp: he's always there staring over it, long before you reach his gate. Seems sensitive to vibrations, scents… who knows?'

Taggle, 'RAFF!' *Stop gassing; let's go and see him!*

As they walked, Sophy mulled things over. 'Can Tracker move quietly?'

Those Swansea eyebrows: 'I'll say! He's goosed Sabrina, and me, and Anna.' Then, realising this was a new word for Sophy, she rather hotly explained, 'While your back's turned he creeps close; then, PHSCHOOSH! from his nostrils, right down into your knickers. Bloody near jumps you out of 'em!'

Sophy titterexploded.

'First time he pulls that stunt, Mrs Madoc hears my shriek from her kitchen and comes up the yard, brandishing a rolling pin. She thought I–' Bronny, re-reddening, began coughing.

'Thought you…?'

'Ahuhahum, actually she never said. Seen an adder? Not that I minds snakes: they've their lives to lead. *Anyway*, Tracker then behaves all butter-wouldn't-melt, doesn't he?'

'Nobody believed you?'

'Not about *deliberately* snot-bombing my bum.'

This so sniggered Sophy, she must go behind a bush…

'They'd only accept his playing Grandma's Footsteps. Until…' The dirtiest Glamorgan chuckle.

'Well?'

'He caught Sabrina an ab-so-lute *PEACH*! I tell you, they heard that squeal in Haverfordwest.'

As they started down the track, Sophy formed a cartoon image: a horse on tiptoe behind a posh pony girl who'd a shoelace to tie, his muzzle discharging like a cannon... Except, was Tracker the typical Thelwell chestnut?

How tall, this creature craning to see; his startling piebald coat and pink-and-white nose made Sophy exclaim, 'He's like an American Indian's horse!'

An arm around: 'You reckon? That's interesting.'

Introductions were conducted over the gate. Though not just tall but very sturdy indeed, even when Tracker muzzle-nudged Sophy's giggling neck she wasn't intimidated: his seemed a wholly engaging temperament – and how his dark wise eyes drew hers.

'As if he recognises you!' *As if they already know each other.*

Climbing the fence to demonstrate trust, Sophy must dodge sharpish when Tracker suddenly began scanning the sky: 'Steady, boy!'

Bronny murmured, eyes shaded, 'Aircraft coming.'

Grey underneath, white above, US Navy markings; four turboprops booming out dark haze. It had few windows; was its purpose to carry weapons? On low approach it looked scarily big to Sophy, but the trio with her weren't perturbed: Taggle's stumpy tail wagged on.

'A marine patrol aircraft. See its number, 716? Well, Tracker always looks out for her sister aircraft, 789: he owes his life to its pilot, Carson Lightfoot. Just let's hear them safely home...'

The machine sank from view; there was its touchdown wheelskitch, then the braking powergrowl.

Now Bronny climbed up to begin the horse's story: 'Know what sort of 'plane a Galaxy is?'

'Only what sort of chocolate bar.'

'It's a humungous transport – far bigger than that 'un just now: Galaxys can literally carry railway engines. Beefier than 747s; not as threatening-looking as B52s, though. God,' Bronny shuddered, 'I hate those nuclear bombers!'

Sophy hated *anything* nuclear.

'One November evening, a year and a half back, a Galaxy came in over the bay – first time I'd ever seen one. Taggle and I had just put the horses to bed when we heard this great growling noise: those engines is 'mazingly loud. Tag growled back, can you believe it?'

'RALF!'

'The sky was clear – it was already frosty – and there loomed that massive thing, looking about to flatten us. I had to tell myself and Taggle that she wouldn't.'

Sophy pictured this little dog, stiff-hackled, looking up to the cloudy-breathed girl for reassurance.

'Now, from here on this is the story as Carson and Sam told it to us, okay?'

'Who's Sam?'

Was Bronny pinking? 'Carson's observer.'

'On the marine patrols? Yes, I see.'


'On landing, the Galaxy men headed for the mess, where 789's crew were getting supper after a patrol. One chap recognised Carson from years before; soon the crews were eating together. Then in came the Military Police, looking for the Galaxy lot. Carson asked what was wrong; the MPs wouldn't say, but they let him and Sam go along with the others.

'Armoured trucks surrounded that 'plane, and troops were aiming machine guns: big trouble.

'It had started innocently: the ground staff had heard this knocking, and assumed a mechanical fault; but when Aircraft Maintenance shut off all the 'plane's power systems, the knocks continued.'

Sophy jumped in, 'The cargo was making noises!' Unsure why Bronny was telling a shaggy dog story, she'd happily hear it through, *then* find out Tracker's tale.

'Somebody asked, was there paint aboard? Because tins which depressurise at altitude get squashed when the aircraft descends, making clonky noises. However nothing likely was listed, so the Head of Security immediately sealed the base: a Code Red for suspected stowaways.'

Sophy frowned, 'But stowaways would stay quiet, hoping to sneak away later.'

Bronny hugged, 'Exactly what Carson and the Galaxy's skipper argued! More likely, they thought, a wild animal had got aboard. The

Head of Security insisted, 'Terrorists!' Suicidal types, spoiling for a fight: happy to blow themselves up, and anyone coming close.'

'Plus a 'plane worth squillions of dollars.'

Bronny's old-fashioned look: 'Perhaps that thought crossed the Boss Man's mind, too. Anyway, foxes *or* terrorists, pest fumigation gas would sort them out, he said.'

Tracker grumbled deeply.

Sophy boggled, '*WHAT?*'

'Carson said, maybe a crate containing Mexican peasants trying to enter the USA illegally had gone astray; were Security happy to gas them? As he speaks Spanish, he and Sam volunteered to search the 'plane.'

'Good for them!'

Boss Man said they should take guns; well, considering what one stray bullet could do to all the fuel still aboard, what a pillock! Anyway, the noise came from a lorry... Any guesses?'

No.

'Well, before they could get back out and reveal the answer, the Boss Man loudhailered them.'

'Saying...?' *She's a brilliant storyteller!*

'"RELAX, GUYS: IT'S A HORSE!" As horseshoe imprints in the lorry's sides had just told them.'

Tracker nodded over Sophy's shoulder; she started, 'Good heavens, it was YOU!' Now she was wriggling with it: 'Enough suspense, Bronny – just tell me everything!'

'Okay; but, understand, this didn't all come out that night. So – Tracker *is* an American Indian's horse: he's from a reservation near the Rockies airbase that Galaxy had come from; his owner's tribal name is Listens Well.

'Now, Listens Well had been complaining about jet fighters buzzing his reservation: this was prohibited. As fighter squadrons are pretty gung ho, likely the pilots weren't punished, but just got a mild ticking off; nevertheless, they had it in for Listens Well. Who, they discovered, owned a remarkably intelligent horse: rather than warden his woodland by jeep, he rode everywhere; thus that horse had learnt loads of stuff.'

'Including tracking...?'

'Correct! And Tracker was docile: "Good as gold!", folks said.

'Well, the pilots started putting stories around: strangers from away, circus people, were looking for smart horses to buy. Next, they spread rumours about animals going missing. Then, one Saturday, they "borrowed" a truck from a quiet corner of the base...'

'The lorry!'

'Importantly, they cut security seals to steal it. They strawed it out, then someone rang Listens Well saying a friend who wasn't on the 'phone hadn't been seen for a while. Once he'd departed in his car, the pilots turned up with a sedating kit.'

'Poor horse!', Sophy patted.

'They intended holding Tracker overnight, to give Listens Well a nasty shock; by making it look as if he'd found his gate open and wandered off, the police wouldn't pay much attention.'

'ROFF!'

'Yes, Taggle: *very* devious.'

'They put the truck with Tracker inside back where they'd found it, wired closed again to discourage snoopers. At least he'd plenty of water and hay, for when the wooziness lessened. The next afternoon, they'd planned, they'd release Tracker at the edge of the reservation: he'd find his way home, end of story. Unfortunately, next morning, enter the Galaxy...'

'...And in went the lorry...'

'...destination West Wales.'

The horse shook his head: he hadn't enjoyed that journey.

'Tracker was very lucky that the boys understand horses. While Sam befriended him, Carson negotiated with the Head of Security: the vehicles and troops left, and there was peace. Carson asked about sending for a vet; however, one had already been called.'

Sophy sighed, 'The security man wasn't completely heartless.'

Bronny head-tilted, 'You'll see.'

'How was Tracker?'

'Not bad, actually. The boys wondered if, used to seeing aircraft, he knew he was in one and was kicking out of boredom, not fear. Not surprisingly he had sore hooves; luckily, he hadn't cut himself. Anyway he soon decided he could trust them, and relaxed.

'When Carson led Tracker out he had a good look around, then apparently decided, "This is different! But that's grass over there, and I'm hungry." So Sam took him off the runway to graze.'

Sophy nudged, 'And ease your poor hooves.'

Tracker nodded.

'Carson told the Head of Security, "This horse isn't badly injured; I'm sure it's recovering from a tranquilliser shot." Then, dear Sophy, his next sentence saved Tracker's life.'

'*How*?'

'Carson insisted that Tracker was naturally docile and wouldn't need sedating for a horse box ride to a local stable; he'd understand what was happening. The Head of Security said, "Then regrettably he'll understand what's happening, when he gets his biggest goddam sedating ever!" He wanted Tracker put down, you see, because quarantine regulations had been breached.'

'Oh, Lord! So who persuaded him–?'

Bronny leaned, 'That nasty asterisk never was persuaded. Sam just let Tracker go, whispering "Make yourself scarce, buddy!" Which he did, helped by a sympathetic flight engineer who re-started the Galaxy's generator unit. While horrid Boss Man was bellowing what the asterisking hell is going on etcetera, clever old Tracker here–'

'He raced off?'

'Nono! Gallop, and everyone hears you. The boys tracked *him*, next morning: he'd carefully put the 'plane between himself and the MPs, then crept quietly off across the grass. Using lawns and flowerbeds to approach the gatehouse, he'd watched from the shadows awhile, and then nipped out alongside a cyclist.'

'*Then* he raced to safety?'

'In which direction, Sophy? That cyclist said Yankee Boy just, Badump!, hopped the nearest fence. My guess, his priority was losing the airbase's lights to get proper night vision, before working out how to put a decent distance between himself and it by next morning.'

'Which, Q.E.D., he managed!'

Bronny muzzle-stroked, 'Actually, Tracker's escape was a superb outcome for the Head of Security: he'd no unquarantined animal to destroy, and evidence that a horse had been aboard the Galaxy was easily erased. Also, why should anybody finding Tracker connect him with the base? What's more, Boss Man was fox-crafty about dealing with the servicemen involved.'

Sophy supposed the bully had threatened demotion, or being posted somewhere horrible.

'Love, umpteen bods knew about Tracker; he couldn't mistreat them all. Accepting that anything more than two folk know isn't a secret, he admitted there *had* been a horse on the base.'

'He *what?*'

'With the cunningest twist! The ground staff, he said, had thought that the Galaxy was stuffed with terrorists; naturally, he'd declared a Code Red. While he prepared to gas the insurgents, the flight engineer discovered a stowaway horse: Carson and Sam, in pantomime costumes.'

'And people believed–?'

'His making himself the butt of the joke was utter genius, because airbase security people are never popular: who'd want to believe someone later insisting there'd been a *real* horse aboard…?'

'Okay,' Sophy accepted, 'so the Boss Man had swept *his* problem under the carpet – but poor Tracker was all alone in a strange place.'

'And the only humans he trusted were at the base.'

The Leamington girl hadn't forgotten him: 'Plus Listens Well, back home.'

'Sophy, the U.S. Military Police don't mess about: Listens Well was told that Tracker had somehow got into his local airbase, "encountered" a Galaxy, and been buried; for security reasons, nothing more could be disclosed. They paid the fellow handsomely, Carson said; but as no horse could replace Tracker, the poor chap donated the money to a disabled children's riding school.'

Flushed red, Sophy's eyes welled: 'Because of those disgusting lies, I bet that dear old man is d-devastated to this day!'

Bronny hugged, 'I know – but try to contain your upset, my love; otherwise, I'll feel so bad for telling you this.'

'You mustn't ever,' Sophy snuffled. She straightened her back, 'I can cope with knowing all of Tracker's story – whatever's involved.'

Bronny's hanky dabbed Sophy's eyes.

Then, 'No local horse sanctuary had taken Tracker in, they discovered, so the boys started searching for him.'

'How?'

'By air, of course. 789's crew cooked up excuses for not landing immediately after sorties: they would mooch about locally, supposedly investigating technical niggles but actually using their fancy kit to scan the countryside. On day five, Eureka! He was safe, and being tended.'

'By whom?'

A finger to Bronny's lips; but Sophy noticed Tracker's head swing: 'Miss Gwinear?'

The older girl grinned, 'Pretty cunning yourself, eh? He'd found the spinney: by day he'd hide there, at night he crept out to graze the lane verges; she met him, out on a moonlit walk.'

'And, because her grandparents had owned a donkey, she had the skills to make him better?'

'The apples and veges, too. And she brought him seaweed daily.'

'*Seaweed?*'

'Proper shoresiders know what a tonic dulse is: it's packed with goodness. When the boys called, politely enquiring after a stray horse, Miss Gwinear produced a happy, healthy Tracker who recognised them straight off.'

The girl patted, 'Clever boy! And so you came to live here?'

'No, not then. Carson and Sam divulged what they dared; Miss Gwinear insisted on telling the Madocs, because if Tracker had an illness...'

Sophy nodded.

'A1 healthy, they reckoned; but, just in case, he should overwinter in Drift Cottage's paddock.'

*Jill owns a paddock!* What else didn't Sophy know?

'Carson insisted he'd pay rent and buy Tracker's hay and treats; he and Sam promised they'd regularly visit. Mr Madoc rigged a tarpaulin shelter, but Yankee Boy here soon realised he needn't hide away: all the base's fliers were on his side – so, he became a planespotter. Because Miss G waved whenever 789 flew over, this one could soon tell it from its sister seven-hundreds – Lord knows how! Hence he always looks up when he hears a seven-hundred coming.'

'When did he move here?'

'Late last spring.' Bronny croaked, 'When Miss Gwinear began to...'

'It was so unfair, her getting ill; the Madocs adopting Tracker must have pleased her.'

'Sophy, the stable isn't a charity: Carson and Sam started paying Anna.'

'They're generous men.'

'Aye. Anyway, by then he'd the all-clear: they could ride him out along the lanes, onto the beach even; I reckon regular exercise, and hearing the boys' American accents, did his homesickness wonders. And, being prairie-born, that tin lean-to over there was – is – all the shelter he wants. If he sometimes lurks inside when it's nice… well, he can get the blues, like me. But normally,' she cheered, 'he *has* to be outside: he's pretty inquisitive.'

Sophy, considering what she knew about horses, tilted her head…

'Oh, all right – Tracker's bloody nosy! From over *there* he can watch Gareth restoring the derelict wing of the Madoc's farmhouse, where he and Anna will live; the west end of that ridge looks out to sea; the other's best for 'plane spotting.'

Sophy tickled, 'I hope you're very grateful to Carson and Sam, Yankee Boy!' Seeing Bronny's expression, 'Do they ride well?'

'Carson handles Tracker like an American Indian: telepathic, the relationship seems. 'Cos while Anna and Sabrina and I have lovely rides on him, and Mrs Madoc sometimes too, we all have to talk lots.'

'Gosh! And Sam…?'

Eyes eloquent, 'Absolute poetry, Sam Goldfire riding!' A deep breath; 'If you hadn't realised…'

The old-fashioned look of an observant child.

'Okay, you had. Well, Sam was taught really formally; Mrs Madoc recognised that, watching him on Tracker. So, because he's lightly built, she insisted he had a go on our top pony.'

Sophy tingled, 'Slipstream?' A spiritedness she'd recognised straightaway.

'Spot on! Well, on his very first ride he simply *flew* Slippy, like Sabrina can – as Heather will, one day. Round the jumping course, straight off, no problem; down the home straight like a firework!'

Heather was obviously someone likeable. 'Don't you ride Slipstream jolly well, yourself?'

Bronny waved, 'Pretty well; but considering how few goes Sam ever got–'

The abrupt turning away, that shoulder set: Sophy put out a hand, 'Tell me, please; number 789 didn't crash, did it?'

A head-shake; 'We'd have heard, somehow.'

'So...?'

'Until early October last year, both boys regularly rode Tracker, and I was going out with Sam – then, absolutely nothing; and 789 hasn't been seen since.' Bronny choked, 'No American can say, dares say, where they've gone. Or if they'll be back, ever. I daren't question anyone pushily: horrible Boss Man would punish people for letting slip even the tiniest secret.'

'D'you think he had the 789s transferred away as some kind of delayed revenge?'

...

'Bronny...?'

A deep breath. 'I can get that emotional, it makes me hard to be with; as the others, bless 'em, have been really tolerant, there's a worry I didn't burden them with. But because you've talked so maturely about sharing difficulties...'

'Try me, please.'

'Towards the end, Miss Gwinear began speaking overtruthfully – like saying how Mrs Dinmore broke her hip because she was so fat. She also got steadily more het up about righting *all* the world's injustices.'

'She went to the base to confront Boss Man about wanting Tracker put down?'

'That's unlikely: had she got past the barrier, apparently he's hellish difficult to get hold of.'

'So...?'

'Who was most wronged?'

'Sophy fingersnapped, 'Listens Well!'

'And if I tell you that Miss Gwinear knew which American airbase the Galaxy came from...?'

'You think she identified the reservation, and wrote to Listens Well saying Tracker was alive?'

Bronny nodded, 'Forgetting she was compromising Carson and Sam. Now folk who care about Nature are considered dangerous in the 'States, so let's suppose that U.S. government spies intercepted her letter: they'd have learnt that a horse *had* been in that Galaxy – a huge security breach. And American defence high-ups would be in-can-bloody-descent about the cover-up.'

'Which was the Boss Man's idea, so he'd have got roasted.'

'My love, Carson and Sam and the Galaxy's crew would have been drawn in, too, for not reporting sooner what they knew.'

Sophy understood: 'But had they, Boss Man would have twisted the truth to heap blame on them.'

'*Exactly*: it would have been, "Damned if you do, and damned if you don't," for the 789 boys.'

'Um, of course it's agonising not knowing where they are, Carson and your dear Sam; and, yes, the airbase security people are devious; but surely you shouldn't go meeting trouble half way, worrying about a letter Miss Gwinear might not have written? Patrolling for Russian subs is a really important job, Bronny; maybe the boys went off on a top secret mission. Wherever they are, they're aware that you're missing them and praying for them, Sam especially. Meanwhile, wouldn't they *hate* you to be worrying about them unnecessarily?'

Sophy gulped, 'You're very caring, Bronny; there's a girl like you at school. So please be careful: they say that Ariadne's heart is too big; is yours? She cries for ages about everything horrible: kittens being drowned, stillborn babies, African famines... People can blow fuses, going on so.'

The older girl crushed, 'Sophy, you'd have made a brilliant younger sister!'

'Gosh, thanks! Now let's you and I send our thoughts to Carson and Sam; and, from now on, Jill and I'll be praying for them every day.'

Bronny sniffed, 'And I'll count my blessings: two new mates rooting for me. I've always had Tracker: because he misses Carson as much as I miss Sam, we've both felt pretty subdued since last autumn – but on our rides, we cheer each other up.'

'Wherever he is, Sam needs you happy, Bronny; so does everybody you work with. Now I've met you, *I* need you happy – and, actually, I think I'll need you always.' *As the big sister I never had.*

# CHAPTER 8

Weeks earlier Jill had ordered a 'phone installation: now she'd the equipment, and poles strode the verge; still, though, no wires. Thus after lunch she and Sophy returned...

It had been a false alarm: Anna, home again, felt fine. Meanwhile, Mrs Madoc fumed: every girl booked for afternoon tuition, bar one, was at a fifteenth birthday celebration – and not one partygoer had given notice. Then, brightening, 'Come and meet Heather Haroldston: you'll get on with her.'

Shaking hands, Sophy immediately sensed a caring nature.

Heather smiled, 'I'm so glad I wasn't invited; otherwise, we mightn't have met.' She'd little in common with the rest, anyway, being far and away the youngest in the class – the same age as Sophy, in fact. 'You're a new joiner here, hmm?'

Shaking her head, 'I just came along this morning to help a little–'

'She and Jill,' Mrs Madoc insisted, 'saved the day. So, Sophy dear, you deserve a free lesson.'

Bronny, leading him into the yard, 'On Tracker, why not?' And Heather could ride her favourite...

Sophy could tell: 'Slipstream!'

Borrowing Bronny's bike, Jill must dash home for her sketching things.

During the preparations, ponies who should have worked that afternoon watched indignantly.

Sophy thought, *Why not ride Tracker? Because he's the biggest horse I've ever met, never mind sat on!* Indeed, she couldn't recall ever seeing a girl – or a boy – her size in command of such a large animal; and she said so.

'Well,' said Mrs Madoc, 'my very earliest riding, when I was tiny, was on big working horses – and, look, he has a special saddle.' Which seemed emphatically arched, sat the rider well forward, and had double stirrups. 'So please don't worry: you honestly won't feel as if you're sitting atop a railway carriage, if that's what you were thinking.'

Sophy didn't; what was more, the saddle's strange surface felt amazingly grippy, as if her jeans were Velcro'd to it.

Heather whispered, helping with adjustments, 'Like shark skin, eh? Pretty jolly come-off-proof, you'll find.' Then, loudly, 'Tracker's size is irrelevant, Sophy: as he likes you, he'll look after you.'

Bronny said, 'Little Slippy, you'll see, is much more of a handful.'

In the sparrowy indoor arena, with Mrs Madoc watching, Bronny had Heather do some basic moves; 'Now you, Sophy!'

Sobered by seeing what sharp wits the other girl had needed, 'Okay!' So, would Tracker understand when she talked each manœuvre through...?

Yes, every time. She half-giggled, 'He's a dream to ride!' So responsive; so intelligent; as Heather had promised, so securely seating her. 'Thank you, thank you!', she kept patting. And those confidence-building exercises confirmed this animal's power: nothing took much effort.

'Brilliant rapport,' called Mrs Madoc; 'but don't let him forget who's Boss.'

When, 'More room to play in!', Bronny opened the gates leading to the paddock, Sophy felt Tracker tense as he trotted the ring.

Having caught Mrs Madoc's wink, Heather called, 'You first!'

The great horse lurched sideways like a train negotiating a junction...

'NO YOU DON'T!' Sophy heaved his head round, keeping him to the arena circuit. Then, opposite Mrs Madoc, she hauled him up, 'Stand STILL!'

He gruntingly obeyed.

She patted, 'That's better!' And saluted: 'With your permission, Ma'am...?'

Those eyes: 'Having won his respect, Miss Fossway – carry on!'

Heather grinned, '*Bravo!* I tell you, I flipping failed that test.'

Sabrina appeared as the girls were taking the pace up: no jumping, just gradually faster circuits, interspersed with stops and turns. Next came joust circuits: riding counterwise, the girls increased speed until passing like expresses... While, unfortunately, Sophy's bottom, thighs, and spine increasingly reminded her brain that she hadn't ridden for some while.

Relief mixing regret, she dismounted so Sabrina could give Heather her jumping tuition.

Now Sophy could study her new friend's technique.

She didn't ride on Slipstream, she rode *with* him: each manœuvre was theirs – but wasn't this pony headstrong! Heather must control his run-up speed; he'd then take them over a jump beautifully while she anticipated the next manœuvre, allowing that he preferred turning out rightwards: on an anti-clockwise circuit, Slippy's pilot would need reins tighter than today, resolute knee-nudgings, the voice firmest.

But, no matter: what a keen vaulter and fluid runner Heather commanded. Mrs Madoc whispered, 'So pretty in the feet for her!'

Tracker jumped a few times for Sabrina to illustrate some point – but such horsework wasn't his vocation: he moved like a trained soldier, not a dance-loving gymnast.

His military obedience wasn't surprising, considering Sabrina's attitude and physique: whether tutoring a timid six-year-old or petulant teen, this young woman insisted on correct behaviour from any, from every mount. This needed strong will and, sometimes, blunt strength.

A grateful Sophy, who'd learned an invaluable lesson. Mind you, Tracker was no more suited to competition riding than she herself was interested in gymkhanas.

About his acting impulsively: plain naughtiness, some would say; but it did reflect his remarkable ability to understand; also, Sophy suspected, he had been itching to get back outside. Slipstream might revel in pole heights, turn angles, and take-off points; Tracker's head was surely full of weather and terrain – hence his regular patrols of that ridge, viewing the ocean and the hills.

*We get on so well because we're natural co-operators.* Whilst the horse must obey her in the artificial setting of the arena, Sophy could imagine whole days in the saddle (her body having got used to that!) without either ever considering who was Boss. Indeed, seeing how much older and more experienced Yankee Boy was, in many situations she could be literally riding for a fall, should she presume to know better what to do.

As for Tracker's size – she thought no more about it.

The girls thanked Sabrina and Bronny for their tuition, and Mrs Madoc for the afternoon; to each she made one key suggestion for improving technique, to be remembered when next they rode.

Horses hitched outside the office to thirstily trough, Bronny sent the girls to fetch the curry kit.

Heather could immediately start on Slipstream, but Sophy must drag over a crate to stand on.

Bronny knew how to engage the Leamington girl: 'When you're trekking wilderness, your survival depends on your horse's health: overlook one cut or chafe, and flies could attack. Frame of mind's crucial, too; if your horse knows you truly care, he'll give you his heart, and share all he knows. The happier you both are, the better your chance of bringing each other safely home.

'You and your fellow riders must give each other similar care and attention, too. Friends can notice slight changes in your appearance, mood, or the way you move before you yourself realise there's a problem: co-operation is key. As with horses, so with humans: that sense of being cared for maintains health far better than medicines.'

'Anything else?'

'Actually, Sophy, one rule will get you safely over the Rockies or, indeed, the Prescellys: *Do As You Would Be Done By*.'

The girl beckoned from atop the crate and then hugged: 'Like that?'

The telephone saved her tutor from complaining re 'something in my eye.'

Slippy finished, Heather fetched another crate to help groom Tracker.

Through the horse, as it were, both girls found it easy to share understandings. Changing topic was as easy as steering a small boat a different way; little jokes bubbled up in that wake of words.

New friendship; Bronny heard it from the office. She had willed these two to click, sensing the need of both for friendship's buoyancy – its compass, too, as they departed childhood's shore to cross the ocean of life.

And she should know.

Fast work, all that afternoon, testing picture compositions. The girls had practised unselfconsciously: easy for Jill's pencil to notice

Heather's natural seat, see what a negligible weight Carol's girl was to Tracker.

Her best sketch? Sophy's alert lean, absorbing Bronny's advice along with her ears-cocked mount, the two about to wheel away and re-try the manœuvre.

Much harder to represent Heather on Slipstream: such easy movers, so seldom still! She'd eventually focused on the girl approaching a jump which Sabrina had had them repeatedly try. Eyes steadying the obstacle ahead; mouth encouraging tautly; frame reinforcing command of reins plus the thrust of those words, whilst anticipating the pony's imminent muscles... And, in the airborne moment, nothing else in that fine young head – for nobody rides well with a mind elsewhere.

Truly, the best compositions did find themselves: here now were the new friends, pampering the American horse with no awareness of being observed – or overheard, except by tufty ears...

'Bother!' the artist muttered, as Heather hopped off her box; *But, no: bless the girl, because now that drawing can't be overworked.*

'Aha!' The youngsters now brushed Tracker standing side by side: a new viewpoint, another balance. Left, a closer human intimacy; the horse, central, head now turned away; on the right, Slipstream – watching proceedings and sometimes, it appeared, whispering in the American's ear.

She'd crept closer, upturned an empty bucket to sit, and was just turning a fresh page...

Tyre rumblings; then a green Volvo estate, roof rack burdened, scattering sparrows and exploding Taggle – where had he been? – into challenging barks.

Heather loudly grinned, 'My Dad!'

'Ah, well!' Jill closed up, stood up, and stretched.

Hugh Haroldston habitually hurried; hence Heather's hasty ''Bye, Bronny!'

However he didn't resist when daughter-propelled toward new friend Sophy, and gladly he met the Drift Cottage artist. But then, 'I'm sorry, we must go now.'

Cheek-pecks accompanied Heather's well-hugged 'See you again soonest!'; then, window-waving, away the Volvo went.

Tracker finished down to his hooves, Sophy led Slipstream to his box.

Now, their turn for ''Bye, Bronny!' She'd seemed, that morning, born worry-worn; now they knew: this was just someone with concerns, bouncing quickly back to health.

They returned Tracker to his field, Sophy allwhile re-living their afternoon; spinneying homeward, Jill gladly reinforced the girl's many positive observations about Heather.

Sophy's never asking after the art mattered not: let the girl's heart sing its feelings, regardless of how leaf shades played with sunlight; let her walk oblivious to her own summer-loved aura... Not registering, either, that Jill wheeled a bike.

Mogulus's milk-thirst they straightway slaked; next, teak-coloured tea for them.

A refreshed Sophy un-flopped from clovery repose: 'Better shower, I s'pose.' Her words didn't exactly shiver, but that cold spray after this heat...

The artist pointed between two apple trees: 'I'll bring you soap and a towel...'

Flinging all her horsey clothes onto the grass, 'AJ, you're BRILLIANT!' For, before returning to the stable with her drawing gear, Jill had dragged out a tin bath, filled it, and left it soaking up sunshine.

'Ooh, so super!' Wallowably warm, it was, like the deep pools retreating tides sometimes leave – in which Sophy loved to mermaid herself, finger-sieving sand while deep-wiggling her feet.

But why, the girl wondered when Jill returned, need she know that Mogulus was indoors...?

Jill's robin, seeing *this* Sophy as a natural animal, swooped to the bath's rim. On her settling lower he flickered onto an island knee, she feeling through those tinynesses which were his claws that minute change in balance as he curtseyed; then he hop-turned there, and sweetly sang.

# CHAPTER 9

*A quarter past six?*

Such an early wake-up; but, sunshine and bacon alluring, Sophy dressed fast.

Breakfast over, she suddenly rushed outside barefoot, toothpaste-mouthed: 'HORTHETH!'

Bronwen, riding Mrs Madoc's hunter, Arrow, led a saddled Tracker; Taggle scampered alongside. 'Time for The Sands, Sophy!'

Bronny clicked Arrow away, Sophy followed; Jill got the bike rolling.

From horseback the spinney's canopy, that green domain of birds, felt much closer; however Sophy's Christmasly intense excitement obliterated other wildlife thoughts.

Sabrina waved as they echo-clattered the stableyard cobbles; how nosily ponies craned to see! Then, that bosky climb towards... The road. Inexperienced Sophy was apprehensive; however they weren't on tarmac long before reining left for the bridleway and, 'Let's trot!'

Taggle bounded; when ra-ther boun-ced Sophy looked back, freewheeling Jill waved gleefully.

Sounds, and her mount's behaviour, said The Sands were near; but blackthorn still glimpsed meadow – then, there before them was the coast road. Jill pedalled off southwards; after furious thought, Taggle ruffed in pursuit.

'All clear!' They clipclopped across the tarmac and started up a marramy dune; into view came the village of Talbenny Haven, and a headland; beyond its coastguard station that narrow inlet overlooked by imposing houses was... 'Creampot Cove', Bronny poshed. On they climbed...

'The Sands, Sophy!'

A smooth mile silver-gleamed by breezed-in waves, where just two dogs people-walked and a silhouette beachcombed: seeing such emptiness, the excitement of both horses!

Dune petering out to their right, the Pembrokeshire Coast Path went skewing up and round a cliff; Bronny said, 'You'll soon see where to...'

Gingerly down the dry sand's seaward steepness, the two dismounted to cross skiddy shingle. Back up, they headed out to meet the sea, Sophy feeling that Tracker loved its clear colours and freshfoamed waves as much as she did.

Eyes scrutinising, they trotted right down its sloshing edge to the rocks of Creampot Point, just below the coastguard station. There Jill, camera clicks, Taggle, and yaps met them.

The artist beamed, 'This lighting!' Under northern Wedgwood blue, iridescent surf-mist drifted inland over tawny wet-mirrored sand; behind, grey-black Druids Head derided Time...

*Wow!* No question about it, now: Sophy *had* to explore there, soon.

Beyond, the north shore of Saint Brides Bay tapered westward towards Ramsey Island; then came the scattered rocks called The Clerks; further out rose lonely and low South Bishop rock, topped by its white mitre lighthouse.

They'd confirmed the shoreline safe; Bronny enthused, 'Warm-up canters, then we gallop!'

Jill nodded, 'Okay; Taggle and I will walk up to where you'll come past fast.'

Sophy patted, 'Time for the real fun, Tracker!' But her jumpy heart wondered, *HOW fast?*

He turned, and caught her eye; Sophy knew that his would be a gallop she could cope with.


The riders felt their horses' muscles gradually loosening; increasing snortishness told them ever keener to be off at the fly. Wheeling their fourth turn, as Bronny passed Jill at a fast canter, 'NEXT TIME!'

They went right down to the south end, turned the horses—

And halted, very firmly: 'This morning's reminder about who's boss!'

Then – 'RIGHT AWAY!'


Sophy had never experienced anything like.

The first moments had a short-train-behind-big-locomotive feeling; then sensations beyonded the mechanical. The gallop became hers as well as his: one girl, one horse, one mutual will.

A sun-shouldered flight, hooves loud-stinging the saturated sand; yet, even at this speed, so high above the ground, she felt secure. Body speed-percussed, Sophy's glances knew Bronny fearless, beautiful with achievement: no camera would understand. And what privilege seeing Arrow's action, every muscle under control and drive of myriad nerves: within that work-sleeked skin such a puissance, life-sparked from nothing but grass, air, and water.

*And Arrow's so aware of us!* Matching Tracker's pace perfectly. *Which isn't stretching her, though...* As Sophy must soon acknowledge.

For the north end turn, FAST WHEEL!'

Not slackening, the horses curve-leaned side by side in thundering battle manœuvre.

Sophy wouldn't have missed that for *anything*; but now, 'BRONNY, GO AHEAD!

Somehow, more beautiful yet: the mare freed to find her own speed, Bronny tensed into a racing position; as Arrow drew away, absolute effort hammering steam from warming sand, Sophy gasped, 'Lovely, *lovely!* Oh, PERFECT!'


A trot-about, sweating the horses down.

Taggle arrived, then Jill, effervescent both: time for lemon squash. Arrow and Tracker got peppermints, and more promised: encouragement to not wander.

Bronny, stripping to a one-piece, 'Coming in?'

Jill un-knapsacked Sophy's costume; while Bron removed saddles, the girl changed. And sighed inside at the other's frumpy black, affronting her shapeliness and that complexion.

AJ helped Sophy up...

Not just closeness to Tracker, but closeness *with*; and, as he moved now, yet more so.

They'd go in slowly; maybe Bronny could gallop bareback like a Cossack but Sophy, who hadn't the leg-length or musculature for imposing her will anyway, was one for gaining confidence in stages. Furthermore, wild riding was much more feasible on ponies – and hadn't the Swansea girl fallen off lots, learning tricks in her stripling years?

Such lovely camera compositions; however, Jill herself must absorb the spiritual essence.

Taggle first spattered alongside, next he hopped and ducked; soon

70

he was bobbing, paws busy, as out the horses waded... When Tracker began tiptoe-swimming Sophy whooped, 'So *special!*'

Afterwards, Jill led the horses to the stream; the riders swam, rinsing off the grit of earlier gallops.

More squash unsalted throats; then clothes on again, and saddles up, for heading back.

Sophy dismounted from Arrow, and Bronny from Tracker, before many jealous ponies.

Heather's class was coming daily that week, building up to the County Show: its snooties watched too, mostly vaguely greenly; but some who'd never ridden noble Arrow shot daggerish looks.

Profuse with thanks, Sophy and Jill offered to assist; but Mrs Madoc was about to announce that, as penance, yesterday's birthday party girls were doing all the stable's chores that morning.

As Sophy and Jill waved their goodbyes, one scowling poo-shoveller unjustly poked her tongue.


CHAPTER 10

That private track down to Mill Cove threaded meadows to accompany the brook; opposite, wind-bent trees showed ever more salt-burn.

To gain the coast path they climbed a field gate; it not betraying their track's existence as a stile would have, wanderers seldom came Jill's way. Who cautioned, 'Always approach here silently, and let any walkers get well past.'

'Coming back, do you pretend to tie your shoelaces until nobody's in view?'

'That's my girl!'

It wasn't, alas, a private cove; that overgrowth-tunnel drifted them sounds of a girl, hopscotching.

Sophy tutted, 'Other people!'

Did Jill recognise...? She whispered, 'You might like them.'

Scowled back, 'We'd rather have the place to ourselves!'

Abruptly onto the glaring sand, she blinked bemused like a burrow-tumbled rabbit...

'So-phee!' Rushing up, Heather kissed coconuttily, 'Normally we resent intruders here, me and Gran.' Living near Talbenny Haven, they loved The Sands – out of season: it wasn't for them, the summer's throng there.

Having waved to the lady Sophy frowned, 'Shouldn't you be–?'

'Anna 'phoned: the rest are spending *all morning* tackcleaning and, pardon me, shovelling shit.'

Heather loved the blue costume; bubbly Sophy complimented her new friend's old gold.

'A lucky experiment! 'Twas yellow, in a jumble sale; I dyed it. Unfortunately...' Pingably tight, because the Pembrokeshire girl was also growing fast.

They swam, rock scrambled, did gymnastics... Sunhatted Granny Haroldston knitted meanwhile, lovingly watching and listening; Jill's biggest brushes bravely tackled a blank canvas.

Into a found sack they threw plastic, plus rope and net bits (polypropylene, apparently). Stinky black sticky tar balls, too: 'Ships,' Heather grumbled, 'need house-training; or, rather, sea-training.'

The other scratched her head.

'What are these, if not tanker turds?'

A relaxed swap-you lunch, Jill reporting satisfactory progress; afterwards, some sunbathing...

Heather, having her back re-lotioned, 'Mum was called Louise; she was so sweet. She made me love Nature: I'm so grateful. Taught biology at the Grammar, *adored* teaching. One morning, when I was seven, there was black ice; Mum said that it wouldn't stop her...'

Sophy stroked sympathy.

'When two years ago Dad said he'd treat me to something lasting, I asked to try riding; he and Gran reckon Mum's genes have helped me get on so well.'

'That's the loveliest thought.'

Hugh Haroldston had always done plumbing; 'Then a Women's Institute talk about renewable energy excited Mum, so he got interested, too; now he concentrates on wood stoves and solar heating. Talk about busy!'

'But...?' Sophy had heard hesitance.

'You'd sussed that we live with Granny?'

'She's sweet, and loads more with-it than mine.' Mummy's mum, emigrated to Australia, whom Sophy had only known for that confusing fortnight after Daddy died. 'Um, does the arrangement let him be *too* busy?'

Heather embraced, 'I'm *so glad* we met!' Then proved as understanding a listener.

Sophy said, 'I'm enthusiastic about solar energy, too: Jill has a tin tub and...'

'That was the Gwinear's trick, originally: Miss G had garden baths as a baby.'

'Was she friends with your Gran?'

'Always. She helped Dad develop the renewable side of his business by ordering a woodburner, and showing it off to every visitor: he got lots of orders.'

'That was kind.'

'*Super* kind, because that was just after Mum died: her belief in Dad, it was, which had always helped him weather setbacks beforehand, so you can imagine how lost he felt, then.'

'Heather, I'll not forget that: if Mummy decides to write full time, I must believe in her.'

'There's Jill, too. You, your Mum, we Haroldstons, and other new friends, all of us have to believe in her art, because she hasn't a husband. Um, or anyone special...?'

Head shaken, 'Mum would have said.'

'Such a waste!'

Sophy tried, country-style, ''Tis. But I can't imagine she'll stay alone, like Miss Gwinear.'

'She *mustn't!*'

...

Heather, again: 'My Dad *was* upset when Miss G went so suddenly. You see, he'd wanted for ages to thank her for supporting him; then, she enquired about solar water heating. So he quoted *really* reasonably for a superduper system, and she said yes, and he was all set...'

'But Heaven had plans for her.'

'I bloody hope so, 'cos the old girl was *so* busy here. I bet she went barging past Saint Pete, and his Host of Highest Angels, straight to the Old Man: "You'd better have a VERY GOOD excuse!"'

Sophy chuckled.

...Then silence, each knowing the other's thought: if snatching life from a busy old lady was unreasonable, what possible excuse could God give for taking parents from their young children?

They'd just agreed to swim ashore when Heather chuckled, 'She's snoozing; why don't we...?'

Sophy assented, as it would be harmless fun. And sort-of intimate, too: *Something rather cousinish.* If not sisterish.

Their sea-shielded costume swap discombobulated, then amused Granny; seeing how well Sophy's styling suited, she promised Heather a new non-school costume; 'But as for the colour...'

'One will consult The Artist,' Heather resolved, acknowledging old gold's drawback: it didn't compliment her complexion, it exactly matched it when sea-wet. 'And,' throwing her new friend a wink, 'don't boys at a bit of distance ever stare 'til they realise I'm *not* in the nuddy?'

An ebbing Welsh lagoon, tropical under the sky's stare.

Intrigued by wriggling heat-ribbons, the friends explored that teasy boundary of shallower and warmer, deeper and cooler. Surfacing sneezily Heather gestured, 'Blazing like this, Dad calculated, the sun heats this water as much as a thousand immersion heaters. The energy pouring down here during one afternoon would, could you store it, keep Drift Cottage warm all winter.'

'Wow! But how *could* you store it?'

'Perhaps Jill should work on that – probably with Bronny, 'cos she's dead brainy too.'

Finally persuaded in, Mrs Haroldston launched out strongly.

Heather, filled with familial pride, 'Gran'll clock up half a mile, minimum: as a girl she did long distance regatta races. Should have become county champion, but the war—'

A crisp splash, a neat bloom of foam... Surfacing, Jill beckoned.

With her I'll-show-you-how encouragement the girls' dives became surer, sleeker, deeper-reaching.

Meanwhile, Granny waded ashore near the easel.

Eventually, Jill noticed: 'I think Mrs Haroldston— Um, could you two stay *exactly* like that?'

Sophy, rock-perched, toes ripple-tickled; Heather, standing, hand on her friend's shoulder.


A family appeared at the top of the beach: 'Our fault,' Heather admitted, 'for splashing so much. But, bless 'em, they're jolly quiet.'

'Very unrowdy.'

'So blond!' With no unpleasant edge, 'German, perhaps.'

'I'm glad you don't mind.' Sophy sighed, 'I hate foreigners being talked about as if the war never ended. Or coloured people getting treated horribly.'

'If every country's citizens decided they couldn't forgive old wrongs, all Europe would be like Northern Ireland. A fine sort of peace, I *don't* think, putting blame on folk who weren't even born at the time! And how far might people go? What if, as a loyal Pembrokeshire girl, I'd have to be your enemy if you were from Carmarthenshire, never mind England?

'That's a weird idea, having to hate others to order!'

Sophy's mum couldn't have discussed Nazism or, indeed, what "Northern Ireland" actually meant. But Heather's dad hadn't, either; Bronny had. 'Anyway,' Heather said, 'typical German visitors here love our un-mucked-up coasts, and Miss G happily shared "her" cove with them.'

'I wish I'd met her.'

'Oh, you already have, in spirit: she'll never leave here completely.'

Sophy quietly sent greetings.

Heather chortled, 'Wherever from, they like acting naturally...'

Evenly brown, the sister and brother splashing in.

'That's the *best* way to swim!' Then, 'Isn't her haircut perfect?'

Sophy ached to say how Heather's hairstyle suited her. But, for honesty, 'Actually I swam like that the day before yesterday 'cos we'd just meant to go walking but then I found the path down to here and nobody was around and the water was so clear *and* it was sunny like this and I'm so glad I did because it did feel *so* lovely.' Her panting look pleaded.

Heather approved, 'A true country girl! Mind, your way with horses omened well. So, Welsh or not, you're One Of Us. Because, in the end, it's always about what your heart thinks – and nothing else matters.'

Jill's painting admired in passing, the parents explored towards the point.

Beckoning as they emerged, Granny Haroldston wrapped the fair-haired two in the girls' towels; they gratefully shared a beaker of tea, then shuffled off along the sand… A respectfully inquisitive distance from the artist, that warm boulder was perfect for sprawling on; close enough to sniff the lovely linseed, they could quietly observe without being bothersome.

How Jill wished she could paint those water babies watching her!

Contrasts were changing; came a breeze. Glad her models were when, at the artist's mimed say-so, the little ones hurried to the sea's edge: 'OHØJ, SIO-FEE OG HED-DA, HUN HAR STOPPET!'

Heather, before diving, 'Not German.'

Danish. Amazingly fair hair; oh, those blue-grey Viking eyes, their arresting glad-to-meet-you frankness never cold! Curtseying, Flora introduced herself; Nils, the younger, bowed. Towels surrendered, 'Dank-yiu!', they raced off to dress.

The boy's cotton-borne scent: so different from Heather's, but as nice.

A rendezvous around the easel: the picture was toasted by Mr and Mrs Gram in coffee, and in lemon squash by boy and girls; Granny Haroldston and a glowing artist sipped tea.

Hiking this biggish canvas here had certainly been worthwhile: with lively brushwork and faithful colours Jill had bestowed on an absorbing view a charming focal point. To convey the cove's enclosed feeling, she'd not shown much open sea, and set her horizon high. The low-tide strand saucered the lagoon in an eye-pleasing creamy sweep; thin glazes let sunstruck sand glow through limpid blue-green. Confident opacity contrasted the rock reef's solidity; her figures brightly blended rose and ochre above bronze and salmon reflections…

Sophy, 'Oh!'

'Mrs Haroldston said I needed you girls to complete the picture.'

'YES!', reinforced the Grams senior; cottoning-on Flora pronounced, folding arms, 'Du to piger skal vaere i denne male!'

Heather nudged her friend, 'We do look naturally right.'

'The happiest picture,' Mr Gram declared, 'for having in it, um…'

Nils whispered; his mum smiled, 'Two sea-fairies. We buy it, please, Madam Jill.'

'NO!' For, surprise overcome, Sophy was smitten by the work.

Though understanding, Heather must gently admonish, 'Heyyy!'

The lady's hands shaped resignation: 'Ah, it's promised to you already? What a lucky girl!'

Prompted governessishly by Heather, a deep plum Sophy said, 'It isn't, Mrs Gram, and I was horribly rude; I'm so sorry. You must take Jill's picture back to Denmark; your family will love it better than anyone else could, because you all saw it created.'

Mr Gram, neutrally, 'But you love it yourself.'

She stood her straightest; 'Jill has to sell paintings; I was being selfish. It was pleasing, seeing that picture produced; it's great, knowing it will live with people who'll love it.'

Heather whispered, 'Good words!'

Jill said, 'It's the same for me: when I like a picture lots, so do other folk – and, Goodbye!'

'Rather like that poem,' mused Granny Haroldston. '*Each a glimpse, and gone forever.*'

Mrs Gram gestured, 'Please…?'

Sat on that boulder, the lady drew them close and recited so animatedly that, although those children knew scant English, steam-beaten rhythm flashed them through Scottish countryside…

> *Faster than fairies, faster than witches,*
> *Bridges and houses, hedges and ditches;*
> *And charging along like troops in a battle*
> *All through the meadows the horses and cattle:*

*All of the sights of the hill and the plain*
*Fly as thick as driving rain;*
*And ever again, in the wink of an eye,*
*Painted stations whistle by.*
*Here is a child who clambers and scrambles,*
*All by himself and gathering brambles;*
*Here is a tramp who stands and gazes;*
*And here is the green for stringing the daisies!*
*Here is a cart runaway in the road*
*Lumping along with man and load;*
*And here is a mill, and there is a river:*
*Each a glimpse and gone forever!*

After letting imaginary coal smoke disperse Flora kissed smackingly, 'Det er et dejligt digt!'

'Yes,' smiled her mother, 'A lovely poem. And, like Jill's picture, a lasting image.'

Negotiations dislike distractions; Granny despatched girls and Gramlings to her encampment for reiving of squash and biscuits. Before following them she assured Jill, 'Hugh will package that painting for you.'

Signature flourished, Jill photographed the canvas together with the girls and the Grams; they would collect it from Mrs Haroldston's after their week exploring Cardiganshire.

Knapsacks had been packed, addresses exchanged... But everything *wasn't* settled yet: Flora pouted, 'Dette male skal have et navn!'

Sylvia Gram agreed: 'Jill must name the painting.'

She couldn't think.

Mrs Haroldston suggested **The Golden Afternoon.** 'Because it's been one, and that title recalls Flora and Nils swimming here.'

The Gramlings hugged her their endorsement of **Den Gyldne Eftermiddag**.

Hans Gram queried Sophy's rubbish sack; 'Officially,' Jill explained, 'this isn't a beach, so the council ignores it. However Nature insists it *is* a beach, and stuff washes up.'

Something came from his pocket; his wife nodded. 'For two girls who are Friends of Nature.'

Five pounds!

They left together, the little ones insisting on each holding a Big Girl's hand.

At the Coast Path junction, farewells: Granny had parked at Colliers' Quay; the Grams were bed and breakfasting at Druid Pool Farm.

Emotional farewells: the girls by now adored Flora and Nils.

Following a stiff back and hearing sniffles, Jill wondered: was Sophy also taking the parting badly because Hans Gram was such a good father? At the next gate, 'Sweetheart, please tell Aunty Jill.'

'I - am - ASHAMED for shouting at the Grams – your customers! You *must* be livid; I'd rather you started showing it. She started weeping, 'I've enough money for the train home tomorrow.'

Jill kissed away tears, 'Sophy, stop it! You actually did me a whopping favour.'

Hesitantly sweeping wet-ended hairs from her face, 'F-Favour?

'Your outburst wasn't *rude*: the Grams saw your true emotions breaking surface – and what better tribute could a painting receive, hmm? Cheer up, love: today couldn't have gone better!

It really couldn't have: Mrs Haroldston had asked Jill about painting her granddaughter's portrait.

The tin bath was sunshine-heated to the brim.

Inspired by solar conversations with Heather, Sophy's brainwave dropped the foot pump in, then hung the sprinkler rose in a tree: henceforth, open air warm showers on sunny days.

# CHAPTER 11

Having flooded the kitchen with yawns while washing up, Sophy headed atticwards. Jill called after, 'Hairbrushing now, or haystack tomorrow!'

Mirror-checking her fringe, *I'm so brown!* Well, she and Heather had been in cozzies most of the day. Girl and reflection nodded, *So lucky, our deciding on Mill Cove!*

Prayers said, she was 'READY!'

Nicely tanned, Jill confirmed, Niveaing the girls' back.

After a long diary entry, how about one book chapter...?

Perhaps another...?'

Adventured beehive-busy, the girl's head which finally tilted to its pillow.

After trying to sleep for, it seemed, aeons, Sophy crept downstairs; she didn't expect sympathy, *But hopefully AJ won't mind me sitting up a while.* Outside it was that mild, and her skin glowed so, in her shortest, lightest, nightie she felt fine.

In the dimpsy, an oil lamp rectangled Jill's table. Paraffin fuming the air midge-free, there she worked, lapping an alert and nosy Puss. Mogulus would have sworn on the Biblius Catticus that he was only checking Jill's handiwork – and *not* contemplating batting the pen away as retribution for his mistress' refusal to play; perhaps, though, he couldn't trust his paws: once Sophy was seated, he deftly hopped across.

'So *that's* why we bought blank postcards!'

Yesterday's report: three lines of news plus a lively ink sketch, dashily brightened with watercolour, of Sophy surveying Saint Brides Bay from The Lookout... 'It's splendid!'

'I thought, your Mum's supposed to be the writer; and wouldn't poor Hannah prefer to have pictures, to help her imagine being down here with you?'

'But AJ, what if the Royal Mail were to lose it?'

'Sweetheart, Carol needs consoling with your news. During that trekking week her days dragged terribly: she 'phoned me most evenings, because.'

'But...' Mummy didn't normally call Aunty Jill more than once a fortnight.

'Sophy, when you've children of your own...'

A redflishflashing 'plane hummed home.

That day's card wowingly approved, Jill had a still wakeful girl put on sandals.

A spinney enchantingly still, the infinitely indigo gaps in its leaf canopy starting to minusculely prickle white; Sophy's dewdance imagined starlight ethereally tickling her glimmering skin.

As she climbed Tracker's fence his wish was obvious, but AJ wondered: going bareback with Bronny there was one thing...

'Doesn't she insist he's *completely* trustworthy?'

Jill conceded; Sophy settled herself, and gently away.

A oneness, ghosting the dimness: the girl might have believed herself become horse, had afterglow not silhouetted Tracker's head. She began to murmur her day to him.

Together they stared out to sea...

A far off ship, twinkling towards warmer waters.

Like a war film searchlight, the South Bishop lighthouse's white sky-wheeling beam.

Around the airbase, myriad ugly orange glares; amongst them moved vehicle strobes, red-splashing the sides of coffinish fuselages.

Tracker turned...

'Stars, stars, STARS!' Reason, here, to learn your constellations.

Shaping the dark farmhouse, Sophy prayed for Anna; this ride's sensations seeming her differently alive, she first-time-ever wondered *How does it feel, a baby growing inside?*

Back at the gate she tried leaning to alight; but, reading his headshake, 'AJ, you must come.'

'Hold me like this,' said the greenwillow girl.

Fingers encircling flawless young warmth, Jill felt every horse-whisper. Inhaling through the still-sea-scented hair silkstroking her face recalled her the tear-taste of tiny Sophy-just-arrived, crying at Life's frightfulness; hearing the child's Milky Way sighs recalled that tiny mouth, once breast-sated, smiling at its loveliness…

In that moment, Motherhood pondered this woman; *But after time, food, and love, how does it feel to try love-holding like this a child of yours – and find your embrace rejected, even your needy touch unwelcome?* Already this girl could, as she willed, give love to others; with time's passing, choice more hers to receive.

How much did it hurt, the fledging of one whom your womb had carried? The jittery come-and-go, love-and-war, hug-and-hate of teenage years? And–

They gasped together; Sophy marvelled, 'He brought us to watch!'

The favourite face of legends, rising now great and amber from horizon pillow-clouds; rapidly paler, it started shining Prescelly's slopes. Against Tracker's neck, 'Thank you!' Then Sophy leaned back – and, so serene for both, that Jill-as-mother touch.

Farewells patted, Tracker stepped silently away.

Glad of her nightie again, plus Jill's cardigan too, the would-be woodnymph; met at the brook bridge, warmth-rumbling Mogulus was willingly buttoned within. Sophy neverminded her chilly legs: how many people in the world would ever ride so magically?

Arm lovingly around, Jill heavened her wish for that ultimate female fulfilment.

Sophy, asleep as the pillow met her hair – still wearing a cat-filled cardy.

A self-extrication most skilful: Mogulus never spilt one feline tickle into her sea-and-horse dreams.

## Chapter 12

Mogulus, pawing the door?

Actually, the climbing rose glass-tapping. Sophy peered the blue: clouds were crossing briskly.

And more wind was forecast.

Many sounds penetrated Tŷ Bach. South sent the girl spinney stirrings, and whinnies of enfriskened ponies; the South-West pulsed her surf-roar from The Sands. All the while, rocks to westward breakfasted on breakers.

An aeroplane overed as she skirred back, engines heat-ripping and wheels down. Landing would be tricky: its pilot fought gusts, you could see, just as a ship's steersman that morning would be wrestling waves for the rudder's obedience.

'So it truly appeared,' the girl related, 'a craft of the air.'

Toast, in the rack, plus *three* cards for posting. Fingers checked for butterlessness, Sophy studied *Moonrider*: delicate lines, and muted movement of dry-brushed colour... 'It's the loveliest yet.'

'I just drew what I'd seen: a night-nymph on horseback.'

'Um, I don't mind sharing my secret with Mum...'

Jill smiled, 'But not the postman? Understood. So, into an envelope with it.'

'With all three! Lest your pictures get franked... Or a sorter falls in love with them, which I would, and they never arrive.'

Before heading for a letterbox... To Tracker's field, of course.

So different, the spinney now! Breeze-swayed tree crowns recalled for Sophy underwater film of divers with seals: hide-and-seek amongst enormous restless seaweeds.

Tail high and mane spiky, on sighting them Tracker did a thundering wind-dance. After over-gate petting Jill smacked his rump, 'Go and show off, then: we know you're itching to!'

A full-stretch gallop up; prancing parades on the ridge. On a 'plane approaching he reared, whinnying; as it overflew, powerful back-kicks started his race back – he ending it with such a skid, Jill insists to this day that sliced turf steamed. Sophy said, 'He *must* get a ride out today.'

As it was too late for The Sands by then, why was a wind-frapled Taggle bombing down the lane?

Sabrina, now, on sideways-trying Slipstream: 'Before teaching starts, we must let off steam.'

So swiftly the two were up on the ridge, tensile spirit under dominant athlete; *'Beautiful!'*, sighed Jill, so glad she'd the camera.

As Sabrina began a perimeter gallop, Tracker came pacing, he and the other calling excitedly...

Now, the home straight. As the horses bore down, ground and girl began to shake: Sabrina had Slippy all out for the best possible photo, and Tracker wasn't tiring...

In the gunsights of those pounding wind-fired creatures, Sophy's heart was in her mouth: such frightening splendour!

But now Sabrina leaned Slipstream for that corner, Tracker keeping station as if he paired a cannon-carriage: like racing trains they nostril-blasted past, hooves pistonbeating.

Bottom-jumping like an exultant tot, Sophy shouted 'OH, FANTAS, FANTASTIC!!!' after the receding clod-flung din. AJ wound on film, all grin: 'If just one shot comes out well...'

By the brook-side corner, Sabrina had eased right down; Tracker circled, noisy for more. He shadowed their trot back to the gate, all indignant snorts; she leaned to pat, 'Yankee Boy, we'd love to stay and play!'

After, by much cajoling of a certain American, the friends had helped her out into the lane, Sabrina hazarded, 'If Anna okays it, what about a Sands outing later...?' Hupping Slippy away, Tag pursuant, 'A message by half past four, all right?'

As time would drag anywhere within earshot of neighs and whinnies, Jill proposed an outing.

After humptibumping, she aimed Bumble northwards; in the back rattled two elderly surfboards, woodshed-discovered the day before by Sophy and Mogulus.

A quirky clifftop hotel lured them to early elevenses: paintings, drawings, and carvings were for sale everywhere, even in the loos. Overhearing Sophy's enthusiasm the Reception girl, silver-pendanted

SASKIA, confirmed the owner's passion for Pembrokeshire arts and crafts.

The relaxed lounge overlooked a white-screeded beach, huge fun today for confident children. Jill got beltingly strong coffee; Hot Choc French Style was intense, not so sweet… Sophyisticated!

Saskia now brought over a lady of blownabout hair: 'I understand you're an artist.'

Jill wavered, 'Actually, I…

Saskia's eyebrows encouraging, Sophy chivvied 'Sketchbook, AJ…!'

Mrs Malator nodded: 'When you've some framed Ribblesdales ready, we'll find wall space – eh, Saskia?'

Her niece.


A wiggly coast; a narrow, closed-in road.

'I saw a cottage with a bright white roof,' Sophy frustered, 'for a moment.'

Jill patted, 'That's *Each a glimpse* again; the older you get, the more it's true.' And recited that same poem; she'd learnt it, pigtailed beside a moany coke stove, on a raw day carrying train sounds up from by Arkholme.

Ahead, now, a magnificent sand expanse with cliffs west-turning beyond; as Bumble browed along the shingle backing that beach, 'So busy!', the girl boggled. How did paddlers, swimmers, surfers, and even canoeists manage to not collide?

'Aye, because you can drive right up to't.'

Non-stop through a trinkety village: out-of-season art possibilities around its harbour, Sophy agreed. 'It and Colliers' Quay could be cousins.'


'How confusing!' Here was a little place called Saint Davids, but the city of the same name couldn't be much further.

'Sweetheart, this *is* the city: there's the cathedral tower.'

'Mon dieu, mais comme je feels une twitte!'

Historic buildings being best kept for rainy days, they reconnoitred galleries. Such lovely pictures, prints, and sculptures; some people sold pots and textiles too. And jewellery: a tortoiseshell cat brooch in one window arrested Sophy; *But by a factor of ten I can't afford it*. She hovered there trying to memorise its perfection until Jill, thrusting coins, pointed out the Post Office: 'Four first class stamps, please; I'm after a newspaper. Rendezvous back at Bumble, next stop Whitesands Bay!'

Though hungry, the girl gladly walked way beyond the café-clustering crowds; shelter found, they changed before breaking out sandwiches. Afterwards, Sophy sunbathed and Jill sketched nearby children.

Molly was sevenish. Edgar, about twelve, was tolerant; if she fluffed a catch older Lowell called his sister stupid, deficient even. Nature had made the poor girl clumsy, but she tried her best; alas, the wind played tricks with their beach ball.

Sophy was summoning courage to join in – moral support for Molly, of course – when the father returned from a walk: they must leave for Dinas 'NOW, so I can listen to the cricket!'

Molly walked silently away between nevermind Edgar and downtrodden Mother; Father impatiently strode ahead; replica bighead Lowell pranced, bouncing that ball.

Sophy, prone again, didn't see it gusted away, didn't hear Molly's 'I'll go!'

It bowled along...

Bomp!, against Sophy's hip.

'I'm fr-frightfully sorry!'

Handing it back she smiled, 'Molly, don't worry. I'm Sophy; I'm sorry you're going.'

'Your name is so suitable! Your costume, too. And–'

'MOL-LEE!' The male parent's face, hatefully red.

'A-And Edgar thinks you're pretty – jolly, actually. Goodbye!' Then, hard running.

*Never before*, that she knew, *has any boy*... She stood up – but arms-filled Molly couldn't wave back. Flopping back down she sighed, 'Each a glimpse!'

Wise Jill, who'd watched, 'Surf time, Sophy!'

It was roaring in.

Sophy waded out rather self-conscious about that wooden board: everybody else had flashy plastic ones. Fortunately, Jill's advice and demonstrations demanded concentration.

Soon both were having a wonderful time — and doing as well as anyone else. Sluicing forward upon that rolling tilt of water, what gorgeous puissance! Now Sophy understood why surfriding girls whooped: the fun, the sensations!

As she strode back after another scorching ride, one more piece of Life's jigsaw... The heroine of an Australian novel had been "addicted to surfing"; reading that months ago Sophy hadn't believed it possible, for all that she loved sea-swimming. Now, she didn't want to miss a single wave; also, every time she caught one she jealously wondered, was its break better for other people?

As for whether different boards were better... After Sophy's had stopped, other children could keep skidding on a bit; but her DREADNOUGHT BRAND was steadfast: several times that session, anguished wails burst across the waves as snazzy modern boards snapped in two.

They had two long goes; after warming up again, Sophy was all for haring back in; 'But,' Jill reminded, 'we're due home within the hour.'

Ice creams disappeared en route to Bumble; but their sea-play had been that thirst-making, Drift Cottage greeted two travellers as desperate for strong tea as Mogulus was for milk...

However, very first things very first: on the doormat, a scribbled message.

Back down in a trice, old swimmers on underneath.

Jill cautioned, 'If it's too rough, or you doubt you'll warm up afterwards, don't go in.'

'I promise.'

'With this wind, I need a head start; see you down there, hmm?' And onto Bronny's bike.

'Just a mo!' The girl hugged, 'Thanks for *everything*, AJ.'

'And to you, for such lovely companionship today.' So grown-up.

Leading a skittish Tracker, grinning Bronny — now completely recovered — rode Mr Madoc's horse, Lamorna: 'A moderating influence on Yankee Boy, I hope, because,' she tutted, 'what a wind!'

Sophy promised Tracker great fun, 'If you're good. Misbehave, and Bronny will turn back.'

He grunted – but good naturedly.

Taggle appeared as they crossed the gusty yard, escort joining convoy.

*

Perfect conditions for testing 702's upgraded gimbal controllers; these automatically aimed the video cameras. Sister aircraft 716 had already "resulted" well; that evening, Surveillance Data Analysis wouldn't be disappointed.

West of Ireland that morning, from 20,000 feet they'd detail-captured a Russian "trawler": such aerial-bristled espionage vessels monitored NATO communications, logged movements of Free World merchantmen and warships, listened beneath.

But that had been with Coarse Control engaged, and the Observer joysticking fine adjustments.

Early that afternoon, activating Automatic Image Finder and telling the Observer, 'Let it be', how 702's Electronics Officer had whooped! With AIF subtly correcting the instruments peering down from the 'plane's belly, pitch and roll of the swift-slicing turbine container ship they'd picked on had been eliminated: for once, The Pentagon had gotten 702 some Real Good Gear!

Now above Saint Brides Bay at 5,000, they'd one last trial to conduct: AIF tracking of a moving land target, resolution set ultra fine.

Both Observer and Electronics Officer scrutinised viewfinders for something suitable: after this long sortie their first beers would taste mighty fine – and the sooner they drank them, the better; also, 702's super-buoyant feel meant little fuel was left: unless they hit **RECORD** soon, the Skipper would be bawling them out.

The EO zoomed, 'Hey, is that the horse Carson Lightfoot rescued?'

The Observer notched even bigger: 'For sure, that's Tracker; how 'bout that?'

Exercise planners hadn't envisaged an equine target; nevertheless... The EO intercommed Skip requesting a Locked Box – tight circling of target – and 702 leaned on her wings.

*

The wind had departed most folk; however, at the south end Bronny and Sophy found Jill chatting to a young mum with a toddler and a son, aged four, who must see the sea demolish his sandcastles.

Emboldened by Mum petting the horses, the boy accepted Bronny's offer of a gentle walkabout; meanwhile little sister reached from her buggy to pat good-as-gold Tracker's very big nose.

Then, despite Taggle's best efforts, barking the waves back... Fortifications no more.

Lamorna had calmed Tracker so far; now, chaffing the wind and knowing their course clear, both horses wanted the off...

They smackily galloped through foamy tongues of breakers, Sophy knowing this was Proper Bronny whooping and cackling alongside. She gasped to Tracker, 'Just listen to her happiness!'

Wheeling about allowed a glance along the white-flinging coast to Druids Head; then for an ear-roaring romp back, kicked spray vapour-trailing behind.

Again at the south end, gentle circling to discuss swimming the horses. Going in a little should be fun but safe – but wasn't that southerly wind powerful!

Indeed: Jill struggled with her pencil to–

From the slipway, a scream... Gust-snatched, away went that buggy on a trajectory which–

Bronny gasped, 'Jesus, NO!'

A decisive snort-jolt giving tiniest warning, Tracker was on his way.

Urging Lamorna into pursuit, Bronny hollered, 'For God's sake, Sophy, HOLD – ON!'

## Chapter 13

The gallop of Tracker's life – and of Sophy's.

At that speed, everyone watching knew, she'd never survive a fall.

And everyone who'd twigged *was* watching: cars had stopped; folk craned from windows; people promenading had rushed for the railings, thence to stare.

Tracker felt supremely happy: here, at last, a REAL TASK. And he was confident of beating the kid's wheeled thing, so the girl could stop it safely. Back home he'd rounded up sheep and steers, darned awkward critters; by comparison, that metal animal was behaving real predictable.

At first Sophy couldn't understand: *We aren't chasing the buggy...* Then she recognised the classic cowboy film manoeuvre: they were heading it off. She bellowed, 'CLEVER HORSE!'

Only, could they work the trick? The buggy had really spinny wheels; hood taut as a boat's sail, it fairly flew along – was yet accelerating, indeed, its springy ride ever twitchier. She prayed, 'Don't let it topple, PLEASE don't!'

They were gaining: having got his second wind, Tracker was going and sounding like an express steam loco – but feeling like a battle tank. Totally trusting his judgement, the jockey-crouched girl juddered to his thundering power, skinny ribcage nearly pummelled airless, her triple-visioned eyes flinching flying sand and horse spittle.

Having more weight up, pursuing Lamorna wasn't yet in full flight; but, compared to her usual best, she was already off the scale.

Neither riders nor horses could hear that rising sound: many voices, ever urging them on.

They'd drawn level: now for a surge to get ahead and–

'NO!', Sophy screamed.

A squall had swerved the buggy: through a gap in the sandmist she'd glimpsed it now slicing knife-swift askew the wind: sometimes level, sometimes two-wheel teetering, it was on a course intersecting theirs.

And, caught out, Tracker wasn't reacting ...

Only one manoeuvre could prevent collision: heart in her throat Sophy left reined, 'Into the sea, boy – and DON'T WORRY ABOUT ME!'

Wind now galing, folk on the front saw the hurtling buggy only intermittently; sometimes, indeed, sand whipped yet higher obscured that headlong horse with its petite rider.

As the chase furlonged northwards, people gathered around a birdwatcher who'd powerful binoculars. All cheered as he reported Tracker catching up, but his woeful 'GOOD GOD!' had everyone holding their breath.

They MUST avoid a crash: full faith in Sophy's judgement, Tracker obeyed. Maintaining that lung-searing speed into the surf, each screeding wave boshed up spray ever harder to see beyond...

Without warning it came rearing, that wall of green-streaked white.

Would that this should help his precious human friend: as that crashing water overwhelmed him, the horse ducked... And he succumbed to those pounding rolling tons satisfied, having felt the child fly clear of—

Head piledriven into hard sand by his own inertia, Tracker blacked out.

'Child, horse – both have disappeared.'

No consolation, him saying the second rider was about to arrive: they'd seen that for themselves. What would they discover, she and the youngster sprinting to rendezvous?

'My granddaughter,' mumbled an ashen-faced older lady.

The birdwatcher wouldn't say what, through whirligigging grit, he thought he'd glimpsed the pram thing do.

Missiling into that seethe, Sophy was thrust deep where dervish sediment tumbled her; survival training remembered, she tucked tight – and, lungs now frantic, prayed she'd soon bob up.

But this child was wave-trapped.

Lamorna hammered an agonised Bronny along; *But at least that buggy—*

'Oh, JESUS!'

Sand ripples bounced and bucked it then, flipping, it slam-landed side-on in the surf...

'WHOA, LADY!'

Here, full pelt, came Heather, who gasped, 'Bronny, I'll help the baby: you find Sophy!'

Sophy, held under by rolling water: helplessly trapped, like a leaf in a river eddy.

Urging Lamorna in, Bronny was astonished by Tracker's head bursting from that roaring whiteness; struggled up, he bulwarked his stable-mate against the breakers.

Sophy, wishing for poor Mummy's sake that this wasn't happening: *So sad, she'll be.*

Stirrup-standing, the Swansea girl searched screamingly, teetering new-soaked when seas slammed into the horses; they, equally frantically, gave voice.

A shout, behind: underducking rollers, Heather lunged for a floppiness being pulsed about…
    'SO-PHEE!' Bronny wept joyously, seeing movement.

Perversely, a tide-rip had freed Sophy from that malevolent undertow's grip.
    As both horses struggled ashore the girl, coughing done, straightened up beside Heather with the weakest smile of relief. Who kissedandkissed, 'Please, Sophy, NEVER, Sophy, EVER, Sophy, scare me like that again!'
    Bronny jumped down and drew the two for hugs; then it hit her: 'Jesus Christ, the LITTLE GIRL…!'
    Waves were strewing the buggy.
    Heather seized the older against her panicking, 'Bronny, RELAX! It was EMPTY.'
    Collapsing like a string-snipped puppet, as the youngsters deftly caught her a familiar Land Rover roared up.

En route to Talbenny Haven for more candles (wise precaution), the Madocs had sighted the Great Chase. Having screech-stopped for Granny Haroldston, Mr Madoc had rattled down the slipway, looped to collect Jill and Taggle, then full-powered up the beach.

A milling of folk, now; although many adults, learning that the buggy had been empty, promptly dispersed deflated. Children lingered, wanting to pat horses and praise Sophy – whose concern, of course, was for Bronny.
    Conscious again, she sat horse-blanketed in the front passenger seat, being blasted with engine heat. In the gloom behind, Granny hustled two shiverers into dry clothes: wise Jill had brought a complete change for Sophy, and jeans plus extra layers for herself.

Slurping Thermos tea, Bronny declared to the others, 'Ah, I'm restored, now!' However, Mrs Madoc was unswervable. 'Love, you passed out: you need a check-up. Talking of which…'

Through steamy windows they watched Mr Madoc look the horses over… Seeing nods and pleased pats, thanksgiving refills were in order.

They felt fine, Heather and Sophy insisted; 'So, may we…?'

Mrs Madoc assented; 'But Jill can't cycle with you: she'd get blown off. I'll ride Lamorna, while you two take Tracker – with Heather in front, please.'

The Land Rover having gruntled away with Mrs Haroldston, Jill plus bike, and Bronny aboard, those remaining now registered an overhead roar: a Marine Patrol 'plane, which had in fact been circling quite a while. Visitors enquired why; locals said you never knew what the flipping Yanks were *really* up to.

The riders were cheered and clapped away; though extremely achy, the girls were happy saddle companions: the incident had bonded them and, pragmatically, each welcomed the other's warmth.

A full gale, this; at Taggle's level, stinging grit flew thickly. Extreme, his gratitude, when collar-hoiked up onto Lamorna's saddle.

At the slipway head, no young mother: probably she was acutely embarrassed about the incident. Someone Mrs M knew could discreetly get the buggy returned.

An elderly gent burst furious-faced from the 'phone box – because, he explained, on learning that no child had been rescued, every newspaper had rejected his "scoop". 'But damn me if you aren't all three the finest of young heroes, so let me salute you…!'

Everyone thereabouts joined in with his 'Hip, Hip…!'

The bridleway's dust devils and shrieking 'phone wires unsettled the horses; they flicked ears like billyoh, even stuttered back legs. Mrs Madoc called a halt for calming; then, 'You weren't talking to Tracker, were you?'

Sophy bellowed, 'How could he hear our words clearly?'

Heather's solution: 'We must sing!'

And Girl Guide campfire songs from then on definitely made a difference. The English girl glowed on hearing Heather's 'Lovely voice…', then giggled at '…considering you aren't Welsh!'

But Sophy wouldn't even minitickle in revenge, lest the other's ribs hurt as much as hers.

The wind on that ridge!

Books talked about the sky growling; a real experience, now. Those tall hedges gave some shelter; at a furnace-roaring gateway, though, Mrs Madoc must dismount again to lead the horses past. The huddled girls had their ears pop; buffeted Tracker growled.

Green mess and twigs in the stable's lane were explained by the shelter belt's cacophony: hissing air ripping at leaves, limbs clashing and cracking.

Crouching parka'd out from the office, Anna mother-henned the youngsters from saddle directly to farmhouse; within seconds they were upstairs, and wholly divested. Pinkly they mug-emptied cocoa while taps gabbled steamily for her; she gathered their allgritty things as, Cadbury-moustached, they started demanding each other's stooping hair in the basin. By the time they'd relaxed into cushioning foam, below them a washing machine's rumble was already rising.

Relaxed, now, truly: as same-aged and same-looking, they'd realised, why be shy?

In adult dressing gowns they glowed stiffly into the flagstoned kitchen, inhaling toasty cotton. Pulley-hoisted on a frame, there were the clothes they'd shed not thirty minutes before; bone dry and folded already, the things last seen in the Land Rover…

But, before dressing, vegetable soup and nutty Bara Gwenith: 'Fantastic!'

Sabrina and Mrs Madoc bustled in, the door gunbooming shut behind them. They'd cosseted the horses; Tracker would stay in overnight, 'Because it's getting wilder.'

Mr M telephoned from Haverfordwest Hospital: though finding nothing amiss, A and E proposed keeping Bronwen overnight; 'But I reckon this storm'll make 'em so damned busy, they'll be wanting her bed back before bloody long!'

Next, Granny Haroldston: 'A tree beside my drive looks ready to fall; if so, it'd cut my 'phone off. So, Anna, simplest plan – may Heather stay the night with you?'

'Actually, Gran,' the girl reminded, 'Jill did say I'd be welcome any time…'

Sophy's beaming smile: no better Weather Emergency outcome was possible!

Their Rayburned clothes pulsed warmth, and how welcome: the evening had chilled enough for mizzle.

Unbelievable, the way that southerly pushed at their backs: other times they'd have scampered, like Mogulus gone barmy; but Sophy ache-throbbed and Heather was still grievously stitched, so they just let Nature longstride them. Meanwhile Sabrina followed with deep-sea-diver gravidity, her knapsack food-crammed: Mrs M well knew growing girls' appetites, and maybe Jill's larder wasn't that well stocked.

Woodburner lit, oil lamps aglow, The Snug couldn't have been snugger.

Jill was delighted to see Heather, and not too surprised; could Sabrina help fetch in the double mattress for the girls to share? The fire's heat plus each other's presence would do much soothing; and she had, anyway, expected Sophy to eschew the rackety attic.

Sabrina codedly agreed that both girls might have nightmares; and what better than to wake from a dreadful dream about your friend, to find her safe beside you? Accepting wine, she admired oil sketches propped about the room; then, 'Will I see your **Golden Afternoon** before it goes?'

Proof positive that young Heather understood marketing.

Departing, she kissed both, 'I couldn't be prouder of you; and, girls, it *wasn't* all for nothing: you both impulsively made the correct decisions. Never, ever, forget that you two would have saved the little one's life, had she been in that buggy – and only you two *could* have saved her life.'

*

Competition between Marine Patrol aircrews was abrasively friendly.

Sure they had bettered 716's efforts, 702's crew wouldn't go and play pool until summoned; that impatient evening they hung about near the SDA's Drinkomat.

The Observer and EO having over the intercom expressed tearful admiration for the kid riding Tracker, the 702s were unanimous: if the footage *was* sharp and steady, their Skipper must ask the airbase high-ups about sending BBC Wales Television a tape. This would boost US Navy Public Relations; also, that boy's courage deserved recognition.

At last, electrilocks buzzed and a hand beckoned: 'Come see, guys!'

But just then their none-too-popular Operations Commander (OPCOM) crashed the swing doors, his expression even more vinegar-drinker than usual: 'Come see WHAT?'

The Tec. Officer offed the lights for maximum impact: 702's footage was the best ever.

The OPCOM kicked his revolving chair back and stood up: 'Guys – NO! Firstly, the capability of your new system is HIGHLY RESTRICTED INFORMATION! Even with reduced image resolution, we'd show the Soviets how STEADY our AIMING is.

'Secondly, remember the wisecrack about a secret three people know: it would only take one clever journalist, and TRACKER'S STORY could COME OUT! A STOWAWAY STOLEN HORSE on ONE OF OUR TRANSPORTS...? Our H.O.S. would LOVE that, I DON'T THINK!'

Having bawled them out, his facial colour dulled from hot maroon. 'Anyway, because your pictures enhanced so good, we now know that babystroller was empty. So, it was ONE DUMBASS KID who took Tracker after it like Paul goddam Revere! But,' he chuckled, belt-hitching, 'what else could you expect from a GODDAM GIRL?' He exhaled, 'Discussion over, gentlemen – Roger that?'

The 702s conceded as wearily as they dared, 'Yes, Sir.' And started gathering their kit...

The OPCOM now raised his palms: 'HOWEVER – those sequences reflect top flying skills, and exemplary intra-crew collaboration. So I'll suggest that UKOPS copies your footage to ALL OTHER Marine Patrol bases, to show what WE can do.'

702's skipper risked it: 'Sir, might it be captioned, *BEAT THAT!?*'

The OPCOM had some humour: he slapped the man, 'Too darned right it might, Fraser! Now, all of you – DISMISS!'

The thirsty EO grumbled, 'Some praise, in the end; but he never offered to buy beers.'

Their last OPCOM would have.

'No.' Then his Skipper side-mouthed, 'But he did say "*All other* Marine Patrol bases."'

'Yeah; so...?' It had been a long day.

'If he meant *every* base, globally, then wherever Carson and Sam are, they'll see our recording.'

*

The spinney roared.

For all its hissing door-draughts, sheltered Drift Cottage was better off than most houses thereabout; and, wholly within thick walls, stove snoring contentedly while sporadic rain rattled the window, that snug made an ideal refuge.

Their black iron friend: the girls rated its hotplate-brewed cocoa superb; when at the glaring open door Heather began toasting wholemeal for her hot-fingered mate to liquidly butter... 'BLISS!'

Sated, Sophy now registered the affable firebox's appetite: that log basket had started piled high. But this provided proof, at least, that by carrying wood home she was truly pulling her weight, as Mummy'd wanted.

Soon Jill encouraged, 'Into bed, girls, for a Stormy Night tale...'

Straight out, as if drugged – and now how sweet and sketchable! The artist set to straight away.

Before long, Mogulus came scratching. Admitted firmly warned re conduct, after a steamy clean on the hearth he compliantly curled the basket's wicker lid... Et, voilà, completed the charming composition for *Scene of Peace*.

So fierce, the wind, in the small hours.

Into that darkness carried crack and crash of branches; from the cove came bursts and booms. Though both children came awake, on sensing the other's soothing skin-proximity an instinctive drawing kiss-close soon had each adrift from thought again.

# Chapter 14

Waking encuddled, neither girl had dreams to share.

Heather table-groped two Dickensian dark green bottles; uncorked, one smelt 'Different, but nice'; the other, 'PHEUTH!'

Her note read, *For if you're still stitchy*; palming stinging, air-bittering liniment into her lean flanks she grumbled, 'Distilled from weedkiller, creosote, and trawlermen's wellies, I reckon. If that's Witch Hazel, this is Witch Evil. '

For Sophy, *Please get H to apply W.H. if you're bruised.* She eased down the bedclothes... Front, back, above, below: all over her slender everywhere were tender blue blotches.

Heather, overruling, summoned Jill...

'Sweetheart, poor you! No riding for a while, I fear.'

At least Haroldston nursing was the kindest.

Almost palpably punchy, that sea-roar filling the little cŵm.

Shredded clouds tumbled a pearl sky like express-swirled station litter, and... 'Heather, look!' Was that great creamy blob wobbling over fifty feet up Doctor Who's *Spawn of Death*?

'Spindrift – sea foam. And it carrying this far, so wodgily, means the bay's heckishly boiled up!'

'Wow!', Sophy wowed. Mind you, that's a huge noise.'

Heather, pensively, 'Even big ships will be galumphing; as for any small boat caught out there...'

Spinney detritus might strew its roof, but Drift Cottage wasn't damaged.

Discovering umpteen dropped apples, the friends jumpered the largest; though all were bullet hard and battery-acidic, back in Jill's kitchen crumbular yearnings were voiced... 'Oh, and every single rose bloom has burst.' So off again, this time gleaning pot-pourri – Heather, after front-stuffing petals 'to antidote my Witch Evil.'

Sophy found the medicine-and-perfume blend redolent of Boots the Chemists.

'And don't you prefer that to me ponging of chemicals and boots?'

Now here streaked wind-wild Mogulus to play *You chase – I climb*. They obliged their best, i.e. stiffly, and sometimes ouching.

No electricity, that morning. On Sophy's portable radio the BBC breakfast-bulletined tugs assisting a freighter near Lundy, and damage all up the Irish Sea. Concerned for a yacht departed Dublin-bound the day before, HM Coastguard Milford Haven were requesting all vessels…

'Oh, dear!' That Heather had been chillingly prescient was Sophy's first thought; but, she realised, her friend's thinking of all poor souls at sea was simply instinctive.

Finally, West Wales police asked civilians not to drive: trees or fallen walls blocked many roads.

To the stable, of course.

Branches strewed the now hoarse spinney; Heather gleed, 'Oodles of Jillyfuel!' Their rain-nuded pale roots strikingly expressive, two fallen sycamores sprawled the brook corner of Tracker's field: thank goodness he'd been stabled.

He was fine; Lamorna, too. After they'd fussed Sabrina said, 'It's time to see someone else…'

This, the story: waiting in A and E, Bronny and Mr Madoc had garnered ever more tales of disruption; Sister, having heard the canvas-screened confession blushed out by those beautiful eyes, had said, 'HOME!'

Thus, being enormously breakfasted by maternally-mooded Anna, was the Swansea girl whose secret had exploded right before her boss's astonished husband: 'I fainted because–'

'You stick with eating,' Anna commanded, 'while I explain!'

Well on the way to mastering stable management, Sabrina Caerwent had recently assumed responsibility for all the veterinary records; while Bronny hadn't long begun her first college equestrian course, having a head for figures she already handled straightforward livery accounts, Tracker's included.

Carson had always paid cash for Tracker's upkeep; since he and Sam had disappeared, though, Bronny had been settling up out of her own pocket – and nobody had been any the wiser.

Her act of faith, that: the boys *must* eventually return. And profound Celtic superstition had forbidden Bronwen from raising The Tracker Quandary with Anna: that could be meeting trouble half way.

Furthermore, with monetary inflation gone mad, those were pretty lean times for livery businesses: the Swansea girl must do anything to protect Tracker and keep her job.

Alas, she'd soon been digging into her savings: Yankee Boy's winter appetite matched his bulk, and his Suffolk-Punch-sized shoes never lasted long.

Bronny's pay was modest but reasonable, considering that the Madocs provided accommodation. She'd been happy enough, living simply and weekly depositing five quid towards buying an old banger – beforehand. A month back her Car Fund had zeroed; not long after, Sabrina had begun questioning Bronny's supposed Lady Diana dieting régime, which was conspicuously going too far...

Half-starved, of course that mental shock on the beach had made the girl faint.

Pressing a post-hospital restorative supper upon Bronny, the Madocs, Anna, and Gareth had blended praise and upbraiding. All her outlay on Tracker would be reimbursed; he'd go on their books as a Working Horse. Mr had grinned, 'Making him tax-deductible!' Then he'd patted, 'All clouds have silver linings, dear Bronwen: because of yesterday's incident we've prevented you starving yourself ill – and, after that horse's selfless heroics, how could we possibly *not* guarantee his future? He'll become one of the family, same as you.'

Belly full for the first time in ages, she'd gone to bed tearfully happy.

Sophy said, 'I'm so glad the truth came out; but, Mrs Madoc, why *did* you send Bronny to hospital? At school, if children faint briefly Mrs Gilder soon has them back in lessons.'

Beautifully ambiguously, 'Dear, how could I tell what condition Bronny was in? While she was unconscious I couldn't ask if there was anything I should know; and, anyway, haven't you just learned how well she keeps secrets? '

Bronny blushed; the Sophy she hugged didn't fully understand, but was convinced that she did. Heather shot Anna a wink; typical country girl, she already knew *exactly* how things worked – and not as misperceived through the distorting fog of playground gossip.

'*Anyway,*' Mrs Madoc finalised, 'what really matters after yesterday is, everybody's safe.' Then, with a deep breath like a page being turned,

'Now, we've storm damage to manage – and, everybody, I want that done without incident!'

The 'phone lines to both farmhouse and stable office were severed – somewhere in the spinney, chances were.

An ash tree blocked Upper Lane: no Haverfordwest road access for the stable or neighbouring farms. As council men mightn't appear for days, Mr M had gone to borrow a chainsaw.

He'd not been first away. Damage already reported the previous evening, Gareth's had been a dawn departure, his van loaded with temporary repair essentials.

Those eager girls: Anna, delighted, 'Of course you can help!' Heather could take messages to Druid Pool Farm, then Talbenny Haven; 'On Slipstream, okay?'

'Gosh, *really?*'

'He'll be specially frisky, but you must hold him back: spindrift can leave tarmac oily. Be especially wary, girl, if you see rainbowed puddles.'

'Righto!'

Horses, the Madocs believed, shouldn't just be ridden for leisure: they should do practical work. Their gig had got postman and doctor through floods and snow; that four-wheeler wagon didn't just give fête rides. It carted bales during haymaking, transported firewood, and from winter shores fetched seaweed for the vegetable plots. The family also collected implements, like ploughs and hoes, and old tackle: having located trace chains, Sophy and Sabrina had a choice of harnesses.

As Mr Madoc sawed off logs, therefore, Tracker would drag them to the yard. Sophy could lead him: that Listens Well had trained his horse for lumber work had been obvious when, the previous winter, he'd helped deal with a fallen larch.

Earlier Heather had, with a gruesome relish typical of bucko girls, overdescribed Sophy's bruises; at coffee time, therefore, the youngster's stoicism was much praised.

But standing and walking, she demurred, much more comfortable than sitting; 'In fact I forget the aches, because working with Tracker's so rewarding.' And reassuringly unfraught: neither the chainsaw's grarr nor its stinksmoke bothered him.

Returning at a quarter past twelve aglow with accomplishment, Heather was told to clang the yard bell: they'd lunch early, Mrs Madoc decided, 'So us can all hear your news together.'

Hearing that tremendous wind-borne roar on waking, everyone local had known its meaning. For Sophy's benefit, therefore, Heather's description of The Sands: the sea mountainous and completely white; stomping waves kicking up spray 'like depth charges' and racing the whole strand right to the sea wall foot despite it being low tide; that shingle bank strewn with mashed debris.

Talbenny Haven Village Hall was now the Emergency HQ of the Parish Council; while trees were down everywhere, the Portfield Ridgeway had priority because the exchange's trunk telephone cable was cut.

Children were biking messages about, even out to Creampot Point coastguard station. This was in radio communication with other emergency centres – including HMCG Milford Haven, now co-ordinating sea searches for the missing yacht, hence all the heliclattering they'd heard.

Heather described a tense situation at Creampot Cove inshore lifeboat station: 'Obviously they couldn't launch directly there or from Talbenny Haven; and, because of blocked roads, they can't get up-coast to Pinched Pill or Solva.'

Around the table, a groan of dismay.

Mr Madoc explained to Sophy that the RNLI's powerful but lightweight craft was kept on a trailer. Normally beach-launched using a special amphibious tractor, in rough weather the ensemble travelled to whichever inlet conditions favoured. Then, 'Heather, are they declared unavailable?' That was the last thing any lifeboat crew wanted.

'No, no! As the route to Saint Bride's Haven is open, Coxswain reckons he'd try from there.'

He frowned, 'Unless things've changed since I was last over that way, that beach track's flipping rough.'

She bubbled, 'They're changing right now! The Rugger Tuggers are over there, clearing the sides and levelling. All working like stink, apparently: if a call comes, maroons *will* be fired.'

Special red signal rockets, set off to summon a boat's crew: no mistaking those stupendous bangs for fireworks or shotguns.

All morning Sophy & Co had ably handled branches, bundled or singly; however, Tracker would never manage the main trunk sections on his own; and unless those could be shifted…

Sabrina opened the post-lunch conference with, 'When's Dai Griffiths and his tractor expected back from clearing work?' The Madocs' neighbour, who farmed just up the valley.

Mrs M shook her head, 'Not today.'

Heather tried, 'Couldn't Lamorna join in…?'

'Aye,' Mr's pipe ruminated bluely, 'if we could somehow yoke her beside Tracker.'

A scrappy-looking jury rig, maybe; but it worked. Pulling power was further boosted for the last really fat tree pieces by also hitching on Arrow, whom Heather barebacked… By four, the lane was open.

Lighting up like a loco after draining his tea, Mr Madoc confessed to being chuffed; cheeky Bronny Cheshired, 'You certainly looks it!'

Now, they stirred, to tidy up on the stable's own land…

'But,' Anna exclaimed, 'you two girls and Tracker have been busy since eight-thirty: have a break, do!'

Arrow and Lamorna stabled, Heather rode Tracker to his field while Sophy walked alongside.

Gate opened, the girl gingerly climbed; yes, she could she bear sitting on the fence.

However, drawing level, Tracker stopped – and wouldn't budge. Heather said, 'He wants you to come.'

Everso cautiously, up behind her friend, and arms around… As he took them up to the ridge, neither girl had known a horse walk so gently.

The bay was a boiling green-white cauldron; spray blasted up over cliff edges as if the sea were being dynamited. As for the far-billowing haze, *No wonder Heather's hair tastes salty!*

A yellow RAF rescue 'copter swooped over them to land in the base; they wondered, had the yacht been found? But, no: presumably after refuelling it blazed lights again, and chopped gustbuckingly back out.

A growling, now: here came a Marine Patrol aircraft, on approach. Tracker watched intently; following his gaze, 'Look,' Heather pointed, 'they're flashing us their landing lights!'

'Why,' Sophy scoffed, 'would a military flight...? Then she twigged: the pilot maybe recognised Tracker, might even be a colleague of Carson and Sam. So, 'Let's wave!'

It boomed over jolly low; from one observation port a lifejacketed and helmeted crewman waved back. Its number was 702; Heather bellowed against sooty turboprop exhausts, '702, 716, and Carson's 789 were this base's Three Sisters.'

Wheelbarrowing the chainsaw, Mr Madoc met them at the gate: 'I'm after cutting up those sycamores by the brook; as I don't want His Nosiness interfering, could you...?'

Leaving someone trough-golloping outside the stable office they demanded, 'What's next?'

'Honestly, now,' Sabrina asked, 'how was that ride?'

Sophy bum-massaged, 'Tolerable.'

A haysack to soften its seat, they hitched Tracker to the four-wheeler. Trundling down, Sabrina demonstrated driving basics; once in his field, an awed Sophy took the reins. And off around the perimeter while the others gathered small falls: not a straightforward exercise, because Sabrina contrived tricky situations; and thus the youngster learned lots about manoeuvring.

Circuit completed, Sabrina said, 'That's ideal stuff for Jill.' So, seen through the gate by her tutor, Sophy drove to Drift Cottage with Heather "riding shotgun", i.e. working the brake.

They composed a raucous work song as that fuel flew over the hedge: Jill's surprise gift, for when she returned from sea-sketching.

Slowly Sophy backed and turned, veryminding Bumble's wing panels... Their rumbly amble back seemed so delightfully story-like, the friends couldn't help leaning into each other.

Sabrina watched them re-entering the field, arms folded: 'Good driving, Sophy!' Indeed; but Tracker's good sense must be acknowledged: wholly aware of the vehicle in his charge, he'd carefully negotiated anywhere narrow, and never tried turning sharply.

Sophy mentally compared Tracker, Lamorna, Arrow, and Slipstream with the hacking ponies. If let out, most of the latter would just moochingly graze; freed, the girl saw those four adventurers taking off – probably to go and race about the beach, surf-cantering just for the joy.

Therefore, kit them out cowboy-style for camping and turn them Prescelly-ward, and wouldn't they be raring to thread the county's bridleways and get up on those moors? To explore from standing stones to Atlantic-panorama'd cairn; and then down to a brackeny dell, there to pitch tents and stream-dip the day's dust away.

Engine cut, Mr M beckoned: 'Let's load it all, logs *and* brash.'

The foresters' term for smaller branches, how the girls relished its onomatopœia: "Brash!" was the very sound of such stuff when flung. Another consignment for Jill, this: Mr Madoc would come along, to choose a storage spot and then show how to construct a drying stack.

Arriving home during their unloading, the artist protested re overgenerosity.

He insisted, 'You've helped us lots; and as for Sophy's efforts today…'

Wagon emptied, Jill asked, 'Finishing now, you two?'

Firmly synchronised, 'Not yet!' Firstly, for fairness Heather must drive the wagon back and park it in its shed; also, as everyone had had a long day, they must help to put the stable to bed.

Their rattling into the yard appeared Mrs Madoc. Not having heard from Granny Haroldston, she'd driven over: two trees down, ergo no 'phone. 'So, might our Lumber Gang be free tomorrow…?'

Mr Madoc and the girls exchanged thumbs-ups.

Goodnighting, Sophy whispered, 'More work, tomorrow!'

Tracker's way of nodding: had he followed earlier conversations?

Jill had wondered, *Might Sophy sleep upstairs, tonight?* But seeing the friends tramping home, arms around shoulders, animated breaths fogging the spinney's stillness as Heather relived her outing on Slippy… 'Getting chilly, girls! But you'll be cosy, in together again.'

A hearthed tin bath already half full, the hotplate's copper pan just reaching simmer again to top it up; a giggly squeezy in-together bath; a candle-lit loll dry, linseed-seduced by sketches of sea-boshed rocks.

Now the brushing of each other's heat-soaked hair, plus deeper contemplation of this fresh art... And though they'd barely cork-sniffed the mantleshelf's opened claret, these emboldened junior connoisseurs agreed, 'They're all RUDDY GOOD!'

Paregorics applied, they dressed, Heather in loaned clothes: their wine-relaxed cook was a touch confused by apparently two Sophies simultaneously gracing her kitchen.

The suppered friends rug-stretched pyjama'd to watch a Debussy concert in the flames, Mogulus too; that scene captured, Jill owned up to sketching the three the night before...

Delighted by those drawings, both girls (the cat was non-committal) assured her they were happy to be sketched whenever. 'Except,' Heather asked, 'will you please draw us separately, sometimes: I'd like to buy a picture of Sophy.'

'Me too!', said the other. 'Um, you know what I really mean.'

'Gladly I will,' smiled Jill. 'But I wouldn't dream of charging.'

Each knew they'd receive something above valuation...

For both, to this day, such treasured possessions.

Last thing, shared prayers: on the missing yacht was a family with three young children.

During the night, each had a chilling nightmare about the other, lost at sea... The waking consolation, then, that comes from sleeping closely.

Theirs now, a Companionship of Hearts.

## Chapter 15

The yacht was safe! Thus the BBC related it...

Soon after clearing Saint Annes, the headland guarding Milford Haven's entrance, its skipper wared that strengthening southerly. He'd too modest an engine for turning back; but northwards, Skomer and Skokholm promised offshore reefs, and tide races infamously turbulent when the wind contraried. So he and his wife and children had sailed their flying fastest westward, to cross the St George's Channel steamer lanes before visibility deteriorated.

Unfortunately, the yacht had had no radio to report that change of plan. So while, sea-anchored south of Ireland, the family had safely ridden out the storm's edge, they'd been reported overdue – and searches had begun along their intended route. Only after an Irish trawler out of Dunmore East had chanced upon *Alcantara* slooping comfortably towards Carnsore were Welsh Coastguards telexed a position, plus ALL PRESENT ALL WELL.

High cloud fuzzed the sun; a gentle south-westerly told The Sands still crunchous.

They called at Tracker's; he'd already left for work. A GPO van was departing the yard as they arrived: garrisoning the reconnected office, Bronny would advise parents that all sessions were cancelled.

The Land Rover must stay for Anna – so, four-wheeler loaded and Tracker hitched, away Mr Madoc drove, his either side apprentices closely watching and learning.

A car could never compare!

Sitting so high, you commanded the hedge banks: the landscape's every feature and the entire sky were yours; and no tiresome engine-thrum, just a jingled clopping trundle.

So closely they approached a pole-perched buzzard before it took off, Sophy and the magnificent bird exchanged acute-eyed looks: Heather reached to nudge, 'Magical, yes?'

Encountering horses, some drivers acted idiotically: handling this wagon required perspicacity and cool nerve. Nevertheless, as Listens Well had taught Tracker so well, on one quiet stretch Mr Madoc could let each youngster take control a while.

How could you not tingle, rolling along with the reins in your hands? Although, just as Tracker wore a weighty harness and knew the wagon's drag, you sensed that burden of responsibility… especially when instinct drifted this horse to the American side of the road: that kept you alert!

Both youngsters appreciated how much easier, driving with a

companion: watching for traffic behind, signalling All Clear to overtakers, working the brake.

A greenbluesilver bay, today; of a ship on its swell-creased horizon, Heather's 'Isn't she a heavyroller?' had it perfectly.

Crunchous surf, certainly. Adults edged its metallic gleam; children ran splattily: much wrack, there was, for playing *Found It First!* But those waves weren't dangerously rowdy, so why wasn't anybody going in? Indeed why, most oddly, was nobody even in a costume?

There was little driftwood on the shingle ridge, but plenty of proof that the sea is the sailor's dustbin: plastic containers, rope tangles, paint cans, glass bottles (mostly unsmashed, amazingly), tar balls... And dead birds, by the hundred: sad compresses of grease-glued feathers, same as those children must be finding.

Then, its reek: oil. Toxically sheening the sea, black splotting and rainbow blooming the strand.

So foul a blow against this beautiful coast! Sophy frowned, 'What caused this pollution?'

Heather sighed, 'You should ask, who? Slicks were really common before there were rules forbidding tankers from cleaning out at sea; nowadays, ships do sometimes get caught and captains are prosecuted – but in rough weather, who can check on what crews are up to...?'

'The filthy, *filthy* pigs, never thinking about the mess they cause, the creatures they kill!'

But perhaps they did: Mr Madoc explained that crooked ship owners told their officers, "Do as we say, or we fire you!" 'Those men wouldn't break the law, only they've families to support.'

Heather patted, 'Sophes, I said things are improving.'

'As older ships are scrapped,' Mr Madoc nodded, 'and people gradually care more about Nature.'

'They must care *loads* more!', Sophy pouted. 'All those poor birds! And how many holidays have been spoilt?' So many, if the whole Pembrokeshire coast had been affected; and what about up where the Grams were, Cardigan way? So far, they'd travelled, to explore these precious shores.

Talbenny Haven.

A canvas cover flapped on a damaged roof; ripped from walls, climbing roses sprawled lawns. Flagpoles had toppled; a lamp-post was well wonked. Atlantic Terrace's missing chimney pots were conspicuous as tooth gaps; that bus shelter where once Bronny had shivered, black-eyed, wasn't one any more.

Forlorn faces, everywhere; but Tracker's chinkling progress along the front did lift spirits: indeed, some cheered children broke from parents to run abreast, enviously asking the horse's name.

Necessarily alert for berk drivers, Heather and Sophy hated not returning every friendly wave.

Sleepy, now, the lane that they'd turned onto.

But an important thoroughfare in prehistoric times, for that skyline ridge it climbed towards was the watershed between Saint Brides Bay and the Bristol Channel. Beyond was a descent to The Spread Eagle.

Well that name described the forked upper reaches of Sandy Haven; this inlet, branching north from the Milford Haven waterway, had like Pinched Pill been tradeless many decades. Trees were steadily dismantling its lime kilns and old wharves, but in pasture doming down to a dull red shore, steadfast standing stones still aligned for a purpose millennia had forgotten.

Sophy was fascinated by what he'd described; few folk, Mr M regretted, showed such interest.

Granny's house, *Bishop's Watch*, was ten minutes' walk from the village.

There it stood: a tall-windowed Edwardian villa, tending to pomposity. Heather explained the name: looking across Saint Brides Bay, the South Bishop rock dominated its panorama. 'From my bed I can see the lighthouse, and watch the ships.'

*How romantic!* 'And make up stories about their destinations, their cargoes, and their crews?'

'Yes; but how did you—?'

'Because it's what I'd do!' And more: imagining herself onto a midnight-rambling ship, Sophy would sail away to many an Isla Incognita.

Mr Madoc prompted, 'And why else does the name work well...?'

'Ah, yes: a Mr Player had it built – and he was good at chess. Clever, eh?'

'A Name For Three Reasons!'

Impatience leaping Taggle down well before the gateway, he yapped ahead to alert the kettle.

Granny's drive was a dreadful mess: it grudged them hardly enough room to close the gate behind them, and unhitch Tracker. While he drank from the clear-trickling ditch, Sophy studied the maple left standing: *Vulnerable and shivery, like a stripped slim girl contemplating an icy pool.*

Mr M left smoking the problem over, the youngsters commandoed through branchtangles to, first thing, deliver Jill's letter; message absorbed, Granny went thoughtfully larderwards.

Hot drinks, and planning.

Tracker would, they decided, drag each chainsawed tree section to the yard behind the house; Mr Madoc would later set up there to produce right-sized logs for Granny's stove.

Cocoa'd and biscuited, Heather and Sophy shot off; shortly the adults heard pushpull bowsawing being hilariously learnt: 'So good for each other,' they agreed.

Quite soon the girls had cleared enough brash for Mr Madoc to make a start.

This was trickier work than yesterday: Sophy took Tracker grazing verges while the machine rivved and gnarred, smoke upsquirting while sawdust downshowered. Goggled, gauntleted, leather aproned, Mr Madoc hesitated before each cut: a heft to see if, relieved of weight, the tree might roll or tip; a check that the falling offcut couldn't bounce or be deflected. Finally, he must be sure of his stance – because chainsaws were 'Vicious, VICIOUS gubbers if you loses control!'

Motor silenced, girl and horse negotiated the wreck, shackled up, and were ready to haul.

Heather was nearly ready to stack logs down the garage side walls when Sophy and Tracker arrived outside, slipped their first tow, and turned back; when, soon, Mr M fired the saw up in the back yard, Phase Two began.

Arriving at elevenses, an urgent repair completed, a very grateful Hugh Haroldston could join in for the rest of the morning. Hard-working but well-humoured, so like Heather, his coffee conversation with Sophy was engaging. '...And despite your bruises,' he concluded, 'haven't you been busy?'

She was spared blushes: Taggle butted in, 'RALF!'

Heather explained how the now remarkably grubby dog had also been grafting, mostly under Granny's sheds: two despatched rats had so far been noisily brought before the girl.

Sophy had pondered those barking bouts; realising what discoloured his fur, the animal's murderous relish slightly alarmed her.

Mr Madoc rewarded a Digestive; she had to smile, seeing Taggle's biscuity grin instantly disappear on hearing, 'It's the ditch for that gubber, later on: he's bloody as a butcher!'

A combined effort got all brash to the bonfire spot; the men then began operating very slickly.

Sophy & Co still having lumber to haul, Heather would start tidying up the drive on her own.


Tracker had just begun dragging the last piece—

Head suddenly up, ears pricked, he halted; rumbling deeply, he shook Sophy off to look behind.

Tummy chilling, she tried following his gaze: 'What is it, boy?'

Feeling as unsettled, Heather lay down her shovel and began walking towards the horse.

Sophy squinted against the sun: what *was* worrying him? An aircraft making strange noises—?

With great sweeping beckons, 'RUN, HEATHER, **RUN!!!**'


## Chapter 16

That groaning collapse now sounding unsurvivably close, sprinting Heather flung herself...

As she full-stretched onto the giant-thumped grass, air-whacking branches smashed down all about; exploding like bombs, rook nests catapulted myriad twigs every way.

Leaves landing whisperily; then, that feathery silence of falling snow...

Sophy struggled up to pat Tracker: he'd shoved her clear, somehow, then stood guard above. Wincing, every bruise made tender again, she stumbled, 'HEATHER?', into wood-flavoured fog.

Who raised a debris-bumped head to spit out grass and foxy mud, then felt her teeth and face – OK, apparently. Her chest's tenderest part so sore, she mumbled 'All here, I think.' Wondering, *What's this powder?*

Scream-alerted, Granny had reached her side door in time to *not* see the impact: a second's fraction before, children and horse were blizzard-obliterated by...

Sawdust.

When she came puffing, flour-fine stuff still filtered down: into it, then, flapping arms and calling the girls' names.

'OVER HERE!' Sophy had Heather's head in her lap: 'She's turned over; I said not to move any more.'

The gasping grandmother knelt, unbuttoned, felt that slim frame for trouble...

'Ouch, OUCH!'

Sophy stroked her friend's hair.

'Dear, dear!', choked Granny. 'That painful, eh, my little lamb?'

'No – but your HANDS are FLIPPING COLD! Heather sat up: 'I'm sore across my... Across my front, that's all.' She saw to her well-greened shirt, re-buckled her jeans.

Dragging his log, needing to know how his young friends were, Tracker the bay roan until–

'CHWLO**OOPPHHH**!' That dislodged most of the sawdust; then, a mighty stem-to-stern wrigglyshake...

Piebald, again.

After cackling madly, they came to reassure the poor unaware creature, 'Everyone's fine!' Still sniggering, though: they'd never forget that sneeze.

'That's right,' Granny stroked, eyes brimming, 'everything's fine. And mumbled, 'Drat this dust!'

That scream had got Taggle barking bristle-backed; the falldown had berserked him into nipping boot ankles, too – eliciting sailory curses, and a kick he did well to dodge.

Right then Mr Madoc had been, wide open throttle, tackling a fat lower trunk section, while Hugh hard-hefted against its moving. The bloodlusting dog, they assumed, had only got another rat: nabbing one soon after elevenses, hadn't he let them know?

Finally, 'She's away!', and a girthy log tumbled.

Mr Madoc set the stilled saw down, raised his visor and, ears ringing, 'WHAT'S - THE - RUDDY - PANIC?'

Hugh ran, Mr did his nicotined best; the dog looped between, strafing with I-told-you-so barks.

Why did that little group stand so still, facing the fallen tree?

Granny, her red rimmed eyes sometimes open, sometimes screwed close; Sophy and Heather huddling each side, hands linked behind the woman's back; Tracker, freed from his log, nudging over a Warwickshire shoulder.

Then, Hugh saw...

The tree trunk had utterly flattened the wheelbarrow, exploding its tyre so violently that nothing remained.

Heather's barrow.

Dropped to his knees before his daughter, the man crushed, 'Oh, Cariad, CARIAD!'

Sophy had never seen a man cry so.


CHAPTER 17

He solemnly kissed Sophy's bewildered hand, 'An infinite debt, we owe.'

'But,' the girl protested, 'Tracker saved Heather's life! She only got clear because he was warning us before anything happened: that meant I called out the moment it started leaning, and Heather could do that amazing dash.'

Granny patted, 'You did an amazing *shout*, girl: that door's double glazed!'

Hugh tried, 'Nevertheless–'

'What's more,' Sophy blurted, 'Heather saved me from drowning, the other afternoon.'

Heather protested, 'No, I–'

'YOU DID! I've not said before, because I d-didn't know how you'd react, having lost your m-mother. But I'd been aching to have it out, and thank you – and then tell other people.'

Sophy had been worried about folk assuming that Tracker's flinging her off had put her at risk when he, wise horse, had wanted her well clear when the sea toppled him. It was the undertow, she insisted, which had imperilled her.

'But,' Heather gestured, 'you were struggling free when I–'

No, Sophy wept profusely, she'd been held under so long, tumbling dizzily and desperate for air, that that hadn't been swimming but only aimless arm-thrashing.

After the friends had shared tears, time for all to fuss over Tracker; he seemed to understand.

Unnoticed, he'd entered the green chaos; now, tail unusually still, Taggle the cat-terroriser, the rat killer, the scandal-magnet, delicately lay something before them.

Heather pulled away from her father; palm-cradling it, she kissed with murmurs the tiny brown head of Granny's front lawn robin. He'd so trusted the girl: he had happily perched, barrow as watchtower, scrutinising the ground while she worked, to swoop fearlessly for food finds, even seizing them from between her feet.

She spluttered grief, perplexed: how could he, that fleet flyer, have failed to escape?

Mr Madoc's leathery finger stroked that downy red breast; thus revealed, the cold cruelty of Chance: shot, no less, by the tyre's air valve.

Hugh fetched a trowel; the friends bid the bird goodbye.

A brew of tea, Granny decided, to deal with the shock – the shocks. And, as they should celebrate Heather's salvation, despite lunch nearing she would sacrifice that monster Victoria sponge she'd specially baked for the lifeboat fundraising tea.

Delicious, Tracker and Taggle wordlessly concurred.

The girls pointed out that surviving a near miss each wasn't so unusual.

The coastguards, they'd heard, had the day before seen a boy cycling up to their station gusted way off the path, almost to the very cliff edge; calmly retrieving himself, he'd never referred to the incident on arrival.

Heather then reminded her father, who'd grown up in Swansea, about the Germans bombing his neighbourhood: several school friends had been badly injured, and two killed.

So, please, no more fussing.

The garden ended in a sunken lawn surrounded by apple trees; beyond its hedge, pasture stretched away.

'Mummy so loved this place.'

For its secrecy; for that blossom-circled sky in springtime; for blue-green glimpses of the bay between its branches.

The children lay together, hands linked, staring into the blue; this, Sophy's silent introduction to Louise Haroldston.

Mr Madoc investigated that treacherous collapse – despite overnosy Taggle's assistance.

He felt the roots' ripped ends, showed the smooth impressions they'd left, peeling from the soil; finding leaves Sophy'd torn from the crown too leathery, 'She died during the gale; no sap's flowed since. Wasn't ever decently rooted, see? While they grew together, this middle tree was protected; once her sisters fell…'

Sophy shivered, 'Her fate was sealed.'

Hugh, for all of them, 'But why didn't this one drop in the storm?'

Mr Madoc turned bright eyes on the youngsters: 'Well…?'

Sophy tried, 'Because it didn't want to?'

Hugh tilted his head; 'Describes the observed effect; sheds no light on the cause.'

'Also,' Heather said, 'why fall today? It's hardly windy!' She stomped one way, then the other, studying the other stump holes: 'Suction, I think.' Enlarging, 'The other trees grew in crumbly soil; this middle pit's clayey.'

Mr M agreed: 'The storm broke her roots, but she stayed flexibly glued in position, as it were.'

'Like a pushed-down sink plunger?'

Hugh nodded, 'Excellent description, Sophy. So, Heather – what happened today?'

'No rain since the storm; the surrounding soil had so dried out, that clay lost its...'

Acely, Sophy somehow knew: 'Glutinosity.'

From crossword fiend Granny, 'Bravo!'

'So this breeze's leverage,' Mr Madoc gestured, 'could break the vacuum under the stump – probably with a bit of popping and sucking. Heather was too busy working, but surely Tracker heard it happen: all horses are sensitive, and he's sharper'n most. Also, he'd heard trees come down the other night.'

The girls spun round: the horse had grunted.

The third tree had been cut up; the drive was clear; dealing with the stumps would need a digger.

Granny called, 'Nicely done, my dears: it's nosebag time!'

A conversational lunch outdoors, rounded off with more cake and mahogany-strong tea. Sophy loved that meal's familiarity, as the Latin origin truly meant it.

For Taggle's ditch-bath, Mr M now deployed Granny's scrubbing brush, its bristles stiff as the dog's indignant growls were loud. He delivered the brick of laundry soap a killer bite; instant regret, on starting to bark green-flavoured lather.

Heather teased, 'It *was* your terrier, all the time! I thought you'd swapped Tag for a hyena cub.'

*

Solva-bound now in his Volvo, a thoughtful Hugh Haroldston doubted Sophy's mother understood how brave her daughter, the other afternoon. Whatever, she also ought to know that as much as Tracker's behaviour it was Sophy's love-loud scream which had saved Heather's life that morning.

Thus, whilst respecting Sophy's wish for no fuss, he'd do something lasting – which she would appreciate – to evince his gratitude.

*

As the waggoners loaded, Granny proffered a suitcase: Jill had invited Heather to stay longer. Next came a cardboard box, 'Against you emptying her larder.'

Posters in Talbenny Haven sought volunteers for beach cleaning the next morning.

'If Bronny doesn't need her bike, might I cycle down and help?'

'Sophy,' Mr M kindly sighed, 'you've no obligations to us! Anyway, as we're deliberately not forcing things with Anna the way she is, lessons probably won't resume tomorrow.'

Heather bounced, 'Then I'd be free, too!'

Hauling over, he strode to the public 'phone, leaving them dealing with please-may-we-pat-him tiddlers; after the kiosk, he visited the village hall. On returning, 'You'll be collecting the rubbish sacks with this wagon.' Normally, somebody loaned a tractor and trailer, but with still so many trees to be cleared...

He'd drive the wagon down for them, then go on foot and finish off Granny's logs.

'That's brilliant, Mr Madoc!'

Pretend wonderment: 'Talk about horses being keen: for some girls, free time means the café.'

Not them.

'Listen, now – that's tomorrow morning *only*: Heather's group might have an afternoon lesson.'

'Okay!'

He asked, 'Home, now?' But he hadn't got back aboard.

They nodded.

He head-shook gravely – then whipped out a pound note: 'Ice creams, first!'

Eating her wafer, Heather wondered: could her group catch up on practice enough to decently account for themselves at the County Show?

He said, 'Every other team must have been disrupted, too; and even if you've not jumped these last few days, haven't you learned many new horse-handling skills?'

Sophy glowed, Sophily: 'Knowledge you might use anywhere, Heth – not just in a riding ring.'

The wagon, parked; the equipment, stowed.

*It's a good opportunity.* Heather asked, 'May I take Slipstream jumping?'

But Sabrina concurred with Mrs Madoc: 'There's quite a morning you've had, girl! Doctor Caerwent prescribes relaxation.'

117

So, Tracker taken home, they ambled back to Drift Cottage.

Jill had GONE TO COVE. Heather said, 'I've had enough of tar today; so, where best to sunbathe round here...? The paddock, I reckon.'

Sophy frowned, 'Must we go back to the stable, again?'

'I meant Drift Cottage's paddock – which Jill hasn't shown you yet.'

Indignation, almost: 'No!'

Heather chuckled, 'Sophes, don't get het up: she hasn't ever been in it herself, yet.'

Honeysuckle so smothered the hedge there, Sophy had never suspected...

Wearing bear's paw gardening gloves, they lopped and secateured into the greenery until–

'A door!'

And, after souses of oil on its hinges and ancient latch, then gentle tapping and chivvying...

Sheltered by gorse-outbursted banks, a maybe acre of wildflowers, once home to the Gwinear grandparents' donkey.

Which, taken most days down to Mill Cove, had never returned with empty panniers: always glad of driftwood, in autumn and winter the thrifty pair had gathered storm harvests of seaweed for manure; and the low tides had seen them plucking mussels, crabbing in crevices, sand-hoiking razor clams.

That north-east corner: what a sun trap! They sickled themselves a grass-nest, then spread the car rug and shared some thirsty squash.

After lotion, down they golden lay to whisper...

And everso sensibly cry together: about Sophy perpetually missing Daddy, and Heather always wanting Mum. Then, afterwards – Wise Sabrina! – the warmth slept them...

Tremendously refreshed, they stretched their downy lioncub limbs in the now lower sun.

All that while, had their spirits been sharing thoughts? For there was a new oneness...

An almost sisterly feeling.

Jill appeared art-burdened and tarry-booted: Mill Cove was filthy, too.

Vehicles couldn't approach it, and that reef kept out boats: inaccessibility was key to its charm. The disadvantage was, removing that rubbish sack by sack on foot would be hard work. Nevertheless the girls agreed about not seeking help, lest more folk got to know "their" cove.

'Unfortunately,' Jill sighed, 'burning plastic and tar produces such foul fumes...'

'That,' Heather grimaced, 'we'd stink ourselves or the stable out.'

'But I'm worried about all the—'

Sophy-ushered into a deckchair, handed a mug, the artist must promise: no more fretting. 'Because,' Heather reasoned, 'tomorrow's clean-up might suggest a solution.'

'Very well!' Tea drained, Jill started, 'I suppose it's time I—'

Another Sophy countermand: '*We're* suppering; but not just yet...'

Heather told of the tree, and her close escape; Sophy disclosed the brink she'd reached when pulled from the waves; the two confessed to flashbacks, since.

Jill said, 'It's all very well, carrying straight on at the time; let's reflect a while, now.

'In both cases, wasn't dear old Tracker heroic? Sophy, he anticipated danger and ensured you flew clear when that big wave came; then he stepped so carefully in the water, for fear of trampling you. Today he heard the tiniest warning sounds from that tree, Heather, and alerted you both.'

Nods.

'I'm sorry you've suffered horrid visions about what might have happened to each other; however, now you comprehend how precious any child's life is – not just to their parents, but to anyone who knows them. Which Tracker understood, or he'd not have chased the buggy. And I can see that there's a mutual bond, now, such that you would never get over losing each other.'

Hands met, and squeezed.

'Nevertheless, you still mightn't appreciate how much your lives are worth to *yourselves*. Girls, you must both learn Tracker's instinct for anticipating danger, must both consciously aim for a long life. First reason: you care about Nature, hence your going on tomorrow's beach clean. The Earth will increasingly need defending against people saying, "If we have to destroy and pollute the planet for the sake of Progress, that's just one of those things." By constantly fighting those sorts of attitudes all through long and busy lives, you'll do the most good.'

Heather chin-stroked, 'Miss Gwinear didn't feel she'd achieved enough.'

Surprisingly, Jill chuckled. 'A great introduction to my second point! The dear lady forgot in her later years how she'd taught through sharing her enthusiasm; that's what you two must *always* do.

'Always you will uphold Nature's importance, of course; but after you, the good work must continue. Chances are, some people will emulate you anyway – but your actively spreading the word might do much more good. Not necessarily through teaching; you might write, might broadcast, get photographs published, who knows? If you become good communicators, people will start looking to you, seeking your advice on what to do for the best.

'Therefore – hopefully you're old enough for a paradox – for unselfish reasons, you must act selfishly. Taking care of yourselves, aiming for a long future in which you inspire many others – your own children included – to continue the everlasting struggle against the selfish grabbers.'

Showers, while the water was warmest.

Heather said that the tin bath did pretty well, considering; but, thinking about her father's solar installations, 'We'd get better temperatures by putting in slates: dark surfaces absorb heat better.'

Worth a try, Jill and Sophy agreed.

In with the Bishop's Watch supplies was Jill's note, confessing *I've never baked much, so could you...?* Voilà, Gran's recipe plus the ingredients: Heather said, 'Now, it's up to us.'

Sombre omelettes plus cauliflower salad; pallid apple crumble with unsmooth custard... Despite appearances, all delicious – and Jill loved being cooked for.

A much warmer evening: after washing up, into the garden. Heather asking, might she try out the tin whistle, Jill fetched it and her guitar; mostly good sounds arose while, from postcarding Sophy's lap, Mogulus purred the sun down.

Aircraft 702 and 716 droned home; 'Back to the usual Tom and Jerry routine with Ivan,' Jill grumbled. 'Better they tried finding that filthy tanker, instead!'

Again, the youngsters would share; too tired for sketching, Jill turned in when they did.

During witchhazeling Sophy suddenly embraced, 'Heather, everything Jill said was spot on: you're indescribably precious to me.'

Meanwhile, outside, many gloomsounds and shadescents to investigate; plus, Mogulus must discover what the girls had been up to.


## CHAPTER 18

Mr Madoc was lining the wagon with tarpaulins; Heather laughed, 'Hey, Tracks, dig your groovy socks!'

Actually, potato sack gaiters.

Mr N growled, 'You'd rather he got oily fetlocks?' Producing two pairs of USAF overalls which had somehow become his, 'Wear these, maid, unless you fancy being de-tarred later – and reeking of petrol afterwards.'

Tracker trotted along the highway, chipper as anything: *Off to work, again!*

Both girls got spells of driving; the bowling wagon's ride not being bumbruise-friendly, whoever was Guard gripped the brake handle against spontaneous cantering – because, as Heather put it, 'He's got such a frisk on him, this morning!'

The Parish Council chairman would oversee operations.

A jovial chap – and just as well, seeing he was Mr Clark: Bronny had warned Sophy to expect dreadful word-play from local people.

Issued with old fertiliser sacks, volunteers boarded the wagon; warned against bouncing folk out, Tracker set off smoothly.

Sophy and Heather dropped groups along the shingle ridge;

everyone alighted, they reconnoitred on northwards for anything particularly problematic. Meanwhile, behind them, full sacks were already appearing.

So cacophonous, rolling that empty oil drum down; then, achy Sophy only just struggled her heavy end aboard. But they'd hardly moved off when it rumbled back out, BOMMM!

Driftwood and held-back tears chocked it good and proper, the second time.

A long lank of expensive terylene cord was miraculously oil-free: 'Could be very useful.'

Sophy, beginning to see well with country-dweller's eyes, readily appreciated that.

At the beach's very end, a huge tangle of trawler net; Heather doubted that all the volunteers together could shift it.

Turned, Tracker brisked to the first stash; Heather now hopped off, gloved, to load rubbish as Sophy eased along.

Greasy, the sacks, and heavy; but, back at the slip, a puffed and very warm Miss Haroldston told Mr Clark as he helped unload, 'At least I'm working on the sand.' For, not infrequently, one of the gatherers would pebble-slither and fall hard: 'Sophes could start a Bruise Club!'

They'd just emptied the wagon when a racing bike screeched up; rugby-striped, somewhat older than them, 'Sorry, Mr Clark: I had to help with morning milking!'

'Perfect timing, actually, Charlie Solva: you can partner Heather.'

Red Rab Farm was east of Talbenny Haven, about two miles from the stable; Heather knew the Solvas quite well: while she and Charlie went to different Grammars in Haverfordwest, they'd both attended Talbenny Cross Junior School.

He included Sophy in every conversation.

*That's considerate; and, even better, I'm relaxed talking to him!* An only child who'd no cousins, she'd previously wared boys, never understanding the creatures.

*But I wish I didn't ache so!* While not jealous of Heather, their taking turns at wagon-driving and loading sacks might have been nice; though, as they trundled and halted, trundled and halted, a thought niggled: Heather had mentioned plenty of friends, but not Charlie; was that significant?

His Triple Team having cleared the sack backlog, Mr Clark asked to view the trawler net.

Heather said, 'Charlie, as you've no overalls, sit beside Sophy; Mr Clark and I'll go in the back.'

Tracker hupped up to a smart trot, Sophy explained the plan to him – rather self-consciously, with that handsome Welsh boy right beside her.

Mr Clark sighed, 'That needs a tractor.'

'There are none spare,' Heather frowned. 'But we *mustn't* let it drift away.'

Sophy pictured Mr Madoc giving his pipe the problem; she said, 'We could surely tie it to something with heavy rope, so that it didn't go anywhere; then, when a tractor could be spared...'

Mr Clark beamed, 'I can certainly arrange that; well suggested, Miss!'

Back, then, towards the slipway, horse turning just as she wished.

Charlie said, 'Good driving, Sophy; you and Tracker have an excellent understanding.'

*He knows about horses!* She smiled, 'Luckily for me, we clicked on first meeting; but is it that difficult, getting results with such an intelligent horse?'

'Not that simple,' he disagreed. 'Reckon there's something special about you.'

Pinking, she turned just enough... he'd reddened, too.

How reassuring: either he'd not realised the remark was complimentary, and caught himself out; or he'd been deliberately ambiguous, but wasn't used to complimenting girls. Either way, his not being over-relaxed in conversation made their age difference seem—

'A–HOYYY!' And arms waved overhead, the sailors' distress signal: called to the rescue, Tracker opened up like a fire-full locomotive.

But here came ripplesand: Sophy warned, 'Everyone, HOLD ON...!'

...And, although badly bum-bumped, she couldn't help chuckling at charioteer Heather urging the horse yet faster, Boudicca-style, from just behind her head.

A thundrous approach, therefore Charlie had to brake very smartly.

A fairly elderly lady had hurt her ankle; Mr Clark helped her aboard while Charlie and Heather folded a tarpaulin comfortable; Sophy's haysack could be her backrest.

Sophy first headed toward the tideline: the smoothest sand there, thus a circuitous but comfortable ride to the slip. Saying 'Gently and steadily now, boy!', she let Tracker set the pace and choose which way.

Most apologetic about the imposition, the lady blocked her pain by engaging the children in conversation. Simple questions, but much learnt: thus, Sophy Fossway's introduction to Mrs Alice Williams.

Arriving at the slipway, Sophy knew they'd taken the best route; Tracker had, Charlie was sure, pulled especially smoothly.

Mr Clark asked Sophy to stop opposite the telephone box; however, Alice Williams insisted, 'No ambulance, please!' But might they make for the Atlantic Café? She assured them, 'I've friends living nearby who can take me home from there – via the doctor's surgery, if after a rest it really seems necessary.'

Nobody would do better at driving on the road than Sophy but, the sea front being busy, Charlie offered to lead Tracker. She was grateful; he, with kind eyes, 'You'd do the same for me.'

Heather whispered warm compliments as the boy stepped down.

The others saw Mrs Williams to one of the café's window seats; profuse, her thanks. 'And well done all, Tracker included, for your excellent work: as dear Millie Gwinear used to say, doing's better than praying!'

There was a turning place further along; en route, Heather congratulated Sophy for answering Alice Williams openly: 'Actually, *she* isn't a nosy-parker; but in this place, if somebody wants to find something out, they eventually will. Thus, better the truth from your own mouth now than a Chinese whisper later.' Of course she didn't point out that – AW was a clever old owl! – Charlie and Sophy now knew lots more about each other.

All of them being keen to recommence work, Charlie was leading Tracker back at a jog; but here was the café's proprietor, Hywel Orlandon, flagging a tea towel. Assuming Mrs Williams had taken worse, Heather's harsh braking screwed train-like screes from iron rims...

Out came sparky waitress Ellie Gugg, with a tray: tea and a bun for Mr Clark; milkshakes and custard slices for the others; an apple for Tracker. He, treat dispatched instanter, nodded conspicuously; his recent passenger, other side of the glass, blew him kisses.

Foreclosed at midday by Neptune's scheduled return, the operation hadn't quite cleared everything.

'Back again tomorrow, then?'

'Thanks, Sophy,' Mr Clark said, 'but a few of us can tidy up this evening.'

Heather, 'I wouldn't have been free, anyway: Mrs and Anna are planning catch-up sessions.'

The Chairman approved: Talbenny Haven was proud of the Madoc stable's achievements at the County Show.

His morning productive, a cheerful Mr Madoc got verbally pounced on by Heather, as soon as he was within hailing distance: 'Can we bring down Tracker and Lamorna this evening to recover a really big net?'

After hearing Mr Clark's description, a head-shake: 'Whilst Lamorna coped with those logs, her wouldn't manage a long haul like that.'

The girls took it well.

'However, I knows a horse who *could* match Tracker for pull and stamina...'

Heated by heartful young eyes imploring, Charlie said, 'No promises, but I shall ask Grandpa...'

...About Aberdare, a shire horse who would be starring in the County Show, and was thus already groomed into magnificent condition. Nevertheless, like the Madocs, the Solva family loved to see horses at work, so Mr Senior might oblige; Charlie proposed that, if so, during the afternoon he would telephone the stable, and Mr Clark, confirming arrangements.

Before departing he shook everyone's hands... Saying, at Sophy's turn, 'So glad to've met you.'

As they jingled, tar-whiffing, back to the stable, Heather explained how special Aberdare was: the Gwendraeth stud had, traditionally, bred railway shunting horses. Exceptionally calm and strong, old Mr

Solva's horse was named after the Aberdare Class steam locos: they'd hauled heavy coal trains. Also, people from Aberdare – an important colliery town – were famously tough; '…and that's tough by Valleys standards, girl!'

Charlie's grandfather, whose whole life was still farming, although he'd supposedly retired. He used Aberdare for hauling, harrowing, and so forth; the horse was, Heather winked, also ideal for mowing small fields.

Sophy willed Grandpa Solva to consent: that would be some spectacle, Tracker and Aberdare working together! And, of course, she'd like to see Charlie again.

Mrs Madoc gave the girls sandwiches; then, 'Feeling fit enough for a private practice session, Heather…?'

So Sophy Bronnycycled back to Jill's, reassured that word would come betimes re plans for later on.


## CHAPTER 19

'An afternoon here…?' Fine by Sophy, carefree in sunflower teeshirt and soft shorts. She would sunbathe later, *And Jill can sketch me.* First, though, a garden amble.

Mogulus came.

Those six small dipped lawns had been veg plots, the girl now saw; whilst the apple and pear trees Puss scrambled about in carried few fruits, pruning might make them bountiful as Granny Haroldston's…

Over the autumn and winter, Jill would have lots to do.

Curiosity satisfied, she was ready to uncover and laze; but, Mogulus insisted, now for the paddock – properly, this time: *There's loads you don't know about!*

Sophy sighed indoors, returning long-sleeved, jeaned, and wellied: dressed to cataccompany.

Moving slowly, better appreciating, *So many grasses and wildflowers; such herby scents!* Now Sophy understood writers emphasising the sweetness of some hay; surely delicious, this would be, to a horse. Alas, the hedgerow plum trees she only now noticed were struggling: the weight of coiling brambles smothering their sun-hungry leaves had already cracked branches.

She sauntered, remembering Heather's hints about Aberdare coming mowing here; *But that doorway would hardly take a tubby pony; and as for a hay wagon, it—*

Mogulus, left-springing, disappeared into high-piled growth.

'How curious!' Sophy crouched Alicely... and found herself peering down a wild creatures' tunnel, ending in – 'Sunshine!'

Curious, indeed: *Daddy would surely have investigated.*

Quietly from the woodshed, the Be Very Careful sickle, a long-clawed rake, those monsterman gloves again.

Hotly, dustily, she hacked and dragged away, hacked and dragged away...

'Oh, wow!', as a field gate appeared. Beyond it an overgrown broad track descended, all thorn on one side while, opposite, Jill's garden hedge stretched away: this was a route for hay carts! *Only, where does it come from...?*

And where had Puss gone?

Gingerly over, imagining the myriad poisonous hungers of those nasty plants which hadn't assailed a human in years; with tum well sucked and hands high, a sideways shuffle down that choked lane...

And, suddenly, Sophy remembered a news image: miserable mud-faced soldiers somewhere horribly hot, surrendering out of bamboo to some crazyeyes, who waved guns and prodded blades: those captives' prospects were very poor, the caption had implied.

Halting, the girl prayed: were Carson and Sam doing something horribly dangerous?


Beside a shallow ford...

Sophy whispered, 'Mogulus!'

She'd known the track must meet the stream; off to her right it went, suckandgurgle, into AJ's garden beneath a huge stone slab which the bank hedge was built on.

So why not tease the artist, only a score of yards away, with a yoo-hoo?

Because here was timeless: her afternoon's side of that ancient earthwork, Sophy wanted to believe, existed in a different age: perhaps that of Owain Glyndwr, or maybe Saint David.

Left, the rill emerged from a steep bank's impenetrable growth: *There must be a spring in there.* She crouched to wash dusty hands and hot face, again wondering, *Why such clear water, but an orange-red rubbly bed?*

The ford trickled contentedly; how incongruous they sounded, that spring's drips, plops, and splashes, all oddly echoey. She murmured to Mogulus, 'It sounds rather tunnelish...'

Then, shivery realisation: *Not a spring.*

She'd found the coal mine.


## Chapter 20

'Pussy, NO!'

But this undergrowth was irresistibly mouse-scented. His co-explorer *must* blaze another trail: 'Mi-AAOWW!' he contradicted, venturing further.

No echo: he was still outside the adit. *And might yet be turned back!* Further along, tussocky grass sloped: up Sophy struggled...

Crabbing across above the thicket to get over that entrance, 'Flipping CRIKEY!' For just ahead of her new-torn turf sagged, indeed blackly gaped: the mine roof had recently collapsed. Retreating, Sophy sat to brain her dilemma.

Anywhen there might be a further collapse, which would bury Puss forever. Perhaps lobbed pebbles could drive him back – but then again she might hit him. What else to try...?

*He hates me mimicking his anti-Taggle growl.* So Sophy inhaled hugely; cupped hands; and roared that loudly, her own neck hairs bristled.

Bumbogganing back down, there was Mogulus back at the ford, glaring gloomwards, his tail lashing superfluffously. 'Bad place, Pussy!' she stroked. 'Let's go straight home!'

Although... 'Ever played Poohsticks?'

Again, 'MRAOW!'

Sophy hadn't won once – not even after they'd swapped sticks.

*What explains that colour, coating every pebble?* A super stir-up with a much bigger stick turned the flow spectacularly orange: highly opaque, and surely mother-explodingly good at staining clothes… *Yes, because there are ginger blotches on AJ's gardening jeans.*

That first evening, Jill had said about finding the shower water iron-flavoured. So, the girl supposed, rust was dissolved in it – *Rather as Cotswold water is hard with lime.*

The mud-clouds cleared… Glossy black, now, those stones. Sophy fished some out, finding them astonishingly light; and, even sun-dried, still remarkably shiny. Looking just like… 'But Jill said the mine ran out of coal, so what's this stuff?'

He sniffed: no idea. Definitely inedible, worst luck.

*Well, proper explorers gather geological samples…*

Jill much appreciated the tea brought by the girl – who, mug drained impatiently, comprehensively worded her guilt.

The artist couldn't frown for long; 'There was only a hedge between us, sweetheart. And,' leading Sophy to the nook she'd been clearing, 'I even watched you, up on the bank.'

'So why didn't you…?'

A loving but piercing look.

'Oh!' It had been a test.

'I knew you'd never deliberately seek The Drift; but one can't curb Pussy's nosiness…'

He smugly misped, 'Mo!'

Yes, horses and hay carts used to pass The Drift to reach the Gwinear's paddock; and, yes, that briar patch on the spinney's fringe hid the lane's access gate; 'So, well done you for working that out. But while you and Heather won't be tempted by the mine, unfortunately other children aren't sensible – nor some adults. That's why, like Miss G, I didn't want people getting near the place.'

'You can always warn visitors, and if people choose to go snooping uninvited–'

'Oh, *really?* So would you say that it was just hard cheese if Heather, exploring a derelict cottage, fell through rotten boards and drowned in its well?'

The child gasped as her spine iced.

In firmest Lancastrian, 'I'm glad tha' understands, now; ergo, that door into t'paddock will get a strong padlock.'

'Hey,' Sophy suddenly beamed, 'Gareth could block The Drift right up with building rubble!'

Jill liked the idea; unfortunately, the mine belonged to Patsy Flange's grandfather, Nigel Cranston: 'I've only rights of way along that lane.'

Sophy pressed her: what harm in asking the chap?

'Because, for profit, the old sod will do *anything*.'

Without consent, Mr Cranston had turned an old barn into a swanky house. Anyone else would have been forced to demolish the place; but, with bribes rumoured, it was given official approval – and had then sold for an absolute packet: 'Classic Cranston manœuvring!

'Sophy, coal is dear; reminded about The Drift, Nigel Cranston might try re-opening it – never mind that he has no mining rights, something Miss Gwinear established for certain. Imagine roaring air compressors and smoky lorries just over our hedge, plus black dust blowing everywhere. And a dead stream, filthing Mill Cove with mud.'

*Horrid!* 'But AJ, you said the mine ran out of coal.'

Alas, that oft-used expression was inaccurate: 'Mines usually close with plenty of coal left; the problem is, the cost of digging it out.'

'So, what has changed since The Drift closed?'

'Excellent question. The Victorians' steam engines burnt lots of fuel, keeping mines drained; modern Diesel pumping is much cheaper, as Cranston could easily work out for himself.'

Sophy pocket-dug, 'And this stuff, from the stream, is what he'd be after...?'

Jill's eyebrows went up: 'Pembrokeshire anthracite, the best in Britain! Water forcing into the workings must loosen the odd lump. Keep these to show your Geography teacher, hmm?'

The artist and Mogulus weeded; Sophy was mastering the push-driven lawnmower.

Jill cleared her throat; over the scrapy blades, 'Miss Gwinear also liked that lane gate kept overgrown because she loved "communing with nature" in the paddock. As I do, too, at secret swimming places.'

She'd known: AJ was all brown, no cozzie marks. *And good for her!*

130

Because she and Heather had "communed" that other afternoon: *Ultra nice!* Half because, on reflection, such a relaxed honesty with each other.

While noting the girl's tacit acknowledgement, Jill withheld this idea: didn't shapely country-complexioned Bronny beg to be painted *alfresco* – and what better setting than that secret little field?

'So,' Sophy supposed, 'the paddock won't ever get mowed.'

'But it should, or the hedges will encroach. So maybe Gareth could enlarge the doorway to take a small cart; I'm sure that, with some shrubs shifted, a bright horse could make its way there across the garden.'

'AJ, Miss Gwinear would *love* horses being used to make your hay; that'd be a sort of communing, too.'

More mundanely, 'Maybe the Madocs would swap my hay for horse manure. And–' *That's Keith's expression, exactly!* 'You've though of another benefit, Sophy...?'

'Fantastic picture opportunities, with horse-powered haymaking.'

Hugged so very maternally, 'Sweetheart, YES!'

Heather reappeared dusty, scuffed, dispiritedly silent.

Shower-pumping Sophy wowed at how well slates in the bath had worked to heat the water... and elicited no reaction. As she lathered her friend's hair – normally she'd bubble with giggles – tears appeared...

'Heather, please tell us what's wrong, do!'

It hadn't been a solo session. Noticing Heather at the beach clean, Marcia Flange, pushiest of mothers, had guessed how the girl might be later rewarded; honest Bronny, answering the office telephone, wouldn't lie. So the lady had insisted, 'Then Patricia will practise, too.'

And, being that sort, Mrs Flange had straight away made the 'phone wires glow: soon pony mum after pony mum was ringing to *inform* Bronny that their daughters...

Anna had capitulated: very well, an open session.

It never rains, but it pours.

Unashamedly lying about it being her turn, Patricia Flange had got Slipstream; Heather, barged aside during bigger girl bickering over mounts, had ended up on Greengrass – the most unimaginative paddockmower. Who'd always before just been bus-sluggish, so the youngster hadn't been prepared for bolshiness: never mind sudden sidesteps, he'd bloody gone and thrown her twice, hadn't he?

As Heather sat on her towel in the sun on the lawn, snuppling tea while Mogulus fawned, Sophy assayed skin marks before dabbing treatment.

Next massaging, Nurse Fossway learned what the snooties had hissed about Heather's tumbles: "Serves her right!" Having had in recent days "So much fun on whichever horse she'd fancied."

Sophy's first ever out-loud swear: 'The bloody bitches! They've no concept of real risks, no experience of hard work… Oh, DAMN them ALL!'

Perking up, Heather now related how Slipstream had proved truly loyal: 'While doing one circuit, he just stopped dead and did this MASSIVE fart; his glance backwards afterwards obviously meant, "Up yours!". And what made Fatsy Patsy LIVID about the incident was that everyone, absolutely *everyone*, laughed like drains.'

As did Sophy.

'Anyway, I've kept the best news 'til last: this evening's on!'

## Chapter 21

During supper, Heather yawned so; afterwards, 'Perhaps I won't come down to The Sands.'

'Then, sweetheart; I'll keep you company.'

'Jill, you *must* see the horses working; I'll be fine on my own.'

The artist disappeared looking decisive; over sinksploshes Sophy thought she heard pedals clanking away.

Soon back with Taggle, 'Company for you; and no wandering beyond the garden this evening, okay?

'RALF!'

That decided Mogulus: off to the paddock, toute vite.

Jill walked a very keen Tracker up from his field, pushing the bike; the youngster cadged a bareback lift.

From within the yard loo Sophy heard Tracker whinny, and soon detected a pulsing; then, through that wooden seat came a vibration, relentlessly increasing 'til her bottom felt strong bumps…

Charlie's voice: 'WHOA!'

As was the wont of Aberdare's ilk, no standing quietly for him; he must regularly stomp, booming the yard.

Coming to the office door, Sophy met hot black glossiness: a locomotive likeness, indeed, enhanced by brassy harnessing – and Charlie's clamberdown, reminiscent of a driver descending from his cab. Leading Aberdare to the trough, 'Introductions not needed, hmm?'

Leaning lest her toes were steamhammered she patted, 'Magnificent!'

'I'll make sure to tell Gramps,' he grinned. 'Where's Heather, then?'

She explained.

'Nasty item, that Patsy Flange.' His mimicked spit a venomous fullstop, Sophy liked the lad even more.

He brightened: 'Gramps says you're welcome to ride Abbey down; or are you still…?'

She nodded loquaciously.

'Aye: a ruddy hard gallop you had of it, folk said. Damned brave – wish I'd seen! Then you must ride him next time, eh?'

*Next time!*

Mr Madoc, Sophy, and Jill led in the tackle-laden wagon, drawn by Arrow; Charlie and Aberdare followed, then Bronny on Tracker.

Though taller and broader than Sophy, the lad looked small up there; nevertheless, he was confidently in control, and alertly so – as Bronny needed to be too for, ears pricked and noses busy, both mounts clearly meant to egg a pounding pace.

Remarking the horses' excitement Sophy sighed, 'Heather should've come.'

Adoring how Aberdare shone like smoked copper in the lowering sun, Jill glittered, 'Hopefully she'll like my photos.'

'Ah, yes,' Mr Madoc remembered, 'Missus wants first refusal on any horse paintings you do.'

Sophy nudged: many horsey folk would see a picture hung in their farmhouse... *Good publicity!*

He asked, unpointedly, 'Charlie all right, Sophy?'

Proudly, 'Doing very well.'

'Us was at school with his gran'fer; that youngster has his instinct with horses.' He turned, 'And didn't you feel an affinity straight away?'

Unintentional ambiguity, Jill supposed.

The girl shrugged, 'Horses apparently understand, when I discuss our tasks.'

Tracker whinnied.

Jill admired, 'And there's your technique: treating the animals as equals. You realised of your own accord that they don't just want to work, but to co-operate.'

Past the Atlantic Café.

He mused, 'Rather how you clicks with Heather, eh? And don't protest that it's nothing like because you two can speak! The better you know each other, the less needing putting into words: you'll see. And, I dare say,' he nodded, 'soon like that between you and the lad, too.'

Feeling Sophy's heat, Jill fired a deflecting question about GWR horse-shunting.

While he enthused, Sophy squeezed AJ's arm: yes, she liked Charlie, and he behaved nicely towards her; but she was his junior by two school years. So—

Here was the pub, and Mr M was passing the reins: would she please drive them down the slip and up the beach?

A nicely-rolling wagon flanked by heftily striding horses: impressive, seen or heard. Far ahead, folk milled expectantly; Mr Madoc murmured, 'Silly gubbers had better keep well clear!'

The buzz between the horses being obvious, Sophy asked when they'd worked together.

He replied, impressed, 'Two year back the Griffin Brewery had them dray-hauling at the Carmarthen Show: did a grand job and looked damned fine, I tell you!'

*

Patsy Flange had orchestrated that needling well: Heather had felt whacked, earlier.

But, deckchaired a sunny while, she was fine again. A little shiver, then she steeled herself: it was time to spy.

Taggle tailwagged madly: *Action, at last!*

Pencil, paper, tape measure… Suppressing guiltiest feelings of trespass, for she was a good girl, up to Sophy's bedroom.

'Grr!' Espionage was difficult: even after borrowing Jill's screwdriver and her torch, the Big Picture wouldn't reveal itself. 'If this were a James Bond film, Tag, by now we'd be well away.'

Getting bored, 'Rumph!'

Pushing him off the page of instructions, and scratching her head… Unnoticed, something fell.

*

Charlie's grandfather had wheeled a whole barrowful of rope from the village; one end of it now encircling the net, he was gingerly descending the shingle, paying out.

White haired, moustached, tweed jacket shouldering cordage, the gentleman reminded Sophy of those quaintly jovial mountaineers who waved from Swiss chocolate bars.

Such resemblance between Solva generations! Jill murmured, 'I'd love to try a double portrait.'

Now jury yoked, Tracker and Aberdare had the rope attached; onto the wagon went the wheelbarrow…

All would be ready – once the onlookers had retreated: stumbling, horses could grapeshot pebbles everywhere; snagged, the pair might lunge sideways. And should the net suddenly free, Mr Solva warned, 'They'll be off like the Light Brigade!' As for a snapped rope whipping back…

Charlie steadied Aberdare; Sophy whispered Tracker last-minute advice; Bronny, now wagon driver, waited to follow.

Nobody heeded a circling aircraft: the American marine boys often curved about this way and that before landing.

With Mr Solva monitoring the net, Mr Madoc could direct; Charlie would command both horses, Sophy reinforcing orders if needed.

Mr Madoc nodded; on Charlie's 'Gently now!' the horses eased forwards and the rope lifted, shedding sand…

'All good!' from Mr Solva; Mr Madoc's train guard wave.

Charlie gave that key command, 'Go to!' The horses tautened chains, adjusted hooves for best thrust, and PULLED.

Nobody breathed, it seemed.

The rope creaked bar tight; a pebble clattered... Charlie tried, 'Go TO!' and the horses superbulged muscles and furnace-roared lungs – to no avail... 'Easy, now!'

Patting Tracker, assuring him they'd soon see what was wrong, Sophy had realised that horses listen as much to the sound of commands as the words spoken.

Onlookers murmured as both men peered: why such enormous resistance? From somewhere, a snorty bray: 'They're bound to fail: Slow Flea is jinxing them!' This elicited a few prim titters.

Sophy didn't try to locate Patricia Flange and her cronies. She looked to Bron, who mouthed, 'They're only jealous!' Subtly indicating Charlie, now consulting with his Gramps; but the Leamington girl never realised. Holding both horses, she had made a lovely photo for Jill and others – though not realising it, as her neck now craned after that 'plane's number... *No, too high.*

'THAT'S the problem, boy!'

Funny, hearing someone's grandfather addressed thus.

Mr Madoc pointed: the net sat on a bedrock hump; during the day, sun-melted tar had drooled; 'And, now that black muck has set again, the thing's glued down.'

Mr Solva sighed, 'We's gubbered, then.'

Perhaps not. Sophy backed the horses; Mr Solva and Charlie heaved rope right over the mounded mesh; far side, Mr Madoc crouched to re-attach it. Then, he must explain with gestures before the horses: they were now aiming to unpeel the net from the rock.

Squeezed trustingly between the animals, Sophy patted them simultaneously: 'Let's make it work, boys!' Then she ducked out to take position on Tracker's other side.

'Gently, now!'

The rope slithered, straightened...

'Hold there!' And this time, maintaining tension meant keeping edging forwards.

'Fastening's good!', said Mr Madoc; Mr Solva, peering rather riskily, ''Er's lifting!' Indeed, the ooing crowd saw the net creepingly rolling, heard shingle shift.

'Hold well!'

Aberdare and Tracker leaned more, stomped one pace then another... Noises came, in combination, from rope and net.

Someone, excitably, 'GO TO...!' Immediately they were shushed.

Another signal: 'Hold well more!' And it jerkily came – with the rope yagging this way, then that...

From Bronny, 'Careful, Sophes!' So close to her feet, those pistoning hooves trying to pull straight.

'Hold well MORE, boys!'

On they strained, the low sun shining sweatmarks to molten iron; but...?

With proper ripe cussing, underdiving Mr Solva's clasp knife slashed deepdeep where twisted stuff was clefted. Then, from the crouch, he still grittily sawing through the last fibres, 'She's there...!'

'GO TO!'

The horses surged; with a ripping THRRACKK! the whole net leapt from the rock. Behind jubilant hooves boosted by a suddenly rugby crowd, that mighty lump shot off down to the strand like a skidding bomb... And Charlie had to bellow that command: '**WHOA, NOW**!'

After he and Sophy had calmed their charges and checked for hurts, they noticed a noise behind them: enormous applause.

*

Finished in Sophy's room, Heather felt yet more uncomfortable clicking Jill's latch.

*

While they took a breather, children were photographed with their horse-heroes.

Shortening the tow to raise the net's leading edge should, Mr Madoc thought, lessen drag on the long, long haul to the slipway; Mr Solva agreed.

While the youngsters were backing the horses a stocky sunburnt gent approached wearing tractorish Wellington boots, sailcloth-weight jeans, and, despite the evening, a sweater; inspired by Dylan Thomas, keen reader Sophy saw *A shipshape fellow with horizon eyes.*

Jack Sound, retired lifeboat coxswain: 'Most impressive, those two working together! And, another feather in his cap,' he winked at Sophy, 'that piebald doesn't fear the sea, hmm?'

Mr Madoc, patting her on the back, 'Both did very well, the other day.'

Charlie ventured a pat, too: 'They did.'

Sophy glowed; Tracker nose-nudging, she didn't notice hissy girl-whispers circulating.

Mr Sound nodded at him, 'The black 'un exercises in the surf, sometimes?'

'Occasionally,' Charlie confirmed.

Mr Solva, typical farmer, warily, 'And...?'

Jack spread palms, emphasising no subterfuge: 'Someone proposed re-enacting a horse-drawn lifeboat launch during the Talbenny Haven regatta, next year.'

Charlie whispered to Sophy, 'That's in August.'

'I said 't'would need calm horses; animals panicking is the last thing you'd want. Told him the ones they used in t'old days was proper carefully trained, too.'

'They certainly had the hang of it,' said Mr Madoc. 'On the maroon bursting, they'd jump their gates and gallop to the muster.'

Tracker The Lifeboat Horse, the Leamington girl knew, would have been out of his paddock just on hearing the rocket's whoosh.

'So,' Jack resumed, 'might these two learn to launch a pulling gig, using a lumber truck, d'you think?'

A traditional timber-transporting wagon.

The horses' quiet grumbles opined that, given sufficiently intelligent human assistance, the job would be a doddle.

The girl saw it in AJ's eyes: more action worth capturing on canvas.

*

Spying assignment – completed!

But a task remained: guiltily shiverful because she *was* a good girl, dog giving her reprobative looks despite being so shamelessly nosy himself, Heather clicked open Sophy's suitcase.

*

Easier work with a shortened tow, indeed.

Mind, the horses were assisted: having brought the towrope's scrag end forward, Charlie and Sophy walked side by side ahead of the animals, leaning into their shared pull with arms out behind. Sophy did her silent best, knowing she hadn't the boy's strength: on setting off Charlie had attempted conversation, but huffpuffed replies had evinced that she must concentrate on haulage.

Both regretted.

At a stream, a halt; the horses drank keenly. Aberdare's reverberant sand stomps made the girl walk that bouncily, a piledriver might have been working adjacently.

The young horse-handlers declined two holidaymaker dads offering to take over, on principle: to get the best from your horses, you worked with them. But those good fellows, noticing some cord tangled into the net, soon had their own towing strops attached.

Setting off again, thanks to those men the youngsters could now pull and talk.

'So,' muttered Charlie, 'not all holidaymakers are useless.'

'Charlie, I'm a holidaymaker!'

'Reckon you became one of us, on your volunteering at the stable. First day of your holiday, wasn't it?'

'The second; that same afternoon, I met Heather.'

'She told me about your father; I'm really sorry.'

'Thank you, Charlie.'

'You don't mind me knowing?'

'It's essential for good understanding, knowing important things about friends. I've heard some of poor Bronny's story already; and, actually, a good deal of Tracker's.'

She learnt about Charlie's older brother, Simon "the Spanner" Solva – who'd never shown aptitude for agriculture, but had passed Royal Navy recruitment thanks to his knack with farm machinery, and was now doing well at sea.

*

Leaving Drift Cottage, Heather told a doubtful-looking dog, 'They'll understand.' She hid the key under the usual stone, having checked nobody was about…

…Not that anybody ever was.

*

Unsurprisingly, Charlie's favourite school subject was geography; history engaged him, too. 'It probably helps that Pembrokeshire's been crucial all through Britain's story, because of her links with Ireland.'

Sophy glanced out to sea; one easily forgot that the Emerald Isle was there, just below the horizon.

'And Pembrokeshire folk know the part geography plays in history; it explains so much.'

'So as well as knowing *where* an event happened, you should know what that place is like.'

'What it *was* like, Sophy. But actually, you should first check if historians have the location correct: do descriptions of the battle match the landscape there…?'

'Gosh, that's a good point! Y'know, I've been thinking about geography and the past, because of the farmhouse, and the mine, and Pinched Pill: they're all to do with ordinary people, like us, just getting things done – who ought to be important in history, too.'

He'd have loved to say that she was important and not at all ordinary; instead, he must nudge…

Firstly, she'd not realised they'd almost reached the slip; secondly, why was that woman talking into a cassette recorder's microphone while a lensman clicked?

'The Pembrokeshire Chronicle, I expect.'

Mr Madoc, 'You two don't want bothering…?'

No.

He semaphored Mr Clark, who promptly closed on the journalists.

Never claiming the clean-up as his idea, the Chairman acknowledged those locals and visitors partaking. Rather than condemn crews or ship owners outright over pollution, he simply questioned if either ever considered the consequences of tank flushing at sea. Concluding, he praised 'The youngsters, whose efforts were key to our operation's success.'

Encouraged by Charlie, Sophy was firm: 'Excuse me, but the horses' efforts were crucial – and they didn't volunteer!'

Before Tracker and Aberdare, Mr Clark bowed theatrically: 'I beg your pardons!'

With alacrity the photographer created a strong composition:

Charlie on Aberdare and Sophy atop Tracker, Messrs Madoc and Solva standing either side, Mr Clark and Bronny with Arrow and the wagon.

Should make for a super feature, Jill reckoned.

The horses truly looked heroic, dragging that net up the slipway… 'The dustmen will collect everything tomorrow, and good blooming riddance!', exhaled Mr Clark.

A tray emerged from the Talbenny Arms: lemonades for Charlie and Sophy, shandies for Bronny and Aunty Jill, Best Bitter for the men: 'With the landlord's compliments!'

So low the sun now, not welly-paddling nippers but fire-nymphs frolicking in amber mercury, seen from the sea front.

Tired satisfaction, shared by humans and animals. Bronny drove; Sophy sat beside her. Behind, back to them, well-placed to warn of traffic coming up, Jill sketched the closely-following horses.

A pleasing music: hoof-beats and jingles, wagon timbers creaking, iron tyres smooth-singing the tarmac. Mr Madoc hummed old tunes; whenever Jill whistled in, at the refrain's end he chuckled something like, 'Blow me if you didn't know that 'un, too!'

As Mogulus liked to with her, Sophy leaned into Bronny.

An arm around: 'Missing your Mum?'

'She'd have loved this.'

Bron whispered, 'And so would Daddy, hmm?'

'How did you…?'

'Celtic women are strong on feelings; anyway, love, my own mood's sentimental enough.'

'For saying about Dad, diolch yn fawr, Bronwen!' Now knowing that, same as with Heather, she and the Swansea girl could talk about anything.

Jill cautioned, 'Tracker's heard something.'

Driver and mate, looking at each other, 'A 'plane!'

It was Number 702, drifting down.

They'd been spotted; for the engines fanned, retarding descent; and two friendly helmets came to a hatch.

As it crossed ahead, all waved back while Tracker snorted; but

Aberdare frowned, as best a horse can: why such fuss over a Noise Bird?

Setting her nose back down and easing throttles, the skipper acknowledged them himself by wing waggling; Sophy whispered, 'Give Number 789 our love, Mister Pilot!'

*

A nice weariness, this, after doing so much good.

Heather and Tag had just crossed the brook when those turboprops voomed; only then noticing the 'plane, suddenly fearful, girl and dog rushed... Out under open sky, hearts thumping, 'PHEW!', the pilot had just pulled up, that was all. Probably a landing hold-off; it happened, sometimes.

But then, that finesse with the wings: the Pembroke girl chuckled, comprehending, 'Our cue, Tag me old mate, to get back to that kitchen and get busy!'

*

Well rested that afternoon, Anna felt bonny: since he'd brought news of a successful operation, she and Mr Solva had talked horses at the kitchen table.

Sabrina came in: she'd heard the wagon far off...

Anna said, 'I'm up to light tasks, and Jill should lend a hand; so let's have Sophy straight upstairs: Heather's left everything ready. Then, George, you and your grandson can head home without him feeling he's shirking.'

As the three reached the yard Sabrina suggested, 'Take Bronny's bike in your van, Mr Solva: tomorrow, Charlie can whizz back down for Aberdare.'

A bat-flitted afterglow; hoping to see "their" owl, Anna and Sabrina wouldn't blaze floodlights – which the horses, their eyes dimpsy-adjusted, would hate anyway. They hung out two candle lanterns, kept against power cuts.

Iron tyres crossing concrete at the lane throat... The blackboardy scrape of brakes touching on... Two yellow oil lamp glares appearing, and tangerine shoe-sparks... Now, just, Arrow's pale star...

Cobbleclatters noisy as train arrival, Sophy firmly braked and Bronny whoaed; Tracker and Aberdare wheeled around and halted, stomping and snorting. Thirsted by enduring evening warmth, three soft mouths were soon trough-slurping deservedly.

'Well done!', Anna glowed. 'We're so proud of– You haven't left Jill behind?'

'What?', laughed Mr Madoc. 'Take off without our tail gunner?'

'Observer,' corrected Charlie.

Still in the back of the wagon, she was – drinking in cheery chatter, hot horses clustered, and candle-glowed walls with that star-sprinkled blue above. Busily sketching ideas for **The Last Load's Home**, while her ears imagined grander: the old Coastal Mail, changing horses.

Sophy had hoped to ostle alongside Charlie; instead, here she was undressing in the farmhouse bathroom – bewilderingly, beside a change of her own clothes.

She'd just stepped in…

Bronwen tapped, 'Sweetheart? Do help yourself to Anna's bubblyubbly; and will you leave the water in, please?'

'Okay!'

'Here's your…' The door – no lock – ajared for a tea mug.

The girl hopped: 'Thanks tons!'

On she'd have lolled, but Bronny was waiting … Dripping rose-scented to the door, 'Ready!'

As at school she'd dry, and dress, with her back to the room.

Footsteps raced up, doored the fog, bum-bumped the world out.

Hairdrubbing Sophy heard clothes flop; next – rather blushmakingly – porcelain rilled; *Although,* she reflected, *Heather and I aren't bothered, grass-squatting together.* Now, the sloop of getting in; then, a settling sigh.

'Blissful?'

Waterrush of turning onto her front, 'You bet, girl, and – My GOD, Sophy: your BRUISES!'

Squeebing the mirror clear for fringe unwonking, the Leamington girl had unwittingly let Bronwen periscope her front; who, instantly out of the water and looking by comparison awfully lovely, contemplated those blue-black marks… Swansea hand on Sophy's shoulder, 'Oh, my brave little Spartan!'

She shrugged. 'Twice daily Heather witchhazels me, which helps;

don't forget, hers truly was a killer stitch. Actually they've eased lots, now; and, Bronny, I wouldn't have missed *anything* that's happened since, even if they do ache a bit.'

*Especially meeting Charlie.* 'I understand; anyway, being with horses helps one heal.'

In steamy silver Sophy watched Bronny back to the bath, clumber in facing away from the taps, and breast herself down into the foam, only twisting about once immersed: *Okay – Bronny isn't at all shy amongst friends, and that's a good example to set me; but, nevertheless...!*

She puckered herself a pondering pout; as she started dressing, the mirror glimpsed the older girl sinking for a hair-dunk.

Top and skirt on, Sophy had her second sock–

Thrashed water, and an explosion of coughs.

Sophy sprang to the bath; hands gripping taps, her friend choofed and goffed.

'Bron, what happened?'

A strawberry Swansea face: 'I just botched a burp! Swamped my nose, and...'

After staring at Bronny's lower back, the younger girl's love-tender touch: 'You were just fussing about my bruises so much, but... Which horse went for you? Bronny, who does *you* with witch haze–?'

Eyes steady, 'Not bruises; won't fade. I hoped you wouldn't see 'em because... Well, my Dad did all that.'

'Wh-*When?*'

Easier talking when active, Bronwen stood up and began strigiling wet off with the side of her hand. 'Not just once. The third really bad time, when I was fourteen, was the *last* time: I socked him back, fists in his face, and my feet... Ahum, where they'd hurt him best. Then, out of that house forever, so slamming the door I bloody smashed the glass, girl! I went straight to a friend's place: Jesus, the relief of finding her at home!'

Settling this overmemoried girl on the laundry box, Sophy started to towel, listen, and learn.

## CHAPTER 22

During sleep, while our eyes and ears rest and our muscles recover, our brains are busy: all the previous day's events are revisited, and then committed to memory.

Every Pembrokeshire night, therefore, Sophy's head had much to do in the quiet dark.

Small surprise, that her final morning dream reeled as a breathless adventure film... *Charlie and I are driving Aberdare, a loco with sparky hooves who can fly; rear gunner Heather has downed Bronny's father, who was flying a German bomber. We're after Patricia Flange, who's stolen a Victoria sponge and was escaping on Greengrass, but he bucked her into an orange stream: there she sits with nothing on, singing Girl Guide songs and drinking liniment. Now here comes Slipstream, who has finished his custard slice, in a lifeboat, to teach Patsy a lesson: up goes his tail; out come steaming tar balls – Oh, no: MAYDAY! The engines are leaking oil; we must land now, only the wings won't stop waggling...!*

Reality was no less weird: Heather's body was hugely oversmall, and far too furry against Sophy's waking skin. Furthermore her friend was close-pressing a wet rumbly nose, and...

'Heather, NO!'

...licking Sophy's throat so raspily that—

'Oh, for HEAVEN'S SAKE, Mogulus!'

'MrrrAAOW!' Unappreciated, he huffed out of bed.

Blearily recognising that oleic pong, 'What are you painting, AJ?'

'Can't you guess, sweetheart?' Setting palette and brushes down, Jill knelt to hair-stroke, 'Heather was away ages ago; you, sleeping on, looked so lovely...'

She nodded, pleased to have done some painless modelling. Staying statue-still was hard work when you were awake: you'd rather be whizzing about.

'When Puss came to see what I was doing and then started tunnelling into your bed, I didn't scold him lest I woke you; in fact if the twit hadn't started that licking, I'd still be painting you both.'

Sniggering, 'You put Mogulus in? Let's see!'

Jill turned the easel around...

The colour-muted dark surroundings were sketchy; her expression serene, Sophy's hair gleamed across the pillow's linen, while her shoulders disappeared brownly under the floral eiderdown. Tucked alongside...

'Maow!' *That's me!*

'AJ, you can obviously do portraits and animals just as well as you can countryside and the sea.'

'Thank you, Sophy. Actually, Miss Gwinear reckoned all good paintings were portraits: don't we talk about the character of a landscape, and discuss the weather's moods...?'

Girl and cat left contemplating, off to brew some tea...

After sipping Sophy yawned, 'Why was Heather off so early?'

'She wasn't, though. I was letting you both lie in, when suddenly Sabrina appeared on Arrow, giving your fellow Belle Dormeuse five minutes' grace. I somehow un-snuggled her from you; away they hurried, Heather still munching her marmalade sandwich.'

'But if that was ages ago...?'

'It's ten to eleven.'

'WHAT?'


Sophy toastmunched, 'You know about Bronny being taken in by her friend's parents...?'

'Kind people; but, unfortunately, she couldn't feel safe living just streets away from her dad.'

'So she moved down here?'

'*Moved?* Sophy, she just packed up and started hitchhiking, and only headed for Pembrokeshire because of happy holiday memories: total madness, I think you'd agree. It was indescribable luck, Mrs Madoc noticing Bron huddled in a bus shelter, and somehow remembering her from a morning trek two years earlier.'

'Perhaps Bronny's being so caring results from Mrs Madoc's kindness to her. AJ, she tried so hard to hide those awful marks: she didn't want me realising how some fathers behave. But I knew, because bad things happen in books. Mind you, Bronny's the first person I've met whose father—'

'She is, Sophy, as far as you know.'

Extremely thoughtfully, 'Hmm.' Then, 'She *says* that she still feels love for him, because although he would get drunk and come home out of control, when he was sober he could be affectionate. That's what she says.'

'But you suspect that was a white lie, so you shouldn't worry overmuch about the world's badness? I'm sure I don't know, sweetheart. Christians say nobody's irredeemably evil; history, and news stories, say me a different truth.

'Accepting that people tell white lies for honourable reasons, it's nevertheless a horrible feeling, knowing somebody's lied to you. But, dare one challenge them? It's dreadful, accusing someone of lying to whom you'd far rather give the benefit of the doubt.'

'I'd always give Bronny that.'

'And she you; so there you are.'

'AJ…? Bronny asked, would I have liked to have had a sister? I said that I loved being with Heather because she seems like one – and, apparently, Heather feels the same about me!'

Jill must hug, 'There's no doubting that.'


The sun lured Sophy's slow breakfast outside with a nightie on, where Jill's coffee joined it.

A grey jet ripped over and then curved to climb, the double-barrelled blue flames which scorched it cloudwards tummy-pummellingly loud.

Able to talk again, 'Do you think 789 will return? So Bronny sees Sam Goldfire again, and Carson Lightfoot can ride Tracker?'

'I hope and pray as much as you – you hungry girl!'

'Hey, I didn't eat anything when I got home last night!'

'You did; but you ate with your eyes shut. Then, down your head drooped… Asleep in the coleslaw, but for us catching you.'

'You and Heather put me to bed?'

'Don't apologise; didn't it prove that you'd made the most of the day?' Jill mused, 'Inviting you down, I did worry that you mightn't find much to do; in reality, my cards to your mum can't keep up. As for friendships, you've completely clicked with the loveliest girl; and I think that Charlie–'

Squeaky springs; a Bumbly exhaust; a red roof.

'YOO-HOO!' Flashing yesterday's postcard for Sophyapproval, Jill scampered to meet Martin The Post; when she reappeared, 'It's for you!'

Sophy read her mother's letter out loud with increasing disappointment; afterwards, pained silence. Then, flatly, 'Mummy's getting on well.'

Jill sighed, 'Not writing your story, though, is she? I blame my anodyne cards.'

'AJ, we agreed you'd not worry her. Because I'm only young, and—'

'Sophy Amelia Fossway, you've worked alongside grown-ups as an equal, and coped with wholly adult situations. That girl your mother's created is… is as useless as a snooty!'

'Um, it should still be a good story…'

Jill now hairbrushed, 'Of its sort, yes, because Carol's intelligent and capable. But, were she to use everything we *could* tell her about the exceptional horses, all the excitements, and the people you've met and hit it off with… Well, even without poor Bronny's struggles, what a yarn that'd be!'

Loving this passion, Sophy warmed, 'Jilly, you *had* to tell white lies: Mummy couldn't understand at a distance how I've suddenly changed – which I know I have. I probably *was* Mummy's story girl when I left home; but the moment Bron came asking for help I just had to, um…'

'Become one of the links in a grown-up chain?'

The girl kissed, 'Exactly.'


Dressed now, 'AJ, did Heather seem okay…? Because of Mrs Flange's pushiness, Patricia needles everyone; but she especially resents someone younger being better, that's obvious. It's also obvious, though, that she simply hasn't Heather's way with horses.'

'Or yours.' Jill sighed, 'That girl's so burdened by her mother's ambitions, she doesn't pay any attention to what her mounts try telling her. One might have pity, but for her poisonous tactics: home life has taught Patricia that bullying gains you advantage – and blow her school's ethics!'

Which were purely theoretical, Sophy knew: according to friends' big sisters, convent girls were consistently the most vicious cheats in sports matches.

'So, considering that everyone should do their best as much for the stable's sake as for their own, and help their team mates to succeed, that viper Patricia's behaviour is doubly poisonous.'

*Jill Ribblesdale, blazing firebrand!*

'Anyway, love, Heather seemed fine; and don't Sabrina and Bronny understand Patricia's game?'

'To an extent, yes; but she's a clever operator.'

'Bien sûr. Sophy, it is only *verbal* bullying…?'

Heather was too good a friend now not to have said.

'Anyway, Charlie definitely has Patricia weighed up: while collecting Aberdare he'll maybe observe Madam's behaviour, and have words if necessary – as I'm sure he would, had you been riding today and got sniped at.'

'I wanted to say earlier: I think he's the nicest boy I know. I haven't properly met many, but…'

'But if you had, you'd still like Charlie best, hmm?'

'Yes, Aunty Jill.'

*Delicately, now, Jilly!* 'Of course, you're bound to think of him differently from Heather; she's known him since her first term in infants. "A friend through school" was her way of putting it.'

'Meaning, they'll grow up to be village mates?' Sabrina and Bronny used the expression.

'Spot on!'

'AJ, what do *you* think of Charlie?'

'I like him for who he is, for how he respects you. I expected you two to click: you both love horses, and are instinctively good with them. And yesterday you were both trying to see the other's point of view which,' those eyes twinkled, 'was good.'

After they'd straightened out The Snug, 'As Heather's class is practising morning and afternoon, and Anna's doing lunch, we can go out today.'

'Okay; but do let's be back for when Heather returns: even if Patsy holds off, she'll be so tired.'

'Agreed. Now, wherever we go, we'll take some of these…?'

The fruit buns quizzified Sophy: no smell of baking.

'While you slept, Alice Williams called – no, she's not fully recovered yet: a friend was driving. Those are to reward your and Heather's beach cleaning efforts; I said you girls would be most grateful.'

'Mmm!'

'Apparently oil's come ashore all round the bay; so no swimming anywhere, I'm afraid.'

Explained, the breeze's chemical tang. Saddened to think how wildlife must be affected, Sophy sighed, 'What can be done, AJ?'

'Alice says that hoteliers and local businesses want the beaches sprayed, but the detergents they have to use damage marine organisms dreadfully. Kete Fort's biologists have begged the County Council to hold off: the winds predicted for tonight and tomorrow could disperse the oil naturally.'

'So, despite the last storm,' Sophy supposed, 'our prayers are for the wilder the better?'

'Beaucoup du vent, oui, chérie; encore un orage – non, merci!'

'Then today we must clean Mill Cove, or the rubbish might get washed somewhere inaccessible: there were sacks left over from yesterday, so we've the wherewithal.'

The gatherage afterwards would be some logistical challenge but, 'Righty-ho, sweetheart! I'll make us packed lunches while you fetch 'em from the stable.'

Knowing that Tracker would sense her nearness, she called by to apologise: he couldn't take part in today's activity. Convincing herself that he understood and didn't mind too much, a happysad Sophy gave him one last ear-tickle, then said goodbye.

Unsurprisingly, she'd missed Charlie; and, since the indoor arena echoed with intense exercising plus the repeated exhortation 'CONCENTRATE!', she didn't look in.

Anna sorted her out with sacks plus tying twine; all went into a capacious hiking knapsack. 'Which you may borrow for the rest of your holiday, if you like.'

'Gosh, thank you!'

Sophy realised on her soldierly tramp back through the spinney that although in human terms she'd never been more alone, she had innumerable birds for company: *A veritable choral symphony.*

Granny Haroldston had called, meantime: with swimming off and winds forecast, why didn't Jill and the girls plus Puss come to stay for a day or two? Here was an opportunity to start Heather's portrait, she'd reasoned; meanwhile, maybe Sophy could do some holiday homework.

*And write to Mum and Hannah.* 'Also, AJ, I expect they've been missing Heather at Bishop's Watch.'

'Aye,' Jill sympathised. A grand idea, indeed: shared cooking duties, and a proper laundry session for bonfiery pillowcases, tomboy-flavoured bedsheets, and everso sandy towels.

'And, assuming *more* extra riding practices...' The artist saw opportunities for her and Sophy to explore places Heather already knew well: Pembroke Castle; serene Bosherston Ponds; Kete, with all its sailing activity; especially special Moel-Rhos Sands. If it really rained, then Haverfordwest for the museum, plus art supplies – and Victoria's, where Sophy could browse out a book for herself.

This Jill kept to herself: she might also treat the youngster to something older-girl pretty, practical though hinting at formality, so inevitably fairly long, which would do well for *her* portrait, when the time came.

'Mrrreu?'

'Relax, Moggo: Granny has no pets.' Respite, for him, therefore, from bristling terrier confrontations.

'Talking of practising, they've a piano over there.'

'Good; there's ages since I heard you play. Although, no doing scales for hours, my love – or homeworking too hard, either. Recently, life's been remarkably serious; we should do relaxing things. Like mooching to the Atlantic Café for leisurely milk shakes, and such like, hmm?'

It really upset Sophy, finding the first dead gannet.

Far larger than gulls, she loved watching these birds of the offshore wheeling above the waves, stretched wings flashing so white; when they plummeted after fish, their last-moment foldup was an origami so deft, in they splashed with Japanese neatness. Now just spear-beaked humps of greasy decay, their starved chicks on a somewhere crag helplessly shivering to death.

Tarred to a pitiful nothingness, here were other species which never ventured inshore, thus only recognised from Jill's bird book: diminutive roamers of the vasty deeps, they bred on Pembrokeshire's grassier islands.

As they bagged rubbish, ever more bird carcases; 'Poor, blameless creatures,' sighed Jill.

'Aren't we, in all this business?'

'Alas, no. The car needs fuel; you must realise that paint, detergent, and farmers' sprays come from petrochemicals. So that their products cost us a tiny amount less, oil companies hire cheap ships; thus, this sometimes happens.'

'I wasn't thinking deeply enough, AJ. …How does one learn to?'

'You pick it up gradually, by always being inquisitive, and suspecting easy answers – especially from politicians. Like Mum, I buy a questioning newspaper; and some TV programmes *are* properly investigative – but the radio tends to tackle the more difficult topics better. Anyway, Sophy, you've started very well; and Mummy will surely keep you heading down the right road. You know, I admire her hugely.'

'Because of bringing me up on her own?'

'And devoting lots of time to you, exactly what she promised your Daddy. Teaching you things, and helping you to make discoveries for yourself: I think those are gifts of her love as important as food, and kisses, and nursing you when you're sick.'

Unlike Sophy to swerve so, but, 'Aunty Jill, how did you decide to not marry, and to not have children, and concentrate on doing jolly well at work?'

A huge breath… 'Actually, I made no such decision; having a demanding job just kept me single, you could say. But once you were born, after every time I saw you I drove away more regretful.'

*Gosh!* 'I appreciate you telling me.' *Will Anna's baby make women she knows have such strong thoughts?* 'And I sort of understand: after spending time with the Gram children, I had feelings inside I've never known before.'

Kissing the girl, *Perhaps like the ones I've been having.*

After lunch a blue-uniformed gentleman appeared; he began probing the wrack with a crook-ended pole.

Sophy hissed, 'Is he Royal Navy? Is that a special detector?' Had a Top Secret gismo been lost off a ship?

'He's a coastguard; that's just a rather flashy boathook.' Jill waved, 'Hello!'

Friendly, perhaps thirty years old, most impressed by their efforts. Saying to Sophy, 'Particularly so, considering all your and Miss

Haroldston's work yesterday. And aren't you still pretty shaken from that spectacular gallop, and afterwards?'

On behalf of the youngster's glowing silence (mostly because of praise from a rescue professional, but partly related to his way of looking at Jill) the artist explained, 'She didn't realise you were observing from Creampot Point that day.'

'Not just observing, young Miss: I was just on calling out a helicopter when my mate spotted you girls emerging! Anyway, so's you know, our log recorded everyone's brave efforts, and heartily commended the horses, too.'

Beaming, Sophy made a mental note: *Tell Tracker and Lamorna about that at the earliest poss.*

'Anyway,' he harrumphed because of Jill's eyes, 'while I'm glad to have praised you and the other young ladies, I've come down here because...' Unfolding a poster, 'Our Yankee friends have recently lost some big distress flares. Fireworks they flipping aren't: these pack such a punch, they're classed as incendiaries.'

Jill assured, 'We've found none today.'

'They say the items were lost well offshore, so they probably won't show up for a few days, but...'

Sophy said, 'We'll keep our eyes open, Sir.'

'I'd appreciate that.'

Jill offered him tea.

'Thanks, but I've more places to check.' Making to leave, 'Err... Have you arranged for anyone to collect these sacks...?'

The girl shook her head.

Jill smiled, 'This was a bit spur-of-the-moment; but you'll understand that when a headstrong Environmental Warrior...' She feigned resignation.

Sophy defended, 'It's not *all* rubbish: that cargo net might do for training honeysuckle, you said.'

He, ruminatively, 'Jolly well salvaged! It's plenty strong – a handsome size, too; rather heavy, though.' Then, did he flash a wink? 'Y'know, if we were in Ireland, you'd pray for help with this stuff from the Little People; but perhaps a big yellow paraffin-burning fairy that HM Coastguard knows might lend a hand, or rather a lifting hook... Call it a shore recovery exercise, we might.'

Sophy boggled, 'Gosh, *really?*'

Jill tried, 'Same as you chaps always arrange when nice timber comes floating in?' She'd loved Miss Gwinear chucklingly describing some of his service's antics.

His twinkling grin, then! 'No comment. Just be prepared to bring pets indoors if you hear a chopper coming in really low, all right?'

Jill, nudging Sophy, 'We'll try warning Mogulus, but he's quite a bold cat: I suspect that, actually, he'll hurry to watch what happens!'

Warmly, 'I know the sort.'

Sophy, delighted that he liked cats, 'If you can't stop for tea, please do have a bun…'

He sampled it, then cap-swept gallantly: 'I already was going to say, so delighted to have met you; but now…!' The girl pressing on him another for later, he departed heartily wishing he needn't.


## CHAPTER 23

Waking at Bishop's Watch, Sophy missed the sisterly sensation of Heather being beside her: the guest room they shared had twin beds.

Because of the new-place undercurrent of excitement, sleep had come reluctantly the evening before; now, *It must be ages before getting-up time.*

Curtains left undrawn, the girls' sunset whisperings had relived the Mill Cove clean-up and those busy horsey hours; then, that friendly sea-beam had started flashing. A ship's lights appearing soon after Heather had drifted off hadn't fired Sophy's nautical imagination, though, for a concern had re-emerged, as she had been fearing it would.

In the end, dog tiredness had borne the child off; now, persistent as a toothache, that worry had unsettled her from sleep.

What worry?

Just before departure the evening before Sophy had exclaimed, 'Hey, you haven't seen my bedroom yet!' So, off up Drift Cottage's curvy stairs – only to spot, on the rug, one of her friend's hair clips.

Hotly flustering, 'Mogulus must have filched that for a toy, then left it up here,' the other girl hadn't even convinced herself.

Sophy would have soon forgotten the business, because Miss H was notorious for shedding clips, and they did turn up in the oddest places; however as they'd boarded Bumble Heather had overemphatically finger-clicked, 'I REMEMBER! I shot up last night to get you clean clothes, then realised your suitcase was in The Snug. Reckon that clip went flying as I bombed back down.'

So Heather *had* already been in her bedroom, albeit fleetingly; furthermore, at that moment Sophy had caught on Jill's face a suspicious expression.

As the day brightened and the swallows in their eaves nests twittered ever louder, there Sophy lay doubt-nagged, her remnant bruises seeming to pulse...

For Heather had also, that evening, broken her promise to Jill, by going up to the stable. Did she therefore rustle them up a snack supper as a guilty penance, for that and snooping in Sophy's room?

But *why* lie about going up there, *WHY*? Could horrid Patricia be somehow manipulating Heather, obliging her to spy on despised Slow Flea, as part of some devious scheme?

Wrigglily trying to get comfortable, Sophy sighted Heather's tikitik travelling clock: *Blinking heck, it's only twenty past four!*

*Oh, why do I mistrust Heather's motives, having so recently said I'd always give Bronny the benefit of the doubt?* Heather had suffered differently from Bronny, but when her mum had died she could have endured as much stress: Sophy gulped, *I've never thought enough about making allowances.* Very well: assuming that Heather's had been white lies, what had motivated them?

Too exhausted to fathom that out now, but still sleep-spurned, Sophy wasn't in a reading mood; she mustn't get up though, lest she disturbed Heather, who *was* the dearest friend, important now as Hannah. And who was rostered for another gruelling day at the stable. So, earpiece in, the Leamington girl started sweeping her transistor radio's dial. What for, she didn't know: the BBC shut its stations down overnight.

As the telescopic antenna touched the bed's iron frame, the waveband marked SW (Short Wave), which at home only ever hissed, positively *flooded* with stations: excited foreign jabberings, monotone Iron Curtain announcers, hammered Chopin pianos, wailing priests praising Heaven knew which gods, burbling Morse code, boomshtiyayiya music – and then, so loud it almost pumped her earpiece out, the very heaviest rock presented by a really rather funny American DJ.

She'd never like thrashy guitars or frantic drumming, and some song lyrics were I-don't-think-I-should-be-listening-even-if-I-don't-understand-them; but Jimmy Mace, The Ace Of Inner Space was so preposterously full of himself, you had to keep listening. Furthermore, here was an unexpected chink in the Yankee military wall where the girl could peep in: the American Forces Network carried dedications for USAF and US Navy airmen and women stationed all across the planet – plus even song requests for aeroplanes themselves! She absorbed its raucous bonhomie wondering if, somewhere, Carson and Sam were tuned in, too – and eventually drifted off thinking goodwill to them back through the circuitry, up that shiny rod, out into the Welsh ether, and away.

Crouching alongside, quizzical of the fallen-out earpiece, seeing Sophy's eyes opening Heather whispered, 'Diddly squat, now the sun's up!' She clicked the radio off and, budging her friend over, 'Why couldn't you sleep, poor thing?'

*My turn for a white lie...* 'I don't know. Um, after you nodded off, there was a ship.'

Heather kissed, 'Always good to watch. Actually, I didn't sleep right through; I think I've been worrying about what's been worrying you.'

It came out hoarsely: 'Oh?'

'I lied to you and to Jill, the evening before: broke my promise about not going out, didn't I?'

'With the kindest motive – so, at worst, a white lie. Thanks to you, I bathed at the Madoc's, and learned important things from Bronny.'

'Then I feel slightly better. If I ask Jill's forgiveness, we'll both go back to sleeping well, hmm?'

Unconvinced, a neutral 'Hmm.'

'And now, Sophes, for a PROPER solar-heated bath...!' En route, Heather showed Sophy a metal cabinet on the landing: thermometers, coloured lights, a glass tube thingy, an electronic display. 'Proof,' she triumphed, 'that we're totally solar heated, hotter than Anna's boiler gets her water, and not a drop of oil burnt.'

Sophy's 'That's *fantastic!*' was genuine.

Now wet-glittering, Heather flung the airing cupboard doors wide; out flooded sun-heat. It, jazzy hair-towelling, then pop duo sillymiming before the bathroom's big mirror saw them top-to-toe dry; as the English girl stretched atop the blanket box to be witchhazeled, a click started something whirring.

'Today's sunshine harvest has started, Sophes: there goes the solar fluid pump.'

'And every time that happens, you're reminded of your Mum.'

'I love you so much for making that connection.'

Disappointment: AJ wasn't down for breakfast.

Hugh Haroldston didn't say, but he was glad: the artist was taking a deserved break from caring for these raring children. Not that they'd at first been fizz-full as he'd expected but, fuelled by Welsh bacon, deep yellow eggs, and damson jam on bara gwenith, they were now day-ready – and mustard keen to take the artist up a mug of tea. He dissuaded, 'She's choosing to let Nature wake her, okay?' Quite unaware that his mother had earlier reached in and confiscated the Ribblesdale alarm clock.

Hugh soon departed, taking Heather to the stable; Sophy and Granny washed up, then sorted the laundry; much amusement, all the while, observing Mogulus's scent-whetted exploration of yard and sheds.

Of the open garage, too, with its aggregation of coiled pipes, cables, and door-big boxes bearing a bird motif and stencilled CHOUGH SOLAR – CORNWALL; and a domed-top metal barrel which Sophy recognised from her earlier tutorial as a water storage cylinder: 'I wonder where that solar heating system's being installed.'

Gran smiled, 'Maybe you'll find out, soon.'

'Might Mister Haroldston properly explain solar heating to me, do you think? What I grasped this morning was really interesting.'

The lady determined, 'He shall find the time.'

Back from the stable via a simply-solved leaky tap, Hugh made the acest suggestion: 'Why not come along as my apprentice? I'm not working far away; the house's owner wouldn't mind.'

'Best way to learn,' Granny agreed. *And Jill gets a day off.* She cut more sandwiches while they loaded up, Sophy having promised to always say if she didn't understand, and to never underestimate her learning ability. Most curiously, Mr H told Sophy that she could bring some special knowledge to this new job; she couldn't imagine how.

He rejected "Mr Haroldston" as too stuffy; Sophy insisted that "Hugh" was overfamiliar; both approved Granny's suggestion, "Boss", as appropriate for a trainee to use.

'Whoops, here's the humptibump!' Sophy anticipated everything behind getting airborne with a frightful racket – but the car turned off before the bridge. As its boxy face bluffed up Mill Lane, 'I never realised that anyone else lived down here.'

He grinned, 'Nor they do. When we arrive at Drift Cottage, Sophy, would you go and open up? The dear daughter forgot to say *which* stone the key is hidden under.'

Special knowledge!

Changing weather, indeed: the sun of earlier was gone; clouds gathered speed. Untying ladders from the roof rack, 'Panels up first.'

At last explained, Drift Cottage having shiny rods protruding through its slates, also a roof-scoop with pipes poking out: Hugh had got this far when Miss Gwinear...

Sophy nodded, 'She'll be delighted to see the job finished.'

Mounting rails bolted on, using his clever ladder attachment resembling a boat davit, he hauled the hefty door-sized solar collectors up, and secured them. With Sophy passing up fifteen mil, elbows, tees, air traps, etc, and looking after tube cutters, adjustables, and Stilsons, the plumbing up top was betimes completed: rain was spotting bigly as The Boss slid down announcing, 'Lunch!'

Explaining while they munched that they'd work in the loft next, he produced survey notes detailing the routes of pipes and wires. On recognising her friend's handwriting, Sophy shed tears of relief: Heather's secrecy, and of course Granny's invitation to stay, were explained.

He hugged, 'If, dear girl, you'll forgive our subterfuge *and* agree to join us, we'll give Jill a great surprise.'

Of course she'd collaborate, cryptically as any Elizabethan spy: *Now be fair Heather and I fellow conspirators in an Moste Worthie Plotte.*

Hugh had all along warned about loud power tools, the pop when shutting off the blowtorch, and so forth; so she always knew what was what, he even flagged small things like flicking the pump on to check its wiring. So what, as she crouched in the loft feeding cables, cobwebs everywhere and a small torch her only illumination, was this unexplained and swelling racket? 'Boss, the collectors are rumbling!' Or was the whole roof?

'They can't be, so don't panic; I'll whizz outside and see what's up.'

Sophy wanted to shout 'Please hurry!', for there immediately inkled the miner's chill fear of entombment. Already of submarines she was resolved *never*, because of a too-realistic war film: faltering lights, the crew's expressions on hearing the hunting destroyer's returning screwbeats...

Not propellers – blades, though: Hugh chortled up, 'It's that helicopter you ordered: come and see!'

Ladder run back up the rainy roof, he stuffed the girl into his anorak and, 'GO!'

Man-scented nostalgic, she clambered monkey-keen and leaned against Jill's chimney.

Yellow-bellied, dervishly rotoring, reverberating the valley, its warning lights sparkled like gems through Sophy's wet lashes... 'What's that wafting orange, Daddy?'

'The shore party's smoke flares. For indicating the wind on the deck, and warning civilians.'

Invisible wire reeled up a helmeted man; now stout tackle descended to coastguards below. Up came... 'It looks,' Hugh exclaimed, 'like a dead elephant!'

How she must shout: 'We did gather plenty of rubbish; they've put all the sacks into a cargo net Jill found.'

Payload secured, as yet hotter fumes poured out the machine rose, then leaned away Doppler-shaking the air. But, incomprehensibly, it didn't go far north before dropping from view: 'Daddy...?'

'I expect your coastguard has arranged a council lorry rendezvous at Colliers' Quay.'

Surely yes: the machine soon reappeared, unburdened.

'That's so good of everybody,' Sophy said. 'A shame about losing AJ's cargo net, though.'

The helicopter was swinging around towards... No it wasn't: 'It's coming this way!'

'Don't panic: you shan't get wafted off. Try waving, hmm?'

The thuppering aircraft came to a hover above the paddock; then, facing her, it executed a bow. She and The Boss waved like mad; it now half-circled with the yellow-suited winchman waving back, then clattered off to dip below the ridge.

'Well,' a chuckling Hugh helped her down, 'that doesn't happen every day.'

The bizarred girl had no words.

'I'll make tea while you dry your hair?'

'All right... Um, did I call you Daddy?'

A nod, eyes all gratitude.

Normality restored by the brew and a Digestive, 'Wasn't that *amazing*? He looked that mischievous, I'd wondered if the coastguard chap was teasing me when—'

A blue Land Rover with extra lights, aerials, and a winch...

'It's him!'

'...Good afternoon, Miss; hello, Mister Haroldston!'

'Thank you so much, Sir, for arranging the helicopter.'

'My thanks to you and Miss Ribblesdale, for cleaning Mill Cove. By the way, is she well?'

'Fine, thanks. We're staying at Heather's grandmother's for a few days.'

'And you're helping Mister Haroldston put in solar heating here: well done!'

He and Hugh unloaded the cargo net; then, saluting Sophy with a wink, 'Didn't forget, did I? So, please give the lady my best regards. Also, instead of honeysuckle, will you say I'd try star jasmine – plus a hardy vine, why not?'

And gone.

'Gosh, Boss, we've so much to tell—'

He tapped his lip: wherever they were supposed to be working that day, it wasn't Drift Cottage. 'Heather will have surmised what the helicopter was doing down at the cove; we'll let her say about seeing it, hmm?'

'Righto, Boss!' *Another worthwhile white lie.*

'More generally, about our coastguard's interest in Jill...'

*Many men wouldn't have noticed.*

'...Well, you must keep mum. Despite the frisson, hmm?'

'D'accord.' *And isn't "frisson" an ace word?* But then a different, an unwelcome frisson: she fraught, suppose the chap bumped into Jill, and let the solar cat out of the bag...?

'Good point! I'll suggest Mum takes our artist out tomorrow – perhaps calling on my cousin, as works at the County Archives, to ask about old photos of Pinched Pill...?

'Monsieur le Chef, ça va absolument!'

By home time Sophy understood how hot water systems worked; moreover she could cut pipe cleanly, do compression joints, even solder simple connections with the blowtorch. Clicking her seatbelt, 'Mister Hugh, Daddy would be so grateful for all you've taught me, today.'

'When you pray tonight, please tell him it's been an honour.'

Heather was delighted that Sophy had been working with her dad.

She'd ridden Trotsky that morning: tip-top, his conduct! Better still, Flange P had been allocated Greengrass, who'd trundled like a milk float. They'd then all had an afternoon of graft, but now most saddles were see-your-face clean, and the show-bound ponies shone like conkers.

Having eyeballed Mogulus conspiratorially – he knew *exactly* where Sophy had been – the girls went up for another solar bath.

Her worrisome night now seeming ancient history, Sophy became as bubble-blissed as Heather. Afterwards heat-bathing stretched on the floor, the friends couldn't help eavesdropping pan-clattered chatter from downstairs: Hugh's account of their progress at 'A cottage near Colliers' Quay' furnished winking Sophy with corroborative detail.

They loved his "brainwave" about Granny taking Jill to the Archives; when Mrs Haroldston suggested, 'Shall we collect Heather in the afternoon...?', said girl whispered, 'Sophes, maybe you and Dad will complete the job tomorrow, and Jilly can join the Solar Bath Owners Club!'

That 'Yes, maybe,' sounded distracted.

'Well...?'

The Leamington girl hissed, 'Haven't either you or your father noticed that Drift Cottage has no bathroom?'

Heather's laughing eyes said, *Think again!*

So Sophy did... 'Jill's larder!' Quite a large room, with half-tiled walls.

'Miss Gwinear included it in the extension, but said she'd only fit it out when she couldn't manage the tin tub. However, she began preparations late last year: that white thing buried by logs in the woodshed corner is a lion's paw bath. Could be got working in a day, Dad says; he tracked down the fantasticest brass taps – shower gizmo, and all!'

'Hmm.'

'Sophy...?' *Why so thoughtful?*

'If Miss Gwinear knew she was on her way out, then she was going to fit that bath for Jill's benefit: she was *that* kind.'

'Maouuw!'

Springing up, absurdly pulling towels around themselves because he was a boy cat, they synchronised, 'Mogulus, where on *earth*...?'

The airing cupboard.

Suppertime Jill, having had an 'embarrassingly restful' day, proposed afterwards trying out pose ideas with Heather.

Heather, who speculated exemplarily about the helicopter's antics.

Jill then said that he'd seemed a good chap, the coastguard she and Sophy had met.

Sophy glanced *très soutilement* towards Hugh.

Excused washing up, boss and mate loaded up the Volvo for the morrow; then, after her solar heating tutorial, Sophy sat at the kitchen table to write notes. Mogulus snoozed beside sock-darning Granny's sewing basket, paws emphatically furled: he'd earlier discovered that her pump-up plant spray was very good at delivering jolly wet water, which discouraged dabbling with balls of wool. Hugh, meanwhile, had retired to his study.

*She's praying lots tonight...* But then Sophy had had lots to tell her Daddy.

At last, Heather could come cuddling, to know more of her friend's day.

A wet wind now huffed, chimneying persistent grumbles; the girls jointly willed this weather to see off that horrid oil. Squalls blanketed across the darkening bay: only fitfully did that flash glimpse. Protective thoughts sent to all at sea, they snugged closer, imagining themselves lighthouse keepers…

Granny reported, 'As you've described before, Jill: tucked together like twins.'

Hugh emerged; perusing Jill's sketches of his daughter as the three shared a pot of tea, he and his mother independently chose the second pose.

What a smile from Jill: 'It's my favourite, too. Early tomorrow I'll do a tracing and square that up; say what size picture you'd like, and I'll get a canvas in town.'

## Chapter 24

No rain, next morning; still a good wind, though.

Two deeply slept girls rowdied down for breakfast like tiger cubs: 'We woke up at exactly the same time, and Heather said, "I'd better go to my own bed now." But, just then, her alarm went off!'

Having noted every item chalked on the kitchen blackboard, the towngoers asked, was anything else required?

Hugh needed some pipe fittings, to be charged to account; Heather requested midnight blue hair clips; Sophy reminded Jill about a 2½ inch scale Ordnance map.

Lunchtime reminisced Hugh's childhood.

As he chortled, sighed, and mused, Sophy heard with increasing clarity Swansea's industrial intonation – that metallic resilience Bron delivered most strongly when acting cocky.

Then, for her life in Leamington.

Lucky for Mrs Fossway, he reflected, the girl adapting to that flat so well. *Considering that, apart from sea and countryside, Sophy loves Pembrokeshire for its roamy gardens.*

Sophy asked, 'Outside the County Show period, in the holidays does Heather usually come along with you when you're doing installations like this?'

'More often than not: same as with Charlie, helping out with the family business is something natural for her. But please don't imagine I resent Heather spending time with you: your company makes her extremely happy, and nothing else matters half as much. Anyway, haven't you been a busy pair on your own account?'

The girl's increasingly dextrous hands gave invaluable assistance, getting that big hot water cylinder into position under the stairs, and fiddlily working around it; nevertheless, they didn't complete the installation that day.

'A good job takes as long as it takes, Sophy; rushing the work results in leaks, which do one's reputation no good. And we'd have been back tomorrow, anyway: sunshine's forecast later. So, while you'll be studying the system's operation, I can check the fluid flow and fine-tune the controller. That is, once we've…'

'Let the water in!' Young as she might be, Sophy had deduced for herself that it wouldn't be wise, filling the cylinder now and leaving it to its own devices overnight.

Heather had practised well on Astral.

Jill had bought her canvas, and ordered copies of 'superb' Victorian photos of Pinched Pill: sailing ships, horses with wagons, people galore. For Sophy, 2½ inch *and* 1:50,000 maps: 'The other's bang up to date on footpaths and bridleways.'

'Thanks, AJ!' But she'd already had her best surprise, on arriving back at Bishop's Watch: there was Bronny.

The Swansea girl had been invited for supper by Heather who, having heard the forecast on the Volvo's radio while going to the stable, had asked Anna's permission to telephone Granny: 'This evening'll be gloomy; so as Jill can't work on my picture…'

Mind, Miss Haroldston's plot slightly backfired.

When Hugh and Sophy arrived she'd just asked, 'Now you've showered, Bronwen, do you fancy cards or a board game?'

Most firm, the rebuttal: 'I'm Cook's Mate this evening, and Jill's postcarding at the moment; as Sophy's already started her holiday homework, why not get stuck into yours?'

Heather was big enough to admit, coming to the supper table, 'An excellent bum-kick, that was.' She'd not written much, but many anotated paper slips eared the family's encyclopaedia.

Bronwen, between the girls: a happy, balanced composition. Jill got her camera; for this candlelight (they were going "semi-posh"), slow shutter speeds and very steady breathing.

Lovely food; wholly honest conversation. While Bronny was so fond of the Madocs and would be ever grateful, she did miss her three young Swansea cousins: living nearby and not chaotically, she'd loved being their babysitter. Thus she so enjoyed the company of these two girls; also, skilfully could she curb any tittering tendencies.

Over pudding Granny asked, 'Bronwen, did Miss Gwinear ever suggest you train as a teacher?'

'Yes, Mrs Haroldston; but university first, she insisted.'

Jill had brought her guitar and the whistle; Sophy did pretty well, dropping piano chords into each tune; Heather later persuaded her father to sing.

Armchair-sipping wine, Bronny offered, 'Moggo and I will just hum along, all right?' But actually she and Hugh sometimes stopped play when proper Swansea banter ignited, as richly boastful and rude – never modest nor respectful, that town of many docks! – as you'd hear down its covered market.

Now and then, surreptitiously, Granny, getting a green light inside Jill's focused viewfinder, gently pressed the button…

Come her bedtime Sophy pleaded, 'Surely you can stay, Bronwen?'

But she'd not realised: during the County Show lead-up, the ponies were unsettled; therefore the stable's girls took turns, bedding down in the office – and this was Bronny's duty night. 'Actually, show or not, I might have kept them company anyway, because of the wind: it calms the nervier ones, knowing someone's there.'

Heartfelt, Sophy's 'I understand.'

Jill had wined a bit, and good for her; Hugh still having things to check, Gran ran Bronny back through the stissing gloom. Who enthused about what good company the girls were, so mature most of the time; 'As for those conversations between you, and Jill, and Mister H: so many subjects covered!' Mizzled hair glistening in the yard light, her goodbye glittered gratitude.

Granny replied, diagonally, 'We loved having you, dear; after the County Show's over, you must give your future serious thought, hmm?'

And drove home wet-eyed, thinking how desperate for Family, the poor girl. *But at least Heather and Sophy will always love her to bits.*

CHAPTER 25

Jill brewed herself tea while the warming-up BBC transmitted its first forecast; as clear skies were expected all day, she must be ready for an after-supper session with Heather. 'So that canvas needs–'

'MAOW!'

Although the cheeky creature never lifted a paw domestically, he was right about Jill pulling her weight: Granny having acted as Town Guide yesterday, she'd laid on a delicious dinner, including Heather's favourite, gooseberry tart with clotted cream.

'What's more,' the artist conceded to don't-I-know-it Mogulus, 'I never helped wash up.' So she cupboarded the dried crocks and then laid the table, tripping outside for flowers. Next, to polish the shoes in the lobby...

Furthermore, Hugh had gone to his study after the girls had turned in; 'Although it was pretty late by then, Puss!' For who'd have denied the two a long evening with Bronny?

'Maouw!'

Hugh Haroldston, exemplary widower father to Heather, surely soon "Uncle" and not "Boss" to dear Sophy...

Now slicing Bara Gwenith, 'Not that he's my sort.'

'Mieuu!'

'But certainly a very good man.'

'Prrrp!'

'Who understands good friendship: grown-ups getting on well

without inappropriate cosiness, which would confuse or mislead children.'

'Ahum, thank you.'

Jill, just not dropping the bread knife.

'Sorry, Jill: I couldn't help hearing, coming downstairs. But, look here, I don't deserve any credit. After Louise died I wanted the least possible contact with anyone; it was Mam who put me straight: introversion isn't an option for a father.'

'But,' she insisted, 'Heather's being so level despite everything is a lot down to you, I can tell.'

An appreciative nod; then, 'For my part, if Sophy had any blood aunts—'

Lancashire impishness couldn't resist: 'I see them now, terrorising the Spanish Main!'

He chuckled, 'You must draw them and their ship for her. But, seriously, Jill, the girl couldn't have a better adult friend. That's Heather's judgement; Mother and I heartily agree: it's different, but your way with children is as good as Bronny's.'

'Thank you. Maybe you guessed, but my approach is nothing like Carol's either, so aren't I lucky that she let Sophy come with me? Especially as the holiday's been rather riskier than—'

'Through no fault of yours. Anyway, Carol Fossway will see that enduring those close scrapes has made Sophy, same as Heather, emotionally stronger and more aware of danger.'

'Aye: Carol should be glad – eventually. And while Sophy already knew, because of losing her father, as people are far more important than things, she now understands how invaluable friendship is in tough situations – thanks to your Heather and young Bronny.'

'Yesterday, when Sophy was telling me about her home life, I tried picturing Carol.'

'That's not so easy: Sophy has her father's look. But bear with me…' After wallet-riffling, 'Here are Carol and Keith, a few months before—'

Bomp! Thump! Two hungries, leaping from the lower landing like corsairs boarding a prize.

Granny appeared looking tired; Heather hugged, 'Sophy and I were preparing you breakfast in bed.'

'A kind thought. I didn't sleep much for thinking about Bronny: yes, she loves horses; but shouldn't there be more in her life?'

'There would be,' Heather pouted…

'…If Sam Goldfire came back,' Sophy said.

The lady shook her head, 'That girl's an expert at hiding feelings! All last evening I never thought of him, yet that young man can't ever be out of Bronny's thoughts for long. She's suffering just like those girls in the last war whose sweethearts were posted missing.'

Involuntarily they all sighed together – even Mogulus.

Arriving at Drift Cottage, 'Are we putting the bath in, today?'

'Unfortunately, it's very heavy: unloading the thing took four of us. However while I fill the system, you could clear around it – and while you do, consider how we might move it, hmm?'

She continued pondering that problem during the first inspection (one drip, easily sorted). This was the *cold* check, Hugh emphasised: some leaks only started when plumbing got hot.

Already the collectors were very warm, but no antifreeze seeps showed in the circuit linking them to the hot water cylinder. Having ticked another box in the instruction manual, 'Righto, girl: switch her to "Run", please.'

The pump thrummed; odd crackles were air bubbles passing through. About the pipework's creaks and tocks Hugh tutored, tentatively touching, 'Glycol coil's heating fast.' Then, clipboarding a form, 'Write down *these* temperatures every ten minutes, please; later we'll work out how much energy we're harvesting. At sixty centigrade we re-check for leaks, then start insulating pipes.'

'Very good, Sir!' This, used in old Navy films, seemed appropriate.

Hugh, from one ladder, was now verifying that glycol flowed equally through the three collectors; scribe Sophy was up the other.

This was the *commissioning*: ensuring that everything was performing properly, then logging settings, levels, and so forth. The information was invaluable; if you were called back to an installation, comparing fresh measurements with original readings quickly told you if the performance had deteriorated.

Sophy had realised that, because of Jill's background, Hugh wanted this system to meet her full approval technically as well as aesthetically; also, a pleased Ms Ribblesdale might become a valuable local ambassador for solar heating.

As he whizzed down for the lunchtime forecast on the car radio, 'I'll chuck up two cushions, and we'll have a "high level" lunch?'

That, she thought, would be a hoot...

The wind, much eased now, was still westerly. Sophy, between mouthfuls, 'I can't smell oil at all.'

'Nor I; so I think you should go and–'

Waving urgently for silence, 'Oh, Lordy: that's Bumble!'

He sighed, 'I don't know that pony, but if it's got loose I suppose we'd better–'

'Uncle Hugh, Bumble is JILL'S CAR!'

'Aha; ahum. Then fasten your seatbelt, Sophy dearest!'

With arms crossed, 'Such dedicated engineers, personally checking the sun's strength! I must say, you do look comfy.'

Sophy, indignantly, 'We haven't been–'

Hugh, indicating that they should descend, 'She's teasing, my love!'

Sophy stepped down, 'AJ, you *knew*! But how? Heather wouldn't have said, nor Granny; and I can't believe that Mogulus–'

'Sweetheart, he's a cat! He couldn't let himself out of the bag, so to speak. No – that were someone else, lass.'

Insistently, 'Who?' *Oh, won't they get a piece of my mind when the time comes?*

'The mirror'll tell thee.'

'ME? With red face, and icy neck, 'How...?'

'A towel, last seen *here*, found pegged out and drying at the top of Granny's garden – and smelling of your shampoo.'

Hugh chuckled, 'Astounding deduction, Sherlock Ribblesdale!'

Sophy, pouting, 'What were you doing up there?'

Jill twinkled, 'You'll see.' Then she came to link arms: 'Now, Esteemed Solar Acolyte, pray teach me about this marvellous contrivance.'

He pretend-cowered, 'Do as Her Ladyship commands, young Fossway.'

'…And I've an idea for shifting the bath. When our neighbour changed their heating oil tank, Daddy and he laid planks across the lawn, and used logs as rollers. Just how the ancient Egyptians moved stones to build their pyramids, Mum said.'

'But unfortunately,' Jill said, 'I've no long timbers.'

The girl whirled about: 'Our ladders, Boss Man!'

Flopping onto the bench Jill chuckled, 'Dropping over for some tubes of paint, I find my house overrun by an Eco Hit Squad; soon, I'm emptying my larder and stripping its shelves and then, straining like whipped slaves, we struggle into position a grandiose bath fit for Cleopatra; so, bless this angel in bluejeans now miraculously bringing mugs of sacred Nilewater tea which shall restore us! Which I must swallow fast, and dash: I meant to prepare that canvas this afternoon, but because your mother's tired, Hugh–'

He'd registered Sophy's look: 'We'll collect Heather, and cook the meal. So away with you, Madam Artist, to concentrate on creative endeavours.'

'That's so kind, and I will!' Drink masculinely drained, the artist jumped up; 'Only, sithee, I haven't begun to thank you both, for such a well installed solar system, already working beautifully. On my oath, I–'

Two F-111s, fuel taps open wide: end of all conversation. So Jill, blowing kisses, skedaddled.

Consulting his watch, 'I'm sorry, Sophy: Tempus Fugit, so Mill Cove is out, now. But, while I clear away, you could visit Tracker: when time's up I'll signal a toot, two hoots, and another toot.'

'Morse code for…?'

'P – as in the Blue Peter flag. Meaning "Ready To Depart".'

But Bronny was already there at the gate, clearly having important words with him.

As Sophy decided to retreat the older girl, noticing her, beckoned.

'I'm sorry to have disturbed–'

'Sophes, it's always lovely to see you; but come and tell us why you're here: I thought you three weren't coming back until tomorrow.'

Had they been gassing so, Sophy hadn't heard Hugh Haroldston's horn?

No; for soon after Tracker had warned them, the Volvo came backing down – and out got a relaxed Boss Man: 'Hello again, Bronwen!'

She beamed, 'All well, Mr Hugh?'

'Forty-five centigrade in the cylinder already.'

'Tidy!'

Sophy kissed Bronny, 'It was lovely talking. And to you,' she patted the horse, 'of course.'

Bronny jumped down, too: 'Time I was getting back.'

'Then,' his eyes sparked, 'you can give us a lift.'

She frowned, 'Mr Hugh, surely you mean…?'

But he'd opened the driver's door: 'Isn't it time you resumed driving lessons? There's a good while since you broke your ankle, girl!'

'It would be so useful for you and the Madocs,' encouraged Sophy.

'Drift Cottage and back twice, hmm?'

'Should you trust me with this car?'

'We trust you with Sophy and Heather, going out riding, don't we…? So, in you hop!'

Bronny only stalled once, and that was doing a three-point turn.

She got out bursting with gratitude; she *would* recommence lessons. 'And now, as a return favour: to save you time I'll lend Heather my bike, and she can bring herself home.'

Squirming back round after waving goodbye Sophy sighed, 'She's so chuffed, Uncle Hugh, she's going back to tell Tracker.'

Actually, it transpired, to remonstrate: 'Don't give me looks, boyo! Driving isn't instead of riding, it's as well as. And if I pass my test and they let me borrow the Landy and a horse box, we two can go exploring those Prescellys you stare at so longingly.' Folding her arms, 'Hadn't thought of that, had you?'

Reluctant grunts: he must admit, no.

She hugged, sniffling, 'Bloody Americans, thinking they know everything – and yet you still can't help loving them!'

# CHAPTER 26

Jill peeped: yes, tucked in together.

After the camera's third clack Heather awoke to whisper, 'Time to get up?'

'Almost. Forgive me, but that's a sweet picture you two made.'

'We maids made,' Sophy murmured. Who must know, 'Feeling better, Heather?'

So joyous, the evening before could have been, with Drift Cottage's solar installation to be celebrated. And Heather's cycle back should have been lovely: a honeysuckled freewheel down the bridleway, then on through the village waving to friends. But actually, a journey of pressure-cooked indignation: *How DARE she?* For Heather had, on setting off, been vilely sniped.

Bronny had been the cause, but it hadn't been her fault.

Instead of reading a novel during telephone answering stints, the Swansea girl had made a thank-you card for Mrs Haroldston: her text had swirled hippyishly; framed by extravagant biro patterns, she had cartooned herself and Mogulus, all danced about by music notes; below had looped, AN EVENING I'LL NEVER FORGET.

All well and good; except that someone, infiltrating the office to re-chalk the morrow's roster and allocate herself a better pony, had peeped into an unsealed envelope...

Patricia Flange had kept her powder dry until five o'clock: 'There goes Heather Haroldston, the Talbenny Toady: "Oh, Bronwen, do come to supper! Bronwen, I'll take your bike home and clean it! Bronwen, let me ride Slipstream – AGAIN!"'

Gleed by Patricia's slur, how the posh clique had then tittered over her description of Bronny's "crummy home-made card".

After a red-eyed ride back, Heather had slammed into the house, torn upstairs, flung off dusty clothes, and stepped unthinkingly into a too hot bath... Leaping out yelping, feet and shins flame red, she'd tripped on the rucked mat and crashed to the floor furiously tearful.

So upset, because Bronny had from the shadows heard that acidic outburst and, Heather had seen, been doubly hurt. Firstly, if anything Bron overcompensated for their friendship, always tutoring the youngster firmly; secondly, such blinkered crassness she'd shown over the love-full card, that spoilt doll-faced snob Patricia Flange, to whom the concept of *doing your best with what you can afford* could mean nothing.

Heather had taken to bed very early after little supper – not even tasting her father's and Sophy's excellent interpretation of her second favourite pudding, goosegog crumble and custard.

Restored by profound sleep, Heather yawned, 'I'm fine, thanks. Anyway, I've only to endure Modom's company this morning, then tomorrow's a day off!'

Because that afternoon the mobile blacksmith was coming; and on the Friday, "The calm before the storm" as Sabrina had it, the Madocs, and farmer friends with horse boxes, would transport the County Show ponies to Haverfordwest. Then, later on, Bronny and Sabrina would head to the Withybush showground in a Dormobile loaned by Mrs Williams: their overnight patrols would reassure any nervous animals.

Heather sat up to see a cobalt horizon; 'And this afternoon's forecast…?'

'Promising, but windyish; however, Pinched Pill should be sheltered. I wondered about sketching you two in your swimmers – not statue-still, but doing something practical.'

Sophy requested, 'Digging for treasure?'

Jill laughed, 'That's something *piratical*: your Blood Aunts would be proud!' And she explained.

Sophy remembered, 'AJ, you never said yesterday what took you right up this garden to find that towel.'

Jill perched on the bed's end. 'After yesterday's breakfast Mogulus reappeared, very yowly. Assuming he'd caught a mouse, I followed him outside – and off he trotted, into new territory for me. When we reached that charming little lawn in amongst the fruit trees, there was the towel.'

Sophy triumphed, 'So he *did* give the game away!'

'I'm sure that hadn't been his intention.'

'MAOW!'

They'd not noticed him enter. Heather husked, 'So what were you showing AJ, Puss? The view?'

Onto the windowsill to stare seawards, shaking his head.

Sophy said, 'At home he often takes you to the stream, though cats aren't supposed to like water.'

'No,' Heather concurred. 'Mind, he loves chasing down the bank after anything bobbing along, and hoiking at it from the bridge.'

'Miaow!'

'But,' Sophy frowned, 'there's no water up Gran's garden.'

'MI-AOWW!' *Oh, yes there is!* And he was right: buried under the turf right up there was a great flat stone; and under that slept an ancient well – which, one day, the Haroldstons would be very glad of.

The artist resumed, 'Puss stomped round noisily a while, then lost interest – but I didn't.' She gestured, 'The island framed by those fruit trees; and, girls, those *colours!* The sea seen from there seemed...'

'A liquid jewel?', Heather proposed. 'That's how Mummy put it.'

'And put it so very, very well, sweetheart. And now I must thank Sophy, because that flapping towel completed the composition.' Sighing, she dreamily closed eyes.

'MEEYU!'

Miss Fossway frowned, 'Why's he suddenly so insistent?'

Miss Haroldston tingled, 'You didn't do...?'

Jill stood up; 'Only an oil sketch; but, okay, I'll fetch it...'

'Only? *Only?*' Heather crush-hugged, 'Aunty Jilly, that's MAGNIFICENT!'

A throat cleared: 'Realising I wasn't the only one awake...' Hugh, with tea and biscuits. 'I was going to tick you off, Heather, for risking waking Granny; in the circumstances, I think you'd better invite her to join us.'

Expressed for the three of them, how deep the effect on the lady of first seeing Jill's painting: 'My dear, it's so hard to believe you never met Louise.'

With soft mew, Puss jumped into the silent artist's arms.

\*

Breakfasted on the previous evening's pud, invited to again stay at Jill's, Heather cycled to the stables zestily.

Before Greengrass she produced a compressed ball of that selfsame crumble; it having disappeared instanter, 'Okay, Buster: your nose knows I've a bigger lump in my other pocket; it's yours, if you behave.

But play up just once and Trooper, whom you detest, will get the bleeding lot.'

Exemplarily obedient, he even picked his feet up.

*

They found the new cylinder's forty-five gallons nearing sixty Centigrade; also, Drift Cottage definitely felt drier.

To Mogulus's delight, his new home now had an airing cupboard – the one feature of Cambridgeshire life he'd really missed; and, until he figured out how to break in, flopping on the toasty attic stairs was blissful enough.

Maybe the bathroom being off the kitchen was slightly odd; 'But,' Jill giggled, lounging dressed with Sophy in the empty tub to prove how capacious, 'from here I can monitor the supper: how deluxe is *that*?' And she pretended to sip some wine.

Sophy, after pondering two holes midway down the side rim, 'It would be extra deluxe, having the taps *here*: topping up the hot would be a doddle.'

'And you girls wouldn't have to take turns at the comfier end: perfecto luxurioso, eh?'

Hearing about Greengrass at lunchtime, Jill chuckled, 'He should be Patsy's hero: like her grandfather, his only motivation is greed.'

Then she explained about the afternoon's sketching: she would like the two wearing bathers, to understand their every movement; back in the studio, she'd depict them in an earlier era's clothes.

Heather nodded, 'We'll be moving manikins.'

'Girlikins,' Sophy tried. 'Because "womanikins" sounds weird!'

Reflecting about beachwear, they knew themselves lucky: snug one-pieces like theirs hadn't existed until recent times. In the past, well-off children had cumbersome costumes, and because poorer parents were often too straight-laced to let their children go naked, many never got to play in the water, nor did they learn to swim. 'How tragic!', they agreed; indeed, tragedy often resulted.

Already swimmered, on reaching the Coal Road's bosky descent to the pill the friends hootyscampered down ahead. Legs lithe, knapsacks ajig, they echoed Jill's being that age, haring with mates to where a beck pooled deeply.

Operations base would be the lime kilns; feeling so floaty relieved of her backpack, Sophy was ready for the warm green-scented sand and—

Heather, pointing to the pub, reminded, 'Because of broken glass, here we keep our gymshoes on, and we *never* dig with bare hands.'

While they imagined piracy, Jill would sketch them searching for shellfish; hence her bringing along a rake, bucket, and spade.

Thirty paces found them a fisherman's bait-worm pit which the ebb had scoured: 'Will here do…?' '…And might we actually dig?'

'Mais oui…!'

Content sighed Jill: those slender bodies harmonised positions so naturally.

Now, Sophy bent in scrutiny while Heather's spade glooped sand, she sketched intensely: her young models were holding their poses brilliantly considering that, tide-drained dry, the whole estuary awaited exploration.

This digging theme certainly had potential for a pair of pictures. In the first, Sophy could dig while Heather rake-rested; in the complementary view Carol's girl would squat, palms proffering finds, while the other's finger sorted species, flicking anything tasty bucketwards.

Fidgets now; *Well, fair enough*. 'Thanks, girls! Off you go – but remember the tide if you cross to the other side, or you'll be walking back via the causeway.'

Sophy, head tilted, 'If we get carried away, we might get carried away, hmm?'

'Good word-play,' Heather levelled, 'but some stupid brats who stayed on the Sandy Haven stepping stones too long last year got swept well towards the Spread Eagle; mind, Pinched Pill doesn't fill quite as fast.'

Sophy relaxed; 'So here's safe?'

Jill smiled, 'Today it should be; and that's the best one can say about anywhere on a coast. Anyway, will you leave the implements–?'

'No, ta,' Heather grinned. 'Thought we'd try mudlarking.'

One word; instant transport back to Lancashire's childhood riverbanks.

A pan of fine sand, the stream bed, ribboned by sun-warmed water.

Heather having pounced, connoisseur Sophy opined, 'This anthracite's even shinier than my pieces from The Drift.'

'There's more mica in it: truly a Black Diamond, eh? But it can't be from a mine up the valley: after an accident yonks back killed some unemployed men digging for fuel, all the adit entrances were dynamited.'

'So this lump dates from when the last ship loaded?'

'I doubt it.' Dropping the piece into the current, Heather showed how readily it tumbled along: 'Cargo spilt back then would be long gone; reckon it's truly sea coal, meaning the estuary cuts a seam somewhere.'

A few more steps; another lump... Inevitably, an Anthracite Hunt. Heather proposed, 'Let's time ourselves collecting fifty bits, then we can estimate how long for a bucketful. Perhaps Jill could build up a stock: she'd surely like her stove keeping going on solid fuel, right through frosty nights.'

'Mogulus certainly would!'

Heather reckoned ten minutes, and wouldn't be far off: like many country-dwellers, she gauged time's passage well.

However, they'd found most anthracite in the last two minutes, thanks to a Leamingtonian discovery: yes, lumps readily rolled along the sandy bed; but if they encountered a dip, in they tumbled and, sheltered from the current, there they stayed. So bait-digger's holes and the scour pits surrounding rocks were by far the best Black Diamond hunting grounds.

Jill was surprised.

The youngsters had earlier yearned to explore, but on they fossicked; and, though the tide was flooding, Sophy still had time – just – to see the top of the pill, to appreciate the irony...

Originally, shallow tub boats could closely approach the Pit Valley adits, shuttling their output down to Collier's Quay for transhipment to seagoing vessels. Then in early Victorian times some ambitious mine owners had bought steam pumps; alas, while draining the adits well, these had discharged silty water.

Eventually, reedy mud had filled the old channels and, it had seemed, mine wharves must be extended to meet the boats, by then having to be half-loaded lest they grounded en route to Colliers' Quay; but by then, also, the railway was coming: steam, which had seemed the local mines' salvation, had in two ways brought about their demise...

*No: that history lesson must evidently wait!*

Jill wondered what the girls were fossicking for; although lovers of the natural world, neither was so engrossed in biology that they'd study shells scientifically... *So, are they captivated by their shapes and patterns?*

Sometimes London mudlarks found amazingly old artefacts; Roman, even. Maybe the stream was surrendering fragments of stoneware and willow pattern, perhaps even pieces of that brown-glazed clumsy pottery she'd first found when gardening with Miss Gwinear: 'Seventeenth century, apparently. Our County archaeologists hope to find the kiln site one day, and prove a Flemish connection.'

'Aye,' Jill murmured to herself, 'probably archaeologising, inspired by young Charlie.' With some success, too: that bucket was getting steadily heavier.

'Ah, well!' Now for a wide backdrop sketch of Tram Gin Hill's wooded slopes.

Meanwhile, the girls' quest gradually took them towards the causeway...

Which furnished good pickings, all around the arches.

From overhead, 'How much per ton, please? Cheaper than my coalman, I hope!'

Heather, shielding eyes, 'I'm afraid this anthracite's spoken for, Mrs Williams!'

Sophy remembered, 'Thanks for those delicious buns! Um, how's your ankle?'

'Much better, bless you. Is that Jill, over near the kilns?'

'Yes; she was sketching us earlier.'

'Goodoh! You look so lovely in your costumes.'

'Actually,' Heather modulated, 'she only wanted compositions, so's to picture us later as historic cockle girls.'

'A nice idea; but I'd prefer you painted thus: two friends whom I know having fun, hmm?'

Enthusiastic nods.

'Only,' the lady pondered, 'that bucket's heavy, and you've walked here from Drift Cottage. Look here: my car's outside the pub; why don't I take your loot, and deliver it tomorrow? You needn't be in.'

Sophy said, 'I'd prefer we were, so you could view Jill's works.'

'And,' Heather flourished, 'see her new solar installation.'

The lady suppressed a smile: *Subtle marketing, considering how young!* Then she thought, *I'd rather see Jill Ribblesdale's sketches of today, today.* To see them fresh, before being worked up back in the studio. Lots of artists did that, and galleries encouraged the practice because it resulted in modestly priced fast-turnaround works; however, titivation was such a threat to immediacy. So, knowing she'd the ingredients, 'Okay – climb those rungs and pass me up your bucket; and can you please give Jill this message…?'

A fresh batch of buns left cooling, an hour later Alice Williams was back at Colliers' Quay.

Jill and the now dressed girls sat on the wall; trusting them not to dawdle, she three-pointed right outside the pub and, 'Hop in, quickly!'

## Chapter 27

Causeway crossed, they climbed, undergrowth glimpsing them the tide's glittering return.

'Thank goodness the oil dispersed fast,' said Sophy. 'There was just a whiff, sometimes, as we hunted.'

Lest Jill asked what for, Heather observed loudly, 'Nice car!'

'So was the old one,' Alice sighed, 'but if accountants insist… This does use less juice, mind.'

A good thing, everyone agreed.

They emerged onto a green dominated by the mast Sophy had glimpsed days before, and Mrs Williams pulled over: 'New territory for your friend, Heather; do show her the incline, too. Tea in twenty minutes!'

Staring up that pole while chequered clouds slid across dizzied Sophy: it seemed to be ever toppling. 'Far too smooth to climb, surely?'

'There's a pulley up top; on days when low cloud clung to the cliffs, men used to be hoisted aloft in a bosun's chair – a bit hairy, eh? You see, during fog this place often keeps in clear air; those lookouts could have seen the mastheads of any ships out in the bay.'

'*Only* their mastheads? That must have looked odd.'

'On misty autumn mornings, from home we sometimes see just bridges and funnels sliding along offshore.'

'Spooky! AJ must photograph that phenomenon, one day.'

As they tramped the track which horses working the winding gin had once circled, Heather elaborated operations in the old days; then they crossed to the south side of the green – and there was the long, straight incline, reaching down to the corner wharf. Officially, it was a bridle path; a really steep one, mind!

Spaced down that slope were pairs of stout posts; Sophy asked, 'Are those to stop cars?'

Heather laughed, 'They maybe prevent loonies having a go; that's not what they're for, though.'

A jay cackling over, mischievously colourful, forestalled the obvious question.

'Such busyness, once,' the Leamington girl boggled. 'So many people and horses, all needing co-ordination; yet very little coal handled, I expect, compared to modern methods.' Remembering that fuel mountain at Didcot's power station – and the procession of lorry-sized wagons a Diesel locomotive had been trundling: so many trains an hour, day and night, Mum had said.

'People needed heat; even colliers weren't paid much, and children got pennies. So anthracite was a better bargain than firewood; easier to store, too.'

Sophy, having sorted her thoughts, 'That's today's lesson: if what people once did doesn't seem sensible nowadays, we aren't understanding how things were then.'

Crossing the coast road, they took a leafy lane; Sophy tingled, 'Does this lead to the villas?'

Already, the first was coming into view.

'Lucky Mrs Williams, being a neighbour of my favourite property!'

But Alice wasn't. She opened the front door, 'Welcome to Anvil House!', to a rather bemused Miss Fossway: 'Are you all right, dear?'

'Confused, Mrs Williams. When I first spotted this house and told AJ how I admired it, she never said it was yours; also, your hall and stairs seem unbelievably familiar.'

Alice hugged, 'All will be explained.'

They changed back into swimmers in a photograph-crammed downstairs loo, then joined the grown-ups on the verandah.

And a green-eyed black cat; absentmindedly Sophy stroked, 'Hello, Daphne.'

She purred, pleased to be acknowledged; the girl gasped, 'I knew your name!'

'Because,' Jill chuckled, 'she's a television star.'

This further confused Sophy: Aunty Jill had never been much of a TV viewer.

No doubts, at least, about what to do with ice-chinked home-made lemonade; nor how to tackle still-warm fruit buns – two each!

Now out onto the toe-lovely lawn, to take in the sea-staring façade: *Why is this house so familiar?*

'Sophy, I'd better explain; or,' Alice Williams mused, 'you'll believe you possess Psychic Gifts. Did you and Mother watch **The Writer's Holiday**, a television play screened last winter?'

'Jolly good, it was! Set in Cornwall, I remember.'

'But not necessarily filmed there.' Alice pointedly looked about.

Sophy's jaw dropped; 'When he was working in his study…' She sprang to peer from the verandah into the room on the right of the front door.

At Alice's nod Heather went inside, seated herself in the captain's chair, and pretend-scrivened.

Her young friend finger-clicked, 'Of course!' Then, though, she confronted the lady politely but firmly: 'But when he looked outside, there was Saint Michael's Mount – and it wasn't a model.'

'His going to the window,' Alice divulged, 'was filmed using a set built in someone's garden on The Lizard. And because I insisted that people shouldn't recognise this house, the BBC did no standing-back shots of it – just close-ups through windows, and tight views of the doors.'

'I'm glad they did everything to suit you,' said Sophy.

'Actually, the BBC were all for keeping their filming here low key: the actors never got pestered. Because it's busier all year round, that would have been a lot to hope for in Cornwall.'

'Such an absorbing story,' the girl glowed; 'and the pace was perfect, we thought.'

'Yes,' said Alice, 'I was so pleased–'

Heather, from the window, 'It's *beautifully* peaceful in here, Alice.'

The lady mused, 'That worked so well, their recording the sound on location.'

Sophy came close: 'When he played the piano to Daphne – was that actually *him*?'

'Yes, dear: he has a beautiful technique. I was there when they filmed that scene.'

'Golly gosh, did you properly meet him?'

'A really pleasant, hard working chap: the perfect choice for that rôle.'

'And this was the perfect setting; but how did the BBC find it?'

Those grey eyes hesitated; then, 'The producer had been here, Sophy.'

'…Um, Alice, did you write **The Writer's Holiday**?'

'I did. Using a *nom de plume*, of course.'

Sophy frowned, 'Wh-Why didn't you say sooner?'

'My policy has been to never say what I do, because some folk are funny about meeting authors. But you can be trusted with the secret, hmm?'

'I promise!'

'Should word spread, you see, there'd be requests to give talks, do interviews… So distracting, so time-consuming, when writing's a slow enough process, thank you! As for being recognised out and about…'

Sophy and Heather synchronised nods.

'When Giles Farber came down to discuss adapting **The Writer's Holiday**, on entering the house he said the story had to be filmed here, for completeness: a television play about a writer writing a story, filmed in the room in which the original novella was written! But I was so wary of the whole recognition business.

'However, I changed my mind – because that question about spirituality burnt inside me: would Giles's viewers sense the special serendipity? Could a camera convey the ultimate appropriateness of the setting?'

Sophy nodded, 'Tinglingly so!'

Jill agreed: 'That play had a tremendous sense of place, Alice.'

Heather agreed; 'But why didn't you set the story in Pembrokeshire?'

'Firstly, and bluntly, a Cornish setting would have more appeal. Secondly, I was throwing people off the scent: wasn't the creator of a story about a Cornish writer returning to Cornwall bound to be Cornish? And—' But then Alice Williams twigged Heather's extravagantly-gestured charade: 'And I think Sophy Fossway should play that piano herself.'

Sophy gulped, 'The one he played? But wasn't it a concert grand?'

Alice, ushering her young friend inside, 'Funnily enough, it still is.'

While Mrs Williams propped the lid open, Sophy hunted in the piano stool for simple, appropriate music; windows opened, Heather stepped over the low sill to re-join Jill and Daphne.

Sophy played with nice sensitivity, but too much awe; then, her expression changed. Realising how powerfully sonorous this instrument could be without harshness or loss of clarity, her fingers became bold; indeed all her lovely body now woke to the composer's liberating sentiments.

Alice quietly went to brew tea.

Recital over and well applauded, a fizz-full Sophy had many questions about being an author; also, she'd something to share.

'My dear, one writes because a story inside one needs telling: there's such compulsion! As for writing well – it means keeping on, revision after revision… A simple formula for success, but a difficult process.'

'Mrs Williams, it was my so enjoying **The Writer's Holiday**, although it was meant for adults, which inspired Mummy's project: her idea is to tell a story in a grown-up style which has such a good plot that readers my age, in fact readers of any age, will make the effort. A springboard book, she calls it, encouraging young people to then try reading… well, absolutely anything, actually.'

A large garden to explore.

The hill behind sheltering Anvil House from north winds, its back garden was further protected by tall red sandstone cross-walls to the villa's either side. Peaches trained across the western one plumped fruits under protective netting; a fine white greenhouse stood against the eastern bulwark.

In which Sophy imagined Mrs Williams dining colonially: *The remains of the day's heat, candlelit curries, and a wind-up gramophone.* Did she sometimes write in there? *I know I would.* And what jungly pleasure to sulter themselves – her, coppery Heather, tame puma Daphne – secretively female within fecund greenery.

Hand in hand, the girls now, dancingly down to Alice's sundial; cheekily, they thought it slightly fast.

Views, there, to envy many palaces. Leftwards, the ridge they'd crossed earlier rolled down towards The Lookout; below the stubby headland straight before them modest waves washed around The Anvil; miles beyond, ever defiant Druids Head. That bluff opposite Anvil Head was The Furzy, Heather said; far behind, the bay's southern shore receded bluely westward from Creampot Cove until hidden by skyline-hunched trees.

So good to be in costumes: as Heather observed, every breezeless nook around this sunny lawn was 'gorgeous warm'. At last, they found one such which Alice's neighbours *didn't* overlook – a sunken lawn, east of the sundial. Backed by dog roses, this was most discreet, and yet you could see out: the low stone wall's faux arrow slits peered seawards. They brown-sprawled within some good long while, spying the sea just as Crusoe and Friday had from their sand-floored stockade.

Recce resumed, Sophy pointed, 'What's *that* for, on the right?' A recess beside a bedroom window housed a handsome ship's lamp; the surrounding masonry was whitewashed. Then she noticed a matching lantern alcove wisteria-lurking at the wall's other end; this one, though, was framed by tar-black stones.

At the verandah's eastern end question-answering Heather tutored, 'What do you see?'

Recalling **Swallows and Amazons**, 'I see why Alice's mast isn't central in the lawn: align it with the white square above, and you'll sail safely through the pill's mouth. So, here was once a sort of signal station.'

Heather was most impressed; 'Thoughts about the other lamp, then?'

Pacing down the verandah, turning, Sophy stared seawards... *But there can't be another alignment; and anyway, in daytime black squares make useless markers.*

Heather prompted, 'A signal station – a bit like a signal box?'

The other fingersnapped, 'Telling sailors it was okay to come in!'

'Bang on! Originally flags had sufficed, because for safety ships nearly always came and went in daylight; when the mine owners got ambitious about upping production, the Williamses planned for night sailings, to handle the increased traffic.

'A green light up the Tram Gin mast told mariners sea conditions were generally okay; approaching ships must wait for a green light, left of the leading lights, before entering the pill. A red meant there wasn't enough water depth; and, if nothing showed, a vessel was putting to sea.'

'Ah, yes: you couldn't tell from the bay if one was on its way out, because of how the inlet bends – and ships couldn't pass in the entrance, because there wasn't room.'

'And, anyway, it couldn't cope with two vessels at once, this little port's handling method.'

'Which was...?'

'It involved rowing boats and horses, apparently; Alice knows the details.'

'Okay – but, whoa! On misty days, how did they know up here how things were down there?'

'Excellent question; the answer is, an electric telegraph connected here with the corner wharf.'

'Making Anvil House *very* like a signal box: ingenious!'

'Indeed; but unfortunately by the time everything was installed, mining hereabouts was in serious trouble.'

That seemed so unfair, Sophy said; but then she registered her friend's expression: didn't they both know that, in many respects, life wasn't fair? 'The mast and the white square are still useful to boats entering the pill, though, aren't they?'

'Or leaving it; so, ever since, except for wartime, Anvil House has always shown leading lights at night.'

'That's, um, pretty generous of the Williamses.'

'Aye; and plenty folk have had reason to be grateful, over the years. The family've always maintained the Tram Gin Top mast, too.'

'Although that's more about keeping history alive?'

'Hmm. Talking of history, wait 'til you see Alice's old maps and documents! Which are best kept for a rainy day, actually; but isn't it good they've been preserved?'

'Plus all the historic loo photos…? I'll say.'

In the house, a timepiece bell sweetly tinged: it was six o'clock.

Alice stood up: 'I interrupted your afternoon's work, Jill Ribblesdale. To make amends, I'll run you all home; and, I tell you what, if I 'phoned ahead to the pub…' Thus the writer invited herself to supper: take-away fish and chips, her treat.

Getting back in the car with their consignment, plus ginger beers and a bottle of house white, 'Did you guess what the chaps have in mind?'

Just after she had entered it, sturdy men had clustered from The Davy Lamp, crossed over and, leaning over the causeway wall, discussed something animatedly.

Nobody had.

As the engine fired, 'The Talbenny Haven Rugger Tuggers play rugby in winter, and form a summer tug-of-war team. They recently lost against some inland Young Farmers who, adding insult to injury, said that our boys should "stick to playing at sailors". Because quite a few of them run crab boats from Creampot Cove.'

Heather bristled, 'That's getting on for fighting talk!'

'Indeed. So, as they're all strong oarsmen, they propose challenging those clodwallopers – and other coastal villages, too – to a rowing boat tug-of-war.'

'But,' Jill frowned, 'judging a contest would be impossible: you couldn't be sure of the water staying still.'

'No; but I had an idea, inspired by what used to happen here with boats a long while back, involving ropes and pulleys. They're proposing to run a trial next week – which might be fun, so I'll keep you posted.'

On the back doorstep…

Granny's cake tin label read, 'Good Luck on Sunday, Heather!'; the addressee insisted they share her gooseberry pie as their pudding, that very evening: 'It wouldn't taste half as nice, otherwise.'

Mrs Williams reassured Jill that, with vanilla essence, plus sherry splashed, custard made with powdered milk would pass muster.

Jill now read a note from Mrs Madoc: '*Dear girls, tomorrow morning could you possibly see to the stay-at-home horses? That would let everyone else concentrate on loading the ponies.*' She shrugged, 'Rather a busman's holiday for you, Heather; but, having missed the weather forecast, we might have been riding for a fall if we'd planned an outing.'

'We'll do it!', they synchronised.

'Then whizz up now to say so,' Alice said, 'while Jill does veges and I concoct a Crème Gallois. And in case Anna's staying home tomorrow, how about asking what you're to do if, ahem, things begin?'

They departed, 'We will!'

'…About Anna, Alice: what good advice – which I would never have thought of.'

'Jill Ribblesdale, don't berate yourself; you've more good notions than many parents I know.'


By really belting, the girls could deliver the message *and* manage a quick hello.

Ears atwitch as they updated him, Tracker kept peering skywards because, despite the sound of engines approaching, most confusingly no aeroplane deigned to appear. Until, eventually…

'An AIRSHIP!'

Not a huge one; nevertheless, something jolly different: neither girl had seen such a craft before. 'A humming silver aubergine' was Sophy's commendable description; as a light boat is wavelet-buffeted, it was being bumped about a bit by evening thermals.

Either Tracker knew about airships, or just accepted this oddity for what it was; contrastingly some stable ponies, you could hear, weren't at all happy.

Heather remembered what she'd read in the paper: 'The silly so-and-sos had better get used to that didgeridoo: after doing something at the base it's giving local sightseeing rides, these next few days.'

'Would you like a trip?'

'It would be interesting; but why should people suffer *anything* engined coming over uninvited, spoiling their peace and privacy? Flying always takes lots of fuel; more oil used means more tar on our beaches. Even if it didn't, even if ships stopped flushing out at sea, more tanker voyages must mean more accidents, and more filthed coastlines: quite honestly, I wish humans had never flown.'

No aeroplanes; possibly, no atom bombs.

Tracker grunted, watching the dirigible depart: for all that he loved these children and the other friends he'd made here – wherever here was – he'd certainly have preferred never to have gone in an aircraft.

Sophy had hoped for some Pinched Pill history over supper, but Mrs Williams wanting to understand solar heating took priority – and kept the Leamington girl occupied, for Heather deliberately took a back seat.

After the meal (confirmed delicious by Mogulus's purry encrunchment of its remains), Alice refused the girls' offer: 'Your Aunty Jilly had planned a walk home via Mill Cove, so you could swim; as the evening's still beautifully warm, take yourselves down now, hmm? We'll wash up, then I'll see some art.'

No wind, now; the shore rocks cooked. Alone together there they swam, then dived, then sunbathed – all in the almost-silence of so much unsaid understood.

Warm enough afterwards for walking home in swimmers, towel-skirted.

Tin tub dragged to where late sunrays still ambered, they hosed it full of hot water; then to squeezily share the thing. The finale was Alice's inspiration: stepped out, each knelt to receive a watering can monsoon; Jill endeavoured to capture that almost religious glee as both, upraised arms wide-spreading shampooed hair, ensured the downpour squeaked it clean. Although, 'We'll be birdsnests tomorrow!'

Teeth brushed and dressing gowned, delighted to have found the double mattress somehow got up to the attic, the friends reviewed Jill's latest work. Heather immediately saw that **Sophy Deluged** was the better sketch of the two just done; Alice, congratulating her honesty, had already bought it. 'But never mind, because your portrait's coming along so well.'

Her publishers, she revealed, wanted her next novel to come out in her own name; furthermore their new house style featured author photographs on book covers – and they had said they wouldn't negotiate. 'However, young Jill, I'm going to hold out for a compromise: I'll agree to my name on the spine, if they use a Ribblesdale portrait.'

Heather goggled, 'You in that historic chair, with the ship's clock and the big mirror behind, would look FAB!'

'Except,' Alice mischiefed, 'I want to be pictured *through* the looking glass.'

The artist chuckled, 'There's genius! She explained, 'As our faces aren't symmetrical, the picture won't quite be Alice as people see her; also, the old mirror's that ripply, it'll superimpose an Impressionist effect.'

Sophy, after a deep ponder, 'An Enigmatic Variation.'

Heather lawnwhirled, 'And Elgar's pieces are portraits of his friends, aren't they?'


Inviting the girls to stay 'after the County Show dust has settled', Mrs Williams departed.

She'd slightly overslurped of wine; Jill suspected that The Law, should the lady meet it, would nevertheless wave her on. Not strictly right; however when a woman recently widowed had just experienced "my best day since I don't know when", surely not wholly wrong.

Picking up the surprisingly heavy bucket Alice had just unloaded, she thanked the girls for gathering easily a winter evening's worth of anthracite; her head-tilt then confirmed where they must climb to.


## Chapter 28

*I mustn't disturb Sophy;* so Heather lay and listened.

She heard dripping; no rain-patter, though, upon slates close overhead. And there was kitchening Jill, talking to guess who; *so our staircase door must have swung open.*

Indeed, because here came paddy tappings up the treads…

She whispered, 'Hello, Damp Puss!'

'Mih!' Glistening fur; silver-beaded whiskers.

Sophy murmured, 'Fogulous Mogulus.'

His shake, 'Mrrao!', sprayed them giggly; when Heather slipped out and crouched to open the window he came leg-rubbing and, louder protests, cheeked her with his dewy tail.

Hooshing the cat back below, both knelt to listen and look…

Fog indeed, the super-dripping sort. A branch stirred; droplets pattered shrapnelly. 'Shorts today,' they concurred: grass-soaked jeans would cling clammily.

Fog: shore-silencing, spinney-skeining. All-muting, indeed: a patrol aircraft's turboprop hum was modulated flute smooth; all the while, the lighthouse faintly mooed.

Jill called up, *'Foo-ood!'*

So wet, the summerlush they wellyswished, there might have been a night tide.

'Look at the stream!' Dense vapour science-fictioned its chilly flow.

'I don't reckon,' Sophy head-shook, 'that Anna will even let us ride to the lane top and back.' The evening before, they'd crossed fingers about exercising two of the stay-at-homes slightly further afield.

'Umpteen paddock circuits, then: we needn't rush back, remember, because Jilly isn't going out.'

She, innocent of the forecast, hadn't tarpaulined Bumble's bonnet; it, after breakfast, had shown no interest in ignition.

'Remember, though, Heth, that you're supposed to relax today.' And were La Flange to discover that Heather had had another "free go" (never mind that she'd been helping out for hours, first), then her friend might suffer bad-mouthing at the showground: what could be worse during Sunday's gymkhana?

Land Rovers shunted horse boxes about the yard, so steam-snorting ponies could be loaded; clipboarded Anna was ever cross-checking the Roster Board.

Dragging out a chair so the young woman could sit and supervise, Heather scolded, 'Honestly, now: saying everything's fine, when the cobbles are *devilish* slippery!'

Indeed.

Animals all aboard, the tack was loaded – plus crucial cardboard boxes of MISCELLANEOUS.

Mrs Madoc's own lists tallied; each driver knew their destination stall row at the showground: now, engines could start.

The last red tail lights having swirled into the lane's whiteness, the yard fell hugely quiet.

It felt warm, and not just because they'd been busy; Heather said, 'The fog layer can't be deep. She tingled, 'Imagine being hoisted up Tram Gin's mast today, to swing in sunlight above a sea of steam.' She chuckled nudgingly, 'In your nightie, so American aircrews brought home photos of A Celestial Creature So Divine.'

Sophy frowned, 'A petrified schoolgirl, truth to tell.' Hardly a match for those religious paintings with jollybottomed cherubs and cherubesses soaring carefree about the clouds.

Anna said, 'I'll 'phone the showground about our lot being delayed…'

She reappeared from the office, annoyed: 'Damp in that junction box on the pole again, I bet!'

Heather zoomed, 'I'll ring from the farmhouse!'

But returned gloomily, 'It's out, too.'

Anna brightened, 'Let's have tea and biccies, hmm? To get over how odd it feels with most of the ponies gone.'

Transparently, she was trying to smokescreen their situation; for Mr and Mrs Madoc had only gone off with the rest that morning because of Talbenny Haven's scheduled surgery: 'If anything occurs, girls, just ring this number and Doctor Clom or Nurse Firebrand will be straight over.'

But now the stable was incommunicado, and Jill couldn't help them, either: her phone still didn't work, and Bumble was kaput.

'Girls,' said Anna two busy hours later, 'you've done a grand job; saddle up Arrow, and you can take turns round the arena. Meanwhile I'll make cocoa – over in the farmhouse, in case the phone's cured itself. After elevenses, I'll watch you exercising while you watch over me; and, before long, my parents should be back.'

But Heather doubted, picturing showground-bound traffic barely crawling all across a fogbound county.

After their drinks, Sophy and her charge set off for the arena;

meanwhile Heather went for Arrow – unusually wearing a riding hat, at Anna's behest: 'You're right: the stones are treacherous.'

A thoughtful Heather, because as they'd sipped and dunked Anna had ha-ha'd, 'If something should happen, girl, it would be *you* having to get help on horseback: Sophy, who's never been there before, couldn't possibly find the surgery in this fog by following instructions.'

And the Haroldston girl had shrugged, what was the problem?

'Because you're the one who's helped with lambing.'

Whilst Sophy knew very little about The Arrival Of Life.

But the Leamington girl, suddenly looking less uncomfortable, had reached from that ancient smoked-oak mantelpiece **Reed's Nautical Almanac**: 'My Daddy told me, although I've no idea why because I was only seven, that it's all in here.'

Two voices, combined: 'What is?'

'Um, how to have a baby at sea – if you know what I mean.'

Heather rolled open the arena's steel door–

Darkness.

Hitching the mare quickly…

The huge-bellied young woman stood stock still on the garden path, hands on that agony; Sophy propped her, palely fearful: 'She's staggered twice.'

Heather, coming against Anna's other side, 'Back to the kitchen is best, if we can possibly manage it!'


CHAPTER 29

The hotplate sang kettles; the table heaped towels; while Anna in the grandfather chair tried reading **Reed's** through pain's tears, Sophy Dettol-punished everything: her build-up to Being Incredibly Brave, which Heather had assured her she could be. Heather, whose company Sophy needed terribly, but who must go for help.

Who, after kissing both fiercely, 'God knows it, all my love!'

Heading Arrow about, still settling into the saddle, 'This is truly life or death, Lady!'

But the mare had hardly started off before she slithered badly and, grunting with fearful frustration...

'JESUS CHRIST!'

...fell onto her side.

In saving Heather's head from the cobbles, the hat disintegrated; getting up hurt-cursing, over one eye the girl was slit badly. Jettisoning the thing's bloody remnants, she checked the stoic horse, now up again... Nothing apparently amiss.

Noticing rainbowed leaves as she remounted, there was why they'd tumbled: creeping from Milford Haven, this fog mingled oily refinery vapours. *And only last night, Jill said about riding for a fall!* Tighting the mare to the grassy edge, 'Just do your best, Lady!'

Arrow bravely did, while frustration sobbed Heather: they should be flying helpwards, but trying to would be suicide...

Then, horrid realisation: 'If it's this bad going uphill, going down to the village will be lethal!' Either over the bridleway's slippery shingle, or on a road made slicky. 'Friend, dear friend, what shall we do?' *Oh for a green signal flag, giving All Clear!*

And then it struck her: 'The Flags, Arrow: THE FLAGS!' The three huge meadows beside the bridleway: Upper, Middle, and Lower Flags, so called because wild irises fringed them. Across the lane from Lower Flags was Talbenny Common, open grassland which stretched along the village's boundary to right behind the surgery; 'And those fields have just had their hay baled!'

Badly aching, she and the grey tarmac-slithered past the bridleway entrance, then Heather was dismounting to unlatch...

The linking gateways between the meadows were open; not one bale blocked the line of sight. Leaping back on, Heather's 'Straight down, Lady!' was redundant: Arrow knew.

All in sight, those three fields; for, the fog suddenly gone, here burst brassy sunlight.

Too tall and elderly to accelerate like Slipstream, Arrow had to gradually gather speed; but her battleship-like FULL AHEAD could, today must, match Tracker's. Ancestors, those strong bones knew, had borne many a hunter, many a knight, many a Roman mercenary into conflict: a mare, she, from the bravest blood line.

Recently risen from the base, it eased engines lest their sound should fluster the now headlong horse: as the airship manœuvred to follow, cameras aboard activated.

*

That first major wave of pain passed, the waters broken, Sophy now noted contraction times.

No longer seeing stars, Anna was nevertheless desperately edgy; no playing the radio for distraction, because sometimes the telephone came back on with a faint ting – easily missed. To pass time, she'd got the youngster making Welshcakes: rather a random impulse, she'd later admit.

As another spasm came, 'Do you – OUCH! – mind the sight of blood, Sophy?'

Sensibly, Sophy didn't bluff; 'Actually, yes.'

'Right; so, please go and fetch down eiderdowns.'

'To soak it up?' *Just how messy is a birth?*

'My love, no! I don't want you bumping down onto the flagstones, should you come over woozy.'

*

Conditions absolutely perfect, they hurtled through the first gateway.

The pains somehow irrelevant, the old horse hadn't felt so yearling-like in years: indeed, her second now wind came as it had way back, when she'd started hunting with Mrs Madoc. Now, to reach her true peak speed, which Heather had never experienced...

'Oh, Arrow, you're simply FLYING!'

Top speed, and therefore tremendous momentum – so as, on entering Lower Flags, horse and rider spotted a tractor smoking towards the third gateway, they must quickly decide: hold steady, or bear away?

'LADY, I'M TRUSTING YOU!' With a Tartar archer's confidence, Heather dropped the reins: she must demand Right of Way, and her most powerful whistle was the one-finger-of-each-hand sort... She BLEW loud as a loco; lungs recharged, she blew EVEN LOUDER.

Hearing her, Haydn Cullen banged into reverse; clutch burning to smoke, he back-crashed his trailer half up the hedgebank, the shock snapping off the Massey's mothy exhaust. Just clear of it, he was, but he'd no time to open that gate: gesticulating his best, he bellowed, '**GOT TO JUMP**!'

Arrow and reined-again Heather understood – and so, snorting with express impetus, thrusting shoes striking spectacular sparks…

The mare soared; after what seemed airborne ages with the girl-child weightless above her, the two landed as one – *Athletic perfection!* – and pulled away left with speed maintained.

Gone from view; but not for a long while from panting, thundering earshot.

'God speed, both!', Haydn murmured, knowing that the Haroldston girl would never ride wildly for fun; then, hearing zoosing motors – 'Good GOD!'

*

'Sophy Fossway…?'

'Anna, I'm frightened that I'll get something wrong.'

'Don't be. If something, um, isn't quite right, that's down to Nature. You'll do your best; I know you always do: Bronny says so. Believe me, I am so happy you're with me because – well, can you imagine Patricia Flange being here? Complaining that she couldn't possibly assist in such unfashionable surroundings?'

She got a giggle: that was good.

*

'DAMNATION!' They'd not cut the surgery's hedge for ages.

They couldn't blind-jump it: Arrow might land on a parked car. 'What the HELL can I–?'

Miracle of miracles, a friendly face appeared – and beckoned.

*

Never before had Taggle's bark gladdened Sophy; now hearing the vehicle herself, she grinned to Anna, 'Crikey, Heather must have scorched there!'

But this wasn't the doctor, or the nurse.

*

Charlie Solva had already leapt from his grandfather's van: who on earth was riding on the Commons, which wasn't allowed, at Cheltenham Gold Cup speed?

Immediately understanding, boots regardless he scrambled up onto a silver Audi's roof; then, arms spread aloft as if guiding a pilot down…

195

Serenely, Arrow sailed the hedge; showering sand and gravel like an exploding mortarshell, she shuddered to a foamy, sweat-soaked halt.

# CHAPTER 30

Unnecessary, Charlie's 'I'll take her!' For, weeping with relief, head redbloody, Heather Haroldston had already doorcrashed Reception.

He patted, 'Brilliantly done, Arrow!'; then, seeing eyes too dull, the now trembling young lad murmured, 'You marvellous, marvellous lady,' and gently backed her towards the lawn.

Heather's storm-in, shrill for action, was unnecessary.

For, on hearing Arrow's arrival, Mr Solva Senior had put his jacket back on and ordered young Dr Clom, 'Forget my ruddy lungs for now, boy; reckon you're needed elsewhere!'

'Doctor Clom,' Heather sprang, 'Anna's baby's really, *really* on its way, and I must go back with you, because Sophy was so—!'

Mr Solva gripped the determination out of her, 'Listen - to - me, girl: you'se bleeding like a stuck pig. How can he deliver a baby *and* deal with your wounds?'

The doctor departed.

The old gent promised, 'When Nurse has done her patching, Charlie and I will drive you back.'

'But,' her concern-ached chest was still heaving, 'what about Arrow?'

Here came Charlie.

While Heather, who'd certainly lost a fair splash of red stuff, was glowing like an overstoked boiler, he was horridly pallid.

Uncomprehending, 'Charlie...?'

He couldn't return her gaze.

Expecting the faint, Mr Solva caught her: 'Best thing,' he murmured. 'Rest the young maid's brain, hmm?' Limping the battlestreaked child onto the floor, he stepped back for Nurse Firebrand.

*

Mrs Williams pulled up in her Dormobile; she was gladly lending it to Sabrina and Bronny for the show: they deserved a nicer sleep than a strawed-down horsebox offered!

A mother and a grandmother, how her arrival reassured Anna; Alice naturally kept her fears about Heather's mission being risky to herself: twice, coming over, the VW had shimmied badly.

Sophy asked, should she fetch Jill?

Alice said no; having held the fort so bravely, this child mustn't miss the birth: 'You'll learn what Motherhood *really* means. And for your faith, my darling Sophy, there's nothing, absolutely *nothing*, better than seeing a human life beginning; such a special bond you'll have with this child. So we'll try signalling to Drift Cottage, hmm?'

\*

Miss Gwinear had taught every primary year about the RMS Titanic; each November, for Remembrance, she'd brought war's realities to that curlew-skied classroom by re-telling her brothers' stories...

Jill instantly recognised S.O.S. sent by car horn.

\*

As Taggle announced the artist's arrival, Anna gripped the chair arms with a *very* strong word – making Mrs Williams declare, 'ACTION STATIONS!'

\*

'A blackout, a bruised collarbone, and stitches? Hardly "Nothing wrong with me", is it?'

Nurse Firebrand fixed her patient a knowing look.

Reddening, 'Actually, I'm really rather bruised, too, Charlie, just as Sophy was.'

'Well,' he sympathised, 'that was a tremendously hard ride.'

She sobbed into Granny's cardigan, 'It was *too* hard for poor Arrow!'

The lady stroked, 'She was wholly aware, that horse, Cariad; her choice, it was, to go out blazing like a comet.'

'Missus is right,' said Mr Solva. 'Consider this: overexertion kills some racehorses extremely young; Arrow in her life had done so much. And wasn't that such a worthwhile last race she ran, for Anna's sake?'

Official morning surgery had ended some time back; the telephone seemed very loud.

Mrs Rudder, the receptionist: 'A call for you, Miss Haroldston.'

Though she had acute hearing, the youngster could only detect something hushed, like the sea moving on a calm day: 'I don't know what this is.'

Alice Williams came on: 'Hello, my brave one; how's that for her first telephone call?'

'Um, whose?'

'Diana Heather Sophy Broadway! Anna and Gareth wanted to show their gratitude to you three heroines; "Arrow" wouldn't do as Little One's first name, so I suggested the Greek goddess of hunting.'

As a hunter had departed, a new huntress had arrived.

*Obviously, Alice doesn't know about Arrow, yet.* Heather steeled herself: 'Do tell them I'm so honoured! The baby's well? And Anna? And Sophes…?'

Surprisingly for a first birth, things had happened quickly; easily, too, much to the relief of Alice's "Gun Crew". A Wren officer in the war, whilst her tackling of childbirth hadn't been the Modern Approved Method, as she'd admitted, it was clear that her jovial bossiness and mildly inappropriate slang had made the proceedings feel well-drilled, even familiar. A tense, yes, but not a fraught moment, therefore, as the baby had emerged.

That lusty, surely healthy wailing until acquainted with Anna's breast: it seemed to summon The World to her birthplace – first over the farmhouse threshold being Doctor Clom, who'd soon confirmed all well with mother and child.

The Madocs had appeared within minutes; Sabrina and Bronny, soon afterwards. Next had come Martin the postman and Paul The Milk, there to make *their* deliveries; after downing celebratory sherries, they'd departed on a joint promise to locate Gareth: doing small local jobs that day, he could be anywhere. They of course would make the news spread faster than fire, notwithstanding that the 'phone had meanwhile pinged back into service.

Alice Williams concluded, 'Everyone's fine, my love – unlike poor you, from what Mrs Rudder just said. Anyway, when can you come and see for yourself?'

Mrs Williams' telephone voice did its own amplification: Nurse

Firebrand said, 'You may say that you're on your way.' Whispering, then, 'Well done, dear!' For, obviously, Doctor Clom had wisely kept the truth about Arrow to himself: for that immediate now, those folk should only rejoice. Thinking about how very brave, those young girls, she and the doctor must later put their heads together – they'd surely both qualify for Red Cross commendations?

Call over, Mr Solva instructed, 'Charlie, escort the young lady out through that Fire Exit, will you? I'll bring the van round.'

Nurse nodded: the child shouldn't see that humped tarpaulin.

Heather, though, firmly, 'I *must* say goodbye to Arrow.'

So the old gent hurried, to remove the sheet and check the poor horse looked well at rest.

As they came out he went inside to call Alice Williams back: she must break the sad news.

Heather, snuggling against the still-warm mare, stroked in private thoughts. Charlie, beckoned to relate how it had happened, spoke finally the best words for this choking girl to hear: 'Grandad says he's never known of a horse dying better.'

Now the old chap was crouching beside them: 'Fulfilled, you see, by the best run of her life. And the bravest, I reckon: as her eyes were so dull when Charlie was calming her, something must've given out a while before.'

'When she stumbled, when I banged my head?' The girl sniffled, 'But if she knew then, and got back up without fuss – that's *so* heroic!'

'And so loving towards Anna, eh? But that makes sense: she was the kindest of horses and, remember, she'd had foals: once a good mother, always maternal. Also, I'm inclined to think, that was her way of thanking Mrs Madoc for such a lovely life.'

'That's how to see it,' encouraged Granny, hand held out: now Heather should come and meet the future.

Mr Solva's telephone call to the stable had pitched extra emotions into the brew; when bandaged Heather arrived there with him and Charlie and her Gran, not long after Haydn Cullen had called and described her jump – about which she'd said nothing at all – sad tears and glad tears inevitably came.

For Sophy, a very special moment up in the non-alcoholic calm of the stable office, arranged by sage Mrs Haroldston: 'Hello? M-Mummy? You'll *never* guess what I've just helped with…!'

Soon after, Jill knew it: this new family now needed to discover itself. 'Let's go, girls.'

With greatly stretched minds much bruised by sadness, both youngsters were in her charge again: each other's company would be far more curative than any factory-made medicine.

Needing to see for himself how his daughter was, Hugh would come to supper at Drift Cottage.

And her grandmother, of course. Who, after the 'phone call to Leamington, had drawn from pensive Sophy some wanting-to-be-shared impressions of the birth, and had encouraged questions about what had preceded.

So grateful, Sophy, for those as-much-as-you-need-to-know-now answers. Thus a wiser child, but no less awed: birth and death were the ultimate Facts of Life, and now she had witnessed both.

'And,' the girl had confided, wanting to have told Mummy, but over the wires wouldn't have been right, 'seeing Diana born seems to have jolted me into a happier mood – permanently, it feels.'

Mrs Haroldston had hugged, 'Dearest, yes: I'm not saying that Heather's arrival cured every sadness of mine – as you know, you can't ever get over losing your parents – but I got a lift I've never lost since.'

Cuddling his daughter in the evening sunshine, Hugh Haroldston asked how she felt about missing the gymkhana.

'The fact is, Dad, I'd already been reconsidering what sort of riding interests me.'

As his mother had suspected. 'Go on, sweetheart.'

'First things first! Listen, Daddy, I swear I didn't ride wildly this morning: I thought about the risks; I trusted Arrow's judgement. But, same as Sophy and Tracker chasing that buggy, we *had* to go flat out down The Flags, because only we could make a difference. Every second counted: supposing Diana didn't start breathing, or Anna lost lots of–?'

'My girl, you did absolutely right; I couldn't be prouder.'

'Of course I'm pained by Arrow's death, but I don't feel bad about it. Because supposing that my fall had hurt me permanently: who'd have dared ask, having seen Diana, what had been the point?'

'Nobody, Heather.'

'However, if I'd overstretched Arrow for a silly bet, how to feel then about her dying? Or about, say, putting myself in a wheelchair? Or, far worse, challenging Sophy to a race which put *her* in a wheelchair – even a grave? How could I live with that burden?'

'Good questions.' Although not the ideal occasion, but…

'Yes, all riding involves risk; but I was gearing myself up to scorch round that course on Sunday, risking my life and my mount's, *not* for the prize, but to get one over on that cow Patsy Flange. Not riding for the love of it, Daddy, nor for the team's benefit; not even riding for my own selfish sake: I intended to ride entirely motivated by hate: to beat Patsy by out-hating her. I tell you, Dad, there've been days recently… If Patsy'd fallen off a horse and killed herself outright, I would have jumped up and down on her body, whooping for joy.'

'My love…!'

'Heather the hate-machine, no better than pilots who'd gladly atom bomb Russia, and damn the consequences: how dreadful, me sinking to Patsy's level! And doubly wrong, because she should be pitied: her vileness reflects the pressure she's under, from her mum and grandad, to win at any cost.'

'Well, thank goodness you see that–'

'If I'd beaten Patsy on Sunday, it wouldn't have ended there. She'd have demanded her own pony; I'd have pestered you like mad for one… Just like the Yanks and Russkies with their arms race.'

'A hate race?'

'Exactly! Hours spent practising, but never for the joy of riding: and, unforgivably, not enough consideration for the horses, to be sure. And meanwhile…' The girl shrugged.

'Carry on, love!' She must flush her system of this poison; for such it seemed to be: such un-Heatherish talk – *And where's it come from?*

'And with me that obsessed, let's suppose that Sophes came to visit: some mate I'd be, wishing whenever we were together that I was off practising to out-do Patsy Flange – at the next County Show, and maybe other events, too. Meanwhile Sophy, bless her, would happily go off on gradually more ambitious treks, eventually overnighters. And doing, also, what Tracker loves best: being *useful*.

'And she'd be right: hurrying round rings doing complicated routines can't compare with ranging high across Prescelly, finding wildlife not afraid of you because you're on horseback. That, Dad: *that's* true joy, I've decided. Forget riding for a prize; instead, be Best Mates with your horse, and go riding with your Best Friends – because what's a rosette, compared to a mate? Of course you'll still always ride your best, and–'

Suddenly asleep, as if electrically unplugged.

Jill, 'PHEW!', unfroze. Handing him a glass of wine, 'I couldn't help overhearing; anyway, it's as well I did: just then, did you hear the front door knocked?'

A rather humbled, 'No.'

'It was Mr Madoc, with a message. Nurse forgot to say: Heather's on adult painkillers at adult dosage.'

'Ones with side-effects? He swigged, 'I'll say! I'm glad you heard that rant, or I might've later wondered if *I'd* been tripping, not my daughter.'

Instinctively rug-tucking the child, 'Wrong word, Hugh. Heather has genuinely had a change of feelings regarding riding – only she was giving it out like a television with everything turned up full. She *has* had grief from Patricia Flange, who *is* under Mummy's thumb; inspired by Bronny, Sophy and she do talk about horse-hiking – even of campaigning to get old bridleways re-opened.

'And her point about usefulness is valid: take showjumping to extremes, and you forget the practical purpose of training a horse to jump obstacles. Meanwhile, do distance riders jump anything they can go around?' She sipped, 'I think not.'

'I'm glad that Heather was, mostly, just seeing reality rather too vividly – but what to do, Nurse Jill? She'll surely need painkillers to get to sleep; but suppose she fires up like that in the night about whatever comes to mind, barraging poor Sophy?'

'Firstly, Hugh, Heather missed lunch, and the poor thing's expended so much physical and nervous energy today, she took strong medicine on a very empty stomach: she *must* tank up with grub before she has her bedtime pills. My other thought was, what about your mother staying overnight, so they could sleep together?'

'Alas, in with Mum,' he chuckled, 'she's eel-wriggly; I've no idea why, but there you are. So let's go with your empty tum theory; and we'll brief Sophy to call on your help… in case her comfort-inducing, um, radiation, doesn't perform its usual magic upon my daughter, hmm?'


## Chapter 31

*I'll let them sleep as long as Nature thinks best.*

However, quietly kitchening at seven o'clock, Mogulus admitted on pledge not to infiltrate the attic, Jill detected overhead murmuration. So upstairs with tea, to discover that her Empty Stomach Theory had been correct: Heather had slept amazingly well, considering.

Now the friends' memories and impressions of the previous day could catch up with each other; Heather wondered how the other horses were feeling.

Jill sighed, 'Mr Madoc said Lamorna seemed to understand, seeing Arrow's empty box. Stood there for ages, apparently, just looking in.'

And making small noises, Heather knew. 'Poor horse! Who'd be feeling pretty lonely, anyway, with most ponies absent; we should visit her today.'

A good idea, the others agreed.

A deep breath; 'Tracker knew already?'

Jill nodded, 'Mr Madoc was sure.' Surmised, 'Considering Mr Solva's suspicion that the fall injured Arrow internally, perhaps she emitted a special cry of pain…'

'I might not have twigged that, being a bit stunned.'

The others exchanged looks, recalling those riding hat remnants: only a bit stunned? This youngster had a tough skull! Jill resumed, '… and as it was calm, Tracker might have heard her.'

Sophy agreed; 'He's always listening for horses' hooves – and he so concentrates, I've suspected before that he knows which animal is doing what.'

Heather concurred, 'Never mind that there was oil vapour about; I reckon that with the stable upwind, Tracker knew by scent that that was Arrow in the yard…' And this gave her an idea.

Dressed, despite their grubbiness, in yesterday's clothes, Heather set off slowly with Sophy.

In the yard, Gareth and Taggle saw to chores; the proud new father led them to the farmhouse kitchen, where Anna was breastfeeding Diana. Afterwards, the friends had turns at holding the tiny child; little was said as each contemplated this helpless yet determined new human...

Heather just assumed that one day she'd be a mother; Sophy reflected on what she'd seen the day before, and thought how much her body would have to change to make *that* possible and bearable; she pondered, too, the predicaments of princesses in history, married off at twelve or even younger.

Baby cradled now, Anna smiled, 'Wasn't she happy with you? When we're better settled, you must come and bath her one evening, hmm?' A good opportunity to mention the christening, and...

'Oh, Anna, we'd love to!'

Anna had liked Heather's idea, so they took Lamorna down to Tracker's field, accompanied by a sympathetically sombre Taggle.

Sitting on the fence so both horses could come close and scent Arrow on her clothes, Heather told them and Sophy all about that last ride – and thus realised for herself three special truths...

Arrow had known which way the surgery lay, though she'd never been there before.

The mare had accelerated down that third field prepared to jump tractor *and* gate – launching herself, indeed, as if loosed by a giant archer.

Her final leap of all had been faultless because she'd had full faith in Charlie.

Sophy then took both horses for contemplative rides.

A calmer Lamorna returned to her box, the girls were about to go when a yellow excavator came roaring down the lane – a bristly Heather noting as it swung round to dustily halt that it oozed oil.

Hearing its accompanying tractor and trailer approaching, Gareth ran to meet it, hand-signalling 'WHOA!' He returned exertion-reddened...

This was Arrow, coming home; he'd not wanted the youngsters to see.

Sophy shook his hand; 'A kindly thought, Gareth: thanks! We are really pleased, though, that she'll be buried here – aren't we?'

Heather managed a nod.

'Ahum, it'll be in the orchard this evening; we'll let you know when.'

Jill had a salad lunch ready; for afters, flapjacks piled a plate: 'Granny called, and Mrs Williams, too. They left together to go on to Anna's – so, do tell: how are Mum and Little One?'

Eyes so bright, 'Fine!'

'Gran said, well done both for sleeping so soundly.'

Heather frowned, 'Funny, them turning up like that – unless they've been conspiring.'

Sophy guessed, 'To get you to the County Show, AJ?' While she and Heather had understandably lost interest, Jill had still, she knew, been keenly anticipating its pictorial possibilities.

Miss Ribblesdale waved a SPECIAL PASS. 'I'm in, early as I like, to see horses being prepared and the traction engines warming up. So, would you young ladies mind Granny cooking breakfast tomorrow, then running you over to Alice's for the day…?'

'Mind?', Heather shrilled, signalling Sophy for two bread slices. 'A whole day at the Fruit Bun Factory?'

Sophy, stolidly, 'I like to think that we shall cope.'

Jill was determined to take the girls far from the drone of that grave-digging excavator.

Heather insisting she was fine for walking, they descended the meadows, and then headed south on the Coast Path: at last, Sophy Fossway would explore Druids Head.

Miss Haroldston gladly modelled as a resting figure looking out to sea; meanwhile, her friend roamed the outcrops imagining mystical – and gruesome – ancient rituals.

As Jill sketched her, the Pembroke girl plied that bay simultaneously with vessels from history books and the Victorian photos in Mrs Williams' WC: coracles and curraghs, Roman galleys, castled mediaeval warships, topsail schooners, four-masted barquentines, Penarth paddle tugs, coalsmoky Dreadnoughts…

Snack time.

Normally, land tapers down to promontories; Heather explained why Druids Head stood taller and dropped sheer: 'It's an igneous rock remnant which the glaciers didn't manage to grind down.' And, being the easiest spot to defend for a long way around, men of ancient had fortified its neck with cross-ditches and parallel walls; 'Of course, both have eroded loads.'

Sophy boggled because, after three thousand years, there was still a fifteen foot drop from wall tops to ditch bottoms: imagining spears thrown and hot rocks lobbed, 'Pretty jolly impregnable at the time, then!'

'Aye; but only a good short-term defence, Miss Camrose told our class: a siege would be tricky because there's no spring. Think about folk bringing cattle and horses here, their prize possessions: as they couldn't have stored much water for them, they must've hoped that any sea raiders would soon give up, and seek softer targets elsewhere.'

Jill tried, 'So the best castle heads, as the maps call them, looked so impregnable, nobody tried attacking: not a nuclear deterrent, but a Neolithic deterrent, hmm?'

Groaning youngsters pelted grass seeds.

After much inland scrutiny via the telephoto lens, 'AJ, now the map's making more sense.'

Whilst ancient ridgeways had linked skyline forts, hamlets dating from later, more fearful, eras hadn't just made themselves invisible to sea raiders, they'd often hidden from land travellers within wooded cŵms. Contrastingly the county's strategic bridges with their prominent approaches appeared hard to defend – but had that been deliberate? Locals might have let invaders chase them onto a causeway, so that their Celtic allies could bottle-stop the enemy before counter-attacking.

Most churches were close beside springs or streams, which seemed rather pagan; Jill outlined Miss Gwinear's understanding of how Romans and then Christians – some of Britain's very earliest, in these parts – had appropriated prehistoric holy places.

On many hilltops were tumuli, conical earthworks called tumps in the West Country; Sophy's far-seeing eyes followed the lane from

Bishop's Watch up to the Haverfordwest to Kete road, where the map noted a **Mound** beside their intersection: surely this was no coincidence?

Jill said, 'Miss Gwinear didn't think so; but try making your own deduction: where does that road begin…?'

'Talbenny Haven, beside the stream; maybe before they built the sea wall there was an inlet which small boats could have used.'

'Agreed; now, where does that lane lead beyond the tumulus?'

Sophy already knew, 'Sandy Haven.' Consulting the map, 'To a creek at its very top.'

'Also only big enough for very small craft…?'

Sophy fizzed, 'Or for the *same boat*, carried overland!' She unfolded more: 'Which would have saved sailing along an awful lot – of awful coast.'

'Aye: you'd have avoided going past miles of Atlantic cliffs, no place to shelter anywhere. And, unlike a sea chart, our map doesn't show the dangerous tide race between Wooltack Point and Skomer Island.'

Unfolding the other way, 'After leaving Sandy Haven, you could have sailed east up Milford Haven for miles.'

'And, from the Pembroke River, walked that ridgeway *there* to a natural harbour on Carmarthen Bay – now called Tenby. Sophy, Miss Gwinear was sure it was the summit marker for an ancient portage route, your tump; it also would have guided boats approaching across the bay into that little stream mouth, wouldn't it?'

After much cogitation, 'Neverminding our family name, it always feels special going along the Foss Way because it's a Roman road; but to think that travellers had been passing along Granny's lane for umpteen thousands of years *before* the Romans arrived…!'

Jill nodded; then, observing her distraction, 'Heather, what is it?'

'There's something in the water.'

'A porpoise? A basking shark?' Rarities, Sophy knew, but they did appear in the bay.

Heather chuckled, 'Rather too yellow for either!' Gun-sighting her thumbs, 'Reckon he'll drift into Mill Cove. Might be one of those Yankee flares, y'know: you'd better go and check.' She'd meanwhile ease herself gently back to Drift Cottage, the others having promised that if the thing had Russky writing, they WOULDN'T TOUCH lest it was booby-trapped.

An American flare, indeed.

Sophy, hair wet, told her friend, 'Stranded on the reef, it was, so I swam out with a piece of rope we found, lassoed it, and towed it ashore backwards.' *So lovely, slipping along like that all in the sun.*

Jill said, 'Though it didn't say not to touch, we tiger-carried it above the high tide line and left it there, hidden under seaweed.'

'Well,' Heather showed them the note from Mrs Madoc, 'you can 'phone the Coastguard and alert 'em when we go up after supper for, um, saying goodbye.'

Another calm, calm evening.

The girls had collected Tracker; Jill bore their imaginative bouquet of wildflowers and grasses. Hugh and Granny had already arrived, also Mrs Williams; when Gareth came leading Lamorna, everyone proceeded to the orchard.

Mrs Madoc had chosen the loveliest spot, visible from her bedroom window and Tracker's field; it was still in evening sun. Arrow had been laid carefully in the rich red soil of her forever bed; the horses, led to look first, were patient while everyone else approached in turn with valedictory thoughts.

Alice Williams began, 'Bronwen and Sabrina are sad about missing this, but Arrow would have understood: she starred in many gymkhanas.'

The Madocs linked arms.

Alice opened a card: 'Sabrina wrote this...'

*Dearest Arrow, your aim was always true;*
*You flew for us – and how you flew, whenever we asked you to!*
*Your own archer, you were, with sinews of such strength;*
*Best judge of when to release gathered power for perfect trajectory.*
*So tough you were, a horse the Iron Duke would have proudly ridden–*
*Who fought to the end, and won.*
*Enter those eternal pastures, dear Friend, with our loving wishes.*

All whispered strong approval of such hearted words; then, it being time to leave Mrs Madoc alone, the group walked the horses back to the yard.

Habit had Sophy glance the Roster Board…

Gareth had amended it: neatly beside Arrow's name, *Out To Grass*.

At the farmhouse, quiet drinks; and, cheeringly, baby Diana. Pages featuring Arrow were bookmarked in photo albums: Jill found pictures of a much younger Anna equally stirring; Sophy loved seeing how the stable had developed.

A long time reappearing, Mrs Madoc thanked everyone for 'The most perfect ceremony.'

Now the men stepped back out into the evening, rolling up sleeves. Working quietly with birds' dusk-songs about them, every swing of their shovels would pour in thoughts and memories; and perhaps even future wishes for, all things considered, Arrow had been a lucky horse.


'Before you go…' Mrs Madoc asked Jill to take up hurricane lamps, for hanging in the trees.

Returning with a request for strong tea, the artist gladly carried a tray back: for all its sadness, that was such an attractive scene.

Indeed, it would inspire an early October sketch of two girls in a dimpsy orchard, featuring a Victorian-costumed Heather twice, as it were. Its title, **Windfalls by Lamplight**.


Jill Ribblesdale couldn't recall a quieter walk through the spinney.

Suggesting the girls turn in straight away, she brought them up her first ever sketches of Diana from the day before…

'We love them, Jilly! You should—'

A Diesel-engined something was approaching.

The artist was soon back: 'It's your Coastguard chap, Sophy. He's just finished his shift, and thought he'd collect that flare now; would you two mind me going down to show him where it is…?

After agreeably-toned conversation beneath their window had diminished seawards, Heather hushed, 'Which coastguard, Sophy?'

'Tallish and slim, with sandy sideburns?'

'Oh, good! That's Robert Hoaten: Gran and I like him.'

# Chapter 32

They slept through Granny's arrival and Jill's departure.

Slipping in beside her friend, 'My French holiday would have ended today, Heth. I know AJ said not to worry about going home arrangements, but she only meant I could stay on to watch you compete in today's gymkhana. So, very soon...'

'Sophes, what if Hannah's parents had booked for three weeks?'

'That would have been fine.'

'And if they'd rented somewhere abroad for the whole summer...?'

'I just wouldn't have gone: I'd have missed Mum too much, and she me.'

'Yep; and nipping home mid-holiday would have been impossible. However, here isn't abroad.'

'Go on...'

'Idea: Jill doesn't drive you back. Instead, I travel with you by train to Swansea, and the Swansea to Newcastle express guard then keeps a kindly eye on you until Cheltenham, where Madame Fossway awaits... Okay?'

'Rather!'

'...And, after a while, you return by rail. You stay mainly with us, leaving Jilly free to paint – and it'd cost nothing, because we two would get organised. We'd borrow a dinghy to catch mackerel, go spud-scavenging in harvested fields, pick blackberries for Gran come August... Jilly might even pay us to properly model as, say, sea spirits or–'

'Ahem!'

Heather analysed that look... 'I'm just saying, really, that you could even turn a profit. Look, the very day that Bronny quit Swansea and Mrs Madoc found her and took her in, she started making herself useful: what an example to us, eh?'

'I'll say!' Then, 'That's an ace plan, Heth, and well worked out; how much did you sleep last night?'

The other chuckled, 'Actually, I decided absobloodylutely *ages* ago that you must come down again; so, as your mum doesn't know us Haroldstons, every evening I've prayed she'll have faith and say Yes.'

'Could we enlist an adult to help state our case, perhaps?'

'Good idea; but do we ask Gran, or would Mrs Williams make a cunninger co-conspirator?'

'I can't decide. So – if Mogulus greets us with miaows, then Gran; if he purrs, Alice Williams.'

'PRRAOWW!'

He kept saying it over breakfast – and so very deliberately, it seemed, that the decision must be deferred.

Before they rushed upstairs to brush hair Granny reasoned, 'Heather, you're due a progress check at Surgery tomorrow. Getting there early's best; why not sleep at Bishop's Watch tonight?'

Heather hugged apologies to Sophy: it made sense. 'Okay; I'll pack right now.'

Sophy Fossway cleaned her teeth, head emotion-swirled: whilst she was looking forward to seeing Mummy again and visiting poor Hannah, Heather's plan for a second summer break was logistically feasible and Bronnyishly practical – and full of potential for new adventures.

Granny's pulling over at Colliers' Quay surprised them.

'Is there a footpath to Gin Lane?' Sophy didn't fancy walking up the pavementless coast road: some folk took that hill like rally drivers.

'Yes; it starts at the causeway end; however, Alice is meeting you here. Possibly something to do with those…?'

Two large wooden black-hulled open boats, near-vertical bows and tapered sterns, floated placidly side by side, moored to rings set in the causeway wall.

Heather boggled, 'Handsome!'

Burly men nautical with accoutrements now came; as they climbed aboard purposefully Sophy remembered, 'The tug-of-war experiments!'

Granny, passing Heather a camera, 'Take some photos for Jilly, do – and have fun!'

'Thanks!', they doorslammed; Heather said, 'See you later!'

Alice Williams came from her car, a neat camera neck-strapped and a jotter pad pocket-peeping. After perfumed greetings, she filled them in.

Talbenny Haven's Rugger Tuggers had only reached the County Show quarter finals, this year. Never mind, though, because other communities were interested in the idea of a rowing boat tug-of-war, a ROWTOW – so now the competition method she'd postulated about needed proving.

If this morning's trials showed promise then after the Colliers' Quay fête, held on the Thursday afternoon, an evening ROWTOW demonstration would be staged.

Sophy, thinking how strong Sabrina and Bronny, 'With a ladies' heat?'

Good question, Mrs Williams thought. 'Although it's very short notice for getting teams together; however, there's no harm in asking him…'

Jack Sound, who'd instantly latched onto the ROWTOW idea. He'd remembered that two naval whalers had been brought down to Milford Haven for the filming of a Victorian era TV drama; after exhaustive 'phoning around he'd found them, desert tomb dusty, stored in a spud grading shed.

Delighted by the retired coxswain showing so much interest, the Rugger Tuggers had invited him to take charge: he'd give the ROWTOW idea wide credibility.

Unlocking his car boot, he beckoned the girls: Heather could manage his clipboard and odds-and-ends bag; two coiled ropes made Sophy deep-sea-diver ponderous. Jack himself lugged a muscle-bulging bucket of chain and shackles, two pulley blocks, and a brass clock thing.

Identical, the whalers were: twenty-seven feet long and sturdily carvel built, with centreboards. Oars swivelled in gunmetal rowlocks; those rudders had a 'goodish' bite on the water, Jack said, 'And their hulls being narrowish to row well promises swift sailing across the wind or running – although in open water they'd be wettish.' Today, though, they sported neither masts nor sails; each did have an iron anchor, a sea anchor, and warps, i.e. ropes, all Admiralty issue.

No lifejackets.

Thirty or so men had now assembled, quite a few from neither Talbenny Haven nor Creampot Cove; all reckoned they rowed strongly.

This being the County Show's busiest day, Jack had expected that he and the men could conduct experiments 'unhassled'. However, like stars to a black hole, numerous folk who'd picked up the buzz were gravitating toward a Davy Lamp already aromatic with coffee, which soon would be otherwise slaking thirsts: the ROWTOW Trial should be good for business.

Alice countered his muttering, 'I'll make you glad for these gawpers, Mr Sound!'

'Gents,' Jack began, 'each boat needs ten rowers. We're after two teams of similar strength – of blokes, mind, who can keep stroke. You'll be dynamometer tested,' he held up the brass clock thing, 'using this.' A spring balance, with which his slaughterman uncle had weighed carcases.

A clinker dinghy was fetched; the spring balance was rigged between its stern and a quay bollard. Jack explained, 'You each row for a minute while your average pull is measured; perhaps not a perfect system, but it's, um…'

'Transparent,' came from Mrs Williams.

He indicated Heather and Alice: 'These impartial ladies will record your performance; I'll do a demonstration stint now. Thirty strokes a minute is a good gig rowing rate, and easily enforced.' He handed Sophy his diver's watch; she, enawed, clambered in and went to the stern. Once settled on its centre thwart he shipped the oars: huge for this size of craft, between them they'd approximate to one whaler blade.

The girl started calling stroke; once synchronised he nodded…

As the second hand reached **30**, 'GO!'

Couldn't Jack row? His huge paws visibly bent the oar blades each time they pulled; balancing their forces, his thick legs braced hard against the bottom boards. Though Sophy had her task, she couldn't help gleeful chuckles as the going-nowhere dinghy bucked about, power-creaked, while sloshy gops rumpled down their either side to wall-splursh; behind her the jigging spring balance ronk-rinked with each stroke until, '…and REST!'

Cheers rang out when Alice Williams disclosed Jack's average pull: he'd emphatically laid down the gauntlet.

On the individual trials starting, the crowd got really loud: out-noised, Sophy must thereafter mark time by thwart-platting a plastic bailer.

Every chap was both mocked and cheered; some had fans: Sophy decoded from between-test chatter the admiration of some off-duty American servicewomen for certain young Welshmen.

While Jack digested the trial results, most participants sought refreshment.

The girls having promised not to fall in regardless of how exciting things got, Alice Williams crossed the road and entered the pub. Emerging carrying a distinctive plastic box, some effort it took, penetrating that now beveraged crowd; but Jack's smile on hearing her plan well rewarded all that polite pushing.

Knots, checked; pulley sheaves, oiled.

Jack Sound whistle-shrilled, 'Ladies and gents, we didn't anticipate spectators, but of course you're welcome. A local lifeboat supporter, Mrs Williams, will circulate with a charity box; as Creampot Cove's retired coxswain I'll be extremely grateful to anyone contributing. Now—'

But applause, then; and, already, many proffering hands.

Another whistle. 'We've not long: the tide's turned. The idea of this stationary tug-of-war, which Mrs Williams inspired,' (more applause) 'is that neither boat can be advantaged. That rope runs between the whalers via pulley blocks; a rag marks its mid-point; whichever crew makes it touch the block abaft their boat wins.

'The crews are...'

Each name got simultaneously cheered and booed by the morning's alcohol.

'Could they please elect captains, (quickly done) and now choose coxes...?'

The captains concurred: they'd like the girls to cox – so could a tossed coin assign them, please?

*It's not so bad for Heather: she must know most of these men.* Ten of whom would be staring at her intensely, reliant on her judgment! But Sophy couldn't decline the request, because she'd be letting her friend down...

Daddy's voice came: *Belay those blushes, girl; just do your best.*

Jack resumed, 'As some fellows who helped prepare these whalers are crewing, for fairness a coin now decides who rows which boat...'

On their becoming Port and Starboard, the Reds and the Greens, raucously partisan shouting began. Heather would happily cox the Port team because for her their colour was the passionate red of Wales. Sophy gladly had Green: Nature's colour, and therefore Miss Gwinear's.

The crews boarded.

Jack, alighting a granite bollard, 'There's NO COUNTDOWN: when I blow, you start. Rowers, heed your coxes; coxes, don't force the pace to the point of confusion. Finally, everyone understands this is a fight to the death...?'

The onlookers detonated as one when he blew: how the coxes had to bellow!

Both crews heaved well together, but neither had smooth return actions; the sweat soon soaking every man proved they gave their all, as did great seethed-up blooms of weedy sediment in the water all about.

The strokes went out of phase, hitherthithering the marker: harder, now, to tell which way the struggle went – until the Reds, noticing the rag averaging in their favour, found extra energy...

Whistling, Jack pointed to Heather's boat; the crowd's cheer echoed about the valley. Celebrating victory, it also confirmed what excellent entertainment such a sea-contest was: talk about a ring-side view!

Beer-keened folk soon asked, what next?

'Nothing, for now,' Jack said, 'because some of these blokes are busy chaps, even on Sundays.' But as he'd ideas for refining the set-up, might some of them reconvene that evening...?

Unanimously, 'We'll be back!'

As the girls fizzed their experiences to Mrs Williams, Jack introduced a young woman who'd a bright air: 'A rowing recruit, from the aerodrome: Miss K.C., um...'

'Kaycee Fleischmann: hi! Cuttin' to the chase, I wanna form a women's team for Thursday. Not for a tug-of-war but, havin' way less payload, if you follow me, reckon we'd stand a chance racin' against men along the creek. Trouble is, we're only eight, but Coxswain Jack thinks two horseridin' gals y'all know might be interested...?'

Alice having scribbled the stable's 'phone number for her, 'Mighty obliged! Now, as for you bee-yewtifully lightweight kids – Heather, would you cox for us? While Sophy steers?'

Looks exchanged, 'Today was the first time–'

Southern-twanged boyish impudence: 'You think you're kinda green? My darlings, us chicks ain't never rowed before; but we's rarin' to have a go – sink or swim!'

'That's the spirit!', Alice approved. 'But, talking of sinking, these youngsters'll need lifejackets.'

'So how 'bout My Marine Patrol friends,' Kaycee gestured, 'kittin' *everybody* out?'

Jack Sound appreciated that. 'Not having buoyancy aids was why I hadn't suggested a race: being ex-lifeboats, I hated to set a bad example, you see.'

A drab green minibus was pulling up; Kaycee, evidently needed elsewhere, waved 'Goodbye, Coxswain! Goodbye, Ma'am! Girls, give my love to Tracker!'

Mr Sound summarised, 'WELL!' I hope Sabrina and Bronny can join in: that Kaycee has a spirit to match theirs. Anyway, let's all to the Lamp and announce that the Fairer Sex, and damned Yanks to boot, have thrown down the gauntlet.'

Alice wavered, 'Jack, couldn't you–?'

'Madam, you *must* come: we're promised a treat.'

Drinks, courtesy of the landlord: firstly, he'd done well out of the Trial Session; secondly, the RNLI box was stuffed solid with money... 'Which, Mrs Alice, is entirely down to you.'


## Chapter 33

Every chap who'd attended the trial wanted to thank Alice Williams: because traditional rivalries aye endured all thought that, with wrinkles ironed out, this contest would catch on right around the county's coast. As for spectators – though exhilarating for participants, many watersports weren't easily followed from the shore; but here was a quayside contest of relentless pressure: a gladiatorial clash guaranteed every time!

Umpteen beered men airing similar thoughts was tending to the tedious: Sophy was squeaking the pub garden's swing, and Heather making daisy chains, when a question turned things interesting again...

Philip Davies was a Creampot Cove inshore lifeboat crewman. Their strongest swimmer, he would go overboard when a need arose; thus his nickname, Dipper. Once, Jack Sound couldn't approach a dismasted yacht lest trailing cordage fouled the propeller; Dipper had swum a towing warp over. Fishing boats often had nets (usually their own) tangle sterngear: Dipper had several times, wetsuited and masked, cut clutter away. Jack, though, had always fulminated: 'Trawlermen should either carry scuba equipment and sort their bloody selves out, or stop going to sea!'

Dipper asked, 'Mrs Williams, did something inspire the ROWTOW idea?'

'My husband's family were involved in the coasting trade; while men like Miss Gwinear's great grandfather improved mining techniques, the Williamses ensured that exporting anthracite stayed profitable by finding cargoes for inbound ships.

'Pinched Pill never suited steamships, because Colliers' Quay couldn't load bigger craft quickly. Unfortunately, here being sheltered had one disadvantage: unless an easterly was blowing, laden sailing craft must be got to the pill entrance before their sails would fill.

'Vessels might be towed out by rowing gigs, which could similarly bring in arriving ships. However rough seas made that really risky: waves would strike the small boats beam-on. Now some minor ports could call tugs out from larger harbours nearby, but that wasn't an option here.'

Heather asked, 'Did having more rowing boats pulling a ship help?'

Alice Williams tilted her hand; Sophy diagnosed, 'You're half right.'

Dipper proposed, 'Get enough way on a vessel going down the pill, and after slipping her tow the momentum would carry her on out to find the wind.'

'Sometimes, indeed, without any worries; but making that turn could be touch and go.'

Razzer Roch the biker tried, 'Applied Mechanics say that, with a pulley mounted on the wharf at the incline foot, gigs could row *up* the pill while towing a ship seawards.'

Men objected: the falling tide's help being needed to take the ship seawards, those rowers would have had the current against them.

Mrs Williams concurred: 'They only tried that a few times: it was, indeed, such hard work; however, the reverse working proved much safer and easier.'

Sophy felt confident enough to contribute, 'The gigs rowed up the pill with the rising tide; going round a pulley, the towrope hauled the ship in through the harbour mouth.'

Heather took over, 'When she was further in, someone on Corner Wharf could slip the rope out of the pulley, and it would be back to a normal straight tow.'

Dipper contributed the final jigsaw piece: 'First thing, therefore, inbound ships must have picked up the end of the towing warp from a buoy.'

'So even using pulleys,' Sophy summarised, 'unless it was calm, gigs couldn't help a ship put to sea.'

'They couldn't,' Alice smiled, 'could they? However,' she smiled, 'horses could help if they were so inclined.'

Sophy got the pun; 'But how could they have towed a ship *and* climbed that steep slope?'

Jack, who'd been quietly following the conversation, produced a compact pair of binoculars, and pointed up the pub garden: 'Solving that problem is *down* to you two.'

From the upper terrace the girls lensed past The Davy Lamp's chimney pots, and out along the pill to Corner Wharf...

Sophy, standing before those men, reminded Alice Williams of the painting, **When Did You Last See Your Father?** The girl began, 'Heather and I had to guess a bit, because looking through binoculars isn't the same as going over the ground...'

Those nods meant, 'Fair enough!'

'Firstly, Heather reckons that the iron loop out on Smith's Point, opposite The Anvil, could take a big pulley. Second, the track out to Smith's Point from Corner Wharf stays wide and levelled well beyond where the tramway sidings ended – and there must be a reason why.'

Heather took over: 'Gigs would tow a loaded ship down from Colliers' Quay; on reaching the point where it could get a straight run out to sea it stopped, dropping a stern anchor; then, by boat, it received a towrope from Corner Wharf; that was attached at its bow.

'The people on the wharf now released the towrope, so it ran straight from the ship to the Smith's Point pulley. Doubling back, it came ashore; it travelled beside that track past Corner Wharf, then went up the incline to one of those pairs of posts. Each post had a pulley; between them these turned the rope *back down the hill*. Thus the horses worked *with* gravity – and, while descending, they couldn't trip over the, um, rising rope.

'Another thing: you needed pairs of posts at different places, because towing out a ship berthed at Corner Wharf didn't take so much rope.'

Mrs Williams beamed, 'Excellent point!'

Sophy, again: 'A ship ready to depart was lined up like a 'plane waiting to take off. Next, the horses got the rope really tight: kept clear of the water, it couldn't snag a rock or tangle with driftwood. On "Go!", the sailors either cast off or weighed anchor, and down the hill the horses went: once going faster than the water of the pill, the ship could be steered.'

Heather concluded, 'After passing the incline foot, the horses kept pulling on the level – on past the sidings and out towards Smith's Point. If the Harbourmaster had done their sums properly, just before the horses ran out of path the ship must drop her tow, anyway, because of the geometry… And, what with her momentum, and her sails starting to catch the wind, she was on her way – and, PHEW!'

Much applause.

Jack's jocular growl: 'What about an inbound vessel?

Heather hopped, 'A buoy was moored centrally in the pill mouth; a smaller buoy tied to it held the end of a *sinking* towrope, for safety, which ran back to Corner Wharf: horses could haul inbound ships in while, again, walking downhill – et, voilà!'

And, she beckoning Sophy, both bowed.

Alice Williams glowed, 'Really well done, girls! The Holmes and Watson of Industrial Archaeology – except, you both must have brainstormed jolly hard to deduce everything.'

Sophy boggled, 'Wow! Were we…?'

Jack Sound shook their hands, 'Near as makes no difference. Indeed, given the right horses, strong pulleys, enough rope, and well-briefed assistants, I believe you two and Mrs Williams could re-enact the launching *or* towing-in operations.'

'In that case,' Heather shrugged, 'it's just a question of the rope.'

'Yes,' Sophy enthused, 'because Tracker would quickly understand his rôle. Plus, Aberdare's descended from railway shunting horses, and you could say that we've been discussing ship-shunting.'

Mrs Williams nodded, 'Horses and their handlers became truly adept at hauling ships out and in. But do consider how labour intensive the method was: men rowing boats and handling ropes; women leading horses; a harbourmaster, co-ordinating everything. So, unfortunately, what with the March of Progress elsewhere, developing that technique only helped extend the life of the coal workings by a few years: everything was soon abandoned.'

That saddened Sophy.

Jack said, 'It's only thanks to Mrs Williams that the incline, Corner Wharf, and the track out to Smith's Point still exist. A few years ago, all were badly overgrown; she persuaded the National Park people that they were historically important – and, potentially, a visitor attraction. So, all the vegetation got what farmers would call a damned good haircut.'

Dipper thumbsed-up: 'Well done, Mrs Alice!'

Sophy glowed, 'Preserving the memory.'

Heather said, 'Reminding us what human ingenuity can achieve, harnessing Nature. Using renewable power, Dad would say: as long as grass grows, we can have horses to work alongside us *and* the fuel to run them on.'

Sophy wondered, 'Mr Sound, would the inshore lifeboat ever need helping out to sea?'

'I suppose you've read of Victorian rowing lifeboats being hauled miles overland to suitable launching places...?'

Heart-stirring stories, indeed.

'Firstly,' he sighed, 'not all such exploits ended happily; nowadays the RNLI rigidly trials alternative ways of doing *anything*. Because no lifeboat mission is successful unless crew and craft return safely, nobody would launch from here without first addressing the question of getting back in. Which was a lesser concern for the old coal boats, you see: yes, they'd have despatched a ship when a sea was running, but skippers could delay inbound voyages.'

An important difference.

'Also, that technique helped pretty large vessels leave Pinched Pill;

ships which, once at sea, could look after themselves. You're asking about despatching a much smaller craft.'

Intently she listened.

'ILBs are ideal for launching straight into surf up to a certain size; but, try taking a light craft out into big waves which are verging on breaking, and she might flip – especially if the wind's fluky.'

Disappointed eyes, now.

'So,' he mimed a telephone answered, 'supposing the sea was pretty lumpy and the wind was up, if a call came through…'

'Her coxswain wouldn't bring the ILB over here…?' It seemed the obvious conclusion.

'Nono, I wouldn't say that; but if conditions precluded launching from Creampot Cove or Talbenny Haven, you'd think very, *very* carefully about not just setting out from here but also regaining this harbour.'

'Mr Sound, what would *you* do if–?'

'Ahem, our Honorary Harbourmistress signals that luncheon at Anvil House is imminent: you young ladies had better cut along!'

Folk having dispersed, Jack Sound returned to that shaded seat, and his Guinness, well satisfied.

Knowing who were the strongest oarsmen, he could select his ROWTOW team – *and* the whaler crew for next year's regatta: determined, he was, to demonstrate an old-style beach launch. With her zest for local history he was sure of Alice Williams' support; enthusiastic about re-enactments, the youngsters should convince the Madocs and Solvas re sending their animals to sea, as it were. 'I've sowed the seed,' he muttered, then drained the remaining prune-dark liquid.

That evening should see the ROWTOW technique perfected, the pulsing pull of the oars smoothed. About Kaycee's proposed ladies' team… even if those Yankee females weren't any good (though he suspected otherwise), just their presence should make the boys perform twenty percent better. 'Hmm…' He drafted pertinent notes, then went in to order lunch and, a nod to Nelson, a lime cordial.

A fit young woman now emerged from under another parasol; moseying close to Jack's table, she swiftly scanned his clipboard and scribbled in a flipbook... Then, sweatshirt and culottes slipped off, in camouflage vest and silky shorts Signaller Amy Heckrottss clicked the beer garden's side gate and, stopwatch started, commenced her cross-country run back to the base.

Jack returned chuckling, having discretely observed the American snooping at his table as he'd intended: she wasn't the only bod thereabouts who'd been trained in certain techniques.

Sipping his fresh drink he nodded to himself, 'Sowed *more* seed!'

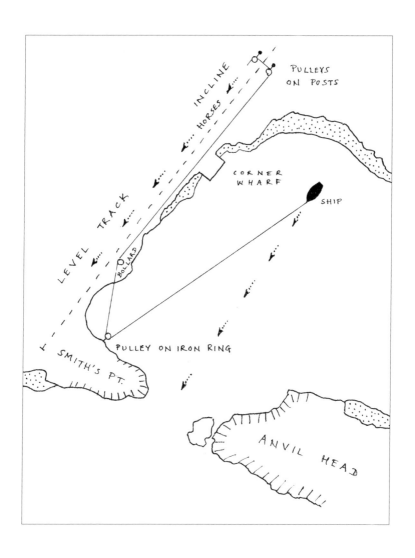

PULLEYS
ON POSTS

INCLINE

HORSES

CORNER
WHARF

SHIP

LEVEL TRACK

BOLLARD

PULLEY ON IRON RING

SMITH'S PT.

ANVIL HEAD

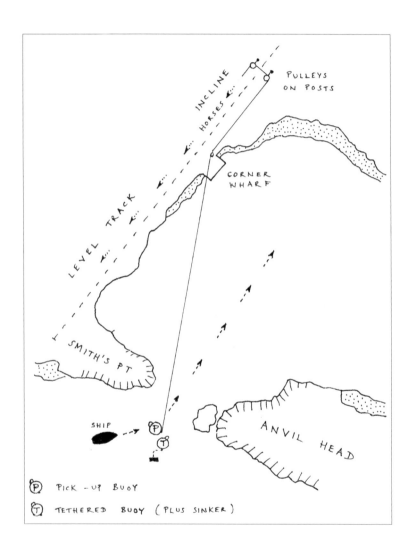

INCLINE

PULLEYS
ON POSTS

HORSES

CORNER
WHARF

LEVEL TRACK

SMITH'S PT

ANVIL HEAD

SHIP

(P)

(T)

(P)  PICK - UP BUOY

(T)  TETHERED  BUOY  (PLUS SINKER)

# CHAPTER 34

Daphne greeted the girls like old friends; they'd already been met by a rich aroma, sweetly seductive as Dutch tobacco, issuing from the Aga.

Normally stood down during summer months lest it overheated this sunny house, Alice's cooking range had been woken up for the production of Fête Cakes. The proud cook withdrew a drum-like tin from its lower oven, raised it like a coronating archbishop, then placed it on a grid. On her tinking the lid off, Essence of Heaven filled the kitchen, making the girls ooh.

The lady sighed, 'Life's cruel, sometimes: unfortunately you'll never taste this one, unless you win Thursday's raffle. But I'm not heartless, so look in the Prestcold, please…?'

A baking tray, screeded with sponge mixture.

Having loaded it into the top oven and set the pinger for twenty-five minutes, 'Lunchtime!'

Tinned salmon; new potatoes; home-grown tomatoes and salad: all Fab, and when cake slices came, steaming and lemony straight from baking, with mugs of mahogany Writer's Tea…

'Mrs Williams, total BLISS!'

An afternoon for exploring.

The friends descended the incline, investigated Corner Wharf, then headed out to Smith's Point, imagining walking with ship-hauling horses.

In a sandy-floored sea-nook some way round the rocks from the iron ring, Sophy duck dived goldenly keen. Overseer Heather falsely classified the tossed-up treasures, outrageous her bluffery: copper rivets were mermaid's ear studs; a flint chip had once tipped Neptune's trident; aeons ago, that polished bottleglass had bejewelled Amphitrite's coronet, and…

Heads history-full they towelflopped, costumed, on Alice's lawn.

Assuring their host they'd dissipated *much energy* conducting research had the desired result: with the tea came paving slab pieces of cake.

Heather then suggested going upstairs to peruse the Williams Archive; but Alice gestured, 'Rest yourselves, now: you've ROWTOW trials to watch on the way home.' *Where you'll hear the gymkhana results.*

'Okay, then,' Heather inhaled, deciding now was a good time to subvert her friend's reticence: 'Sophes would actually like to, pretty please could she, try out your Writing Chair, because I said it felt so special the other day?'

'Sophy Fossway,' the lady kissed, 'why so shy? Few girls might aspire to be pilots, but all should want to visit the cockpit during a flight; even if you don't think you'll be a writer, you must try the chair, contemplate the view, study my pictures… And browse my notebooks, Cariad, why not…?'

A while later Mrs Williams knocked and entered; 'How right you look, sitting there! But you didn't…' She opened the window, and beckoned.

Laying hands gently over the girl's eyes, that flawless sea-scented skin so reminiscent of long-ago swimming-mad summers, 'What I hear here, Sophy, and what that helps my ears go on to imagine, they *so* inspire me!'

So still, the girl; then… 'Wagons going downhill, brakes squealing; coal, rattling into a ship's hold; later, the creaking gin. Shouts; and horses, excited about towing a ship – or about going home at a cold, wet, day's end. During a storm, a sudden pause, as if the wind holds its breath: that's The Smith raising his hammer… Then he brings it down and, CRASH!, The Anvil rings…'

Alice withdrew her hands, knowing those eyes stayed closed for the relish of imagination.

And now she tried imagining, tried picturing that lovely maiden form transformed: Sophy, become a mature young woman. *At least as happy you are now,* she prayed, thinking how much love flowed already between the girl and Heather. Forgetting herself, 'Hopefully, happier in future.'

Turning, instinctively putting arms about, 'Gran Alice, I can't help missing Mummy; but I know she's so glad I came to Pembrokeshire. And you've all become such brilliant friends that I am, I promise, *really* happy to be here!'

Alice Williams hugged back, 'We feel so lucky to have you here, Sophy Fossway.' *So glad of these chances sent to give you love.*

'Mieu!' Daphne, suddenly there to rub round legs.

Early evening.

While the whalers barely floated, that dinghy was busy: pertly-lifejacketed U.S. servicewomen in high-cut shorts were testing each other, co-ordinated by Kaycee Fleischmann. Who, on spotting them, 'Gangway for our British sisters!'

The girls threaded the throng, embarrassed by applause; Alice followed.

'Hi, guys! Well, we got our butts in gear, recruitment-wise, so we've ten of our own rowers, now; and, great news, Coxswain Sound has okayed us to train this evening.' Flourishing a clipboard, 'Not bad results, huh…?'

Indubitably, Thursday's "Davida and Goliath" race would be worth watching.

'Ma'am,' the American turned to Alice: 'as we've sourced safety gear, could the girls come out, uh, kinda now…?'

Consulting her watch, 'An hour's practice? I'll warn people by 'phone.'

'That's swell of you!'

Heather queried the lack of water; Kaycee beamed, 'Honey, observe Empowerment at work.' She called out some peculiar-sounding surnames; then, 'Coxswain…?'

He nodded, 'Take either boat; return 'un as you finds 'un, hmm? And I'm not Coxswain no more.'

'Mr Sound, our ex-presidents are always "Mr President"; reckon you deserve parallel respect.'


The girls and two sinewily petite young ladies embarked; next, eight American Amazons descended the steps and waded over.

With Heather watching for obstacles, the whaler was pushed out beside the causeway; when its keel grazed, the two women and Sophy rocking together wiggled it free. Once the tide's rise was well under her, the other rowers vaulted aboard.

Kaycee, quietly, 'Our initial aim is synchronisation: we get good with a gentle stroke rate, and build on that. So, steer straight down the creek, please, Ensign Fossway.'

'Aye, aye, Sir!'

Amy Heckrottss winked, try "Chief", next time.'

Heather began, 'And, IN!... And OUT!...'

They moved off cautiously, but co-ordinated.

Nearing Corner Wharf Kaycee stopped engines; while they drifted, two pairs of rowers exchanged places 'To improve our trim.'

Boat turned, Sophy held the tiller fixedly midships; Kaycee soon after having swapped the centre thwart ladies to balance power side-to-side, she declared herself 'Happy with this consist.'

Sophy observed, 'Jolly thorough!'

Amy, sagely, 'Nobody who isn't shouldn't have nothing to do with aircraft or boats.'


Swirling but lazily, as Pinched Pill's filling flat waters rose silently towards downreaching branches, a Leamington imagination cousined it with those serene Thames stretches which the London-bound train glimpsed after Oxford... *But I'm not in a summer dress, and this isn't a steam launch.*

Heather's metronomic calls; mechanistic oar-obedience; efficient Kaycee, infectiously determined. The rowing might be slow, but Purpose frissoned: the Women's Whaler was getting to walk well. *But,* Sophy thought, *when she does run...* These female warriors would surely row like Vikings; and indeed aptly, for several surnames sounded Scandinavian.

Sophy pictured a plunder-hungry dragon prow carving across the North Sea: *As Kaycee finesses a fate-filled sail, our battle-tautened crew white-thrash grimacing swell to Heather's racing pace, and my steerboard slices us straight, destination the Western Celtic coast.*

Doubly appropriately, for the Vikings had conquered and settled Pembrokeshire, giving its islands Norse names; indeed, as Mr Gram had teased Welsh-and-proud-of-it Heather, 'The original Harald of Haroldston might have bloody well been Danish!'

Triply appropriate, indeed; the Normans, who'd ringed Milford Haven with eleventh-century castles to guarantee their sea-command of Ireland, had been Viking by descent.

On the next run down, Kaycee upped the stroke rate; on the return...

Heather felt the pill itself take notice as they cut the water swift and symmetrical: the spirits of its trees and rocks surely heard their relentless bow-wave and driving blades. Now also beating time on the elderly boat's timbers she sensed them, sensed the whole vessel, come awake too; and, she couldn't help it, she cackled to everyone, 'I tell you – IN! – she's truly – OUT! – with us!'

Ashore, binocularing Jack Sound murmured, 'Going like a bloody minelayer, that lot, soon!'

When the girls were landed at the quay, much hearty clapping from gathered watchers.

Mind, some men seemed subdued; others, if not awestruck, were perhaps affected another way by so much female puissance.

Jack gloated: firstly, Thursday promised a proper Battle of the Sexes, welcomely boosting the RNLI's coffers; secondly, if the airbase authorities would agree, why not a mixed crew for the regatta's beach launch demonstrations next year? *The spirit of Grace Darling, and all that.*

After their ROWTOW training session, Jack asked the men to indulge him: could they now row out through the pill mouth, and go a short way into the bay? It was, after all, a nice evening...

He knelt, peering over the gunwale; he leaned well back over the stern, trying to re-shape the vessel's wake; note after note scribbled itself into his pocket book.

Like Jason hardening his Argonauts, he had the oarsmen row into the swell, across it, then with it – next, down with the centreplate, and all those tests repeated.

They creamed back, with him well pleased – once he'd heavily scrawled two words:

*SANDBAG BALLAST.*

Granny having earlier collected Taggle, she dropped Sophy and him at the humptibump bridge: he'd see the youngster back to Drift Cottage, then take himself home.

A terrier blessedly contemplative for that walk: neither radaring for rabbits nor barging rushes after bank-dwellers, he trotted contentedly, stopping placidly with her to peer at swirling water-weeds, or eavesdrop gossiping reeds.

Droning turboprops: number 716, again. Sophy waved, but wasn't noticed: 'Never mind, Tag!' Never mind, because she now felt somewhat closer to the Marine Patrol aircrews, even to Carson and Sam of absent 789: Kaycee was pals with their pals, and even knew about Tracker. So though Bronny had literally missed the boat when it came to rowing on Thursday, she and Ms Fleischmann should get acquainted.

Tracker's ridge appeared; on spotting them he paraded back and forth ridiculously showily, almost the prancey-pranciness of a poodlish circus pony.

She agreed affectionately with the dog's humphing stare: 'Silly old thing!'

Those were the Bramley trees surrounding Arrow's resting place; Sophy prayed for the poor horse, and a mistress who'd grieve a long while yet; 'And God bless Sabrina for that poem.'

Reaching the brook bridge, 'You could go home, now, boy!'

But he'd have none of it.

*Is this chivalry, or...?* 'I s'pose you've earned a Digestive for escorting me.'

'RALF!'

But on emerging from the spinney she must commend his protective intuition...

No Bumble.

'Well,' she reasoned, 'Jill was burning keen to go sketching.' *But to be almost an hour and a half late...?'* To reassure herself, 'We'll brew tea, and polish off the best of the broken biccies; that'll teach her, eh?'

'REFFF!'

'Remembering, mind, that this is Mogulus's house: best behaviour, hmm?'

Grudgingly, 'Ruff!'

She lifted the special stone... No key.

'But,' she whispered, 'I saw Granny hide it here this morning.'

To her dismay, though, he didn't seem bothered; worse, when she tried signalling that they must creep away and seek grown-up help from the stable, he trotted to the back door and nosed at it...

It eased open.

Sophy's insides turned over: *Who on earth…?*

And now the wretched terrier was entering, giving his usual 'Here I am!' bark.

Springing behind the honeysuckle, the frightened girl must spy in bladdery agony.


## CHAPTER 35

A face peered out…

'MUMMY!' Within microseconds Sophy was hugging; then she was tugging, 'I've GOT to GO! Come with me and, while I'm in Tŷ Bach, TELL me what's HAPPENED…!'


'Firstly, Mr Haroldston's letter disclosed more than Jill had about your "little adventures". Praising you, yes; but also revealing them as rather hairy escapades.'

'Well, Jilly and I hadn't wanted you to worry about–'

'And didn't I realise it, then?'

'Back home I *would* have told you, gradually, about those events – which each began without warning, Mummy, and we just got caught up in them. It isn't as if Heather and I deliberately tried risky things, like parachuting, is it?' Emerging, Sophy washed hands in the tin bowl kept outside.

They went to the bench; Carol drew her daughter close: 'You're evidently none the worse for what's occurred; in fact, you look tremendously well. And now, lest you're worrying, I haven't lost my job: things were so quiet, Mr Collett agreed to unpaid leave this week.'

Sophy kissed, 'That's *brilliant*, Mum! Every cloud, and all that.'

'Actually, darling, I've not lost out. The afternoon I was stuck on the story, I polished all Mrs Fenny's silver; as it's a task she *loathes*, yesterday morning Ffyldes delivered a hamper so big, you must help me unload it.'

'Wow! Although, where is the car…?'

'At the stable: this surprise was Granny's idea.'

'On reflection it *was* a good one, even if I did think that a burglar–'

'MEEYEW!'

Sophy scooped him up, 'Begging your pardon, Brave And Faithful Moggilulius: if there'd been intruders, you'd have come and warned me, hmm?'

'Mao!'

'Um, Mummy, talking about cars – where's Jilly?'

'A Mrs Willis is very kindly lending her a Dormobile to explore up the coast in, so we've Drift Cottage to ourselves until tomorrow night.'

'Lovely Mrs *Williams*, the writer, whose house is full of family history: Heather and I were with her today. In my knapsack I've some *fabulous* fruit sponge which we helped her bake; you and I *must* buy raffle tickets for her *massive* Dundee cake. By the way, me being at Thursday's fête is *compulsory* because these American ladies have–'

'Sophy, darling, STOP!'

'I'm sorry; it's just that I'm just so excited to see you. I *love* Heather *and* Jill: they're *brilliant* friends, and I'd do anything for them – and for Bronny, too; but *you're my Mum!*'

'And,' that unique hug hugged back, 'you're my Sophy, and you always will be.'

As the evening goldened, they walked Taggle home.

Tracker seemed so pleased to meet Mummy, Sophy wondered if that to-do earlier on had meant he'd known something was afoot; *Or perhaps that should be ahoof.*

Mummy had already met Anna; now, hello to Gareth and the Madocs. Meanwhile Sophy had to peep sleeping Diana: 'She's already much less wrinkly, I reckon.'

Carol drove cautiously back through the spinney; on arriving, 'Let's not unload just yet.'

This wasn't like Mum! 'Because…?'

'Cake, and apples, and towels need taking down to the sea, don't they?'

Where for secrecy's sake they swam silently as swans, and barely whispered after.

To best relish the returning dewy meadows, Carol went barefoot.

After such chatter-rattled suppering, 'Let's talk more once we're in the bath, hmm?'

'You surely don't mean…?' And Sophy shot there to look.

Trying those taps, how delight squeaked the steam-veiled girl: even with the magical uplift of Mum appearing, this was still something wonderful.

Sweet gardengloom infiltrating their unlit window, what deep-draughted swishulous comfort this Edwardian iron Dreadnought afforded! To fête its re-launch Sophy tinily sipped Carol's wine as she explained: on seeing Granny Haroldston's car depart that morning from her bedroom window, Anna The Conspirator had telephoned Hugh Haroldston, and he had come to plumb.

Sophy said, 'He's jolly nice, as well as really practical; y'know, I'm sure you'd get along.'

Astounding her daughter, 'We've already met.'


Detesting Sunday dawdlers, Carol Fossway had left Leamington at 6 am. Through Worcestershire and into Herefordshire she'd seen little more than milk lorries; the Welsh Marches miles and many on the A40 had reeled off easily, 'Because our car got going better and better: remember Dad's saying?'

'"Steams well, once the soot's blown from her tubes."'

Kissing a bubbly back, 'Exactement! Alors I met Granny and Hugh here for a late coffee.'

*So much has happened behind the scenes!*

'And, like you, I got taken on as Plumber's Mate – fortunately remembering lots from my many times helping Daddy. Which made Hugh say what a chip off the Fossway block you are; isn't that pleasing?'

Yes.

'A good man; a good business, he's got. An excellent father to Heather, isn't he? Not overtomboying her as if he'd rather have had a son, but just making her aware of opportunities. The Women's Liberation message, pretty much.'

Recalling one of Hannah's mother's spikier friends, 'Without the man-hating?'

Cottoning on, Carol patted a daughtershoulder: 'Are such women truly liberated?'

'Good point, Chère Maman!'

A snug room, indeed, that eve, with so much sun-heat stored; after towels, by a candle's light they rug-sprawled, often together silent to better hear each other's thoughts.

The night ahead needing nearness, soon they lay spooned close beneath one sheet; a single, a familial breath-rhythm swiftly slept them both.

## Chapter 36

On through the morning they drifted, child and mother, down deeper than dreams—

Until Mogulus, protesting on his stomach's behalf.

Carol yawned tall and pale to the kitchen; she fed Puss while the pot drew, then huffed him outside again and took their teas back to bed.

Sophy all-told the birth, then, and had much to ask; Carol recalled the time of carrying this girl her arms nestled: its joys, its worries; 'The *huge* importance to Daddy, darling, of you coming to us.

'People think their child's birth proves love completely, but that's easily said. I'd rather think of all that Daddy did for us *after* your birth: hour upon hour, day upon day of love being proved; like his keenness to spend time with you, to teach you things.'

'I was reminded of that, working with The Boss. He could have installed the equipment here much faster by himself; instead, I had to learn all the whats *and* understand every why. And...'

'Yes, darling?'

'When we'd finally finished off, he went to brew tea; meanwhile, I climbed the ladder again. Hearing fluid flowing, collecting heat for Jill... it was so pleasing, my having helped achieve that. Then Puss came up and joined me and, cuddling him, I explained what was happening; and tears came, Mummy: I realised I was actually telling Daddy about the solar equipment, just as if he were there. But happy tears, because I'd had the next best thing to Dad instructing me himself – Heather's father doing that.'

*Thank you so much, Hugh Haroldston.*

'It was even lovelier, later re-living that moment with Heather, who understands about Dad as no other friend can. She had this loveliest of thoughts: that with my tears I'd been thanking Daddy because he sort of *had* been there. She said that while her father is a good teacher, I was only able to take it all in because I'd learnt how to learn by being with Daddy – just as she'll forever benefit from her mum's teaching skills.

'And, Mummy, that tied in with what Jilly told us, once, about Miss Gwinear so deeply influencing her pupils that while she hadn't ever passed on her, um, birds and bees DNA to anybody, many people like Jill carry Miss Gwinear's *mental* DNA – which will go to their children, and others they, um…'

'Engage with?'

Sophy kissed, 'Yes. Anyway, back to what Heather said about people living on in their children: we've discussed it before, Mum, but now I've so clearly seen it for myself.

'One evening when we were helping with supper, Heather came into Granny's kitchen and plonked down some runner beans – and froze for a moment, like a cine projector jamming… Then, Pop!, she remembered what needed doing next, and was off back out.

'And I knew, deep inside: I said to Gran, "Your daughter used to do that." And she gave me the hugest hug, then we had a happy cry together.'

*Gosh!* 'You're a good girl, Sophy. And…'

'Don't move, Mum: I want to hug *you*!'

But Carol Fossway insisted: 'There's something you must see, right now: it's proof that others think you're good – and brave. I'm fetching it from your bedroom, where you were meant to find it last night.'

\*

Despite Heather being out of the gymkhana, Hugh had still visited the County Show that Sunday.

Admiring old steam machinery early on, he'd found Jill Ribblesdale sketching – and sketching unstoppably, so he'd fetched her a coffee. He'd then called on the stable girls, wishing everyone well; while intending to listen for announcements and hurry to witness crucial equestrian moments, his main purpose for being at the showground that morning had been commercial research: should he in future hire a stand at this event?

Other small heating businesses did, and plenty of people showed interest; he could display wood stoves attractively, and the Chough Solar Energy collectors from Cornwall were so neatly designed as to bear close inspection. Furthermore, outgoing Heather was now old enough to assist in such a situation.

Although, what if a sales push proved too successful? The business was just himself, Mother taking messages, and Heather his sometimes mate: taking someone on would be a huge step.

Announcing the U.S. military presence there was a line-up of obese vehicles, blary music, and some overglossy servicewomen giving out stars and stripes flags to children.

A camouflaged marquee was set up as a demonstration field communications centre; alongside were a massive aerial-flaunting truck and thrumming generators. Within, while Pembrokeshire's topography rippled round hot green radar screens, Hugh had aired his ideas for improving solar control units with one American chap who'd really known his electronics.

Technician Officer Felix L'Hermitte had enjoyed talking without having, for once, to keep saying, 'I'm sorry, I can't disclose that.' Welsh people were understandably curious about what the Marine Patrol guys did; however, one *had* to obey the rules: who knew, certain "civilians" might be plain clothes plants, working undercover for the Head of Security. Anyway, Search & Rescue operations not being classified, he could ask Hugh, 'Say, might that have been your girl one of the RAF yellow choppers did a favour for, the other day?'

Hugh had replied, hoping not to tempt Fate, 'A friend's daughter, actually.'

'Is she here? That crew are about today as our guests; reckon they'd gladly congratulate her for gathering all that marine garbage. A-And,' Felix had indicated a fridge-sized tape machine, 'we might obtain clearance to show her some video footage: these days, every sortie gets filmed.'

'Unfortunately, Sophy isn't.' Then, his neck prickling, 'D'you mean to say that that airship recorded my own girl, on horseback, going hell-for-leather to fetch the doctor from Talbenny Haven?'

Before Felix L'Hermitte had been able to reply, a white-gloved hand had touched Hugh's arm: 'Begging your pardon, but was this the poor horse which died afterwards…?'

The Lord Lieutenant's wife, invited by its Head of Security to view the airbase's exhibits. '…Because if there's has any film of that ride, I'd *love* to see it, having heard Nurse Firebrand's account. And that was your daughter, Mister…?'

'Hugh Haroldston. Yes – that was Heather. '

'Well then, we *must* see the recording! And then there's this other story going round, about the girl riding into the surf…?'

'Heather's friend, Sophy Fossway.'

The lady had beamed to everyone, 'Hit the jackpot, haven't I?' Who, more than any other woman in Pembrokeshire, had CLOUT.

The HOS had had to think very hard about Security Implications, all too aware of his wife's social aspirations: how could he refuse this lady? He'd grittingly enquired of the Technician Officer, 'Have we have any footage?'

Felix hadn't been able to resist: 'As you were advised the other day, Sir…'

Face purpled by internal conflict, the HOS had waived public disclosure restrictions – with all personnel present registering that *If-the-Pentagon-ever-enquires-this-never-happened* look in his eyes.

Following Felix's high speed jeep trip back to the base, the Lord Lieutenant, his wife, and all the County Show high-ups had been shepherded into a Command Post truck; soon afterwards, an exhibiting Craft Calligrapher had been given two express commissions.

And so, after the gymkhana prizes had been awarded, the committee had announced two Special Certificates of Commendation for Outstanding Feats of Horsemanship; and scrolls had been received on the young riders' behalves by hastily-tidied Jill Ribblesdale and an extremely proud Hugh Haroldston.

Who had been horrified to witness on that screen what a frightful risk his daughter had taken; and who had, straight afterwards, tearfully hurried to his old Volvo before the press could give chase.

*

At first unsure how she felt about her certificate, 'It's beautiful.' Crucially, Sophy now learned that her friend had been awarded one, too; 'Otherwise, I'd have felt awful.'

*So fond of, so loyal to, Heather Haroldston!* 'Sophy, I'm wondering if those incidents, and the tree falling, could bind you two close right through your lives.'

'I'm sure of it.'

'So I can't wait to meet this girl; and as she's at the stable this morning...'

'Okay; but first, who won the trophy that Heather would have competed for?'

'Alas, the notorious Patricia Flange – and haven't I heard tales about that one?'

'It isn't entirely her fault, how she is; and, actually, Mum, that's an excellent result: Patsy was being pressure-cooked to win, and she has; but she can't go lording it over Heather, because she didn't beat her. Also, that was a victory for the stable.'

'You almost seem ambivalent about someone who's been pretty nasty to you, too.'

Sophy boggled, *Mummy's been so well briefed!* Just how long a letter to Leamington – letters, indeed – had The Boss written?

It never occurred to her that whilst Drift Cottage's telephone hadn't been connected, Jill might have sometimes called Leamington from other places. Knowing that while those postcards had been fun, Carol had ever ached for more news of her only girl.

They'd breakfasted; now, despite Mogulus gleefully attacking the broom, Sophy was managing to sweep the kitchen—

An utterly unexpected noise sent her running, 'MUMMY...?'

Curtly, from within Tŷ Bach, 'Answer it, you twit!'

'...Um, hello?'

'Phone box bips; then, 'Sophy! Drift Cottage's first 'phone call ever: an historic moment, eh?'

'Yes; though the ringing first flummoxed Mogulus and me. How are you, AJ?'

'I'm fine; I'm exploring Dinas. Yesterday, guess what...?'

'Um...'

'I met little Molly and her Mum – who bought my Whitesands drawing straight from the sketchbook, thank you very much!'

'Hey, that's brilliant!'

'Anyway, I'm 'phoning because – CONGRATULATIONS! You'll tell Heather the same, hmm?'

'Of course. Thanks for collecting the scroll, and sparing my blushes; you didn't have to say anything, did you?'

'I did, via a microphone, to quite a flipping few folks, I'll have you know. I said you'd be honoured, and would be very pleased about Heather's bravery being recognised, too.'

'Spot on, Aunty Jilly!'

BIP, BIP, BIP...

'Any news for me?'

'Mrs Williams says, would you contribute a portrait session for the fête raffle?'

'Oh! I thought she'd just ask me for a framed sketch.'

'You're jolly good at faces; if you display samples of your work, lots of people will buy tickets – and I bet you'll get some commission enquiries, as well.'

'Actually, by Thursday many folk will have seen sketches by me of you and Heather: after yesterday's presentation some journalists were insisting on having you two photographed – but Hugh refused, outright.'

'So...?'

'That was when Jan Caerfai chipped in: she's only Missus Lord Blooming Lieutenant of Pembrokeshire! She suggested that if I'd drawings of you two in my sketchbook, they would do.'

'And that settled the argument?'

'Magically, because *she* had spoken, the newspaper people suddenly agreed.'

'AJ, getting two of your drawings in the next edition is fantastic free publicity.'

'Indeed; what's more, Jan has asked to visit Drift Cottage; and, like it or not, she has huge social influence: should she buy a painting, other County people would want a Ribblesdale too.'

Sophy chuckled, 'What a hoot, if the terribly-with-it Flanges wanted their Perfect Patsy's portrait done by you!'

'Gosh; I hadn't thought of that. Well, I couldn't paint her – not if she insisted on sitting there slumped all stroppily in my dining room, with a face like a smacked bum on her!'

Huge tittering; more coin bips.

'I'd better go, sweetheart: someone's there outside. Anything else can surely wait; I needn't ask Mum how things are, hmm? Goodbye, sweetheart; and about the raffle – tell Alice, Yes!'

Useful things, telephones.

Sophy gave Mrs Williams the good news; on calling the stable to tell Heather they'd soon be along, Bronny advised, 'Tuesday morning, you've a rowing practice.'

Then Charlie rang: 'Grandfather's been approached about Aberdare giving rides at the fête; could we meet to discuss the idea...?'

Wise Carol Fossway: 'Darling, I know we talked about going off to do things together, but you'd warned me about the rowing already; and, as for people wanting you to help with wagon rides – that's some responsibility, so you should feel honoured to be asked, hmm?'

'If you really don't mind...?'

'Sophy, wherever we go the scenery's new to me; and, like Jilly, I can be gathering useful material, whatever you do.' Also, Carol should see for herself her daughter's confident way with new-met children and adults: about this Jill had communicated enthusiastically.

Could telepathic Tracker interpret every message the 'phone wires carried? As he fussed like bonkers over Sophy, 'Mum, you'd think he already knows about the wagon rides, and—'

The terrier, an attractive gold-tanned girl of Sophy's age, and an older boy very Celtic in looks.

Heather grinned, 'We guessed why you were held up.'

Charlie took over, 'And I realised I'd not said about Tracker sharing Thursday's work with Aberdare: I thought I should straighten that out with Bronny and you, Sophy, as soon as possible.'

The Leamington girl chuckled, 'You mean with *him*, Charlie: he knew something was up.'

Heather said, 'Mrs Fossway, shall I show you the stable while Sophy and Charlie sort out arrangements with Tracker...? That sounds absurd to you, perhaps, but he must be in on the discussions.'

'From what I've heard, Heather, Mr Tracker can understand, and handle, anything – a James Bond of horses. Except, he can't drive an Aston Martin.'

Charlie said, 'He doesn't need flash cars to go fast! Eh, Sophy?'

'No, Charlie.' Just two words; but how the girl glowed them out.

Carol so hoped to click with Hugh's girl; for Heather's part, her friend's mum *had* to be A Good Sort; thus, they leapt into conversation like old friends.

The terrier trotted alongside, not trying to gain attention. Firstly he didn't think he could; secondly, for all his canine self-centredness he sensed the mutual need.

Much of Sophy Heather saw in Mrs Fossway: eyes, intelligence of course, near-identical hair; other traits, therefore, came from Keith Fossway. To whom the Welsh girl now reached towards whenever she prayed, promising to ever do her best for his beloved daughter.

Hesitantly out of the office…

Recognising need in those eyes, Carol embraced, 'Here's the generous girl who's done so much for my daughter: dear Bronwen, it's lovely to meet you!' And – talk about catching people off their guard – on sighting another young horsewoman, 'Surely this is Sabrina, Roman spirit of the River Severn?'

'How acely pagan!' boggled Bronny. 'No wonder animals love you, with such a fundamental name. Whyever hadn't you explained its Welsh importance before?'

'Because,' Sabrina smiled, 'I didn't know its background: I'm sure Mam and Da just chose it because they liked it.'

'Nevertheless,' Heather reckoned, 'it was destined for you.'

Carol, hastily, 'I only discovered last week how *Sabrina* originated, researching my novel.'

Heather hopped, 'Does everyone down here play a part?'

Hesitantly, 'Hoping none of you mind, I'm using all your names: they go together so attractively.'

'That's fair enough,' Bronny nodded. 'And never mind that your characters won't have our personalities: the story's the thing.'

Sabrina said, 'I'm sure we'll like the people Carol's imagined.'

Heather's pantherish smile: 'If not, we'll sue the pants off you for deformation!'

'And maybe,' Bronny ear-tweaked, 'for defamation as well.'

'But you won't,' Sabrina faux-sighed, 'because Mrs Fossway will deploy a clever clause, like those flashed up before films start.'

Charlie, arriving, glinted, 'A really sharp clause.'

Catching his pass, Sophy scored the try: 'For the sharpest of clawses, it's Mogulus you want.'

Plans confirmed, mother and daughter departed.

Granny would deliver Heather plus her kit at six o'clock; she'd stay until at least Thursday; invited to supper that evening, Bronny would hopefully bring a sleeping bag. Furthermore the Fossways needn't worry about food: Gran would take care of that. So they'd a free afternoon; 'However,' Carol said, 'after all yesterday's driving…'

'Let's walk to Druids Head, Mum, so you can see how all your story locations link together.'

'And, later, Mill Cove?'

Of course!

By the afternoon's end Carol looked – and felt – considerably browner. She walked home relaxed, and nicely thoughtful.

As well as Heather's influence, was it partly down to those older, spirited girls…?

Or a sudden spurt of mental growth…?

Might recent escapades have fundamentally shaken Sophy up…?

Whatever the reason, her child now readily voiced passion; and passion now powered many of the girl's actions. Up at Druids Head, how she had vivified the Pembrokeshire landscape; and then in her Mill Cove diving, such striving: to curve beautifully in air, spear neatly, ever further the underwater distance.

Her so-sunned daughter, surely fortnighted taller and stronger.

Granny dropped off Heather plus a sturdy iron pot; then, away to feed Hugh.

The stew needed a bit more simmering, then just-picked herbs snipped in right before serving; 'Our responsibility,' Miss H said, checking what veges.

Sophy announced, 'Here's your guest, Mum: take her into the garden, and drinks will follow.'

Bronny's top and skirt were Anna-lent; with her hair up, she was transformed. An overall glow suggested punitive soaking and scrubbing; came confirmation, 'After every County Show, my skin's in a right state: I got out, just, feeling like a pincushion!'

'Well,' Carol proffered cold-beaded cider, 'it was worth it. I behold a beautiful young woman, with shining eyes as bright as her mind.'

The youngsters had found candles; its central vase overflowing honeysuckle and fern tips, green and sweet that supper table glowed. Facing Carol in the other carver, offsetting their excitability with careful responses, how regal Bronny seemed to the girls...

Upon whom, a wildplant coronet they then bestowed: 'Hail, Flower of Glamorgan!'

Carol beamed, 'Actually, I'd seen Fair Bronwen as a Shakespeare heroine, disguise now divested as we near the play's end, thus just received of her rightful regalia.'

'And so,' Sophy had to know, 'She is Queen of...?'

Heather, knowing the thrust of those garden discussions, proffered her orange juice glass: 'Her own future!'

## CHAPTER 37

The forecast had worried Jill: would fog bring on overstrong recollections of Arrow's last day?

Though she'd slept well back in her own bed again, she woke feeling feverish; *Ah, well – I'll take some paracetamol, and hope for the best.* But, on sitting up, *That's odd!* The room itself was hot.

A bump; from beyond the curtain, 'Mroo!' Echoing the distant lighthouse's lament.

The artist chink-peeped, then padded off for her camera.

Amusing and beautiful, a sight worth capturing: Fogulous Mogulus, his coat aglint with droplets, whiskers diamonded to their very tips.

Intelligent Puss, comprehending that wagged finger: on being admitted he wasn't to rubby round his mistress, invade the attic, or storm The Snug where Carol slept. Heading straight to his kitchen kipchair, he started undampening himself.

No, Jill wasn't ill: regardless of that thick mist, this was a warm old morning. Contemplating the white-veiled dripping calm, she hoped that this heated humidity differed sufficiently from the other day for the girls to not reminisce unduly about Arrow.

Appearing softly, great effort descending the stairs to not wake Carol, the girls were morning-joyous as ever, though bed-cooked too.

'A wind-waiting day for sailors,' said Sophy, stepping under first. 'Beautifully calm for this morning's rowing practice, mind.'

Heather, as they shower-shared, 'Does your body ever feel as if it's, you know, waiting?'

'Not yet, mine hasn't. And I'm not impatient about changing: I like this me.'

'I like my me, too; and, of course, I really like your you.'

Momentarily switching from shampooing the other's hair to shoulder massage, 'Ditto.'

'Bless Bronny, for talking to us so openly at bedtime yesterday about what changing's like.'

'Yes; like the acest big sister.'

'Shame she couldn't stay the night here, at home with us.'

A day steadily warmer and ever more humid – until, after lunch, Heather's nicely described tropical mizzle set in.

In costumes now, tasked with taking fogulous photos: Sophy bearing the umbrella, protecting the expensive camera from that pixyish precipitation; Heather approaching cobwebs closely, crouching adjustingly towards bejewelled blooms, before clicking.

Then, 'Freeze, sister!' The viewfinder edged nearer, scrutinising the perfection of Sophy's eyes, ever more sharply, until defining each mist dot adorning their bashful lashes... Clack! 'A cracking photo, that'll be.'

The other's turn, soon: Heather hadn't noticed her careless morning-washed tresses grow serenely silvery, then begin to seed crystal beads... Agreed with herself about the picture's composition, Sophy held her breath and pressed: *Even crackinger, I reckon.*

'Hey, how Ace!' Where the stream emerged from under the hedgebank's stone slab, mist skulked; above that chilly pool's outflow, whisps rose lazily to drift with it. Having got Sophy to tug up some tall grasses, Heather had her sweep that thick switch of seedy heads through those sullen clouds, wafting reluctant vapour all about: 'That should look so serene, with a slow shutter speed!' Then, 'It's nippy, I know; but would you...?'

Flipflops shed, didn't want them stained orange, Sophy got in warily. Toe-prickling water licking around her knees, her lower torso winced *No deeper, please!*

'Gently downstream, fingers spread, combing the mist, could you…? Perfect! Now thoughtful, like the lagoon girl in that lush chocolate advert…? That's bang on: slow and beautiful does it!'

Meanwhile, dense ochre bloomed up all about.

Reaching the bridge, 'Gorgeous actions, Sophes! Only, what's wrong?'

'Jolly rubbly underfoot.'

'But you always kept looking serene; a professional model couldn't have coped better.'

Turning Cockney urchin, 'La, milady: me feets ain't turned berlue wiv cold, they've ferlipping gorn horringe!'

'Why bless you, child: so they have!'

Now out, Sophy glanced upstream… And pointed, 'Hecking heck, the stones I disturbed have all turned black!' She flopped flat, craned an arm underwater, then slap-rattled her catch onto the planks: 'Cracking good coal – no doubt about it, eh?'

'Yee-hah! A Black Bonanza for our Jilly.'

'Before we fetch her, shall I hoik out more?'

'Better hadn't: The Management won't want rusty blotches, even on your second best costume.'

Instantly a Tennessee Mary-Lou, 'Ain't that the truth? Rusty Blotches is a low down varmint, and my Mammy says I mustn't never have nothin' to do with hium!'

'Amen to that, Sister!'

'Using that long-toothed rake, we shouldn't get splashed.'

'We oughtn't,' Heather owed. 'But,' tomboy pragmatism, 'we would.'

'Hmm.'

'However, rust-splattering our oldest undies can't matter, because who'll ever see? And, anyway, orange-dyed knicks could be fashionable.'

'AJ,' Sophy explained, 'we reckon the stronger flow in winter dislodges anthracite from the mine; it gets washed across the ford, and into this reach.'

'So,' Heather posited, 'Wouldn't it be looking a gift horse in the mouth, to *not* grab it for you? It'll all end up washed out to sea, otherwise.'

A good point, Jill allowed; 'The straight-through migration rate must be sparse, mind: I only sporadically find lumps at Mill Cove.'

'Meaning that if we mine your Black Diamonds, it might be ages before we can again?' Sophy shrugged, 'So what?'

'It's no justification for *not* doing a dredge now,' Heather insisted. 'Coal isn't cod: taking some today won't affect future replenishment. In fact,' the inveterate ditch urchin pursued, 'if we hoik out even a half handy amount of anthracite, Jilly, your next harvest should - be - bigger!'

Sophy, though so wanting this to be true, 'Hang on – we can't make the mine produce more coal!'

Heather, patiently, 'Have you asked yourself why winter spates shift much more stuff? It's because the faster water flows, the more it bowls everything along with it…'

Her friend did a little leap: 'If we deepen the channel, the water goes slower; and so there's more chance of coal pieces settling to the bottom, not whooshing past seawards like leaves blown down a lane!'

Carol Fossway must hug, 'That's my girl!'


Paper reserves placed ready, pencils wedge-whittled for quick capture of moments, Jill was all set for a run of drawings, themed **Nymphs Of The Stream**: a handy title, this, hinting at other sketch series to come: **Nymphs Of The Field**; **Nymphs Of The Shore**; **Nymphs Of The Spinney**.

A double opportunity, this: stripped near-naked for watery work, both girls' every muscle movement would be readable; also the artist was determined, through the unconscious interplay of actions, to interpret the now instinctive co-operation which told of mutual affection.

Here they larkily came, squealing a barrow of tools, perfect models indeed in only lastyear knickers… Plus clompy adult wellies, against the chilly water.

Though how the incongruity wanted her to, *Mustn't snigger!* Lest they came over bashful, and this charming chance would be gone forever.

'Mummy, can't you come and…?'

'Darling, although it's stopped mizzling, the garden bench won't dry for ages. I'd *love* to work outdoors near you, but not if it means damp clothes and soggy paper.'

Heather compromised, 'How about a deckchair in the front porch?'

Mogulus, evidently disagreeing, 'Miaou!'

Taking a moment to locate him, Carol scoffed, 'What – work in that clammy old shower hut?'

'MIAOUW!'

The girls darted to look; Sophy called from the window, 'You owe Puss an apology: it's bone dry in here.'

Heather grinned out, 'You're so slim, Mam, we can fit in you, a camping chair, *and* a card table!'

'Mah-oh!' *And me!* The writer, he'd decided, needed an inspirational muse; also, her warm lap was the best snoozing place he could think of, that afternoon.

Working upstream from the footbridge, they'd first dredge for the coal most at risk from being washed away into the brook; by operating facing into the current, the sediment they disturbed would waft off behind them.

Sophy's earlier wading had distinctly tinted the soles of her feet; though unconcerned about ochred undies, neither girl wanted her nicely tanned skin blotched orange; thus, to be on the safe side, the coal must be washed underwater.

'By me, using the sieve,' Sophy resolved; so Heather began raking lumps to the side of the channel, whence her shovel could scoop them.

After its submerged strumble, for final rinsing each sieveful went into a fishbox sat on the stream bed; the friends from time to time clambered out, drained this, and tippled the accumulation into the wheelbarrow.

Heather, raking, could study her friend at work.

A circular motion, next a jerk flushing loosened mud away and re-levelling the pieces; a to-and-fro rumble plus a spell of twist/untwist; then, straightening her back, Sophy raised the sieve and, one deft movement which swung, lifted, *and* tipped, flew that batch into storage… And, after the shortest moment of relief, spine arched other way, the girl grabbed the implement back off the bank and gestured for a refill…

*Definitely more stamina than when I first met her!*

An effective system, all right: eye-sizing the barrow's black shiny pile with commendable accuracy Heather crowed, 'Only five minutes per bucket's worth!'

Sophy boggled: getting that quantity at Pinched Pill had taken an hour; furthermore, there'd been much tramping about the river's rippled bed, too. Here by the footbridge, 'Wow, you're still raking from the same patch!'

Her friend grinned, peering roundabout, ''T'isn't beginner's luck, either.'

'But,' Sophy pointed to the willow whose branch cranked over the water, a favourite water-watching perch of hers, 'just for a change, why not try there?' *I might rest against the tree from time to time, which would be nice.*

'Righto! First, though…' Having pertly galumphed to the woodshed for some rope, Heather said, 'I know everything weighs less underwater, but surely you'd still rather not…'

Sieve suspended like a submerged baby's cradle from that tree bough, all Sophy's effort could now go into strumbling: She joyed, 'This is *much* kinder to my back!'


Half way through the afternoon, Hugh called. Impressed by their industry, he nevertheless upbraided the girls: 'You didn't fix a price first?'

Jill, bringing teas, 'They'll be fairly rewarded.'

The youngsters explained how their technique had further developed.

Mud-cemented, the anthracite lumps nestled in the stream bed snug as cobblestones; despite experimentation, they'd found no better extrication tool than the stone-rake. However, strumbling no longer involved Sophy stooping with numbed feet and hands. Having (almighty racket!) hammered the rusty bottom out of an otherwise sound galvanised bucket, they'd then strapped the sieve beneath: et voilà, a strumbler! Sophy could dunk it in while either kneeling or sitting on the bridge; a twisting motion rumbled and rattled the coal nicely.

She now wondered, 'D'you see those reeds waving in the current…? Could a paddle wafting back and forth make the sieve twist?'

'Perhaps.' But Heather thought the up-and-down motion during strumbling equally important.

While agreeing with his daughter, Hugh praised Sophy's aspiration re designing a strumbling machine; 'But has this flow enough oomph to power one, do you think?'

'Just watch this, Boss!' Leaning from the bridge, Sophy lowered the shovel, blade facing upstream… Immediately jerking back, its shaft struck the plank, BONG!

'And,' Heather enthused, 'see how water now piles against the blade!'

'Good demonstration,' he nodded. Out of his pocket came tape measure, notebook, and pencil.

Blade area calculated, Sophy must dangle the spade again for him; lying alongside, Hugh pushed gradually harder 'til he balanced the stream's thrust with the handle vertical.

The channel's width measured, from side to side they sounded its depth; then multiple games of Poohsticks derived the average water speed, he noting there'd been no rain for some days: a stream's flow when spating told you nothing about normal conditions.

Sophy said, 'Look: Mummy's having a breather!' Having waved, 'Heather and I were determined not to disturb her or Jill: we could sense them both getting on so well.'

Surprise overcome – he'd simply not noticed Carol there – he smiled, 'Industry in quiet places, indeed: when I arrived, I doubted anyone was in; then I heard you empty the sieve. Hmm, your Mum's got a good writing spot, Sophes: secluded, but she can watch you girls at work.'

For not calling coal-dredging play, Sophy liked Heather's dad even more.


Carol hadn't been writing for some while; she'd just been observing.

Heather's father could uncle Sophy much better than could Keith's brother Ralph, who seldom visited and anyway had scant idea about how to even speak to the girl, never mind talk with her.

Hugh Haroldston: kind and, yes, handsome – but not cocksure with it: that, Carol detested.

Fresh paper clipped into place, pencil notionally observing man and girl conversing, Jill had been glancing over from time to time to see what Carol made of it all... *Now she's realised I've been watching her!*

The spell broken, *I might as well do a brew.*


'Daddy dearest,' Heather crept, 'Might you stay and help us?'

'I'm hardly dressed for the task.'

'No; nor could you wear quite as little as us or,' she Cheshired, 'there might be a falling out.'

Making Sophy go beetroot red.

'But surely you've your soldering jeans in the car, which Gran says must soon become gardening shorts?'

'I believe you're right.'

Hands on hips, 'OF COURSE I'm right, twice over.' Heather explained to a frowning Warwick miss, 'I'm his daughter, plus I'm The Female of the Species.'

'Okay, smarty-pants,' he countered, 'consider this: If I help with strumbling this afternoon, up goes the coal cleaning rate. However, strumbling will continue to be your process bottleneck: if you and Sophy were both scrabbling raw material out like Swansea dredgers, I couldn't possibly keep up. However, if I applied my *brain* on your behalf, we might end up really shifting paydirt.'

Carol husked, 'Can you honestly afford the time, Hugh?'

Brandishing his notebook, 'From a mix of many ideas, a concrete plan has already emerged.'

Sophy was determined to nail that hint; *But if he proposes rumbling and sloshing the coal clean with a concrete mixer, why study the stream so intently?* Unless a mixer might be powered by a water wheel, not a puttering motor... *Hmm; but you'd need sprockets and chains, like on a bike, or belts and pulleys – and how many hours, days perhaps, to put everything together?* Stumbling in various directions, her head kept reaching dead ends – so she wisely retraced steps to the basic premise: there must be rumble and slosh...

And, lightbulb moment, *Rumble and slosh are all we need!* In the simplest possible device for processing coal like a concrete mixer, with the stream providing power and rinsing mud away: thinking aloud, 'A round cage, like a hamster wheel. Dipping into the water, with paddles to rotate it.'

Just as sketched there in his flipped-open book.

Heather peered: 'Amazing agreement between you two! And here's the Anthromatic coal washer's best feature: you needn't build it.'

Sophy gulped, 'WHAT?' Only in science fiction could machines construct themselves.

Heather chuckled, 'Never nosed round our sheds, have you? Fact is, Dad isn't good at throwing things away, Gran's old Kleenomatic washing machine included – inside which is a perforated stainless steel drum, perfect for letting water in and mud out.'

He cautioned, 'The outer barrel would need chopping about carefully: mustn't harm the main bearing.'

'So,' daughterly decisiveness, 'I'll phone Gran re someone else for supper, while you two head home – after Sophes has packed for an overnighter, in case the project overruns.'

A policemanly hand on the shoulder: 'Shouldn't Sophy's Mum have a say in all this?'

'Sophy's Mum says,' said Sophy's Mum, 'that separately these two might fall asleep a deal earlier tonight – rather than in together, whispering 'til all hours.'

Both, 'Oh!'

Carol pacified, 'Your secrets are safe: my hearing's not *that* good. But,' she smirked, 'Mogulus's continual glancing up with twitching ears told me that, last night, whatever you two did…'

…They struggled not to redden…

'…it wasn't kipping, not for a good long while.'

'Well, it'll be nice and quiet here for you and Heather this evening,' said Jill. 'That phone call earlier was me being invited out: remember that hotel up the coast…?'

Sophy advised the others, 'The owner wants to display Jilly's pictures.'

Cottoning on to Hugh and Sophy's plan, Puss wanted in: he sat expectantly in the Volvo. When The Boss got aboard and started up, he who normally scarpered upon hearing any engine except Bumble's just blinked serenely and then claw-hooked the seat, anticipating corners.

Carol, waving goodbye, marvelled 'Cool as a cucumber!'; Heather saged, 'He'll have his reasons.'

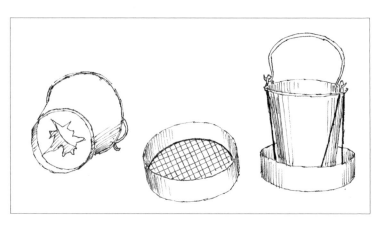

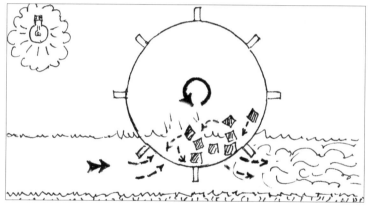

# CHAPTER 38

A purposeful Puss, certainly. Saucer of milk drained immediately on arrival, he miaowed for the door; past the garage he padded, far-staring, Sophy's anxious 'See you at supper?' going unanswered.

Gran winked, 'Not a cat for going hungry.'

Glass porthole removed first for safety, the washing machine's outer panels were soon off.

Sophy screwdrivered; The Boss's spanners tackled bolts. This wasn't scrapping, the girl understood, but dismantling; as Granny's current model was also a Kleenomatic, many components should be compatible – the motor and pump, certainly: 'Should save us lots on spare parts, over time,' said Hugh.

They could have worked faster, but for that constant – and essential – traffic of questions and answers.

Barrel removed from carcase, Hugh decided against sawing out the drum and its hefty bearing. Instead, they'd just cut enough casing away to let that shiny cylinder curve into the passing water. 'Leaving it like a steamboat's paddle box, d'you see?' He went for a marker pen.

From nowhere, Mogulus. Peering at the thing's innards, he yowled concern; then, mystery urgency hurried him away again.

And Sophy twigged: 'Forgive me, Boss, but would paddles stubby enough to rotate inside the barrel produce enough power?'

He slapped his head, 'Damn it, NO! If History's great engineers are watching from Heaven, they'll be guffawing their socks off at how you've shown me up.'

'Actually, Puss spotted the problem.' Then, eyes serious, 'My Daddy wouldn't laugh. He'd know you have lots on your mind; nobody that busy gets everything right.'

Her hugging him was so heartening; he patted, 'So kindly put, Sophy. Of course he's watching us, same as Louise is.'

Unnoticed, Granny radiated approval.

'The electric jigsaw will do for that circumference cut. I'll get safety gear; mustn't forget protection against that poxy epoxy dust, either.'

From inside a swamping boilersuit with sleeves tightly taped, a bobblehatted, gloved, and goggled Sophy, ears defended against Hugh's Concorde-roaring vacuum cleaner, must capture that vile powder with the latter's nozzle.

'Here goes…!'

Initially alarmed by the implacable vibration, Sophy sternly reminded herself how carefully they'd set everything up; furthermore, that cutting machine seemed incapable of running amok; *Unlike a chainsaw.*

Detached from her surroundings like an astronaut, her breathing sounding startlingly loud, this was surreal. Allowing herself quick glances away from the shrieking gizmo she aimed, she contemplated the man beside her "concentrating like hell" lest that sharky blade, reciprocating invisibly fast, should lose its line and splinter into shards. *His goggles and mask make him a ruthless, soulless alien.*

And did so so unfairly, for here was a kind man proving he'd do anything for his daughter.

And for this girl, too.

At last, 'STAND BACK!' And the barrel body parted from the end Hugh steadied, clattered a roundabout dance, and lay still.

Now he hunted the dust-hungry nozzle everywhere – including all about giggling Sophy; having knelt for her to return the favour, 'HOO-RAY!', he switched the vacuum cleaner off.

Un-astronauted, her voice was a stranger's to her ears: 'Well done, Boss! I was–'

Granny ordered, 'You're showering NOW, girl: don't give your precious skin time to even THINK about itching!'

Made to strip outside, she assiduously faced the kitchen door against the infinitesimal just-in-case of somebody in the field. Now, more goosebumped indignity: she must stoop for perusal to her very hair roots – and was then dispatched, behind more stung than patted, 'Be sure you'se THOROUGH!'

So huffy, that Miss waiting for warmer water, until glimpsing the mirror…

Despite every precaution, in improbable places she truly was, Mrs Haroldston's description, white as Dusty Miller: *No wonder Gran had me undress outdoors!*

Just as she'd have made Heather: treated like one of the family, indeed.

Foamy marathon over, dried and dressed again, 'I'm sorry for sulking, Gran: I didn't appreciate how filthy I was.' And straight to the sink, where waited (planned penance) a stack of pots and crocks.

*

A new atmospheric dryness, window-peering Heather noticed while Carol's mother-love towelled her dry, was unglistening the garden.

The sky patched open while they ate; as they mugged down tea, the last foggy rags went.

'Yes Heather,' Sophy's mum sensed the thought, 'we should visit Tracker.'

*

Good old Gran: a swiftly-scoffable supper – and they were excused washing up!

For paddle blades, Hugh cut down six pine pallet slats; narrow-shanked screws driven through the drum's drain holes secured them.

'So, Sophy: how to hang this contraption off the bridge?'

The very question she'd intended asking him. Thinking out loud, 'As it's experimental, we'll be lifting it in and out a lot; that means a strong pivot... A gate hinge?'

'Giving you a swinging arm; but might a balanced beam be better? You'd push on one end...'

Gleefully, 'And up she'd rise!' Then, following his hinting eyes, 'What – commandeer Heather's old seesaw? I know she's outgrown it, Boss, but...'

From the kitchen window, 'Side with sentiment, and you're stuck with the sediment! Straight after breakfast tomorrow, Klondike Kate, your fellow coal prospector expects Anthromatic Limited to deliver an operational nugget tumbler.'

With a look Hugh knew was Keith Fossway's, 'What size spanner...?'

*

They followed the horse's gaze... Astonishingly, here came a yapless Taggle; then Bronny, stomping along with eyes fixedly down.

'We'll leave you in peace,' Carol offered, but that head-shake....

They'd been pondering the hairbrush; now Bron noticed it herself: 'Rather tizzed, when I set off.'

Heather murmured, 'You meant to bring the curry kit.'

Carol's give-it-to-me gesture.

'Yes, Mam: you curry Bronny. But,' Heather was climbing the fence, 'Tag and I had better take Yankee Boy off, or he'll get jealous.' Up now and glowing in the low sun, 'We'll just walk, I promise.'

'Be sure you only do, bareback and no reins!'

Watching them go, Bronny smiled quietly, 'Obviously has secrets she's bursting to share with him.'

Carol, who'd never been friends with a horse when young,

256

contemplated that youngster chattering away to her ambling mount: 'Bless me, yes!' And started brushing.

'…Um, what's Leamington like?'

'Pleasant, but not a patch on this.'

'Under an hour to Oxford by train?'

'Easily. That's where Miss Gwinear wanted you to try for, Bronwen?'

'Yes; although,' rich chuckle, 'as for what I should study at university – one week she'd be for botany and I'd back psychology; next time she'd propose biochemistry, to get a better grip on pollution; politics, I'd reckon, with the same end in mind.'

'Always a problem when, like Jill, you're a good all-rounder: she could have read Geography.'

'With respect – come off it, Carol! You handle any topic going round the supper table.'

'But at your age my knowledge was lamentably, embarrassingly narrow.'

'So becoming mates with Jill, having hols on her folks' farm and such, broadened your mind?'

'What's more, it was thanks to me reading her New Scientists that I clicked with Keith: I could appreciate from the start what inspired him.'

'What *had* inspired him, until you met. Look here, Carol, Sophes was obviously a great talker and listener from an early age; surely you were the same? It's most appealing in any girl, eloquence combined with a generous ear.'

'Well, I–'

'If you'd never met Jill, I'm *sure* you could have still conversed interestingly with Keith; anyway, with your looks he must've been smitten straight off.'

'What happened was surprisingly sudden,' Carol conceded. Anyway,' she sleekly deflected, 'surely with your character, and your beauty…?'

'I get asked out.' Bronny scuffed stones. 'But.'

*What a sigh!*

'I get fed up explaining to boys that–'

Wise Carol; silent Carol.

They'd reached the ridge now, Heather still gassing away to Tracker at the same rate; radiating fondness, Bronny watched them a good while. Then, 'Always, *always*, it's the not knowing...'

'...God, Carol, you're a good listener!'

'I'm so glad you wanted to talk. Earlier, were thoughts of Sam bothering you especially badly?'

'No; I've been tizzed all day, remembering dear Arrow. The Madocs, too; nothing said, but I knew.'

*How it hurts, having a big heart.*

'And you're a ruddy good pamperer, Sophy's Mum: that brushing's done me wonders. Mind, I should have expected that: Sophes was *so* caring when we shared a bath.'

*Remembered as importantly for her, I'm sure.*

Suddenly a kiss, spaniely clumsy; then a piercing two-finger whistle and, hands cupped, 'HOME TIME!'

So Heather, shuffling a bit forwards, had Tracker trot; and when he left it late and stopped sharpish before the gate just to see what would happen – even the nicest horses are mischievous sometimes – with great presence of mind she vaulted his lowered neck, knicker-clipped his ears (*Serves him right!*), and just managed an acrobat's landing, 'Ta-dah!'

*

The steel pipe seesaw frame needed adapting: the big flanges they screwed onto its legs would spread the load when it was coachbolted to the bridge timbers.

Having already decided how to bolt the drum bearing housing onto the beam, they could start tidying up; but that wasn't that for the evening: it was best, a flagging Sophy knew, to now sort out the nuts and bolts they'd need, and assemble tools for the morrow.

When they finally came in, Gran had scribbled, GONE TO BED.

Sophy yawned, 'I must, too!'

'Of course,' he nodded, 'but say quickly – was that more fun than doing solar work?'

'Hard to compare them; but it's all engineering – which is the key thing, surely?'

'That's my girl!'

After praying, with special mentions for the lighthouse keepers and sailors out there, an apprehensive Sophy lay back: *Drifting off won't be easy without Heather here.*

*

'Will you come and say goodnight?'

'Call when you're ready, darling.'

Heather did – from Carol's bed in The Snug: 'I don't feel like sleeping upstairs, tonight.'

'Promise you won't eel-wriggle?'

Already out.

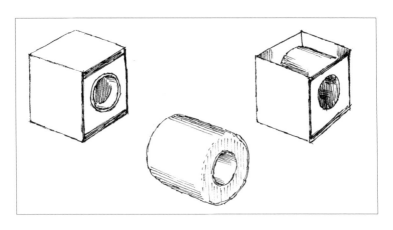

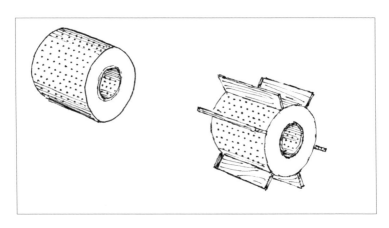

# CHAPTER 39

The next thing Sophy knew, Gran was toe-tickling, 'Fried with bacon, or scrambled with ham?'

Lithely out of bed, for Jilly she'd have been *A Springing Nymph*.

Pewter the previous evening, a bay now blue under a sky which was… Nose pressed to windowpane, Sophy searched: *Cloudless!* Even above the Prescellys. What better than a warm still day, for engineering in that stream with Heather?

Movement in the haze beyond the lighthouse became a patrol 'plane; it took a half-curious swing round a yacht leaving Solva, then carried on homewards. The girl followed it down, so familiar the routine now: the wheels unhatching, big ones first; those plank-like wing flaps extending, making it settle back in the air; now the propellers would be re-pitching, the exhausts starting to voof… As it slipped from view, she was visualising the whitepuff scandalised shriek of tyres meeting tarmac—

With a jolt, 'Carson and Sam!' She'd never prayed for them the evening before. Dropped to her knees, elbows on the sill, into those hard-clasped hands she whispered strong wishes.


Driving over to Drift Cottage, Hugh said, 'Sorry I can't stay today, Sophy.'

'Don't apologise, Boss: you've been so generous with your time.'

The telephone had beaten them there: arriving, Hugh learned that he was bringing Gran for supper – and for the Anthromatic's official unveiling.

He nodded, 'A proper project, this is, now you've a deadline.'

Heather, coolly, 'I'm sure the four of us can manage—'

'Jilly must paint,' Carol insisted, 'so the three. And, I'm cook today.'

Before Hugh left, 'for inspiration' he leaned from the bridge, holding the drum muscularly.

It obliged with a few water-gleamed revolutions; nice to see, certainly, but the question remained: had the stream enough power to get coal clean?

That morning's balmy valley sporadically heard sawing and hammerbangs. Mostly, though, in a murmured garden boots streamsplashed, brace and bit munched grain, and tinsnips crimped; plus, only for the sharpest animal ears, pencil-scribble and turn of page.

Support structure installed and balance beam mounted, an express squash break; afterwards Jill suggested to the loinclothed *Jungle Girls* of her sketches, 'Vests on, until the postman's called?'

Next, for the block and tackle. Proposed by The Boss, it offered easy depth adjustment: using a pebble-weighted bucket for bias, either girl would be able to raise or lower the loaded tumbler single-handed.

Cunningly now the carpentering amazons brought proper coffee and shortbread out to the artworkers; who, concentrations thus completely broken, wouldn't mind helping bracket on the drum, then positioning the completed assembly...

Et voilà: The Anthromatic.

Sophy's fizzing pride, hugging Heather: *I helped build that!* Utterly eclipsing her previous peak achievement, quite a complex Meccano model made slowly with Mum.

Jill heated with a rush of love for these young spirits, reading in those expressions *So much more we can do in future, together!*

That red van was perfectly timed: the postman could photograph the four with the contraption. Anticipating his 'But what's it for?', cunning Carol gave it a naïvely mumsy pat: 'The girls think it'll look nice, going round.'

True, as far as it went.

Martin departed, Heather chivvied, 'That's enough admiring, Sophy: now to get the thing going.'

Jill objected, 'One moment!' She shook hands with both, 'Excellent progress, ladies: stick at it with the same gumption, and you'll make this machine work really well.'

'Hear, hear.' Then Carol Fossway, heartily patting both disrobed backs, felt over-dryness; she pointed loudly to the cottage, 'Lotioning, NOW!' And got Jilly's agreement: an early lunch made sense.

Laden tray set down, Heather asked, 'While we nosh, can it go?'

'Engineer's thinking,' Carol approved. 'New machines need running in.'

Feet-braced Heather lowering away, Sophy gauging inclination while checking nothing snagged… *Dusted with powder soot,* Jill thought, *two of Nelson's gundeck boys.*

After a munchy while the artist opined, 'You can see that the six paddle arrangement gives the water a good grip on the drum.' Keeping this to herself: *The water which meets the blades, that is.*

Heather nodded, 'That's very Brunellian, y'know: the Great Britain had a six-bladed prop.'

Carol tried, 'One can't hear frowning, Sophy darling, and I don't see you frowning; but inside you *are* frowning, hmm?'

'I always thought the drum would, um, plash. Like a water mill.'

Jill knew: 'Not while it's not working. Idle, the blades match the speed of the current.'

'Okay, so…' The girl got in and waded over.

'Fingers off the sharp edges, Sophes! 'Use,' Heather lobbed a batten offcut, 'a brake shoe.'

As the drum slowed, water rumbled around it; sure enough, Slurp!, Slurp!, Slurp!

From over her shoulder, Sophy's GRIN!

'Not so much the bare bones of an engineering education,' Jill sniggered Bronnily, 'as the bare bum of one.'

Heather defended, 'But she isn't–'

'Poetic licence,' Carol tickled.

'…Sophy, *now* why are you brooding?'

'Idling, it wasn't exactly whizzy…'

'…And, braked, it's even less so,' Heather agreed. 'But don't let's get knickertwisty about that, now.'

Jill backrubbed, 'Heather's right, Sophes: wait and see. If there is one, you're good at thinking through problems. And,' winking at her old college mate, 'it isn't a race.'

'Mioh,' said the cat.

'Indeed not,' came reply. 'Although races have their places.'

Mogulus approved of this turning thing which disturbed the stream's flies: hateful irritating things, so difficult to catch; and, whatever the sort, they tasted disgusting. So this afternoon he'd not just supervise the youngsters, but assist them: *I'll purr them encouragement…*

However, 'Don't flop on Dad's sketches, Isambard Kingdom Puss!'

Carol and Sophy chortled together: a stovepipe-hatted tabby, paw sporting a fumy cigar.

Drinking after-lunch tea, another Sophy frown: 'When you brake the drum, the paddles obviously have to fight the friction; now I don't doubt that rumbling the coal will take power; but except for the pieces jostling together involving friction of sorts, I'm unsure *why* they will.'

Her friend saw that Jill knew... 'Once we're rolling, old butty, us must fathom it for ourselves.'


After morning hours of being still, she *must* exercise: 'Back by six to help with supper, okay?'

This gladdened Carol: away out, Jill couldn't get roped in by the children. But, seeing sketching stuff entering that knapsack, 'Aren't your eyes tired?'

'I don't intend on anything complicated; but if I don't take these, I'm bound to spot a good view.'

'She doesn't know about Sod's Law, yet,' Sophy said. 'Mummy, it's like... If you hope to discover a new swimming place, you must pack your knapsack only thinking thoughts about going sunbathing.'

Confused Carol shooed, 'Without wishing you a good or bad afternoon lest I get it wrong, Jilly, au revoir! It's your life, and your luck!'

The girl suddenly kissed, 'Mummy, because your life is mine too, I'm so lucky you're you! If you were differently-minded, we wouldn't be here.'


The Moment of Truth...

'One each at a time?'

'Okay; but, after you!'

Sophy dropped the first piece in; for the word *cantankerous,* an instant new meaning: it perfectly described the sound of coal tumblewashing inside that metal containment.

Pausing at twenty bits, paddle-beats already satisfyingly slurpy, and streaky mud clouds wafting away, they took turns to peer in on the clattery process – quite unaware of amusing Carol's camera with views of prominent netherwear absentmindedly patterned by ochred handprints.

The friends simultaneously solved that scientific riddle: what made work for the drum was coal climbing up inside; plus, you could see the braking effect, could hear its friction, when clustered lumps slumped back down.

Having glee-pointed down-channel, 'Look at that orange!', Sophy was baffled at Heather's braking the Anthromatic to a stop, then spragging it with a wedge: 'What's up?'

'Nothing, except it's time for a research plan.' Grabbing pad and pencil, the Welsh girl drew a humped graph: 'Empty, the drum turns fastest; load overmuch coal, and she won't turn at all; with just the right amount aboard, the mud rumbles off nicely.'

'And we get the most, um, I don't know what the word is.'

'Throughput.'

They needed to conduct a series of trials; having recruited her mother as Project Scribe, Sophy had a suggestion: because "Mrs Fossway" was stuffy, but "Carol" was too matey, and Jilly was right about plain "Aunt" being too jolly old-sounding, 'As you're working hard at writing, and there's already "La plume de ma tante", may Heather start calling you "Tante Plume"?'

'Well, that would be delightf–'

'Which, being translated into English,' Heather pogoed, 'is Aunty Plum!'

Sophy must rush for Tŷ Bach, there to snutter safely.

Resistance was useless; Carol sighed, 'If you insist.'


Heather resolved, 'For each test, we must know how much coal.'

Sophy frowned, 'What – weigh every fill with Jilly's kitchen scales?'

Carol said measuring the anthracite by volume should be accurate enough.

'Plastic flowerpots!' Heather rushed to where Jill stashed them; she and Sophy quickly opted for a simple tally system, using same-sized containers filled level. Now the experiment proper could begin: a one-pot fill, then a two, then a three…

'Having agreed what "clean" means,' Carol recommended, 'so that you're consistent, deciding when to stop the machine.'

Bigger loads taking longer, the girls left Aunty Plum in charge. First, they scrabbled more coal up; next, they commandeered the old incinerator. Basically a metal dustbin with a perforated bottom,

Heather proposed standing it beside the stream: 'Because the sun should warm the thing well, it should make an ideal coal dryer.'

But, no: they realised that emptying out fuel afterwards would have meant reaching deeply, and therefore dirtily, down inside the incinerator with the stubby shovel. So, abandoning it where they'd intended to set it up, back to using fish boxes.

Seven potfuls making the Anthromatic painfully slow, they ditched that trial; Carol suggested, 'To help digest the results, how about a brew-up?'

Heather winked, 'Plus Digestives…?'

Sophy sat back: 'A four-pot charge is best, then.'

'But,' Carol cautioned, 'does that graph tell you everything?'

Heather twigged, 'There's also how long emptying and refilling take.'

Her Aunty Plum turned the page over: 'I timed that, too; pretty consistent, you were.'

Soon, consensus: four and a half pots at a time was optimum. 'That's at this depth setting,' Heather reminded. 'Now we must re-set the beam, and start testing again.'

Sophy doubted they'd see much difference: 'Basically, it's the stream's speed which dictates the drum's spin rate; surely the Anthromatic must rotate so many times to clean a batch, and that's that?' But while the others went indoors to wash up she stayed to keep watch on Trial 2A, prepared to be proved wrong; indeed she was *sure* the stream could work harder for them – somehow.

She'd try studying the industriously plashing device differently, as Jill did with her paintings: by backing away, eyes kept firmly on it…

Squealing with shock she toppled backwards, bottom-landing hard; meanwhile with a scrapyardy clang the girl-skittled incinerator bounced over the bank edge, and sank with a morose burp.

'RUDDY HELL!' Envisaging a dreadful smash-up with the paddle blades, a veryhurting youngster struggled to her feet… 'Phew!', the thing hadn't rolled downstream quite far enough. She calmed Heather, now approaching fast, 'I stupidly knocked that old burner in, but it hasn't affected the Anthromatic.'

Hands on hips, 'Oh, hasn't it?'

Hurt, indignant, 'NO!'

Carol, panting, 'Is she acting concussed?'

'NOTHING has happened to me, or...' A sploshy crescendo made Sophy spin about.

The Anthromatic now whirled like a crazy cement mixer, paddles ablur as if steam-powered; it was so punishing the coal, a dense ochre wake seethed seawards. She boggled, 'Eureka!'

'Never mind trial and error: thanks to your one big error,' Heather whooped, 'no more trials!'

'Yes,' Carol kissed, 'talk about stumbling upon the answer!'

Sophy folded arms: 'We've an answer, yes; but what is it?'

Heather, now lying flat on the bank to peer, 'It's about *properly* harnessing the stream: before, lots of water bypassed the paddles. Now the burner's nearly blocked the channel, most flow's squeezing through the space above – and hasn't that put a shift on it?'

'True; but,' Carol prompted; 'is something extra happening?'

The two using pallet slats to close those splashy gaps between the incinerator's ends and the bank...

'Oh, WOW!' All, but *all* the flow now breasted that bomb-like metal girth before curving into the path of the paddles, making them gallop even faster; wetly drum-tumbling over itself, the coal emitted a silvery roar. Most respectful of those whirling blades, her fingers skimming the rushing fluid's skin, a spray-drenched Sophy shouted, 'THE WATER'S DROPPING – AND ACCELERATING!'

Carol, with fresh tea and Jill's tattiest towel: 'Let's get you warm again!' *If not clean.*

Heather began, 'We force all the flow to go past the drum...'

Sophy, 'And the water backs up. Exploit its falling, and we get maximum power.'

'A dam is out, though: if the banks overflowed, we'd flood Jilly's garden.'

'A weir, then, with a central slot. And ideally,' Sophy curved her hand, 'a shaped chute, with sides, to keep the water pushing the paddles round 'til it reaches the lower level.'

Heather frowned, 'I think it's called a flume, the thing at the end of a mill race; but I might—'

*A race!*

Both girls looked at Carol; Sophy stamped, 'Mummy, you KNEW!'

Heather moderated, 'Jilly did, too. Anyway, didn't us finding out for ourselves feel great?'

Her mate pouted, 'Only thanks to my accident,' rubbing a bum with an uncomfy memory of it.

'Darling, you'd have got there in the end. And,' Carol gulped, 'Daddy would have been so proud of you – and your Mum, I'm sure, Heather, for both persevering with the experiments. Talking of which, why don't I do a re-load?'

While she fetched her wellies the girls found they had to do a victorious dance-about, Sophy's throbbing fundament momentarily forgotten.

'Seeing as we've so much oomph, now…' No measuring for Aunty Plum: she just shovelled like a navvy, then they lowered away – making Heather hoot, 'Just LOOK at that mud coming out!'

Sophy wowed, 'Feeding the thing will keep us so busy, once we've built it a weir.'

Intending to caution 'If Jilly agrees to the idea', Carol saw the pointlessness.

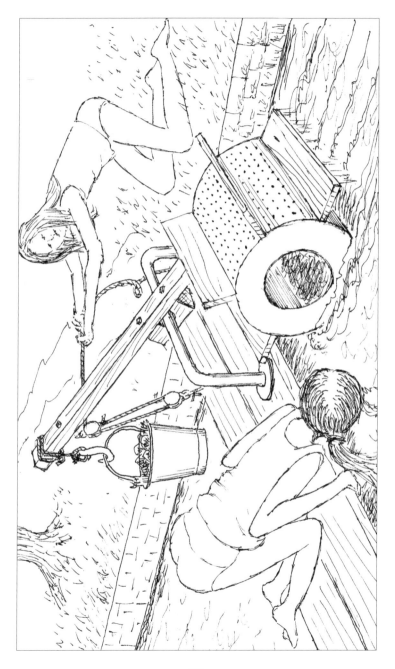

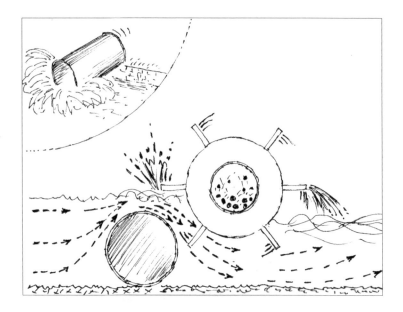

## CHAPTER 40

Promises, promises! Early that afternoon, Mogulus the would-be Engineer's Companion had fallen deeply asleep.

Seeing on waking how very far the sun had moved, anxiously he hurried cottagewards: had someone started supper? A crucial question, because he always got fed after the humans ate: any delay to their meal was, therefore, a grave matter.

No need to panic: Carol was preparing meat; already the cooker was hot. Good eyework having won him a long white drink she stroked, 'No girls to play with, Puss: they've gone swimming.'

'Maow!'

'That's right: never mind.'

*I can still go and see what they've been up to.*

*

Jill grinned, 'Congratulations, you two: what splendid strumbling!'

That baffled them both: *How does she know?*

She pointed, chuckling: some way offshore spread a great area of buff-coloured water.

'Actually,' Heather sniggered, 'Aunty Plum did that.'

Sophy swallowed, 'I n-never thought about the pollution.'

'Whatever,' Jill chuckled, 'it did me a huge favour. D'you see all these elephant tracks in the sand…? I'd not been here long when an utterly obnoxious family appeared: standing behind me while I drew, making ignorant remarks; swinging on that willow branch and breaking it; always, all of them shouting. But then, while they were swimming, the brook suddenly turned brown; and, my dears, you should have heard the screams! Thought it was sewage, didn't they? That sent 'em packing!'

Sophy, amused but not satisfied: 'I know the mud's only a form of iron, but I don't like the idea of upsetting the sea, as it were. Instead of your nightmare family, suppose that some nature-loving people had come down?'

Heather knew: 'Like the Grams. Horrible, to have spoilt their afternoon.'

Jill's voice was studiedly level; 'Are we abandoning the Anthromatic project, then?'

The Fossway brain squirmed, 'But it might get you all your winter fuel…'

'…And although we aren't stealing nasty Nigel Cranston's anthracite because he hasn't the mining rights,' Heather gloated, 'getting the stuff free from his mine does appeal deliciously.'

Indeed; thus poor Sophy got even more discombobulated.

'Off and swim, girls: as the sea's always inspiring, I've a notion you'll devise a solution. Anyway, do watch how the tide's dispersing that brown splurge: soon gone, I reckon, and no real harm done.'

Within the low tide reef they discovered the entrance to a girlable gully, and must investigate.

Some storm-smoothed boulders so shallowed its floor in places, like seals the friends had to skin-slip over; eventually, at this long rock trench's far end, a handsome-sized secret pool rewarded their exploring.

After much diving, they sun-soaked side by side in its shallows.

'Did you mind Mummy mentioning your mum?'

'Sophes, I really liked having my missing her linked with you missing your dad.'

*Yes: sympathy in balance.* 'Got to tell you, Heth: I had a big catch-up prayer for Carson and Sam this morning. I saw one of the Marine Patrols, and suddenly realised–'

'I saw the same 'plane, and that made *me* pray! So,' Heather kissed, 'we're bang up to date with thinking about the boys, hmm?'

'And caring for Tracker, if we visit this evening?'

'Okay; but if that's the plan and,' Heather stirred up to an amber kneel, 'we've to brainstorm Dad after supper about the Sediment Problem then we,' she flop-launched towards the pool's other end, had better SHIFT IT!'

*

*I'm bored.*

Drift Cottage was such a good exploration and hunting base and, unlike Cambridgeshire, no hated roads constrained his peregrinations; thus, since arriving, Mogulus had seldom wanted for pastimes. That evening, though, he got fed up waiting for the humans to get their eating-from things wet and then dry again – what *was* that about? – and come to the stream.

When the friends did appear, therefore, they found him springing back and forth across the narrow neck of The Mist Pool, as the girls now called it: the masonry-walled pound the stream entered on coming under the bank hedge. This would have been rectangular but for those two projecting ashlar piers which, pinching its middle, almost made it a figure of eight.

After they'd chuckled at those feline antics, Jill tutted 'I must clear this area of plants, soon.' Indicating the wild irises growing thereabouts, 'They are pretty in spring, but I shouldn't tolerate them.'

'Mioo!', Mogulus agreed from the far bank.

'In fact...', and the artist was off to fetch boots and tools.

'Because mud collects round anything's roots,' Granny explained. 'So, before long, self-seeded trees could be destabilising the walls.'

Hugh rumbled Volvowards, 'Reckon I'd better get wellied, too.'

Sophy, quietly, 'We were supposed to be discussing...'

Her mother kissed, 'Your machine's just over there; wait and see, hmm?'

Heather beckoned, 'Those flags can be replanted further down-stream where they'll cause no harm: let's get containers for them.'

Her day spent mostly drawing, the artist relished some physical exercise in the evening's cool; also, she and Hugh could together manhandle those tenacious rhizome clumps with ease.

He stood in the stream, clearing beneath with a spade while from the piers her fork prised; as plants tore free he craned them over to the girls' fish boxes on the other bank.

As the first pier end cleanly emerged, Granny called, 'What's that deep cut?'

At the stonework's very point, a vertical gouge: neat; evenly deep, deliberately made. Hugh probed about the other pier… 'Aha!' There was a corresponding groove.

Warwickshire has many inland waterways; Sophy exclaimed, 'Just like those places on the canals, where the repair gangs can drop boards in to isolate a section.'

'Okay,' Heather understood; 'but why the need to seal off a tiny pound six feet square?'

Her Aunty Plum's 'Good point!' sounded uneasy: her daughter already had two pairs of rusty undies and an ochre-leoparded vest; just when the Anthromatic project might peter out because of Sophy's pollution concerns, answering Heather's question might require industrial archaeology of the wettest, filthiest sort. She sighed inside, *Mustn't discourage, though.*

Mrs Haroldston's different tack: 'Without worrying *why* somebody wanted stop boards, that pound closed off from the stream would make a pretty lily pond.'

Sophy tingled, 'How deep might it be, d'you think, completely dredged?'

Her mother muttered, 'You would ask that.' *More blooming mud!*

Heather chin-stroked, 'We'd have to dig a test hole – underwater.' *And how messy would* that *be?*

Sophy fizzed, 'What about keeping fish, like the monks used to?'

'They'd escape,' Jill folded arms, 'first time the beck spated. So, instead, consider stocking it with girls, eh? Separated from the main flow, with those overhanging branches lopped back…'

Heather jigged, 'A plunge pool for us, which the sun would warm up a thundering treat!'

Hugh reached to cuff, 'LANGUAGE!' Then mused, 'Hmm: thirty-six cubic feet per foot depth: potentially, that is a *thundering* lot of captured warmth. Which a heat pump would–'

'Boss,' Sophy seized his arm, 'could this work? We isolate the pound from the stream; we set the Anthromatic's pivot frame up on that pier; we take the paddles off the washer drum and fit them onto a separate wheel, which we flume the stream to. Meanwhile, on the other side of the divide…'

'Gubber me,' Heather hugged, 'you're a thundering GENIUS! That way, all the washed-off mud gets trapped in the pound!'

He beamed, 'Well done, our Sophy!'

'Mao-ooh!', Mogulus protested.

Jill stroked, 'It's okay, cleverclogs, Mummy agrees: half the credit to Sophy; the rest to you for luring us here.'

Heather said, 'I'd wondered how we'd build a weir; now, no we don't need one: that's neat.'

'As you say,' Granny nodded, 'No weir. But how to close the pound off? Judging from those recesses, the boards were hefty ones – nearly railway sleeper thick.' They had lots of timber at Bishop's Watch, but nothing approaching that size.

Heather frowned most frowningly.

Superstitiously, Sophy did as before, except for first checking there was nothing behind: pondering eyes fixed on the gap between the piers, she began backing slowly away; meanwhile her friend settled cross-legged on the bank, brow wrinkled…

'Two brains,' Jill observed, 'under pressure.'

Sophy jolted, 'There *won't* be any pressure: we're not draining the pound.'

Heather finger-clicked, 'So a coffer dam in corrugated iron would do! And Gareth salvaged loads of the stuff from a barn the gale flattened.'

'We've timber,' Sophy asked, 'for a support frame?'

'No problem!'

Carol's hands on her daughter's shoulders: 'Pray, who might "we" be? Do you forget that the Anthromatic only exists thanks to a certain skilled engineer?'

Sophy, sighing, apologised to The Boss for being presumptuous; Heather harrumphed, 'Sorry!'

Hugh waded down-channel to peer deeply… 'Actually, if Jill will donate that incinerator as an ad-hoc water wheel, fixing the paddles to it shouldn't take long; nor should bolting its bottom onto the drum's drive pulley.'

'But, Hugh…!'

'Relax, Carol,' he grinned, 'and hear me buy time: these mudlarks must first dredge the gap between the piers, with a good margin either side, to discover if there's a sill: we'll need to know, for designing the dam.'

Jill, firmly, 'And you young ladies *won't* be doing that tomorrow. Carol was cook today; and, as the forecast's good, she must have a day out somewhere lovely – i.e., completely mud-free.'

'Indeed,' said Granny, not to be contradicted, 'Carol must take a walk *now*: she hasn't been out at all today. The girls can whizz up to see Tracker; after browsing Jill's sketches, I'll see them to bed. Meanwhile, I'm sure Hugh won't mind helping Jill tidy up.'

No rush home needed to prepare for the morrow, he explained: 'The answering machine's not caught any calls since yesterday.'

As much as cats can, Puss smiled: his paw-play with that buttoned box at Bishop's Watch had worked.

Jill breezed, 'Actually, Hugh, might you nip down to Mill Cove? Walking back with the girls, I clean forgot about the rubbish sacks I'd filled.'

'Gladly – unless Carol intended seeking solitude there…?'

The lady in question shook her head: 'If you'll wait for me to fetch a sweater…'

When they returned, Granny handed Carol a folded sheet…

TIDES IDEAL MOEL-RHOS SANDS TOMORROW — H SAYS FAB PLACE AND POSSIBLY SURFY. NOTHING SAID TO BRON BUT WE KNOW SHE COULD HAVE DAY OFF — PLS WILL U INVITE HER TONIGHT IF U APPROVE? XXX S.

P.S. (V CHEEKY) IF U LIKE INVITE BOSS TOO THEN VOLVO WOULD FIT US ALL IN.

'Their plan,' Granny hahummed. 'However, we're now implicated – eh, Jilly?'

In whose hands, a bowl of egg and cress sandwich filling.

# CHAPTER 41

Backdropped by dramatic cliffs, that glorious beach which looked out to those wildgrown tide-raced islands wasn't at all thronged, thanks to the long walk down.

That long walk, during which Taggle had burned off many miles' worth of excess energy, ever egging everyone on; thus, when they reached the strand, he behaved with exemplary obedience on the lead, and even calmly volunteered to guard their dry sand encampment while they swam.

Carol and the three girls had a marvellous surf-session; then, leaving Aunty Plum to "scribble" and Bronny to sunbathe, Sophy and Heather went exploring in cozzies and gymshoes.

They took the terrier along, and were so glad they did: as they were passing a shallow sandy pool and waving hello to the girl of about three who was brownly paddling in it, all splashes and chuckles, he it was who spotted a lunatic black labrador hurtling along the beach on a direct collision course... and, reckoning this the only sure-fire strategy, launched himself ballistically towards the out-of-control creature.

The labrador was that crazy, it didn't heed the girls' screams of panic as they jumped to protect the unaware child, never even registered Taggle approaching like a cannonball, and thus neither slowed down nor took evasive action; consequently, with the most almighty biffing sound, the two dogs collided.

Tag having the lesser mass, he glanced away from the impact point and, seeing many stars, went tumbling across the hard sand...

But he'd saved the day, by deflecting the mad dog from its original trajectory: it, its speed hardly diminished, pistoned past the pool's margin, carried on another fifty brainless yards, and whanged into a jazzy windbreak, skittling the elderly people within off their camping chairs and wrecking their picnic...

And, having scalded itself badly by toppling the oldies' primus stove and kettle, the insane thing, again running fast, now looped round through a game of cricket, and would have no doubt caused more damage and hurt on its way back up the beach if the stocky gentleman at the crease hadn't deftly caught it smack in the middle of its fevered head with his bat.

Such a blazing row, there was, when the unapologetic owners of the labrador arrived to confront the equally unrepentant foundryman who'd floored it; but that fracas was far enough off not to bother the girls. Sophy was too busy calming poor little Jenny, who now sort-of understood what might have happened, and Heather her mother Karen, who definitely did: 'My God, she could have been killed!'

'Well,' patted the Pembroke girl, 'thanks to Tag here, she wasn't.'

Reading the lady's feelings, identifying a fellow felophile, Sophy must point it out: 'Doesn't this incident prove perfectly that there are both very good and very bad dogs? I'm not exaggerating when I say that Taggle would have died, if necessary, to save Jenny's life.'

'Reff!' He delicately licked the little girl's hand as she stretched tentatively to stroke his head.

'Yes, I see that now,' the lady conceded. 'So – as his owners aren't here, how do I express my profound thanks...?'

Heather grinned, 'If you've any biscuits, he'll be the one eternally in *your* debt!'

Having beachcombed all of Moel-Rhos Sands, then reconnoitred further, Hugh's lunchtime report: 'Beyond that headland is a smaller beach. Reaching it's rather a scramble; but the waves look as good, and only one family was on it; plus, chaps, there's a Monster Artefact to ponder.'

Those people had gone; the whole of that beach Hugh had "discovered" to themselves, therefore... Except for a distant boy – rugby wasp-stripes, jeans, and wellies – who was busy at something amongst large boulders.

Heather identified that crook-topped iron post: 'A steam engine crankshaft!'

The ship, Bronwen concluded, had foundered very many years before: there was scant other evidence of a wreck.

Sophy, perusing the map, 'Is this called Albinoni Bay because...?'

He nodded, 'A very early paddle steamer, she was.'

Clearly her wish, in the water Hugh behaved wonderfully daddishly with Sophy. Striding out to have his daughter straightway declare war, with a tickly waist-grab he hurled that cackling waterwitch into a bursting wave; he then repulsed a giggly Fossway challenge similarly – indeed, Sophy being lighter, he could fling her considerably further. And, immediately, Heather again…

During a ceasefire for bodysurfing, 'Sophes, doesn't Tracker at The Sands seem YEARS AGO?'

Eventually chilled by that romping whiteness, they strode ashore – Sophy delighted to see that Bronny, surfing further down the strand with Mummy, had changed into the bikini lent her by Jill.

After squash, the three girls felt like sunbathing – and talking, of course.

Hugh started changing; anticipating his need to beachcomb, as had Taggle, so did Carol.

Bringing the rucksack, she sought dry driftwood for Jill; Hugh, too, until finding a twelve foot plank his shoulder must go under: 'Highly useful, this!'

They got quite near that industrious lad before he noticed them: politely, his local accent strong, 'Do you have a knife, please?' Having discovered a truly handsome length of rope and spent ages on untangling, he'd found it was looped under a boulder, was trapped.

Hugh had; 'But first…' He fiddled his plank's end under the stone: 'When I lever, Carol, will you watch? Meanwhile, young man…'

'I promise I won't try reaching under unless your wife says it's safe to…'

Success – when, darting like a mongoose, Tag it was who snatched the rope free.

They helped the boy to coil his superb prize; then Carol asked, 'Could you do with a drink?'

Rhys Morgan, Moel-Rhos born and raised. Originally Merchant Navy, his father worked on Arabian Gulf oil refineries for months at a time; Mrs Morgan was secretary to 'a large farmer'.

Lucky that his grandparents lived close by, Rhys helped on their smallholding for pocket money; crewing on Grandad's diminutive potting boat out from Saint Brides Haven, more coins for him after the fourth crab: 'The one which pays for the petrol, we calls 'un.'

No surprise, Carol thought, that his beach trips were more about treasure than leisure.

As they approached conglomerated knapsacks, towels, and lotion-gleaming females, his way of gulp-joking 'Three m-mermaid daughters!' suggested that this only child hadn't close girl cousins, either.

Hugh, carefully explaining about not being the lady's husband, appreciated shapely Bronny towel-wrapping herself; readying for an overawed shaking of hands, 'Now, Rhys, this is—'

'You're Heather Haroldston! I recognised you from the newspaper; mind, I'd already heard about your amazing gallop through the Peninsula grapevine.' Turning, 'And you were just as brave, Sophy Fossway, riding into the sea. Gosh, fancy meeting you both at once!'

Cheekily, affectionately, 'And you're honoured to meet me, Bronwen Landore, just because *I'm* from *Swansea*! Bloody nice rope, by the way.'

They gave Rhys plus his rope a lift home via Moel-Rhos Post Office and its ice cream freezer. Waving them gratefully away, 'I wish we weren't busy tomorrow: I'd have loved to have seen your horses working at the fête! Anyway, if my grandies can't manage the Talbenny Haven regatta, I'll work on Mum to let me cycle over.'

'If she does,' Heather called back, 'Take care in the lanes!'

'Her wish is his command,' Bronny whispered to discretely nodding Sophy – then foghorned over second gear acceleration, 'I said "DELICIOUS MOEL-RHOS SANDS!"'

'Aye,' chuckled Hugh, seeing through. 'Hooray for Albinoni Bay!'

Drift Cottage contingent safely home, he dangled car keys: 'To the stable, please, Chauffeur!'

Clicking her seat belt, 'Would you mind, only as far as Tracker's turning? Sabrina mightn't have found time for him, and anyway I've lots to tell.'

She backed down very well. After rorping on the handbrake, a suntanned smile: 'That – was –smashing!' *Being treated as one of the family.*

He knew: 'And you were smashing with the girls – unlike lots of young women, who'd pay almost any forfeit not to play the big sister.'

She sighed, 'But Heather and Sophy are so loveable; the only time I've known them squealy, which can irk, was today – and that, because you giving them the Full Neptune got 'em so excited!' She sighed, 'Actually, I got jealous watching those games because Dad never–'

Disbelieving the rear view mirror, she flung herself out: 'Yankee Boy? TRACKER?'

Hugh hurried after: where the heck was this alert animal who was always there first?

She grinned back from the gate, 'Panic over: he's up on the ridge, with Sabrina.'

'Phew! On to the stable, then?'

Head shaking, 'I'll stay here, please, to catch up with both. But before you go – I didn't thank Mrs Fossway for our conversations.'

He ribbed, 'Talk with her today, did you? Can't say I noticed.'

Hands on hips, 'Mostly about university, actually.'

'Good! She's a savvy lady; I'd been wondering for a while – Mum had, too – what would be best for you, with your brains; I'll gladly pass your thanks on.'

'Do give my love to Gran, too, Mr Hugh. And, one last thing,' with a cocky wink, 'I can only ever be a chauffeuse.' Turning, she blew a ripper whistle; then, for a huge-armed wave: 'YOO-HOO!'

CHAPTER 42

The Second World War had ended on 15th August 1945.

Ringing their school bell like blazes, the Colliers' Quay children bent its bracket; and, of course, The Davy Lamp caroused rowdily; but most resounding in memory, to this day, is that railway detonator which got tossed into the beach bonfire at the evening's end: "Such a big bang, it blew the gubber out!", as old Mr Solva loved to recall.

To formally celebrate Allied victory, however, the hamlet had to wait: it took weeks, months sometimes, for servicemen and servicewomen posted overseas to be repatriated and demobbed. Only when all who were going to had safely returned – some who'd been prisoners of war needing much recuperation – did people feel like planning a Proper Do.

It is now unclear why that original 1946 Celebration of Peace was on the first Thursday after the County Show; but as country thinking favours "Same again, only aim for better", and memory's a funny thing, by 1980 plenty of folk were insisting that Colliers' Quay fêtes had *always* been held on the Thursday afternoon following the County Show weekend, "since before Victoria's reign."

This, Sabrina's strategy.

Driven by Mr Madoc or Mr Solva Senior, Tracker and Aberdare would do turns with the wagon, Charlie and Sophy making one guard & ticket collector team and Heather and Bronny the other. Led by Sabrina herself or, eager accomplice, Kaycee Fleischmann, placid Lamorna would take three littluns at a time on shoreside ambles.

Early in the day, the wagon would be towed over by Land-Rover; taking the old Coal Road, the horses could avoid those unenjoyable lanes. Later in the afternoon Charlie, Heather, and Sophy must lead them over the causeway and up the path to Anvil House, then head back down for the Rowtow.

Previously a stable, Alice's garage retained its hayframes and water trough; Charlie was volunteering to sleep above, like a stable-lad of old. Accordingly this time the girls rejected the Guest Suite (own bathroom and a great view of Saint Brides Bay) in favour of the stooped-roof maids' attic overlooking the cobbled carriageyard.

Jill *would* have the Guest Suite, please; and she would bring painting gear, aiming to capture the next day's dawn. She'd be supervising the youngsters, as Alice was so tied up with the fête; Bronny had originally offered, but Sabrina had spoken to the artist: 'I'm hoping to persuade her down to the evening hop.'

Carol would help set the fête up; then, some folk being attracted to that celebrating hamlet and its hinterland for the wrongest reasons, she'd head back to Drift Cottage and hold the fort, Davy Crockett style, with faithful Trapper Mogulus.

Only one planning hiatus, there'd been: notwithstanding the gents' intention to posh it up, Heather had blazed, 'We're NOT wearing jackets and joddies: they'd be too HOT!' Sophy had backed her, privately reasoning that *Sloppy jodhpurs look so sorry, and ones drawn on tautly get stared at far too much.*

Kaycee's transatlantic solution had been, 'Going as cowgirls: they've got jeans; me and my pals have plenty check shirts and hats! And won't every kid love pretendin' they's ridin' a stagecoach?'

Casual, and loose-fitting: Bronny'd approved on the girls' behalves; 'But,' she'd finger-wagged, 'we Brits draws the line at spurs and six-shooters! As for you, Charlie – how about a flat cap, cords, and a kerchief?'

'Tidy, Bronwen!' And NOT American.

Later Heather, mind half elsewhere, 'Charlie boy, a cat flap should really suit you.'


A lovely morning, Nature seemingly unaware of how ominous the forecast.

When the girls and Charlie came past Drift Cottage with three brightshining steeds, Jill and Carol took such proud photos; then, through the gate and away.

Such joy, together climbing that rise: the jingle of links, glittery brasses dancing, grassy breath tasting the breeze – and, now, views over the hedgebanks.

Sophy wondered if Miss Gwinear had ever come that way on horseback as a girl.

'She certainly never rode on a haulage pony: the drift closed long afore. Not a good combination, anyway, going-out dresses and laden coalbaskets. But,' Heather smiled across, 'wouldn't a friendly ploughboy like Charlie Solva let a poor good girl, traipsing dutifully to Colliers' on onerous errands, up onto his horse?'

'I'd have even welcomed an apprentice witch like Patsy Flange – for the pleasure, later, of pushing her off into a pigpond... arse-first, of course, to best see her face!'

As the cackling subsided he continued, 'But you're forgetting: Miss G's grandparents owned a donkey.'

Heather's words pictured them: older Henry leading the animal; clean-pinnied Millicent in one pannier basket, circumspect sailor in creaking crow's nest; opposite, her counterbalance, cautious and much the quietest Tudor.

Sophy sighed, 'Her poor brothers! I'm sorry for forgetting them just then, 'cos I know she never did.'

A pause on the ridge; inevitably, for the vista was stupendous.

In gin-clear air, all seemed closer: Prescelly's heathery Cerrig Lladron peak, emerald dairy farm pastures, duller green windbreak tree plantations, pale spreads of barley; then, apparently floating above Saint Brides Bay's luminous blue, rugged Skomer, gannet-glaciered Grassholm, and the lonely Smalls lighthouse far beyond.

Sliding the steamer lanes, eyes now imagining travelled past South Bishop… And pictured an other Ireland, there, unseen but more than mirage, saint-fabled beyond that sharp horizon brim.

Lots learned in the previous two weeks, Sophy sighed, 'This clarity can't last.'

Charlie pointed past Ramsey's peak at vapour piling: 'There's our later trouble, sure enough.'

Three horses; one stomp.

Down into the woodland, Charlie first: 'I'll warn you about troublesome branches.'

Heather exhaled, 'Quite the gent!' Then, 'In places, Sophes, you'll be flat on Tracker's back.' She mutterchuckled, 'Seeing as he's half-giraffe.'

Charlie's scold put up a pigeon: 'If Yankee Boy later on bites your bum, Heather Haroldston, you'll be wholly to blame.'

Sophy, again here thinking of bygone children labouring, 'Charlie, if we'd been born when Miss Gwinear was, would you have wanted to work with horses?'

'Lovely, when it was like this. But every day, any weather, always up very early…? And tilling each acre meant miles walked, steering the tackle. I think that this autumn, Sophy Fossway, you should come to an old-style ploughing match.' Loving saying her name.

'I'd really like to!' *But HOW?*

Heather, palming sycamore leaves aside; 'Then how about a job horse-hauling boats, as they did here?' She patted Lamorna, 'You mightn't have had the stamina, girl, but Tracks and Abbey would.'

He twisted round, 'D'you know how they did it?'

'Old Jack Sound and Alice Williams helped us work it out… Hey, chaps, shall we forget the fête stalls, hoppit earlier, and go up to Alice's via the shore and the old incline? You'd understand the system, then, Charlie.'

Aberdare coughed, pointedly.

Heather, apologetically, 'You *and* the horses.'

'Anyway, Charlie,' Sophy said, 'Let's do as Heather says, for their sakes. After all that hot tarmac, I'm sure the three would like a splash-about in the shallows.'

He had just called, 'Limekilns, ho!'

CRATATATASH!, a chair-stacked farm trailer bouncing a rutty gateway.

DAP!, DAP!, marquee guy rope irons going in.

BUPP!, SKRAK!, TUZZZZZ!, was an amplifier being tested; then, across the hot salty flats...

Heather gasped, 'That's lovely music! Stirring, too.'

Three pairs of large pointed ears agreed.

Sophy knew: 'Hamish MacCunn.'

Charlie thumbsed-up, 'Gramps has this piece on a record.' Then, the round kiln walls strangely echoing his frown, 'I hope it's not too prescient.'

Heather, fooling neither her mates nor the horses, 'Remind me what it's called...?'

'*Land of the Mountain and the Flood*', he and Sophy synchronised.

The gents looked splendid: one in a red waistcoat, one in a yellow; both, cravated, wore brass-buttoned jackets, twill trousers, mirror-buffed boots.

Heather simpered, 'La, but if it isn't the Duke of Wellington and The Count of Monte Cristo!'

Charlie's Grandpa, crisply, 'Calamity Jane, I presume.'

Mr Madoc ahemmed, 'Now, before we get whoever's hauling first between the shafts – what to do with these Lifeboat donation boxes?'

Charlie pointed, 'Hung from the wagon's lamp brackets?'

'Good man! Hop aboard: in the box under the bench seat are wire and pliers.'

Coming along on their trial trip before heading home, Carol complimented 'the smoothness of the ride – and the coachman, too.'

Even in those outfits, jolly warm work for the girls – but so rewarding, because children loved travelling "just like the Queen". And rewarded, too: twice over from the thronging Davy Lamp came trays bearing shandy and lemonade.

The horses were good as gold: Aberdare didn't flinch at some idiot's mongrel barking manically at him, ('Should have stamped on it!', Heather had growled); when a vintage car backfired close by, Tracker just shook his head.

But didn't the creatures get thirsty? Sent to the pub kitchen with buckets, a returning Sophy worried, 'It's rather brownish water.'

Mr Solva Senior sniffed; 'That's the Guinness, m'love. A dash each for the boys is a small treat without bad consequences, see?'

Grabbing a break from the raffle stand, Jilly fizzed, 'We've sold so many tickets! And as for folk complimenting those portraits in the paper…'

'They were smashing,' Charlie said. 'I cut 'em out, to keep.'

Heather nudged; Sophy tingled.

'Anyway,' Jill held out the knapsack, 'In case it pours, Sophes has Anna's sailing oilskins, and the army cape should suit you, Heather. Charlie, you must hope it holds off 'til Anvil House: there's Hector's waxed jacket hung behind the scullery door, as Alice says you can wear.'

'Righto!'

Sophy peered, horse into nosebag, 'Anything else?'

'Your older costume. Mum says, wear it underneath for the Rowtow.'

Charlie nodded, 'And hadn't you better warn Sophy to take off her watch, and empty her pockets of money?'

Jill mock-thumped, 'Not now you have!'

Sophy frowned, 'Because of the extra weight…?' Then she recalled the fate of coxes after races.

Jill cuddled, 'As they wouldn't dare fling Heather in, Sophy, because she's still recovering, they really shouldn't dunk you.'

Charlie said, 'I'll speak to Mr Sound.'

Fête-lured trippers busied the causeway: wagon work over, the friends' safest route to Anvil House was going to be via the incline, anyway. Setting out across the sand Heather wondered, 'Why in this heat did these boys want their heavy harnesses kept on?'

Sophy shrugged, 'Pride in the day's work?'

Charlie tickled Aberdare, 'They're pretending to be stalwart boat-haulers, summoned to the harbour mouth.'

The girls knew from coal hunting where the stream bed was firmest; all three horses enjoyed splooshing across. But then Aberdare and Tracker again came over determined: instead of continuing to the far shore, they'd rather follow the water down.

Heather reasoned, 'If it's nice for their tooties...'

Charlie concurred; 'But mind, the tide's turned: us mustn't let these saddles get soaked.'

Contentedly they stroshed, negotiating beached boats, buoys, ropes, and sinkers. Far above swirled a yiarking gull-throng; yet miles higher, mares-tail clouds were frisking quickly in.

'Look,' Charlie showed Sophy, 'they're not riding thermals: as Gramps predicted, wind coming before rain.'

Heather halted Lamorna, cupped ears, then caught up again: 'It must've been blowing in the Bay a while already: big waves are already breaking, out and round.'

'But maybe they're not down to this wind,' Charlie muttered pensively.

Sophy studied The Furzy's skyline trees: yes, their tops were moving well, and– 'Isn't that Jack Sound, waving from Corner Wharf with an, um...?'

'Funny looking thing,' Heather squinted.

'A surveyor's whatsit,' Charlie said. 'With a wheel which–'

Which just then came loose, and frisbeed down into the water.

Sophy, seeing Mr Sound's reaction, 'Charlie, is it floating?'

'Hard to see; I think so.'

Bringing Tracker hard alongside Lamorna, 'Heather, have the knapsack; and now, please take my clothes.' *Undressing on horseback ought to work!*

Reddening, turning Aberdare about, 'This isn't for us, mate!'

'Charlie, WAIT! Underneath I'm in my swimmers: I put 'em on in the pub loo, lest we got short of time later.'

Creak-cricked by bubbleups, the tide's olive dark inflow was invading the ripply sand fast, overrunning furrow after furrow; mid-stream, meanwhile, foam streaks charged towards the causeway arches.

For show, Kaycee had equipped Lamorna frontier scout style: her saddle carried rolled groundsheets, its pommel sported a coil of cord, the very stuff Heather and Sophy had found during the Talbenny Haven beach clean. Urging Heather to pass him the latter, Charlie looped an end: 'Here, Sophy, as that's quite a current…'

Her friend having jumped down, Heather headed Lamorna and Tracker shorewards.

The rope waisted Sophy safely, she hoped: *I should be able to slip free, if it snags.*

Eyes already pleading, he asked, 'Promise me that you'll give up, rather than take a silly risk?'

'Yes, Charlie.'

Heather, 'TARGET IN SIGHT!'

He pointed, 'Wade in diagonally, Sophes, so the line can't get in the way; if you have to swim, just head straight for the wheel. Shout "Go" to be brought in: "Pull" might sound like "Help" to anyone watching. Shout properly for help, and you *know* I'll be straight there.'

Thanking him with her eyes, tummy feeling funny, 'Here goes…'

*So warm!*

It was soon grasped away, that thought, as pushy fast water piled, gobbling, against Sophy's legs. Such wild turbulence she felt about her feet: halting to adjust the rope, immediate undermining staggered her.

Charlie called, 'Turn sideways to the current!'

That made progress easier – but not easy, for bait diggers' pits were everywhere. Mind, that hurtling flow had one bonus: the big and therefore well-equipped shore crabs scuttlebowling past were too busy dodging hungry flatfish – *And can't they whizz!* – to bother with indignantly nipping her toes, punishment for territorial infringements.

*This is the stream bed.* For here her costume touched in, usual breathtake; then, next step, she was waist deep, and–

'SOPHES, HERE IT COMES!'

Leaning, 'I CAN SEE–!'

It collapsed, then, the sand ridge she stood on: toppled splutteringly into frothy flotsam, she breast stroked powerfully with her arms while her legs skew-kicked to avoid the rope. No time to think about how fast being swept upriver, the girl plugged away towards the wheel…

'GOT IT, CH–!'

The estuary gargled into her throat as this time Sophy was grabbed right under; then the something-caught rope, tugging harder, flipped her upside down... *But, dammit, I've STILL GOT THE WHEEL!* Squirming about, she found the surface, belchcoughed hippopotamusly loud and, hugely relieved to find her tether free again, bellowed 'GO!'

His end of the cord tied to Abbey's harness, Charlie turned right around to face backwards; his 'Mate, I'm really trusting you!' got rumbled acknowledgement.

*Sophy's sweeping along!* They must take her in tow very carefully, this so-important girl... Suddenly certain, *Here's how!*, he kneed gently, 'Easy back!'

Aberdare obeyed; Charlie coiled in rope until, 'Whoa!'

Heather gaped: Charlie was backing Aberdare obliquely *away* from Sophy; *Ruddy good horse-handling, mind!* Then she understood: he couldn't haul their mate out until she was as far upriver from him as she'd managed to at first wade the other way; crucially, when the time came, the rope mustn't snatch.

Again, 'Easy back!', now letting rope run.

Heather prayed, 'Good Luck, both!'

Shouting 'HERE GOES, SOPHY!' Charlie started gripping, braking the rope...

*Christ, his hands'd be scorching if it wasn't wet!*

...until, 'WHOA!'

The lifeline linking Heather's two friends was suddenly taut: good old Charlie having arrested Sophes like a 'plane landing on an aircraft carrier she was, tidestream bow-waving about her, now swinging shorewards on its radius. 'Bloody well done!' she murmured, eyes wet; hastily hitching the horses somehow, she hurried to the tide's edge.

Expecting to be snatched like a sack from a mail train, Sophy had wriggled herself around in that silent swiftness; she'd been floating on her back, left hand trailing Jack's wheel and right hand behind her head gripping the rope, when the pull came...

'Phew!', because the rolling surge beneath her *did* buoy her face clear, as she'd hoped; in this manner she was towed in, contemplating further sky-changes quite calmly... Except, her submerged ears only heard bubbleburble: *They might be calling to me, so I'd better indicate I'm OK...*

Above a weedy-headed pill-nymph whistling ***Messing About On The River***, Heather Haroldston's face was suddenly moon-peering down.

Sophy, belly-rolling, grounded: she was in barely a foot of water.

He was suddenly helping her up, a puffing Jack Sound, to whom she handed the evidently precious wheel. 'Flipping, *flipping* well done, girl! Meaning all of you, of course – and Aberdare!'

She smiled, 'It was fun!'

'Maybe; but my heart turned over when you lurched under, I tell you!'

Heather nodded lots.

'Anyway,' he harrumphed, 'I'm SO glad you're all right and I WON'T forget this HUGE favour; but,' checking his watch, 'as to what I was about – I'll explain after the Rowtow, hmm? And off he hurried.

Her first ever hug with him: 'Thanks, Charlie! So glad you thought of the rope.'

His first ever, back: 'Stopped my breathing, though, a moment, you did.'

Heather embraced both, 'Brilliant work!' Then, arm round Sophy, she shot him a prim look...

He backed away, 'I'll see you at the wharf.'

She half peeled herself, then held her hair up; Heather brushed away weed and twiggy bits before hankying that goosy back dry... 'Okay, Sophes!'

Costume right off.

'Hello – what's this?'

Sniggered, 'You've seen it plenty of times before.'

Heather deftly plucked, and passed it over a shoulder...

A heart-shaped anthracite pebble, rainbow-deckled with flecks of mica; water-polished glass smooth, being wet made it glitter metallically: 'Oh, how *precious*!'

Passing her friend her shirt, 'It'll be safest in your button-down pocket.'

Sophy and Heather having explained the old-time boat handling, they seemed pensive, those horses huffing up the incline, well glad of only carrying youngsters.

As they climbed, ever more breeze; and gusts, now, trampolining over the treetops. Charlie said, 'A northerly's better, though, than that last blow: Anvil House is sheltered by the hill; Jill's place and the spinney will sit tight, too, while the ridges either side cop it.'

*And the stable,* Sophy thought.

A gale-rowdy Tram Gin Top, where looking up the mast was almost swoonifying: it flexed and recoiled as if those weren't low clouds racing across, but charging myth-creatures which each tugged hard at it. Sophy, scampering back to her mates, 'Whoo, how weird!'

Heather said, 'Tracks watched you jolly carefully.'

Charlie chuckled, 'Ask nicely, and I'm sure he'd winch you aloft.'

Interpreting that look, 'Sophes would likely ask emphatically nicely to NOT be hoisted.'

'Correct; and I don't care who calls me cowardly.'

Charlie, hotly, 'Nobody ever could!' Neck-craning, 'Can't think who'd persuade me up there, either.'

'But,' Sophy mysteried as they moved off, 'someone's climbed up recently.'

Heather gasped, 'If that was a dare – WOW!' Then, 'How do you know?'

'It's only visible close to: a thin cord loop going right up and down again, tied off to that cleat.'

A pilot line, precursor to heavier rope, Heather was sure.

Charlie, peering behind, 'Actually, those grass marks suggest someone used a tractor to lower it.'

'Well, while they were about it, I hope they checked the pulley,' Heather sterned. 'From right up there even a flag coming adrift could cause trouble, never mind somebody in a bosun's chair – who certainly would just be some body, afterwards!

Sophy shivered; then, 'But *who* rigged it?'

And why?

At Anvil House, not just Jill to greet them but Sabrina – and Kaycee, too: 'Coxswain Jack sure sang your praises! As y'all got delayed, we'll tend these guys while you go eat.'

# CHAPTER 43

Before setting off again, to Alice's garage – where Sabrina tutted, 'We've pampered the three, and they've definitely all they need; the boys won't settle, though.'

Sophy, contemplative, 'The noise from the woods aside, what's that deep grumping sound?'

Charlie, impressed, 'A heavy ground swell: really long waves, stirring everything right down to the sea bed. Usually caused by mid-Atlantic storms, so they're much more common in winter – but a familiar enough phenomenon to these two, so…' He shrugged.

Now Heather: 'About them insisting on bringing their harnesses here: might they, um, be like children's comforters – something reassuring in an unfamiliar place?'

So Sabrina fetched the things, and hooked them where Tracker and Aberdare could reach to sniff… 'Well, blow me down! Heather Haroldston, go to the top of the class!'


With Talbenny Haven's vicar presiding, the Rowtow competition was less profane than the practice sessions – but beerier, far noisier, and lots more profitable for the RNLI: Charlie, trawling the throng with blue boxes, had to twice run into the pub and unload.

Anonymous boats no longer; remembering a famous Victorian naval trial, paddlewheels against propellers, Jack had had signwritten on their bows *Rattler* and *Alecto*.

The Rugger Tuggers trounced their challengers: the Solva Boys, a farmer's team, and the Peninsula Paddlers from Kete, that sailing-keen village at the western end of the Milford Haven waterway: Kete, where Hugh went occasionally to meet the *Josephine,* a keen-hulled cutter-rigged ketch which sailed over from North Cornwall bringing him his solar heating components. A coin deciding, Sophy coxed them in the heat and Heather in the final – and neither got dunked afterwards.

That victory hadn't just been down to muscle power. The wind now strong and the pill full, a brisk chop was piling in, and rebounding from the causeway wall confused and highly uppity – discomforting for the farmers, to say the least. But, such a sea often being encountered at

Creampot Cove, the Rugger Tuggers had ridden it confidently, never missing a beat: so much for "playing at sailors"!

Lurchingly perched in *Alecto*'s seesawing stern, a Sophy glad of being lifejacketed and oilskinned without and sweatered and costumed beneath. With waves slapping in hard and every oarsplash wind-whiffled, of all those on the water that evening only she and cape-tented Heather had stayed anywhere approaching dry.

Because of the pill's angriness, no rowing race between the Miss Americas and the Rugger Tuggers, Jack regretfully announced – at which, someone shouted 'Here's an idea, then…!' And he reacted, 'Don't see why not.'

To each boat he allocated five Rugger Tuggers, two half-teams matched in strength; Kaycee then evenly assigned her lady rowers…

Brilliantly-conceived, this contest was; for both boats' proud crewmen were aghast at the thought of being blamed by the females aboard for not delivering the necessary power.

'…three, two, one, GO!'

And, coxing *Alecto* and *Rattler* respectively, Heather and Sophy must shout louder than ever before.

How long could this sea battle last? Sweat gleamed the gasping rowers' faces; soaking spectators with spray, their oars seemingly thrashed out steam as well.

Inexplicably taking sides as if born alleged, folk bellowed to out-blast the weather; such was the press of bodies, two wall-standing men got sploshed in. For *nothing* mattered more, in those bucking, backheaving lungburning minutes, than where that dangling rag on the water-wringing rope was…

Which eventually began creeping; and the crew saw; and, with Sophy bellowing 'HEAVE, HEAVE, **HEEEAVE!**' her boat surged…

The whistle, the flag: *Rattler* had won.

Detonating a vocal boom: one fiery ambiguity, elation and disappointment. Loud as the simultaneous discharge of opposing great-mouthed cannons, it momentarily out-roared the valley's raucous sky.

Sophy and Heather, equally heroic mascots, were shoulder-borne by American girls across the applauding causeway. Gangwayed into the pub, they were upstaired to Jill, who'd been sketching and photographing from a front window – and mugs of Horlicks, a bath, and radiatored clothes.

Bar sounds from below loud and clear through the floorboards, the hoarse two rested throats as they soaped and splashed.

Outside, away fumed unnoticed Patsy Flange: never such adulation for her, at the gymkhana or after; *Yet all those pipsqueaks did was bloody sit in boats!*

It bothered few, a bar towel covering one beer engine; then, another ran out. A third dying faded smiles and waned the hubbub… Conversation ceased, as if guillotined, when the Western Warrior Best Bitter pump broke into brassy screaming.

Someone, incredulous, 'We've drunk the gubber dry!'

Upstairs, young eyes goggled.

'There's bottled ale, yet,' calmed the landlord. 'And, thanks to last month's Christian campers, before you gubbers could sink all my ginger beers you'd have burped yourselves to death!'

Tittering into tears, the girls got Jilly going.

Commanding special respect for the Lifeboat funds she'd raised, Alice could get away with, 'Is an alcohol drought that dreadful?' She reasoned, 'This is a rough enough blow for someone somewhere to need help – whether you're rostered tonight or not.'

Farming voices protested, 'But Mrs Williams, we aren't lifeboatmen!'

She countered, 'Everyone sensible stands by in weather *this* bad – everyone! Because, who knows what help might be needed, or where? So… The soft drinks are on me!'

As the seagoing contingent cheered and Jack shook her hand, savage raps on the window and Charlie shouting: the marquee was in trouble.

'Talk,' Heather chuckled into Sophy's sud-rimmed ear over the sound of the bar emptying, 'about having your point proved!'

Sophy; who must unbath, go to the gust-rattled window, and peer.

The sky now so cloddily dark, rain was surely imminent; and flings of spray constantly showering the road suggested the wind had plenty more to say. Her eyes tracked across the causeway… On that dim far shore two hauled-up darknesses were the whalers, settled for the night: *I'm pleased Jack christened them; even if I don't understand those names,*

*I like both. I'm sure the boats do, too: it felt safe aboard either this evening, despite the bumpitiness, because they seemed happier. After all, they say boats have spirits, like us; and could any human gladly go through life literally anonymous? And here's a coincidence: when he's happiest, Mogulus is a proper old rattler!*

Thinking a prayer to those craft didn't seem strange: *Thank you, both, for serving us so well and seeing us safe, today – and please forgive those farmers who have no time for seafaring, and boats. I know your sort of craft has saved a lot of sailors' lives, because Jack said so; even if you aren't as young as you were, wouldn't you still do your best for anyone needing help at sea?*

Seeing spinal chill-twitches as the girl pressed a storm-ear to the glass Jill said, 'Get dressed now, sweetheart; then you can open it for a proper listen.'

Sophy had sparkled up the taps; Heather, tidemark awayed, 'I'll cut the light, now, and we'll hear much better.'

Jill undid the catch…

A lucky lull let them distinguish the clasheting of the wood they'd descended that morning from the hissroar of The Furzy's conifers; from Saint Brides Bay, all the while, the groundswell's relentless arrival: piledriver thumps and profound growls.

'It's worsening,' Sophy whispered, 'as Alice said it would.'

The three prayed for all people at sea; then, before that southbound catspaw they'd spotted spray-cresting in could come slamming, Sophy latched the casement closed. As Heather snapped the light back on, the lobby was a-clatter and a-chatter again; and suddenly, below, instruments were thrumming into tune.

Jill guessed, 'They've struck the big tent; the band will play here instead. I know Jack planned demonstrating knots in the other bar this evening for folk who didn't fancy dancing, but I'm sure everyone'll rub along together.'

Together, 'Please could we…?'

'Girls, I've beds to get you and Charlie to – after, no doubt, the horses have heard your news.'

But she did allow the three a lovely listen from the lobby; and when the guitar, banjo, and piano strummed up a Scottish air into which the drummer and blazing accordionist ignited like fireworks, an Irish *I step*

*– you step* wasn't enough for the girls: they grabbed Charlie and Jill for a whooping, circling jig.

Jill, who knew: *So infectious a tune, they'll remember it all their lives.*

When Alice came back, they all left reluctantly. In vain the girls waved to Sabrina and Kaycee, dancing together: amazing, that neither had found a man to partner them. Hunching out into a squall the five passed, piled outside the Lounge Bar window, the pulleys and shackles of earlier plus enormous coils of rope: Jilly pointed, 'There's Jack's stuff!'

Sophy remembered, 'He never said what all his measuring this afternoon had been about.'

'And some of that rope looked like Gramps's,' Charlie frowned.

Heather, as they dodged spray again, 'You were dead right about parking way up the village, Mrs Williams!' Even the Volvo had off moments in damp this bad, so Jilly's Morris…

Charlie peered silently into the dark west as causeway spray spattered shishing Bumble's screen.

'I didn't see Bronny; did you see Bronny?'

'Actually, Sophy, Sabrina said Bron wasn't coming, because of this wind. She was dropping down to see Mummy for a bit, then going back to watch over the ponies.'

'Poor thing, missing that music!'

'Yes,' Heather snuggled back, 'but with American flyers there tonight, maybe she'd have been too reminded of Carson and Sam. Whom we must pray for, at bedtime.'

Sophy yawned like a cave; Jilly said into the mirror, 'Better do that now, perhaps.'

Charlie prayed his own huge private thanks to Fate, for sending Sophy Fossway to stay with Jill Ribblesdale.

## CHAPTER 44

Although, even with furniture cleared, that Public Bar was only a third of the marquee's area, nobody grumbled; the pervasive wartime bonhomie was boosted when the Americans got everyone hoedowning…

So very much *not* the planned dance! That year, pretentious County types had successfully pushed for the fête's first ever all-nighter… Ending supposedly with a dawn dip, but everyone local actually expecting a throwing-in epidemic; and then, all to The Davy Lamp for a thumping good breakfast. The ambitious committee had, another first, named this bash: ***Pushing The Boat Out!***, posters proclaimed.

Previous evening dos had been squeezeboxed country dancing in the village hall; this time, after the folkies had packed up the wee small hours were to have been boogie-thumped away, so a big tent had to occupy the bleak shingly green right by the shore, well away from houses. Local boatmen had muttered about the weather risks; the posh lot had paid no heed.

Decision made to strike the marquee, the local partygoers had rushed to help, presuming that everyone would likewise muck in to salvage the evening; however, the disco man and the mobile bar lot had both packed up and roared off. The latter, hired because they were friends of well-connected friends – quite some bone of contention already – had even refused The Davy Lamp's landlord a deal on the beer they'd brought along.

So this dryish do would end at midnight, as dances always had; but ticket-holders were welcome back at five a.m. for breakfast, on one obvious condition: strictly no swimming.

While familiar tunes came filtering, in the Lounge Bar Jack Sound demonstrated knots to attentive holidaymakers… until the ILB station telephoned.

The band was hushed; after hanging up, he stood in the lobby so all could hear. 'Some ships out there are running for cover, worried about cargoes shifting. Locally, we've a mystery: the Jasmine, a tanker anchored northside of Saint Brides Bay, has been struck below the waterline. There was a boom like the Bell of Doom, apparently, and her hull's badly dented; but she's not shipping water, so her skipper's sitting tight.

'So, what hit her? Probably one of those freight containers reported lost overboard months ago by that Polish merchantman – unpronounceable name, you remember the one – which was on contract to the Russkies. Whatever, the thing's evidently a serious hazard to navigation, drifting barely afloat; hopefully, now it's embayed, this blow will bring it ashore.'

Someone had to ask: 'And it's carrying…?'

Jack sighed, 'I thought t'was Cornish folk as had the wrecking gene! Please don't fantasise, because Eastern Bloc container cargoes are often very nasty – typically explosives, acids, or poisons. So, if it does get beached, give it a WIDE BERTH – and please spread the word about that.'

Sabrina, who'd been studying Kaycee's reactions, wasn't surprised when, as the band struck up again, 'Sorry, honey: I need to use the payphone.'

Gale regardless, tobacco smoke needed dispersing.

Demo over, the settle beside that ajar Lounge Bar window was ideal for Jack. His ropes were just outside: bringing their ends indoors, he could begin joining them up, checking that each new splice ran a pulley cleanly; also, he could regularly break from ropeworking to cock an ear, contemplating those sounds carrying from the outer coast: *Exceptional swell, that, for summertime!*

At twenty to midnight, the telephone again; this time, the musicians were immediately quiet.

'An Irish coaster, the Mary-Kate, reports fuel contamination; she's losing power, and can't hold course for Fishguard…'

The rocks of Strumble Head were, therefore, eyeing the ship hungrily.

'…So, the Saint Davids lifeboat has launched.'

In the man's voice, much concern – but not just for those poor sailors and the men going to assist. If a ship off this stretch of the coast should Mayday now, either the Milford Haven waterway's Angle lifeboat must slog many miles out to the search area, headwinded through the island tide races…

…Or the Creampot Cove ILB's coxswain must commit to launching from Colliers' Quay or Solva – if he believed both his vessel and her crew could cope.

If.

On everyone's behalf, 'What needs doing, Coxswain Jack, to prepare for a launch?'

'Nothing at all here, Miss Heckrottss. The far shore's ferry slip is clear: I checked it this afternoon. And Solva's harbourmaster will have done likewise. But,' eyes casting firmly about, 'the lifeboat can only launch, there or here, if the route is open. So…'

A farmer, indeed he of the original rude remarks, stepped forward: 'You need coast road patrols, each one a Landy with chainsaws and a beefy tractor: leave that to us.'

The landlord temporarily halted the men and women coming keenly forward: 'ATTENTION, EVERYONE! Here'll be Jack's headquarters, tonight; so, to keep the pub's 'phone line clear for his calls, will anyone reporting in please use the payphone? Its number is—'

Ear-clobbering, now building-shaking reverberation froze everyone – nearly everyone – dead still.

'Jesus, those are CHINOOKS!' Amy sprang for the lobby, 'If they've been ordered in, then—'

She rebounded off an enormous US military policeman, and would have fallen over if he hadn't seized her, python fast: 'Heckrottss, round everyone up NOW!'

In that thunder-flogged silence, mute farewells; from the pub's rear, surly bumping of an unlatched fire exit.

*

The base's regular aircraft went unremarked; resigned to them, one only wished visiting afterburnered show-offs like F-111s soon elsewhere. But, as with a Galaxy's grinding whine, the Chinook helicopter's flog-flogga-flog-flogging of the air was unignorable.

The horses detected it first: whinnystomps had Charlie clatting tricky stairtreads by torchlight, glad of companionable Daphne velveting down ahead: 'What's all this fuss, now?'

Across the yard, the girls stirred as one.

'Are those helicopters?'

'Horribly huge ones, Sophes, and flying bloody close to the deck.'

Together peering through that low window… Two flashes, acknowledged with their torch: no panic, whereas three would have dressed them fast. Heather resnuggled, 'Good old Charlie.'

*Just horribly huge,* Sophy worried, *or huge and horrible? And, whichever, why so scarily low?*

Along the landing Jill remembered Lakenheath sorties shaking her Cambridgeshire skies; *But what lifting loads hereabouts are so heavy yet inaccessible, only Chinooks can handle them?*

Alice recalled wartime Whitehall: that brittle shelter banter between her and her Wren friends as German V1 Doodlebugs stutter-rumbled closer.

*

Sabrina had fretted about their using the fire exit.

'Honey, I needed air – and reachin' the front door through that scrum would have been…'

'Okay; but why bring your kitbag and my stuff?'

'I thought we might take a walk.'

'In this gale?'

'It ain't rainin' yet; so, c'mon!'

Thus, beside a dull-gleaming chop shore-breaking stroppily, they had larked off teenagerishly toward the limekilns, and–

Whackering low through the pill's mouth, three hearse-dark machines, mainline loco big and with two huge rotors each. First the valley's bend canted them over; then, stressed blades pain loud, their hard pull-up cleared them the pub plus The Pinch… Banking south-eastwards, they dipped beyond–

Gone.

Kaycee whistled, 'Neat flying!'

Still stomaching rotor echoes, kerosene-tasting Sabrina bristled, 'But our poor horses, up at Alice's…!'

'I know, I know; but, honey, tactical flyin's a crucial skill: goin' in that way is how the Russians would try jumping us.'

Sabrina's spine stiffened. 'Um, has something big begun? Those whatevers hadn't lights on.'

'Chinooks. And, darlin', there ain't nothin' to worry 'bout: our base has just gone High Readiness, that's all, because the goddam Head of Security is paranoid.'

'Some connection with that lost container, is there?'

That hand's touch meant, *I wouldn't lie to you.*

'...Hey, look: there's a police raid on the pub!'

'Sabrina, flashin' red cop lights mean *our* guys: like I said, base status has changed.'

'You knew they'd be coming, didn't you? And now, you're deliberately not going... Kaycee,' the young Welshwoman said carefully, 'I like you lots: please be *very* careful. Bronny and I have good friends from your base; they've just disappeared. Maybe they were somehow disobedient, and now they're being punished somewhere hidden; whatever did happen, it's a horrid situation, with Bron loving Sam so deeply.'

Kaycee hugged hugely, 'Both Carson and he are fine; but I can't disclose where they are, or what they're at.'

Sabrina had to kiss the American, 'That's amazingly good news! Oh, Kaycee, *please* can I tell Bronny? '

'Okay; but just say you overheard Carson and Sam being talked about, all relaxed like, in the crush at the bar – and make it clear you never saw who'd spoken, huh?'

'I *promise*! Oh, talk about making Bronny's day!'


## CHAPTER 45

Rug-flopped Bronny's spine stretch made sphinx-perched Mogulus claw-hook her sweater: 'No, puss: don't fall off my tum – not after sitting out those heliocrappers without crinkling a whisker!'

'Mou!' *I heard and saw that sort many times, back in the flat lands.*

'You can stay the night, dear; I didn't think I had to say.'

Detaching the cat and sitting up, 'I would love to, Carol, because it's been super: the talk, that chess game, and your spoiling me.'

'I only brushed your hair, and rubbed your back.'

*You mothered me, Sophy's Mum.* 'About Anna ringing, saying the ponies coped with those 'copters: for all that, this gale isn't in the stable's favour, and...'

'You've a feeling in your bones? Then you must certainly go, Bronny; but how about coming back for breakfast here?'

'Oh, I'd LOVE TO! But, Carol, because of this weather, can I call you in the morning?'

'Of course; and, as it is so wild out, I'm telephoning Anna now to say that you're heading home, and you *must* promise you'll call me on arrival.'

Mogulus waited by the sighing door, eyes made to blaze by the night's liveliness; when Bron was togged, he scrabbered up to her shoulder.

She tickled, 'Hitching a lift to the hunting grounds, eh?'

'Mioh!'

Indeed, no; for he ferlumped down at the brook bridge, there to yowl at the chuckling channel.

*In the animal world, everything means something.* 'Message received, Moggo: you're worried about this water.' *I can't think why, though.*

'Meeah!' Job done, he galloped for home.

Bronny pondered the restless spinney's being so deeply dark… Then the coin dropped: *No sky-glare from the base, tonight!* She stomped off, wondering why not.

*

Kaycee could somehow see extremely well – unbelievably well. She murmured, 'There go our round-up team…'

Three minutes.

'Two spooks, full camouflage gear, are stationed in the pub garden: good viewpoint, guys!'

Out came a small box; she raised its antenna.

Way down the shore, that torch they'd hooked onto a whippy branch glimmered.

'Because of the wind,' Sabrina hissed, 'it *does* look like someone moving about!'

Convincingly enough for those dark figures to soon pad past that limekiln, in whose dipped top the two young women crouched stiffly still.

Kaycee, after a wisely-timed while, 'Let's go!'

*

Three Chinooks, obscurely arrived into a darkness so unfamiliar: no buildings blazing, nor floodlights staring, nor runways glittering a triangular mile.

A recent recruit peered, 'Why the blackout?', as the bus passed the guardhouse barrier, cut its lights, and fell behind a night-visioned escort jeep.

Came an unseen reply: 'So Russian satellites can't see what's moving, nor—'

'But tonight's so overcast, like before snow in Nebraska!'

'NOR, prairie girl, can any Brits.'

'WHAT? The Brits spy on us?'

From another seat, 'Betcha this rookie ain't realised that WE spy on us!'

Someone else: 'While other guys of ours are checkin' on *you*.'

*

Jack might just rest his eyes…

Sabrina breezed in, 'I missed the end of the dance!'

'We noticed. So, why…?'

'As here was heaving, I thought I'd call Bronny from the green's 'phone box, to see how the horses were, but it wouldn't take coins; I was using the one up the hill when those helicopters walloped over: talk about WOW! Then, walking back down, some buses whooshed past; what was that all about?'

'The Yanks were ordered back to barracks; I don't think your friend got aboard, though.'

'Actually, Kaycee's on a two-day pass: she's staying with me. Couldn't bear that smoky fug, so she went outside when I did; then, get this, she said she'd walk back to the stables, in this blow: isn't she keep-fit mad? Anyway, what's happening now?'

He explained.

Sabrina knapsack-dug, 'Then here's handy, perhaps: some VHF radios. Kaycee borrowed them from work, for the fête; we didn't need them, though. Apparently settings X, Y, and Z can't interfere with normal channels.'

Jack sighed, 'Nice thought; but there's no signal here, unfortunately.' He clicked a set on: just hiss.

Producing a music-stand-like thing with a cable, she twittered about putting it outside…

'VLCC OCEAN GOLDRUSH, YOUR ESSO TERMINAL BERTHING DELAYED UNTIL 0600 BECAUSE OF TUG AVAILABILITY. PLEASE CALL PORT CONTROL AT 0300 FOR…'

Jack absolutely boggled; so did others. Handing it to Dipper Davies, 'Will you try raising our boathouse, Creampot Point coastguard, or Saint Davids?' Meanwhile, Sabrina here needs a cocoa.'

In the pub's kitchen, 'That was ruddy well acted, as a dippy girl: our drama group could use you. So…?'

'The base's Head of Security has almost flipped over this possible Russian container: he thinks it might be carrying something really, really important.'

'He was alerted, of course, by the Jasmine's Mayday: the Yanks monitor everything.'

'Luckily, just before the base went to war footing, Kaycee's immediate boss, who's much more level-headed, cleared her for voluntarily assisting the RNLI.'

'Guessing her capabilities, she'll be well handy if there is a call-out.'

'Unfortunately, two American undercover men are prowling.'

'Who might suspect Kaycee's motives, and be aiming to win gold stars from this security nutcase by hauling her back to base?'

'Not giving them the benefit of the doubt, she and I gave them the slip.'

*How those eyes gleam!* 'Good show.'

'Using some amazing binoculars, Kaycee spotted them spying on this place: she thinks the Head of Security is worried about the inshore lifeboat doing a rescue from here, and finding that container before he can.'

Jack quietly growled, 'And towing it in for salvage, in this weather? He – Must – Be – Mad!'

'No comment. Anyway, the moment those choppers start container hunting, Kaycee expects, the Saint Brides Bay airspace will be closed to all other traffic, rescue sorties included.'

He stared, 'I don't see why the RAF's yellow 'copters should bother those big Cheroots.'

'Well, here's a scenario: the Head of Security fears that that isn't the real Jasmine out there, but a Soviet ship in disguise…'

Masquerading had been a common enough wartime trick, he conceded.

'Anchored near the container's estimated position, the Jasmine declares a problem; the coastguards immediately order other craft to keep well clear.'

Exactly what had happened.

'Hidden under tarpaulins on her deck is, say, a motor cruiser; this, set adrift before dawn, then starts sending Maydays: the engine's kaput and one crewman is genuinely injured. Unfortunately, the Jasmine reports, she can't go to help: her problem demands the crew's undivided attention...'

'Coastguard wouldn't ever ask a ship already at risk to assist, anyway.'

'As the Chinooks' downdraughts might tip that motorboat over, the airbase calls them all home; now a midget submarine can launch from under the Jasmine, and go after the container undisturbed; once located, its divers hook on steel cables.

'To buy time, when a rescue helicopter comes, the motorboat's crew act all incompetent: it takes ages to haul the stretcher case up. Then they ask, can someone be dropped aboard to help when a towing vessel arrives? All deliberate time wasting, of course; meanwhile, the Jasmine is winching the container into a secret underwater compartment. And, later, with her repairs complete, she steams serenely away.'

'Ingenious!'

She blushed, 'Only Kaycee and me speculating, Jack. So go on, say it: far too James Bond.'

He gruffed, 'Reckon it's enough inside the edge of feasible for a paranoid Yank high-up to set out his schemes accordingly: I've met quite a few Special Forces chaps, and they all seemed at least *fairly* bonkers: the crazier the mission concept, the better they loved it, was my impression.

'Anyway, Sabrina, if our lifeboat *did* have to attend an incident without Search and Rescue helicopter support, we'd just be reverting to how things used to be; except, that is, that we've these three damned clever radios, and Kaycee's help being offered – who's presumably hiding from those skulkers...?'

Sabrina nodded: 'For the moment, in the back of my van.'

'Then might I borrow it for, say, twenty minutes? I need to talk to your friend.'

Producing keys, 'Dark blue Escort, parked outside the school.'

He was quietly closing the side door behind him—

'Jack, WAIT! You and Dipper mustn't ever name Kaycee over the radio; instead talk about, um, Heather's friend Cerys.'

'Okay; and if I, ahem, happen to see her, I'll give cariad Cerys your love, eh?'

\*

After Bronny had crossed the Mill Brook, ever more thrashing and clatting overhead; small stuff was pattering down all about. She was sure, even before her torch showed how trunks swayed, that should this wind worsen, at the least branches would be shed. *So unusual, such summertime trouble twice in three weeks!* Passing Tracker's lane, 'I'm glad you're safe indoors tonight, boy.'

Lights were on downstairs: she looked in on the Madocs who, offering cocoa, 'Stay to hear the news, girl.'

Afterwards she said, 'I doubt it helps that ship Jasmine much, being close under Solva: there's a monstrous roar the swell's making.'

Mr M agreed: 'She'll be riding something vile, held across it by the wind; running her engines will only relieve her anchor, and give no comfort to the crew.'

'I'd welcome the racket, for myself: rather that, than just the chains rattling and snatching, and waves keeping whacking home. Anyway – I'll go now and, before turning in to kip, show the ponies I'm near for them.'

But he blocked her: 'Hark to me, now: we *should* be fine, because Gareth checked all the roofs last autumn; but please take one of his safety helmets.'

Although no slates came flying, Bronny was glad she'd heeded him, for the air itself assailed her: a viciously twisting gust, she heard it vaulting the wall; then its skewing updraught, whack-filling her parka, skittled her hard onto the cobbles, CRACK!

And gone as fast.

She ouched up, and felt the hat: it was badly split. 'Bloody hell,' she muttered, 'I could have done a Heather.'

Or worse; and so, going back in for another hard hat, she didn't refuse a tot of rum.

It was thickly overcast; with no airbase glow, the yard was horridly dark. Before Bronny's bruise-limped round of their stalls, she hung up a candle lantern: a night-light for the ponies, and one proof against power cuts.

She kennelled restless Tag, using the standard trick of tossing in a crumbled biscuit: after that frantic, exhausting effort to locate every last shortbread molecule, he'd sleep.

Gale locked firmly out of the office, she was getting herself jimjammed when a paw door-tapped…

'TAG, go to BED!'

But an answering squeaky hiss had her suddenly shooting bolts back: 'Pussy, is that you…?'

'Hass!'

'VINCEY!'

Black face, tortoiseshell markings, bent-tip tail: the stableyard's mouser Vince, short for Vincenza. A great mate of Bronny and Sabrina's, gone missing ever since Carson and Sam's disappearance. A cat with little voice; as piano, indeed, as Mogulus was forte.

After much milk, and umpteen how-I've-missed-you cuddles, Bronny sighed, 'Oh, Vincey, I've had such a fab evening with Carol – and now you've come home! But I can see you're so tired…'

By the time the Swansea girl was settling down, camp-bedded, the cat, curled up on the office's IN tray correspondence, was well away.

*

Carol had poured out some Islay malt whisky, Keith's special treat tipple.

Through that tawny lens, she spoke into the embering stove: 'Dearest, how wakeful you would have been tonight – with the sea so near, and this awful storm, and the poor men out on that ship.

'I'm sure you're proud of all Sophy's done recently, and are loving how she's changing: more interesting, more intense; more outgoing, too. Also, darling, I hope you approve of my trying to write.

'Keith, about Heather's father: as our daughter and his will surely be important to each other for ever, do he and I have any choice but to become friends, and friendly friends at that? Because—'

Some soft sound from the window, which wasn't wind-made.

She everso stealthily peeped…

Resting from the wildness, perfection of hunting purpose: an unblinking Little Owl.

Quite unafraid, though Carol's face was so close.

'Athene!'

Goddess of wisdom.


## Chapter 46

Dipper Davies had been busy with the Lounge Bar's framed Admiralty chart, which depicted the coast from Saint Annes Head to Dinas Island.

He'd posted the weather reports of various shore stations; his taped-on notes located the *Jasmine* and the *Mary-Kate*, ditto the Saint Davids lifeboat's recently-reported position; most encouragingly, a Royal Navy minesweeper was steaming hard down Cardigan Bay to rendezvous. Dipper said, 'She'll do the tow; but our boys will be crucial as go-betweens, taking her line to the coaster, and standing by until the Grey Funnel Line have everything in hand.'

The back of a brewery poster carried time-logged summaries of VHF messages – the latest from Creampot Cove being, SEA STATE WORSENING.

Sabrina queried his added, SLATES.

'A house near the lifeboat shed is losing them.'

Flying slates could be lethal, both knew.

'When Jack brings your van back,' he asked, 'you'll be off home?'

Shaking her head, 'I want to stay and help.' How could she leave here while Kaycee was out there somewhere, busy on the RNLI's behalf?

He shrugged, 'For the moment, there isn't much…'

'Actually,' unfolding it, 'Jack said we should use any spare moments to study this.'

Dipper, 'Let's see,' spread the diagram on the bar… 'So *that's* why he spliced all those ropes together!' He shot a look: 'Hear much about the Rowtow practices, did you?'

'Recently for me it's been nothing but County Show; so explain away, please.'


'…And, with those hints, your young friends worked out how sailing vessels were horse-launched from this pill.'

'So Jack hopes to lay on a demonstration, one day? That would be fascinating: people loved watching Tracker and Aberdare dragging that massive net; and didn't folk ever photograph our horses at the fête?'

'Plus,' he winked, 'their female attendants.'

'Oh, Phoo! But, seriously: why, tonight, should Jack press on us his plans for an historical re-enactment, when we've a possible lifeboat launch to think about?'

Back with them, the landlord peered: 'An alternative plan for launching it?'

Dipper, emphatically, 'NO! The ILB either goes pissing out of this pill under its own power, pardoning my language, or doesn't set off at all.'

When Jack came back, though concern wrinkled his brow, his eyes twinkled. 'Kaycee's lodged with my friends who live by Tram Gin Top; excellent radio reception up there. As for her special binoculars – well, I tell you, they could be fiercely handy!'

Sabrina tried, 'Because you're expecting...?'

'Never,' a finger wagged, 'try anticipating the *nature* of trouble: Fate has trump cards as'll always catch you out. My father's rules were, first, most expect trouble when things are already difficult; second, before committing your crew to a plan, share your thoughts with them and insist they share theirs with you; thirdly, keep reconsidering how you'll get back – or what you'll do instead.'

*Useful rules, if the stable ever runs long treks!* 'So the super-long rope is part of a fallback scheme?'

He sucked through his teeth, 'Well...'

Dipper didn't see how: 'Thanks to the farmers' gangs, the ILB can get here, no problem. Should its launching tractor break down, an ordinary one could see that trailer into the water, even with the pill choppy – and its coxswain obviously wouldn't dream of launching unless both outboard motors were in tip-top order.'

All true, Jack's look said; 'Well, Sabrina?'

The horsewoman contemplated the older man: *"Horizon eyes": Sophy's absolutely right! Which, for all that he's clever, Dipper doesn't have – yet.*

She wouldn't be rushed; she went to study that old, beautifully engraved chart, plus all the notes the younger man had attached. 'It's about getting home, isn't it, Jack? Suppose the ILB had engine trouble while she was out there: then, with a headwind funnelling through the pill mouth, the tide running out strongly, and perhaps even a boat in tow…'

He beamed, 'Well fathomed! Yes: I reckon that, rather than the Creampot Cove crew spending hours sitting at anchor or skulking under the cliffs, waiting for conditions to improve, your horses could haul 'em in.'

Dipper shook her hand with much admiration; 'And, I should've realised, a rescued craft might well need warping over to Corner Wharf.'

But came a thought, and Sabrina's smile stopped: 'How to get the rope out to the ILB, though?'

Dipper, straight away, 'You'd have it placed ready! We'd use a biggish dinghy, good freeboard, to take a sinker out into the middle of the pill, plus a buoyed riser with the rope end carbine-clipped on, and we'd drop that tackle as far offshore as we possibly could.'

'That's right,' Jack nodded, 'you've got it!'

'So,' Sabrina fizzed, 'when do we start?'

Jack policemanned a palm, 'Nobody does *anything* unless Creampot Cove's coxswain likes the idea! So,' he nodded at the VHF radio, 'let's find out.'


The ILB coxswain approved; a team was formed. First, they must get Jack's "super-hawser" to Corner Wharf: Sabrina could drive it across the causeway, then it needed ferrying along the pill's northern shore.

They realised, coiling it into her van, that the operation would need something larger than a dinghy: the combined weight of those spliced-together ropes was tremendous.

Hawser loaded, 'We're ready!'

But Jack beckoned them indoors: 'Hear me out first, eh?' He spread that long paper roll, this time other way up, revealing a different diagram. 'There's no deflection from the main objective, which is getting that hawser buoyed in mid-channel, ready for the ILB's return if she is called out. But just supposing that conditions change…'

'As I've already said,' Dipper started, 'she'll never need a hauled launch–'

'No, lad, she won't; but that's a bloody nasty swell: the ILB might do with picking up our tow far further out than these fellows can safely put a buoy down.'

'You're surely don't propose risking your own life to—?'

'By revising the plan, I don't need to!' Jack's finger stubbed, 'Yes, we drop our sinker, mid-channel, as far out as is safe; but we *don't* clip the hawser end to its buoy. Instead, we fit a shackle to act as a runner. The hawser goes out from Corner Wharf, loops through that, and comes back ashore; when the ILB sets off, she takes the hawser end with her, which now has a decent-sized pick-up buoy attached. Keeping mid-channel she carries on past the tethered buoy until, when all the spare hawser has paid out, she drops the pick-up buoy. That should stay safely aligned thanks to the wind, which we aren't expecting to shift from north any time soon; thus the ILB can, coming back, be hauled in from a good way…'

He meant, from a good way beyond The Anvil; but local boatmen had ever been loath to name that rock.

Sabrina halted her Escort before the causeway's end, exactly where a torch showed her to.

Down below, *Alecto* waited at the water's edge; rather as a cable-laying vessel takes on its burden, she floated patiently while the hawser, snaking hand-to-hand out of the van and over the railings, was fed aboard and, once again, stowed in one neat, if enormous, coil.

That craft couldn't be easily rowed, such was the size of its consignment; two men hauled on its painter while two more pushing askew stopped it grounding.

On *Alecto* arriving below Corner Wharf, scant surprise for anyone that Jack had much earlier prepared an old sinker with a newly-buoyed riser rope; now he had the runner shackle attached to the ensemble, and securely seized.

There were enough fellows there to bodily lift the coiled hawser out of the whaler and lay it on the shingle. By reverse process of what the causeway had witnessed, the line was fed up onto Corner Wharf; head end made off to the centre bollard, it was re-coiled again until Jack was left with the tail end – which he now threaded through the sinker riser's runner shackle. Tying a bowline in it, 'This end of the line stays here, with us, while the mid-channel buoy and its sinker are put in place.'

That iron sinker, the flywheel off a Diesel engine, was damned heavy – but everyone understood why it needed to be. How they struggled and cursed, those men, to get it settled on two crosswise timber baulks at *Alecto*'s stern.

Now for the riskiest bit: lifejacketed and taking waterproof torches, four rowers and two others threw in bailing buckets, then boarded the whaler. Having securely stowed the riser rope and marker buoy they set off slowly, men up on the wharf paying the hawser out for them.

A difficult wait, for those on shore: nothing could be seen once black *Alecto* was past a score of yards away, for she wisely showed no lights, heading into that storm-boomed darkness.

The bow man, who'd cat-like vision, could best read their surroundings unaided; while it was a calm enough ride for the moment, soon it wouldn't be: coupled with hearing its approach, seeing all of an encroaching whitecap, albeit most gloomily, told you much more of its intent than partly glimpsing it in a glaring beam which left you night-blinded. And his fellow in the sternsheets, checking by feel how the hawser fed through that omega-throated shackle, knew the importance of the dark to their silent oarsmen: best chance, it gave, of early-sighting Alice Williams' leading lights – initially as weak glimmers, he anticipated, threading the raucous storm-swung treetops which crisscrossed up above…

'There they are!'

And the four steadfast fellows pulled crosswise awhile, riding them loblolly, to align their keel with that shining path.

They were now losing the valley's lee, and that northerly started sailing them out: oars only needed dipping henceforth to keep the one white light astern above the other; indeed, not much further on the whaler must be sea-braked as she began to confront the wind-steepened backwashes of Anvil-slamming swells.

A bow man no longer: to lighten the boat forward so she shipped less wave-slop, he must crouch now back-to-back with the foremost rower and peer ahead from that position, those warnings to his fellows becoming ever more important as yet taller and more energetic crests came at them…

Until, the bucking now so bad that the lookout struggled to bale while the others swore badly for being so badly thrown about, the oldest oarsman spoke: 'That's the best us can do!' At which, two torches went on to ensure there were no tangles.

Their best, two rowers did, to hold steady while the sinker got blasphemously prised and pushed towards the starboard gunwale; then, it blooshing in with a great backblast of spray, the torches signalled "Job done!" shoreward, then extinguished again, and sudden oarwash strengthed *Alecto* clear as the riser raced down after and, Whomph!, there went the mid-channel buoy.

Now to warily turn well away from that buoy before the wind-defying row back, their stern man keeping them east of the leading lights' alignment, this time, to avoid overrunning Jack's hawser.

At last regaining shelter, they lit a torch once more to see their final shivery way in to where mates waited, the old coxswain amongst them throat-tight with backslapping gratitude: 'Ruddy well done, lads; and thanks, everyone! Let's get this boat back along, then we'll to the Lamp again for some sleep before the party folk reappear.'

# ALECTO'S TASK

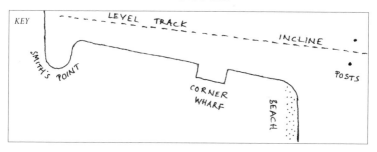

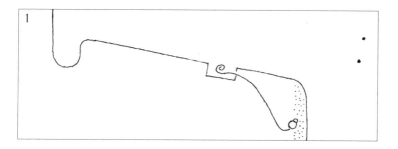

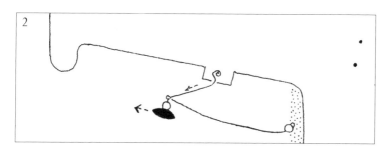

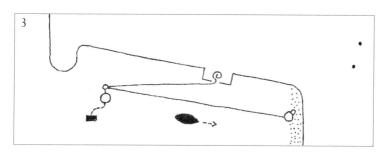

# CHAPTER 47

So well was The Davy Lamp hullabalooing at half past five, few customers heeded that tingaling bell; but then the landlord bellowed, 'JACK SOUND – TELEPHONE!'

The clock ticking; Jack's mumbled, 'Yes, I see; how many...?'

Hanging up, 'That was Creampot Cove. A yacht sheltering under the Caerfai cliffs has gone and found that cursed container, if that's what it is. She's lost one bilge keel; damned lucky not to capsize! Propeller shaft's mangled, too. All she can do is limp downwind, half on her side. Coastguard's only getting an iffy radar track: she'll likely come ashore on The Sands in about four hours, they reckon – if she stays afloat.'

Four adults aboard.

'Tommy Warren on the Saint David's lifeboat hasn't long set off back from Fishguard: the Mary-Kate so worried everyone, they had to shadow her all the way in. So he can't help.

'Creampot Point Coastguard Station has contacted the Jasmine; no surprise, they don't reckon much to either of her own boats in these conditions. In any case, what would her crew do if she sprang a big leak, with her best boat away?

'...No, the ILB station *hasn't* fired maroons, yet: an RAF helicopter's going to have a look at the yacht. ...No, just to *look*. Think about it, man: that vessel's desperately unstable; a 'copter's downdraught might easily drive her under!'

'...Actually, I'd give them zero survival chance, wherever she came ashore with them still aboard; so, almost certainly, the ILB *will* be launching from here: finish your breakfasts quickly, anyone who's minded to offer assistance.'

A buzzing clatter overhead, but nothing like the night's thunderous assault.

His old eyes tracked its sound: 'There goes the yellow helo; us'll soon know what's what.'

Razzer Roch, fast biker and technology enthusiast, had one of the VHF sets switched on and, with headphones, was trying to pick up the helicopter's dialogue with the airbase... 'My bloody GOD!' And he tugged at that lead, to free the plug and put the loudspeaker on...

'SAY AGAIN,' came the Creampot Point coastguard, clearly not wanting to believe what they'd just heard. 'MESSAGE MISUNDERSTOOD, OVER.'

It was the ILB coxswain: 'I REPEAT, THE ILB IS UNSERVICEABLE. WE HAD JUST TOWED HER OUT OF HER SHED, EXPECTING A LAUNCH CALL, WHEN THE CHIMNEY STACK OF A NEIGHBOURING HOUSE COLLAPSED ONTO HER. WE KNOW SHE HAS RECEIVED MASSIVE DAMAGE, BUT WE CANNOT GET CLOSE FOR FULL ASSESSMENT BECAUSE THE ROOF BESIDE THE CHIMNEY IS NOW SHEDDING SLATES DANGEROUSLY, OVER.'

The crowd had parted, letting Jack reach Razzer's side; he whispered; Razzer nodded, twisted knobs, and, 'Davy Lamp Inn to Creampot Point, over…?'

'GO AHEAD, RAZZER, OVER.'

'Please stand by for a telephone call from Jack Sound re alternative rescue strategy, over.'

'MESSAGE RECEIVED, RAZZER, OVER.'

'And out.'

'Jack,' the landlord said, 'use my office, if you want to gather your thoughts.'

'Aye, I will, thanks.' Then, 'Razzer, bring that VHF along, please.'

'Everyone else,' the landlord bellowed, 'into the Public Bar, please, and polish off your food pronto: until further notice, here's back to being an Operations Centre!'

# CHAPTER 48

Quiet, in the dawn, but clear: 'Don't you dare climb my wisteria, girl!'

Kaycee shielded her eyes, deeply impressed. She had crept from Jack's friends' house unnoticed, negotiated Tram Gin Top green and the lane without one dogbark or even a bird disturbed, passed the garage (wherein already grumbly horses), and eased through a heavily-latched side gate…

Now Alice was leaning from the right-hand bedroom window, 'Anyway, it's my help you'll need, not Jill's: she'll have to go with the girls.'

Stage whispering, 'Roger that!'

'Be down soon.'

From right by her feet, 'Miaou!' *Pretty jolly stealthy, I must say – for a human!*

The American jumped: 'Say, pussycat, how long have you been following–?'

'Mieo? *What's your connection with that yellow machine?*

Now Jill's sash window, on the other side: 'A quick breakfast for everyone?'

Charlie, 'Gets my vote!', appeared around the side of the house. 'So Kaycee can tell us all why the horses woke me when that Sea King went over: ordinary 'copters don't normally bother them.'

Ten minutes later, as Alice led Lamorna from the garage, the boy horses watched jealously.

'You'll be off soon, yourselves,' she promised.

The others helped her with that well-found saddle; most importantly, she pommeled the coil of cord which had kept Sophy safe the day before.

As she set off, did the haltered mare following soberly sense what responsibility impended?

Tracker and Aberdare started stamping soon after Lamorna's departure; putting harnesses on them had no calming effect. A quarter past six being early for Alice's neighbours to get an unrequested, highly seismic, wake-up call, Jill and the girls and Charlie must quickly get ready to go.

*

Hitched to the base of that wind-shaken mast, Lamorna grazed, her ears busily twitchy; Alice, meanwhile, tied the pilot line to the end of her rope with great care: *One mistake,* she reminded herself, *and the whole plan's kiboshed.*

She wrapped the join with tape: it *must* feed through the top pulley smoothly. Cleating the coil's other end, 'Here goes, Lamorna!', and she started hauling.

The horse watched, not disinterested but not stopping munching either: she loved long grass with a salt tang.

*

*What stomps, now!* Using Alice's downstairs loo, last minute, some yards and two thick walls away, Sophy again felt as well as heard the horses' impatience.

*

'Easy now, Alice, girl!' She'd spoken to herself, but they'd been dear Hector's words.

'Yes, Heck, I know: Festina Lente!' A motto much quoted by him: in English, Hurry Slowly! So she festina'd lente, and… *Success!* Slipped snake-easily round the pulley, the rope end was now heading down again; soon she'd the tape undone and the pilot line detached.

*

As they clopped Alice's drive Sophy squirmed round: 'AJ, I reckon Tracker knows where he's going!'

'Happen aye; and isn't it amazing how he and t'other insisted on bringing their harnesses yesterday, as if they'd already an inkling? However, for all that he still only goes on your say-so, remember: right soon we've the pesky coast road to cross, and right steady is how we're to descend that bank.'

'Tight reins!', called Heather, sat behind Charlie on Aberdare.

*

From a carrier bag Alice withdrew a large emerald cloth, unfolded it, spread it on the grass, and stone-weighted it against blowing away. Now for a period of contemplation, with conspicuous chin-scratching: 'Here it is, Lamorna: the original flag flown here, advising ships to prepare for entering harbour. Rather fragile, I know; but might we fly it for old times' sake?'

Lamorna liked the grassy colour; but there her engagement ceased: it wasn't cold enough for a blanket, and surely that was what the thing was.

Next, out came two lengths of rope, plus something in garish yellow plastic: the swing seat from the pub's beer garden. Quickly secreting that item under the flag, Alice began measuring and knotting.

They'd just crossed the road, and were cutting across the south side of the green, as instructed loudly expressing doubts about what Alice was doing, when the horses came over disobedient.

Sophy tried reining in, Charlie too; but the boys had made up their minds: side by side they struck north across the green's eastern edge.

Jill, having an inkling, 'Let them go, both of you!'

Agent B, newly assigned to the airbase, supposed the old lady to be an eccentric individual who walked a horse as if it were a dog, and hoisted huge flags in gale winds, just because she liked to.

Agent A, who'd worked locally a while, suspected differently: 'That person there is a published writer with a pro-nature agenda – she's actively anti-oil-industry.'

'That woman supports green terrorists?' Who might be clandestinely funded by the Soviets, for anti-capitalist purposes.

'Oh, no: nothing like that; she writes protest letters about marine pollution. Blames refining companies for not demanding higher standards from shipping lines, stuff like that.'

'Then I kinda see her point, considering how beautiful this coast–'

'AND she's friendly with the females from that riding stable. Including, therefore, Subject S.'

Meaning, the civilian with whom Target K had recently buddied up. 'So d'you reckon Target K might–?'

'Target K's breaking cover RIGHT NOW!'

On Alice signalling, Kaycee had leapt from her hiding place to pelt across the green. She wore Hector's heavy mackintosh; she'd those special binoculars looped round her neck; in her backpack were the VHF radio, water, and rations.

The agents now moved fast too, on the opposite side of that broad space; however between them and the mast were Tracker and Aberdare. Suddenly very belligerent animals indeed, they snaked about stompily before the men, threatening with hoof-drags and snorts.

Agent A bellowed, 'Call them off, you damned kids!'

Sophy shouted, 'I can't control this horse, mister; nor can my friend his: there's something about you they don't like.'

Charlie insisted, 'This isn't normal behaviour!' He tried, as Aberdare half-reared, 'Are you from the airbase?'

Agent B, perplexed, trying to see past the horses to the mast, 'Kinda; why?'

Heather's turn: 'That's what it is, then: Aberdare hates the smell of guns – even the oil.'

'And for Tracker,' Sophy lied, 'it's aeroplane fuel.' *Although, actually, maybe that's true.*


Kaycee, after quick but careful knot-testing, 'Is Lamorna ready?'

The horse approached as Alice bundled her decoy flag away... 'We both are!' She dropped the slip knot over the pommel, tugged it tight, and, grabbing the halter, 'Gently, now, girl!'

The rope followed, and rose; the swing seat dragged across the grass, lifted, yawed across to clatter against the mast base...

'Lamorna, WHOA! Now, Kaycee, get aboard quickly!'

The American men didn't notice Heather heel-jabbing Aberdare's flank, riling him more than he had already riled himself; Jill, who did, started doing the same to Tracker.

'Jesus, A,' B called across, 'What are we going to do?'

'B, I can't think! But for Christ's sake don't use my codename any more!'

Charlie muttered, 'A stands for afthole; B stands for bustard.'

Heather so cackled, she almost fell off when Aberdare had another front-feet tantrum.

Sitting on the swing seat, a length of cord rope loosely looped around the mast as a steady, Kaycee commanded, 'Lift off!'

Before Alice could say 'Go to!', Lamorna had already begun smartly walking away...

...And Kaycee ascended, 'YEE-HAH!'

Agent B, somehow dodging Tracker, came sprinting: 'Please stop that, Ma'am, right now!'

Alice blazed, 'How DARE you? This is part of a RESCUE MISSION!'

He showed no sign of desisting: he was going for the rope.

Like Miss Gwinear, Alice had had brothers; she, too, had played cricket, and got pretty good. She'd a nice round stone in her pocket; 'In the NAME of ALL that's DECENT...!'

The man dropped howling to his knees, clutching a part of his person somewhat above them; meanwhile Lamorna, looking round, judged Kaycee's arrival at the mast top very nicely – who bellowed down, while busily tying knots to secure herself, 'GOOD HORSEY – CLEVER HORSEY!'

Agent A now dashed, drawing a knife; Alice shouted up, 'KAYCEE, HE'S GOING TO CUT–'

'ALICE, LET IT GO!'

Alice did; as the man sprawled, locomotived flat by a surging Tracker, he saw the wind-caught rope end rise away: Kaycee was coiling it in.

Before the two stunned agents knew what was happening, each found themselves pressed to the ground by the front hoof of a great horse.

The riders dismounted; Jill, staggery after Tracker's antics, 'Alice, what can we do with–?'

From far above, 'Hi, guys!'

The couple who had taken Kaycee in overnight were now approaching.

The wife panted, 'We set off when we first heard shouting – and saw everything, just now.'

The husband pointed to the telephone box on the edge of the green: 'I've called the police; if there's spare rope, I'll effect two citizen's arrests, and you riders can be on your way.'

Agent A exploded, 'Now see here, fella–!'

The man crouched beside him: 'No; you see *here*: I'm a retired police detective. Whoever you are, matey, my word as a witness holds good with the local force.'

Kaycee had now sorted herself out; not so easily done, swaying about up there. They faintly heard, 'This is Cerys calling Jack Sound… Target in sight, Jack, so please stand by for bearing and range, over!'

CHAPTER 49

They departed full of admiration for Alice, and willing Kaycee to be safe: despite her being petite that mast was bending a lot, and shuddering in gusts far worse than they'd ever seen before.

On reaching the incline head and seeing the bay's wildness, immediate realisation of how frightened those poor folk on the yacht must be, which Kaycee's shouts had confirmed was 'In a real bad way';

the explosive violence of that thundering shore must unquestionably be fatal.

And so down the slope, at first so apprehensively: though the horses stepped confidently, the busyness of their ears and those great heads casting about told of their being on heightened guard. But the descent gradually left the gust-clattered trees behind; and it dulled, the coastboom rolling in from westward: as did the human talk, surely horse thoughts also turned to that impending task.

Two Rugger Tuggers were busy at the middle pair of posts, lashing a hefty pulley block to each: 'One horse can wait here; we'll check his traces while the other goes down to fetch the hawser up, after getting the hauling procedure confirmed.'

Heather said, 'Because Abbey's stronger, Tracker has to lead: overall, that'll strain the gear less. So you swap with me, Sophes, and accompany Charlie; when Abbey gets back and the hawser's been fed through the pulleys, he can link onto it again and Tracker will go in front.'

Jill said, 'I'll follow you two down on foot.'

Sophy must hold Charlie tightly as Aberdare clumped downhill; neither minded. She peered keenly past his shoulder, puzzled by that familiar sound; as the thronged shore below Corner Wharf came into view, there was one of the whalers – *Which one?* – from which blue chainsaw smoke seemed to be, 'HEY!', drifting up...

But, of course no: Charlie, seeing more easily, 'They're cutting up old bottom boards from other boats; someone's prising slats off pallets, too. Reckon they're making a temporary foredeck, so she doesn't ship much water when her bow gets overslopped.'

Studying the sea beyond the pill mouth, Sophy thought "overslopped" understated Charlie's true expectation. She saw, now, that it was *Rattler* being prepared; the whaler looked quite different in character with her two wooden masts stepped and those red-brown sails furled around them: older, certainly, but more adventurous, too.

From Colliers' Quay, the sound of an engine racing down; the snarling chromed shape which appeared blurred the causeway, braked, and halted briefly at its far end; then a staccato roar climbed it on out of the valley.

Razzer, obviously; 'But why did he stop back there?'

Charlie recognised a hurrying figure: 'That's Dipper Davies, back from Creampots because the ILB couldn't launch: Jack'll be so glad to have him aboard! But don't ask me what sent Razzer blasting north after dropping Dipper off.'

'Why are those people filling sandbags, Charlie?'

'Reckon Jack's adding ballast: extra weight inside, see?'

'I don't understand; won't that make Rattler sit lower in the water, letting more of it come aboard?'

'Yes, Sophy – and no: weight her down low, right near her keel, and she won't roll so much: that'll keep her drier; and, sailing, she'll be good to carry more canvas.'

Greenhorn Sophy marvelled that the whaler might safely carry *any* sail, in that wind.

On seeing the horses arrive at Corner Wharf, Jack, down on the shore by *Rattler*, climbed onto a shingle-stranded tree trunk: 'Attention, everyone, please! You've all been helping make preparations without knowing the plan; I appreciate your faith in me, because until very recently *I* didn't know exactly what the plan was.'

He waved a VHF set: 'Thanks to an extremely brave volunteer up the Tram Gin Top mast,' (many murmurs) 'we know where the yacht is and we're tracking her; we *were* in touch by radio, but her battery's just failed. She certainly can't be approached by a helicopter; what's more, the crew don't have the option of abandoning, drifting astern, and being picked up from the water, because one of them has a suspected broken leg.

'Talking of helicopters, someone at the base did have the human decency to suspend their Chinook flights: that was pretty galling for those wretched people on the yacht, having aircraft which couldn't help them buzzing all about the place searching for the whatever-it-was they hit.

'So here's the idea: I propose to rendezvous with the yacht and take her crew straight off; an RAF helo can then pick them up from Rattler, and the injured party will be got away to hospital. Our target's not far north of Blackreef Point; the sooner we set off, the quicker we intercept. Also, the better our chance of getting back here on a broad reach: I'd rather sail *out* close-hauled, while we're lighter.

'...Certainly, I intend sailing. Firstly, there's little point in rowing

322

when there's ample wind: sailing's faster, and boats of this class have voyaged for weeks in the Atlantic in winter, so that sea shouldn't worry her – and this simple rig couldn't be safer, because there's no boom to hurt anyone's head. Secondly, we've four people to rescue, and after they've transferred from the yacht we still want to maintain a good freeboard. Having ten rowers aboard would ride us deeper.

'So: I want six crew, strong but lightweight, to sail her out and give us sufficient strength for manœuvring under oars when we've got close.'

Nearly everyone there stood forward.

'First, anyone with children must step back.'

Quite a few.

'Ditto if you're married…? Or engaged…?' He then gesticulated, 'Robert Hoaten, no: your sister and your niece depend on you.'

Jill, seeing that good man torn by conflicting emotions, felt for him.

Jack's next question: 'Now, has anyone remaining not done any sailing at all…?'

Twenty or so men and women were left.

'Okay – the crew are…'

Seeing some expressions, knowing what might get murmured back and forth, 'Attention, everyone: I want Amy Heckrottss with us because she's proved herself as an oarswoman *and* she's a medic; what's more, she shouldn't be here because the airbase is supposed to be sealed, thus she may already be in very hot water. So, who here will say that her actions haven't shown the right spirit, hmm…?'

Silence.

'Good; now, let's get on…'

But people pointed: a red-light-flashing camouflaged vehicle was pulling off the causeway's northern end.

Amy sighed, 'Guess I won't be coming after all, Jack'

Someone, fixing binoculars on the pebble-stumbling figure, 'Relax, now: that's Felix; he's okay!'

'Righto; so, while he's getting here – Robert Hoaten will be in charge of this launch, shore-side.'

Who, equipped with a tin megaphone, started making his way down to Smith's Point. From there he could watch *Rattler*, and would also be seen by the horse crew on the incline; furthermore Jill, positioned close by him, would supervise the pulley there, probably the hawser's most crucial turning point. So, between them, he and she could monitor the whole procedure.

A Jill now perceiving Robert differently, knowing that the little girl she'd seen him with, so strong the similarity, so evident the love and commitment, hadn't been his daughter but his niece. Thus collapsed, many imagined barriers.

Felix L'Hermitte was someone else who shouldn't be there at Corner Wharf; he'd brought a video camera for Amy to record the rescue with.

Jack said, 'Reckon we'll be a bit busy for that caper, thanks to the sea's mood this morning.'

'So could we just strap it to your mast? This is the waterproof, fully automatic model the US Marines use on landing craft.'

'Then, yes, by all means – at its own peril, of course.'

'…Finally,' Jack announced, back on the tree trunk, 'it will definitely be easier for us to be towed out, rather than our trying rowing, because that's some rough old water near the pill mouth.'

His head tilted wharf-wards, 'However, Charlie and Sophy, we don't want to be powered along as if you're after getting us into the air: we'd likely suffer a dreadful dousing. So please just taxi us out to Smith's Point, where the wind should take over and take us off, all right?'

'Aye, aye, sir!'

'That's all, then – except, as soon as you youngsters get the hawser up to the turning posts, will you please tether both horses until it's time for the off, hmm?'

Turning round, Charlie and Sophy found Aberdare's drawbar already fastened to the end of the huge coil of rope.

A glance back as they departed showed it paying out obediently…

The high trees were now moving so much, even from low on the incline the leading lights glimpsed at them.

'It's so dull,' Charlie said, 'they won't just use them homebound for finding the pick-up buoy.'

'How'll the lights help on the way out?'

'By keeping to one side of their alignment, Rattler won't run down the mid-channel buoy.'

On Aberdare climbed, the hawser's resistance increasing: ever more weight to haul uphill; ever more dragging friction. By no means defeated, he nevertheless began snorting like a locomotive.

Halting the horse, Charlie dismounted; 'Stay up, Sophes: you're much the lighter, and you've that knack of encouraging.'

*

How Robert cursed! 'There's some trawl net coming down on the tide, as will foul the hawser: I must swim out for it, or Jack won't be going anywhere.'

Jill, already stripping, 'You're not going anywhere, Mister Coastguard: you're in charge! Anyway,' her bikini revealed, 'I'm ready to go, *and* I've brought a towel – I've even got a lifejacket, thanks to Kaycee. Are you as well prepared?'

'Well…'

'I hand-haul myself out along the hawser, tie the net to it using a loose loop, then pull it ashore?'

'That should work fine; but please be very careful, Jill: that's a nasty sea.'

'To think, Robert Hoaten, that you were going to do this without a lifejacket, with your sister and dear young niece dependent on you – while I've only a cat, who can happily look after himself…!'

'Jill, don't talk rollocks! You've *many* human friends,' he kissed, 'who need you.'

*

Tracker was undeniably strong; Aberdare, travailing beneath her like a steam-heated machine, indeed, was truly powerful. Also, he seemed… *More male – or do I mean macho?* Sophy didn't think she was imagining; presuming that Abbey understood about her liking Charlie, he was surely going at his task with a Tom Jones swagger, trying hard to impress her.

He twisted his head, though, to throw her a reproachful glance.

*Okay: I'll call it gusto. Not showing off; but certainly flying the flag for your master, hmm?*

Not just no refutal; actually, a subtle but definite nod.

Noticing how much the rope was dragging, disappointed men who'd hoped to be in Jack's crew now hurriedly dispersed themselves down the track to pick it up and walk it along; Aberdare thus assisted, all were soon pacing smartly.

On the horse reaching the posts, the Rugger Tuggers began setting him up with Tracker for the launch; meanwhile Robert sent word along the line of those who'd just assisted: could they please, in pairs, post *Rattler's* spare oars under the hawser? Though not expecting friction to inhibit the animals, heading downhill, he would on the offchance like everyone standing by to again lift that long rope clear of the ground.

At the twin posts, all was now set.

Sophy looked down the incline; now the launch was imminent, it seemed steeper. 'Tracker,' she said, 'please do exactly as Charlie says: he's in charge. And,' turning, 'you too!'

Heather patted Aberdare, 'One stumble, boys, and we could all five be in big trouble; and I'd never forgive you horses if anything happened to either of my friends, d'you hear?'

Against the far side of Smith's Point a louder wave crumped itself to flying whiteness; they didn't know it, but just then aboard *Rattler* Jack was reciting Sir Francis Drake's Prayer.

*

'Lord God, when you call your servants to endeavour any great matter, grant us also to know that it is not the beginning, but the continuing of the same, until it be thoroughly finished, which yields the true glory; through him who, for the finishing of your work, laid down his life for us, our Redeemer, Jesus Christ...'

'Amen.'

*

From Corner Wharf, a cheer.

There came Jill from the water, flinging a sizeable mess of nylon net down onto the rocks near the pulley; she climbed up to receive from Coastguard Hoaten a wrapped-around towel – and a huge hug.

Another, louder, saucier cheer.

Suddenly, though, they saw Robert summoned by his radio; message received, he megaphoned, 'STAND BY FOR MAROONS!'

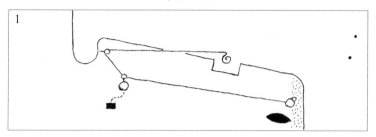

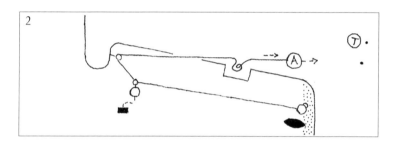

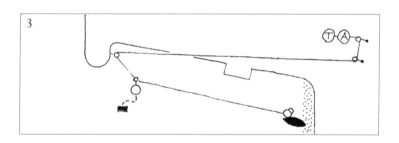

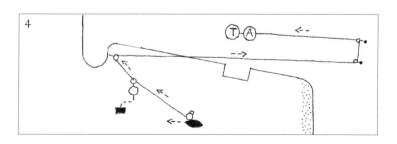

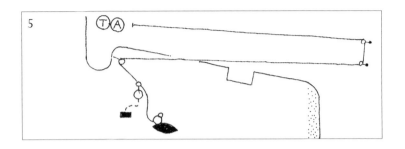

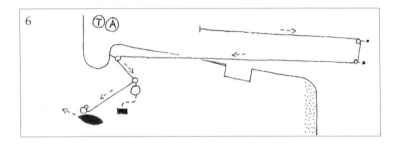

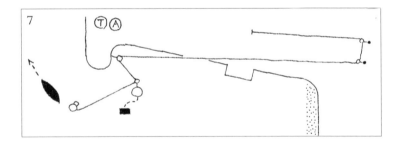

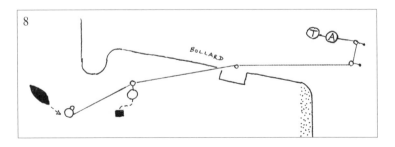

## CHAPTER 50

From Tram Gin Top, two thumping booms and hissing climbs…

'WHOA, THERE!' The girls were very glad of that tether behind them as their noddingly keen muscle-ticked steeds jolted forwards – not out of nervousness, but on the strength of the self-urge to be away.

Meanwhile from all about echoed dog barks, pheasants a-panic, horse neighs, gull screams…

One Rugger Tugger said, 'Good old Razzer, flying up there to signal those poor yacht people about help being on its way; they'd have not known, otherwise.'

'Aye: Jack's committed, now.'

'Us bloody all is, boy!'


Robert Hoaten's shrill whistle, calling for readiness.

As the Rugger Tuggers loosened their tethers, the two horses stomped and champed.

'Easy, now!' Charlie leading Tracker by his bridle, the pair crept forwards, hardly more than leaning into their harnesses. The girls just patted approvingly: no more encouragement needed for now.

Like slow electricity they saw straightening tension flow along the rope: down the long hill, along the path, out to Robert and Jill on the point, round the pulley and then across to the mid-channel buoy; as it disappeared from view on its way inbound to *Rattler's* bow, the youngsters imagined the whaler creeping forward, too, as her stern rope tautened back to that stranded tree trunk…

The green flag from Jill; megaphoned by Robert, 'RIGHT AWAY!'

'Go to steadily, boys!'

'Wish 'em God Speed for us, when you reaches the Point!' One of the Rugger Tuggers, who were keeping at their posts to see the hawser through its two turns. The other, 'So much for "Pushing the Boat Out", eh?'

They departed like a freight train: first very slowly but, with each second, slightly faster…

Such a difference, indeed, with gravity on the horses' side; additionally, the more hawser had turned back down the hill, the more of its weight was with them: soon, Charlie was trotting beside Tracker.

Heather's 'There she goes!', pointed to *Rattler* appearing from behind the trees, cutting such a brave sight, her wake dead straight. As Jack was intently and unswervingly looking ahead, one of the huddling crew must be fixedly watching aft, advising their alignment with the leading lights.

Sophy felt so proud, on Alice's behalf.

And mustn't Jack only look ahead? Though still some way back from the pill mouth, he was already working hard to hold the whaler steady through side-punching seesaw waters: those waves would, no question, have been pig awkward to row through – and very wet, without that temporary foredeck shedding so much boat-basting spray…

Thus, 'Enough, boys, enough!', Charlie didn't want them any faster, and huffed that he was glad for the ascending rope's drag; Sophy and Heather, mind, found this grudgingly checked pace punishingly bottom-bumping.

Taxiing out, just as Jack had asked for.

Down a channel emptying fast: the water depth at its entrance was ever lessening, exposing more of that black fissure in The Anvil's outer face.

And, all the while, swells came rolling across the pill mouth to slam that obdurate reef, so far crashing themselves harmlessly into froth and noise…

So far.


Both living outdoors, Tracker and Aberdare knew every sound which came and went with the sea's moods; what was more, their large and ever vigilant ears could detect sub-sounds of wind and water which humans couldn't.

When Heather and Sophy felt from both horses, simultaneously, grumbles of disquiet, those wise youngsters together suspected it: 'The Anvil's going to ring.'

Charlie, checking where she was, 'But Rattler can't stop now!'

'So,' Sophy knew, 'we must go for take-off: Heather, do a–!' As her friend shriekingly whistled, she gesticulated as best she could.

Robert Hoaten, immediately realising that a very much larger wave was on its hungry way in: from Smith's Point came his metallic 'FASTER, FASTER, **FASTER**!'

Charlie, 'GIDDUP, **GIDDUP!**', must let go and step back; as Tracker and Aberdare powered groundpounding past him, 'TAKE CARE, BOTH, and...' But by the time he'd swallowed that gulp, too late to say anything else. *For Maisie's sake, Lord, look after those precious girls!*

Sophy saw the men far below jump to it: they would help the horses fly! Those oars got smartly hoisted waist-high, then shouldered; the up-rope, thus liberated, went slithering ever quicker over their shiny shafts.

Oh, yes: the horses accelerated, then; and, thereby tightened, the down-rope cleared the ground. Yet less friction meant yet more acceleration: now the up-rope straightened away from those oars, became airborne...

As their mounts surged headlong down the steep bank, both girls got tummy-in-a-quick-lift feelings: take-off, indeed.

'G-Good luck, Heather!'

'Love you forever, Sophes!'

Out there a great wave was approaching; but now here came a thrust of rowdier air, rousting through the trees to their left: a roaringly powerful squall, which might drive *Rattler* swiftly past The Anvil and into the relative safety of the bay beyond...

But only if they could get her far enough from the land's lee to capture it, to exploit it: **'FASTER, TRACKER!, FASTER, ABERDARE!'**

*

Going like a minelayer now, hey, Jack?'

'You reckons? By God, girl, just you wait 'til we finds that wind!' *And we better had find it soon, or...*

*

The two great horses reached the incline foot at full thunder; on down the level track they went, same pace, knowing that only through their efforts could that black boat water-knife her brave humans to safety.

*

Though Jill's now fast-turning pulley almost mesmerised her, she saw how the hawser emerging from the water was tangling weed, twigs and stringy bits with it: they might cause a jam.

She scrambled back down right beside it, so she could keep the rope plucked clean: *Let nothing threaten this venture!*

*

In these two horses pulling, what puissance! The feel of Tracker's gallop, the sound and the tangible spirit of Aberdare just behind Sophy: she wouldn't ever forget this. The girl longed to turn, to just glimpse Heather and Abbey; that was impossible, though, because she'd overhanging oak branches to duck – and must dodge, too, the numerous dangling dead twigs which her horse was snapping like stalactites and sending whizzing every direction.

So intent, her and Heather, on the ride, they never saw *Rattler's* moment of finding the wind; but they certainly caught, WHAP!, the sound of that lionspaw pouncing her sails – just as she was closing on the mid-channel buoy.

*

Of course nobody on shore could hear Jack's sudden instructions, trimming sails and repositioning the crew to counterbalance that northerly's huge shove; and truly huge, it was, despite the reefed rig.

Suddenly bow-creaming and white-waked, the boat was now beating the horses, was running the hawser down – and would soon be overrunning it, possibly fouling it; what was more, once *Rattler* had passed that fast-looming orange buoy, that same rope which had blessedly brought her to find the wind might then snatch her back, slewing or even capsizing her...

Amy, immediately understanding, whipped the slack of the line inboard–

And Jack's swift knife slashed it through: 'You was right, girl: 'twas the only thing to do!'

Although, both knew, that there was now no chance of a tow back in afterwards.

*

Though still out of sight west of that bluff, it was so loud, now, for the deep-hearing horses, the liquid shudder of that steep-hilled inromping green. They didn't understand what that noise from the boat had meant; but how much easier to run, now!

Instantly, so different a ride; what, the girls wondered, had let the horses suddenly gallop faster?

And faster still, feeding each other's keenness: speed was intoxicating them both.

*

It was spinning, now, like a mill bobbin, Jill's pulley; but the rope, though racing, had obviously slackened: 'Robert, something's WRONG!'

*

So much spray was billowing inland on the bluff's backwind, only then did Sophy see where they were – how near oblivion. She screamed…

*

And Robert Hoaten, whirling round from watching that wave with a head full of prayers, 'CHRIST, the horses are running away!'

And taking those children with them.

Jill, what can we—?

She knew, and was already reacting: 'Tell them to—'

He, understanding, grabbed the metal trumpet: 'FOR GOD'S SAKE, **HOLD ON!**'


## CHAPTER 51

So many realising eyes, so many people suddenly praying…

Jill grabbed the net, and lump-jammed it into the pulley sheave's nip…

In a screeing smoke of nylon the wheel seized, and the rope stopped dead.

All up the track and down again, a wild wowing sound as the hawser snapped straight, water heasing from its crushed fibres; the posts up the hill thrummed with shock, and every watcher heard metallic cracking as the horses' trace chains knacked bar-tight.

The animals reared, eyes popping, wheezing like Vulcan's bellows from being harness-winded; impetus drove both riders out of their saddles to whump against their mounts' necks…

Then came the rope's rebound, which reverse-staggered Aberdare and Tracker drunkenly; both girls bottom-bomped very firmly back where they'd been a moment before…

And it was over – with all of them very shaken but safe, and only slightly hurt.

The quickest of dismounting hugs, then a rush to the track's end

333

– and no nearer the sea than that, for in carved the great wave now, terrifyingly magnificent, the stacks and spurs west of them white-bursting its landwards extremity to depth-charged oblivion.

Watching *Rattler* creaming past The Anvil, her bow high-riding heaped spume, Sophy saw why Jack had ballasted her; he mightn't be flying much canvas, but the wind's force on those drum-taut sails must be tremendous: the whaler's windward rigging looked violin-tensioned and her masts clearly bent; miraculous, surely, how nothing aboard had surrendered to such forces.

And nothing must, for the frothed seaspace this boat crossed was falling, keel-troughing her – sucking her, seemingly, towards that approaching waterwall.

'She's *really* going, now – but why doesn't Jack steer them *that* way?'

'Because,' Robert gasped, having just reached them, 'the wind's on her wrong side.' Shaking his head, 'By Christ it's bad luck, the sails setting themselves so; but Jack daren't gybe: never mind losing speed with the wave almost on them, that shock loading of everything going over at once might carry her whole rig away.'

'So what can he–?'

'WE,' Jill roared, 'will **PRAY!**'

Monstrously loud, the wave's near edge ripped past below them; just before its spray clouds obliterated their offshore view Sophy glimpsed a dullshiny hull, far-tilted, teetering mounded green – then, nothing.

Where the whaler had been seconds earlier, a headlong avalanche of water which would have swept the boat up and slammed it broadside against The Anvil. So easy, witnessing that **BOOM!**, to imagine her utter destruction, ragdoll bodies flung far aloft along with broken boatwood by that sky-hurtling white column…

Which now descended, energy spent, upon Anvil Head's salt-burnt rabbit pasture: a coldboiling cataract, it swept back down to the reef uprooted gorse, torn clumpgrass, loosened stones that smashed themselves apart.

A detached moment for Jill: the arresting spectacle of Nature's artistry…

Then, the next second, such a mind-frosting truth…

No *Rattler*.

# CHAPTER 52

Then, through Charlie's tears, 'THERE SHE IS!'

As Jack's voice crackled from Robert's radio, 'ARE YOU ALL WELL ASHORE, OVER?'

'Yes, boy, but for a few bruises. And you lot, over…?'

'THE SAME. NOT QUITE WHAT WE PLANNED, I KNOW — BUT IT WORKED, OVER!'

Robert, seeing Heather's pleading look, pressed the button for Sophy: 'H-Hello, Jack? From all of us, including the Rugger Tuggers, and the horses too, God Speed, over!'

'BLESS YOU ALL FOR OUR LIVES! SHAN'T SAY MORE NOW — GOT A HARD SAIL AHEAD. AND OUT.'

Though pointlessly, all cheered; the horses, who'd dragged their way over, whinnied too.

And suddenly Robert was laughing: 'The cunning, the jammy SOD! Because of the way he went tipping over that bloody great wave, when he was in the dip behind he could put his helm over, and get the sails across, before the wind caught Rattler again – d'you all see?

They did, and must again cheer; for now *Rattler*, cutting whiteboiling across the gale's face with her crew leaning the starboard gunwale against her other-canted masts, was indubitably going like a minelayer.

Heather whooped, 'She is thundering well FLYING!'

With such speed, in such a sea, the whaler was soon but a grey rumour; after passing the promontory called Red Cliff and turning north-west, she was wholly stolen from view by a steely curtain of rain.

Sophy groaned.

'No, no,' Robert Hoaten heartened her, 'rain that hard is a really good thing: it'll flatten the sea.'

Heavy rain, aye, and quickly arriving at Smith's Point.

'Leave the hawser for the moment,' Robert suggested, holding hands with hunching Jill, 'and let's find shelter!'

Trace chains cast off as well, three quiet youngsters led the horses back along the track; each sensed that the others were praying for everyone out there – on *Rattler*, aboard the yacht, crewing the damaged *Jasmine*, too.

Past dripping eyebrows Sophy peered up the incline: 'Poor Kaycee, up that mast in this!'

Charlie patted, 'At least she's trained for such tasks; mind, I'm glad she's got Hector's coat.'

'I get the impression he would have been, too.'

Heather nodded, 'Yes; he was a great old chap. Very teasing, sometimes, but that was fine.'

'Um... Is Jack Sound married, or has he ever been?'

'What on earth made you ask that, Sophes?'

Back at Corner Wharf they hitched the horses beneath that thickly-leaved natural umbrella which was an old crouching oak, and splattered over to investigate... a Pirate Encampment, apparently.

Fully occupied with the launch, they'd not noticed other activity. Assisted by Felix, his jeep shuttling the causeway and cautiously journeying the pill's northern shore, some typically practical Pembrokeshire women had pressed *Alecto's* masts and sails into service as a bivouac shelter.

A driftwood fire burning well nearby, everyone could dry themselves and, courtesy of The Davy Lamp, enjoy a second breakfast.

Once people felt restored, Robert Hoaten spoke: 'I'm hoping some of you can stay on, because Jack must get *Rattler* back in somehow, and his planned method isn't workable at the moment. Maybe low tide'll let us reach the sinker buoy and puts things right; if not, this northerly might drift us the hawser out using another buoy. But, either way, there mightn't be enough time to set up for horse haulage – in which case, we'd need lots of people pulling that rope towards the causeway while Jack steers in on the leading lights.'

Somebody shouted, 'We're all staying, Robert!'

Nobody dissented – so that was that settled.

'For now,' he resumed, 'Kaycee's occasionally sighting Rattler, in rain lulls, making a run well out west into deeper water, where the waves aren't so steep. A while, it'll be, before Jack tacks, and she begins talking him towards the yacht – if her radio and those binoculars hold out, that is.'

Felix, immediately, 'I've spare batteries for both with me; but if I try getting them to her, I'm afraid our security people – they're surely maintaining surveillance – will intervene.'

Jill said, 'Let's send Sophy on Tracker to Tram Gin Top with some food: a lone girl being least suspicious, when Kaycee hauls up the basket, batteries included, those watchers should be none the wiser.'

Heather thought breakfast would only recharge Kaycee for a bit, though; 'She's tough, but it must be miserable up there: she'll need relieving soon.'

Felix sighed, 'On her coming down, it would be operation over, I'm afraid: the equipment she's using is… well, she shouldn't really have it. And she certainly shouldn't use it to assist civilians, as far as our Head of Security's concerned.'

'What,' Sophy blazed, 'not even to help rescue people at sea?'

'Miss, I'm on your side as much as Kaycee and Amy are – that's why I'm here when I shouldn't be. But until you've met our HOS, you can't understand the attitude we're up against.'

# Chapter 53

As Tracker topped the incline, Sophy saw that Alice was also encamped.

Did Jack's friends, the Buckleys, own that posh stand-up-insidable tent? It was pitched north enough of the mast for the writer to have Kaycee in sight from within.

Lamorna had been considered, too; she was hitched in the rain shadow of dense blackthorn. Sophy patted, 'I'll take you over there soon, Tracks!' But first, as instructed, straight to the mast: 'BREAKFAST, KAYCEE!'

'YOU SWEET ANGEL OF MERCY!' Down came the rope, plus the pilot line: 'KEEP HOLD OF THAT, AND PAY IT OUT TIGHTLY AS I HAUL UP, HONEY; OTHERWISE, THE WIND MIGHT TIP MY FOOD OUT.'

Sensing being watched, *Your batteries, too; and how awkward might that be?* Knots tied, 'GO!'

Consignment arrived, 'MY COMPLIMENTS TO THE CHEF: THIS'LL KEEP ME EVER READY!'

Leading Tracker to shelter, Sophy called back, 'EAT SLOWLY, NOW: DON'T VOLT IT ALL DOWN AT ONCE.'

'ROGER THAT!'

Alice had a folding chair, a thermos, even her writing wherewithal. A torch, too, for exchanging Morse code messages with Kaycee: 'Lucky, isn't it, that during the war I learnt lots about signalling?'

'How is she, Alice? Your communicating must be brilliant for morale.'

The lady sighed, 'She seems cheerful, but I think she's cold.'

Sophy started explaining why Kaycee couldn't be relieved—

Mrs Williams suddenly coughed fitfully, clutching her throat.

Horrified, the girl came close; between hacks Alice whispered, 'There's someone outside.'

Flattening onto the clammy PVC groundsheet, Sophy lifted the fabric edge to peer... She reported, 'Green wellies!'

Not military, then. Alice, unzipping a vent flap, 'Come in, why don't you?' Then to Sophy she hushed, 'For once, I'm glad to see a journalist.'

In came the Pembrokeshire Chronicle lady: 'Sorry for the subterfuge,' she spattered, removing a natty so'wester hat. 'But, having twigged that this rescue mission wasn't getting official US assistance, despite all their capabilities, I'd an inkling that if I asked straight out what was afoot you wouldn't let on, because of your loyalty to whoever from the base is helping. So, yes, I snooped; but I promise, I wouldn't dream of—'

A nearby beefy American male voice had wheezed, '*JESUS!*'

Peeping, the lady whispered, 'Another would-be eaves-dropper...?'

A barrel of a man in battledress, chest badges proclaiming him of elevated rank and highly decorated, stood wetly and miserably between Tracker and Lamorna; they both trailed bitten-through hitching ropes. Whichever way he tried moving, they'd have none of it. He growled, 'What's wrong with these stupid creatures?'

Alice Williams, deducing who this was, 'Perhaps you don't remember Tracker; he obviously remembers you. And he won't ever forget what you planned, when – through no fault of his own – you found him aboard one of your 'planes.'

Beside her, the journalist's sugary explosion: 'Gosh – you're the base's Head of Security, aren't you? Being that muddy makes you much more Tough Guy than when you do public liaison briefings, I must say!'

That un-grumped him a bit.

'But,' she continued, 'don't you know to never call horses stupid, to never even *think* it? Try seeing things from the perspective of these two: they're hugely loyal to Sophy, here – and, as far as they're concerned, you might mean her harm. So just explain that you're offering help with the rescue, and once they see she's happy about that…'

Sophy rushed out into the rain and, shaking the man's hand, 'Look here, Tracker and Lamorna, he's here to *help*!' And, despite knowing that he wasn't, 'This is the gentleman who kindly arranged a helicopter to take the rubbish off Mill Cove, and now he's going to–'

Alice, pointing upwards, 'Do the chivalrous thing by relieving Kaycee Fleischmann on lookout duties up that mast, as soon as we've Lamorna ready to hoist him.'

The journalist bubbled, 'Oh, this will make a wonderful cover story, and how proud your wife and children will be: camaraderie and equality in one fearless action!'

From his walkie-talkie, Kaycee's emotion-cracked voice: 'HEY, SIR, PLEASE DON'T COMMIT TO THIS RÔLE IF YOU NEED TO TRAVEL ABOUT, CO-ORDINATING OUR RESPONSE TO THIS EMERGENCY. I MAY BE WET AND COLD UP HERE, BUT I UNDERSTAND ABOUT YOUR HAVING TO DO WHAT'S RIGHT, OVER.'

Struggling to make his grimace smiley, 'Negative, Fleischmann: We - are - swapping! With an extra-channeled radio, no reason why I can't keep watch *and* supervise from up there, huh?'

Alice, now all sweetness and light, 'Look here, any of your assistants you need close by are welcome to share my tent; before Sophy and Lamorna send you aloft, would you like a drink of coffee?'

Holding the lady's look, 'Most kind of you, Ma'am, but I should take station as of immediate.' Turning with a gulp to the girl, 'Ahum… to confirm there are no hard feelings, I'd like Tracker to hoist me. D'you think he'd do that, Miss?'

Thinking how the mast was gyrating and vibrating with svelte Kaycee up there, and wondering how much – rather how many times – heavier this man was, 'Once I've told him how brave you're being.'

Within minutes of the Head of Security taking over up top, a USAF Sikorsky was on station out over the bay, monitoring *Rattler's* progress; thus relieved, the RAF's Sea King headed to the airbase for refuelling.

Saturated camouflaged characters having appeared on the green from all quarters, one of them loaned Alice a walkie-talkie so that she could take Kaycee and Sophy home for hot showers without the three of them missing any developments. They left Tracker patiently grazing near Lamorna; he and Sophy should head back down the hill before too long.

Soon returning with freshly-brewed tea and a welcome snack for everyone, Alice and her younger friends found large military vehicles now clustered about the place.

A happy Felix L'Hermitte, already assured that neither he nor Kaycee would be disciplined, was getting a steel lattice tower erected; on this would be mounted a set of patrol aircraft surveillance cameras, complete with automatic lens wipers to keep them rain-free. He radioed the Head of Security, 'Once we're operational, Sir, you can come down, over!'

'NEGATIVE, L'HERMITTE. I OWE IT TO THOSE WELSHMEN: WHILE THEY'RE OUT THERE, I'M STAYING UP HERE, OVER.'

'Don't forget Amy Heckrottss, Sir: she will, I'm sure, appreciate your solidarity as well, over.'

'MY GOD, YOU DON'T MEAN SHE'S OUT IN THAT...?'

'Makes me mighty proud to be in a mixed unit, Sir!'

'L'HERMITTE, MAKE SURE YOU GET DARN GOOD FOOTAGE OF THIS RESCUE, D'YOU HEAR? I WANT ALL OF AMERICA TO BE PROUD OF WHAT THAT FINE YOUNG WOMAN IS DOING, OVER!'

Kaycee's eyebrows: 'Hard to believe it's the same man! You guys sure did a brilliant job of puttin' him on the spot.'

'Mieu!', said Daphne, who'd picked her way over to the tent, after a long time spent just watching and listening; *Those horses played the crucial rôle!*

*

The rendezvous in the bay went amazingly smoothly; just after the Sea King had taken the yachtsmen off *Rattler,* the American Sikorsky lowered hot food and drink to the whaler.

While Jack and his fellow rescuers refuelled, a coamer engulfed the unattended yacht's cockpit; it tilted and, in seconds, was gone. Some aboard *Rattler* groaned; the old coxswain counteracted, 'While she stayed afloat, she was another hazard to navigation; we were never towing her in, and,' he grimaced, 'she'd have been smashed to matchwood, going ashore. And anyway, Amy's airbase pals are taking the search for this whatever-it-is that seriously, perhaps they'll use divers and a Cheroot to salvage her, just to be sure she doesn't drift about underwater, with her sonar echoes leading them on a wild goose chase.'

At which, they heard again that deep Flogga-Flogga: rescue of humans over, the three monstrous Chinooks could resume their hunting.

Though weary, Jack wouldn't show it. He chuckled, 'It's the shift change: out they come, and we'll soon go home, eh?'

Amy suddenly frowned, 'Coxswain, Sir, did you hear something like a big church bell ringing?'

*

Alice, Kaycee, and Sophy had, with delight, watched operations on Felix's television monitors; the journalist, meanwhile, had been unbelievably busy: interviewing locals and Americans, writing notes, sending reports to both BBC *and* ITV from the red telephone box: this scoop was going to make her name.

All the while, the Head of Security had stayed up that mast, despite its liveliness; he'd certainly had a wilder time of it than Kaycee.

They'd just heard Jack report, 'THIS IS RATTLER SAYING WE'RE OFF HOME NOW, OVER!', when Tracker once again broke free. This time he went straight to the mast's foot, there to stand grumblingly and staring at a point part way up it.

Alice immediately gesticulated to Felix, 'Tell your boss to abseil down NOW!' She hurried over and, putting her ear to it, 'My God: you can hear it going!'

The HOS had got about a quarter of the way down when, emitting pistol-sharp reports, the mast's top half began leaning: a crack was opening, soon so large that everyone could see it. As gravity swayed the man away from the upper section, that increased leverage worsened matters; however, with nothing to brace his pointlessly paddling feet against, he couldn't lower himself further.

More loud noises: half way up, the great wooden pole was bending like a knee joint. Alice patted Kaycee, 'There's nothing we can do, but pray. If it keeps giving out gradually, maybe he'll be able to...'

'Sure,' said the young woman, 'because he's done plenty parachute jumps. But, even so, if it ends up giving out completely, just after he's hit the ground the mast will fall on top of...'

CRACK! And the masts's top half was tilting quickly, hingeing down like a railway signal arm. The big American, dropping fast below it, 'GUYS, I'M SORRY I–!'

With a whoofing thump he landed across Tracker's back; immediately, the horse sprang forwards, just getting himself and the man clear before the toppling white pole walloped deep into the wet ground behind them.

Only blacked out for a second, Colonel Thaddeus Fibflinger came to feeling very sore; miraculously, nothing seemed broken. Feeling hands supporting him, he ungripped the horse's saddle and, slipping backwards to the ground, stood wobblily.

Ignoring medics rushing up with a stretcher, he went stiffly to address the animal face to face: 'Guess I'm always goin' to owe ya one huge favour, my friend!' He turned, 'Could somebody please get a veterinary to check this horse over, soonest? My belly might have saved my ribs, but with my weight I sure hit this fella hard – and I feel mighty bad about that.'

Moments later, he was arming those now-swarming medics away: 'Will you please stop fussin' over me? I can see that L'Hermitte has important news.'

Felix announced from the Comms truck steps, 'Rattler's taking water, Sir: she's struck that underwater object herself – and it *is* a freight container. A-And at least one of its doors is loose, and banging when it rolls, apparently – which explains some of the audio we've been detecting. The Sea King is going to take her crew off but, meanwhile, one of them has volunteered to swim across and attach a buoyed line, so we shan't lose the container again – apparently it hardly shows above the surface at all.'

Alice nodded, 'That'll be Dipper Davies.'

Thaddeus Fibflinger said, 'The guy deserves a medal – Dammit, I mean, an *EXTRA* medal!' He turned to Felix, 'After the RAF have evacuated that vessel's crew, bring in a Chinook straight away, please.'

'For lifting the container, Sir? Umm… Shouldn't we first evaluate its status?'

'I beg your pardon: I didn't make myself clear. No – the Chinook is for the Rattler. The least we can do is get Coxswain Sound's boat safely back home, after all he and his people – out there and down by the shore – have done this morning.'

## Chapter 54

On Carol slept; wind eased, The Snug's stove's flue pipe was quiet.

Rain blatted the attic roof and battered garden greenery, gutters gargoyled to vomiting; but thick walls plus heavy planking and lush rugs overhead were so muffling, her ears only imagined a plush Pullman railing fast, white vapour clouds and lush scenery hushing past.

No travel clock ticked, even: quickly she'd learnt in Pembrokeshire that the stomach of Mogulus would rouse one quite soon enough, every morning.

*

With Vince now enblanketed alongside like a little sister, on Bronwen slept.

Rain drumming was nothing to one who'd grown up beside a straining railway gradient. In her little years, steam had shaken her dreams all night: the Castle class locos, especially, blasting like furnaces and similarly dark-glaring, too. Then, the consistent disappointment of Diesels; but at least the noisiest, twenty four pistons hammer and tongs – they'd thrown sparks after dark, too – had had proud Western names: Champion, Yeoman, Firebrand…

*

Fellow travellers daughtered Carol's dream: Sophy, Heather, and a love-eyed Swansea girl.

*

Trains of thought, passing Bronny's pillow: Hugh's kindnesses, Carol's deep-reaching care…

In a lull between two Vincenza, though not quite sure why, knew she must take her leave.

*

Mogulus stayed there, sheltering from the rain but watching what it did: this was, he knew, what he must do.

*

What of Taggle? A long, long while earlier Mr Madoc had beckoned him to the farmhouse, fisty threats whispered against his making noise.

*

Rain.

Turning garden paths into sliding, bubble-popped canals; saturating the spinney floor and downing yet more green detritus; speeding, muddying, and deepening the Mill Brook…

But then that flow suddenly ceased, there at the spinney bridge where Mogulus dutifully watched; and he, barely believing it, began to worry.

Approaching at a soaked trot, 'Hess!'

This hadn't happened since the flat lands: another cat on his territory. But Mogulus didn't arch and hiss; realising that they could read his thoughts, he recognised a fellow soul.

He slipped out from under that fallen tree and joined the other on the bridge. Ignoring the downpour both peered, contemplating the thin trickle below: so much precipitation, very little flow. 'Maow!', said Mogulus; 'I don't like it.'

Vincenza looked east: 'Up there; upstream.' She hissed, 'I'll go.'

And Mogulus saw that she should. Trouble was brewing; should a human come, his loud voice could get their attention. But he conceded uncomfortably, wondering if the she-cat appreciated how big this trouble, so powerfully portended, might be.

*

Bronny: so happily slept; so saddened on waking to find Vincey gone. Or had last evening's sentimental mood dreamed the little friend?

'No!' For there, on the blanket, brindly hairs. Sitting up, 'Where are you, Puss?'

Other questions: 'Why's it so quiet?' So quiet, apart from the loud, loud rain. 'Why so *late*, and nobody's woken me?' Indeed, why was nobody about?

*Where's Sabrina?*

And where was… 'TAGGLE?'

Feeling adrift without power, like last night's coaster on the news, she hustled clothes on, then donned Mr Madoc's old mucking-out mackintosh and her own puncture-repaired boots.

Splattering into the farmhouse, 'Taggle, you'll get FOUR BISCUITS for finding Vincey!'

He was off out of that door like a rocket.

Then, into Mrs Madoc's arms: 'Why's everything *wrong?*'

*

Carol, up now, hadn't been too concerned at first about this Mogulus-free morning.

Before breakfasting she'd tried calling him from both doors; but, having done so well with supper scraps last night, she'd decided he was surely tucked up somewhere comfortable, sitting out this shocking rain. *Maybe with a mouse or two for nutritious company.*

But, what if he weren't...? *He's a dear Puss, and Sophy would never forgive me if he were in trouble, and needing help: I'd best go out looking, soon.*

*

Saturated, that Pembrokeshire soil could absorb no more water; rain, now, on landing, immediately trickled brook-wards. Down lanes, across meadows, between myriad crop stems in the fields, over woodland floors...

But still nothing passed under the spinney's bridge.

Saturated air, too: all windows and windscreens were steamily streaming, that morning. Thus so little seen from passing vehicles, or from the houses they passed: therefore water, there where it shouldn't be, and in such quantity, was out of human sight...

But not out of animal minds.


Here came the she-cat again; alas, also, that trouble-loving dog.

Mogulus sprang fretfully to interpose himself; however, it seemed the two had a truce.

Vincenza stared upstream: 'Bad! Water; WATER!'

Taggle barked to her, 'Come!'

But then the three heard it, dull through the downpour: the door of Drift Cottage, and 'PUSSY? MOGULUS?' called worriedly.

He said to the she-cat, 'Come with *me!*' And to the dog, 'Go and tell it: TROUBLE!'

## Chapter 55

Mrs Madoc turned off the wireless: 'Well, what a risky carry-on! But good old Jack Sound, eh?'

Bronny, eyes welling, 'And Amy, and those brave chaps; and everyone back safely, thank heavens! Plus, on shore, our two young girls with Charlie, and Alice and Jilly, and your fantastic horses helping – and I'm sure Sabrina and Kaycee were involved, too, although the Beeb didn't say... And through it all, I slept!'

The lady hugged, 'Bronwen, don't feel bad about that: as they said in the war, "They also serve...". You had to be here, girl: if there'd been problems, we wouldn't have coped without you. And think: if they hadn't intercepted that yacht, and she'd beached at Mill Cove, Mr and you and Carol might have been first on the scene.'

This was true, Bronny saw. 'Anyway, isn't it good to know the panicking's over?'

But here came Taggle.

*

Hearing scratches, Carol unlatched; two animals inrushed.

Never having even heard of Vincenza, she didn't know the tortoiseshell; indeed only its miaows initially confirmed the second bedragglement as Moggo. As Jill's cat showed no animosity towards the other, she fed both, then fetched her hairdryer: its slow speed shouldn't be frightening.

It wasn't; moreover, restored, the tortoiseshell's fur confessed a familiar scent: 'Been with Bronny, hmm?'

'Huss!'

After reccying from Jill's study, Mogulus returned to the kitchen. The girl's mother had been ruddy good to him and the she-cat; now, with good reason, to be unreasonably demanding: 'Miao-wow!' *We want the wood stove lit!*

She stared back, incredulous: she'd understood.

'Mieu-oh!' *Lit NOW!*

'Mogulus, yes *of course* my softy daughter would do that for you: for you, she'd do absolutely anything.'

'Heah?' *Please?*

That settled matters: Carol couldn't refuse Bronwen's little friend.

*Ah, well: I'll be staying in to stoke it for them.* She had contemplated a waterproofed walkabout.

*

The rain wasn't easing; but deep in the spinney, far under it, something was.

Was submitting to the pent pressure of three hours' rain – which had completely submerged Mill Lane and the meadows either side, had flooded part of Tracker's field, and was now backing deeply up under the humptibump bridge, even into the parish above…

A great muddy bubble erupted from The Mist Pool. The massive second, following soon after, was a phenomenal release of long-ago air: the whole surface domed and then thousandgallon burst, farflinging also pondweed, russet mud, and coal.

Carol would have heard that waterbelch, had she been outside; and she'd have surely gone to see, just as inquisitive Romans from Pompeii had once approached a newly-smoking Vesuvius.

*

Taggle had brought Mr Madoc in with him.

Who'd been going round the stalls, distributing some feed for the interim: only Sabrina or Bronny knew exactly how much of what each pony got. He said, 'I don't reckon it's rats exciting him, and he's surely over those maroons, by now.'

Mrs said, 'Vincey came home last night, and slept with Bronwen; but as she'd vanished this morning, we sent him to find her.'

'Judging from that orange mud on his paws, he's been poking around beside Jill's stream.'

'Riff!' He had, and with good reason: after leaving the cats, curiosity had made him retrace Vincey's scent and find that great new shouldn't-be-there lake; then, sniffing and digging and afterwards cocking his ear into the stewy pit he'd made, he'd assured himself that something *really ruddy rum* was up.

Bronny, guiltily, 'Look here, I should start on stable work. Tag couldn't have really understood when I said about looking for Vincey; he's probably just fizzed up because of a bloody squirrel, and–'

Mrs Madoc, putting the receiver back, 'Jill's line is up the creek.'

Indeed.

Immediately, that changed things: 'Shall we take the Landy, Mr M?'

'Roff!' *Bad idea!*

'There are probably branches down, so walking will be faster. Let's get ourselves some hard hats, girl – and a rope.'

'REAFF!' *GET A BLOODY SHIFT ON, THEN!*

*

The two cats were amusing company; not amusing-entertaining, though, but amusing-intriguing.

The tortoiseshell was a less demonstrative but also less demanding companion, being satisfied with unpampering human company: she'd curl passively on your lap while you wrote. Amazingly, egocentric Mogulus tolerated this without apparent jealousy, he who always came over possessive when either girl had long cuddles from her.

Restless Mogulus: he frequently hopped onto the windowsill, peered through the murk, and then flopped back to his place next the hearth; the complex noises he and the other subsequently exchanged seemed suspiciously like conversation.

*

The belching had become rhythmic; the mess thereabouts was worsening fast, with each eructation being bumpier. And, besides that sulphurous air, now water pulsed out too; indeed before long, more was welling into The Mist Pool from that mysterious source than The Drift fed...

And ever more water, until Jill's garden channel was violently torrenting: brown-seething, coal tumbling.

Thus, while waves kept thundering grey-green onto Mill Cove's reef, their white spumes were soon overspilling into a turbid, black-lumped lagoon.

## Chapter 56

'AT LAST!' After having its distributor cap, HT leads, and sparking plugs baked dry in Alice's oven, Bumble had fired.

Jill shouted to the girls and Charlie, 'As we can't raise Drift Cottage, let's trundle over and check what's what. You won't be taking the horses home 'til this rain's at least eased, so that means fetching extra hay back, okay?'

*

Faster belching: a demonic fountain in Drift Cottage's garden, now, a hydraulic volcano flobbing out slobbery mud clods.

Filthy streamlets snaked across the once-were flowerbeds from where the gobbed muck was landing; out of a channel become shark-toothed turbulent, water burst-bombed.

Further down, those unseen stonehollows could no longer percolate the stream away as they had for so many years: it went rippling across Jill's track in a widening swathe.

*

Curtaining rain stung the pill's surface into grey froth.

Mid-causeway, they only saw tarmac-dancing water ahead and behind, nor anything distinguishable on either side.

An unsettling illusion: their lone car in wet infinity, without destination…

Happily, Heather was soon dashing for Jill's paper and a Chronicle.

*

'That swell sounds even more ominous, with the wind eased.'

'Easier on the ear than bloody Taggle, though!'

His manic routine: hurtle down the track, skid a U-turn, bomb back, frantically barking, *Come on, COME ON!* But, this being typical behaviour for any terrier at a walk's start, Mr Madoc and Bronny just strode smartly, sometimes cursing the slidy washed-mud surface.

*

Five yards of Drift Cottage's approach were now under water.

*

As they second-geared out of Colliers' Quay, the screen magically cleared; Jill said, 'That's odd!'

Charlie had felt the change: 'Cooler rain, suddenly.'

Making them the first people that morning to properly see out of their car, approaching the humptibump bridge. Screech-stopping, Jill window-cranked, 'Look at that thundering FLOOD!'

Pierced by her telephone poles, disappearing into the spinney fifty brown yards wide…

Having wholly drowned Mill Lane.

Heather gasped, 'Your house!'

Sophy wailed, 'MY MUMMY!' And burrowed, gasping sobs, against Charlie's chest.

*

Mr Madoc peered: 'No wonder he had forty bloody fits! Where's the bastud brook gone?'

Bronny studied Taggle's antics: 'For now, he doesn't care: it's Drift Cottage he's worried about. Let's go and check that Carol's all right; seeing he's so fizzicated, I'll use the rope as a leash.'

But Bronwen Landore wasn't brilliant at knots.

'You go ahead, girl; I think I hear a Morris coming – which is Martin The Post, probably. I don't like this situation, so I'll hold whoever they are here until you report back.'

Bronny unpocketed a lifejacket whistle, gifted her by Kaycee: 'This'll easily carry here from the cottage. "O" is "Okay"; "S" is for "Stay where you are."'

'Sweetheart,' he hugged, 'TAKE CARE: just look at Taggle's hackles. And now imagine my wife's going after me, if you gets in a scrape.'

*

Almost at the boil, the kettle on the woodburner, thus at its most raucous growling and bumpeting.

Carol loved this comforting steam-song, reminiscent of childhood High Tea in Scotland. Into the kitchen, therefore, to clatter together the wherewithals for Proper Coffee – her Writing Fuel.

*

Almost at the boil: thus one might describe Gwinear's Conduit.

One hundred years of silted idleness were over; once the remaining plug of mud had dislodged, it could again do what it had been built for: conveying water freely.

With deep grumblings that last underground blockage eroded; even before its loosened detritus burst, airborne, out of The Mist Pool as if mortar-fired, all wild animals around had detected that hydraulic disturbance – and turned fearful heads.

*

Master of nosiness, Taggle nevertheless sensed a need for self-preservation that morning. Something over there was holding back bigly, but wasn't holding back at all well: couldn't the girl feel that? Never mind fearing for the woman in the cottage, she should worry about herself – *And me!*

'Tag, STOP IT! Stop tugging, and stop barking: can't you see,

350

the brook's somehow diverted itself into Jill's stream? And that's the oddest noise from over there; shut up, and you'll hear it too.'

'Reff-UFF!' *I effing well CAN hear it!*

'Oh, diddums: all upset about putting your tooties in muddy water, are you? Well, I'm not carrying you, buster, because that orange stuff stains clothes – and this water isn't that deep, anyway.'

'ROUFF!' *It flipping well will be!*

*

It was the artist's Morris.

Mr Madoc blocked its path, comedy-film-policeman style; then he saw Jill's expression – and splashed over, realising that, in the back, Charlie and Heather were struggling with Sophy.

'Mr Madoc, thank heavens you've realised about the flood, and are stopping people like the postman going further! Sophy's been in such a tizz about her mum these last two miles, so please tell us – is Carol up at the farmhouse, or has she gone over to Granny's?

'How big a flood, Jill? Carol's still at your house, we're supposing; Bronny's not long gone down with Taggle to check.'

*

Now the kettle was whistling like an old express; but Carol, having had such a neat story idea, was at the kitchen table, furiously scribbling. She shouted snugwards, 'I'll be there soon, pussies!'

Mogulus and Vincenza weren't bothered: having selective hearing, they could tune that whistling out. Both now on the windowsill, through the glass they heard, faintly, in one direction, the young woman arguing with the dog; meanwhile it held their stares, what had once been the stream.

*

Anticipating Sophy's wrenching from her friends to flee the car Mr Madoc shouted 'JILL, CATCH HER!'

The woman did her best, but missed; stepping slightly from the track's centre and bracing his arms *so*, as the fleet child jinked to cross behind he, 'SORRY, GIRL!', twisted, his lightning foot full-sprawling her: not nice Rugby tactics, but… Standing the poor youngster up again, he hand-clamped that 'MUMMY!' - screaming mouth.

A weepy Jill kissed those poor grazed hands; her hanky unsplashed that miserable face. Beckoning the others, who'd hung back, 'The

351

brook's dammed somewhere up *there*. Carol's in my house, we think; she should be fine, because it's some way above the valley bottom. Bronny's gone down; she doesn't know about the flood above here, but Taggle's with her and his instinct's pretty good. The LAST THING Bronny should hear, Sophy Fossway, is any shouting which might make her turn round and come back this way: Mr Madoc reckons she's either past the point of greatest risk already, or soon will be. So, girl, do you promise not to scream, or bolt, if he frees you?'

The girl nodded; he let go, making pained apologies for that thuggish tackle. Then, 'You should know very soon that your Mum's safe: Bronwen has a whistle, and we agreed on signals. So let's all try listening, and—'

A crushing rush, just like a large tipper lorry unloading at once; then, a profound roar.

\*

'Mao-OH!' Mogulus and Vincenza, the only witnesses.

The jumpy belching of The Mist Pool was no more; now there rose from that stone-walled sump a shining coffee-coloured arch of fast water, fully six feet high. Utterly incapable of containing such torrenting, the whole of Jill's garden channel immediately overflowed.

A brown wall of water rushed across the lawn; then, a filthy lake having formed in no time, that deluge seemed suddenly to remember allegiance to gravity – and made a surging lunge seawards, through the hedge bordering the track.

\*

'RIFF-IFF!' *Each for themselves!* The terrier gave an almighty tug on the rope; whanged leftwards as the knot gave, he shot sideways across the camber, and tipped over the embankment's edge. He disappeared from Bronny's view bomb-bouncing down through bracken…

…As, surreal shock, from the other direction came a vile tide, instantly fillbooting and then on up past her knees, rising relentlessly.

# Chapter 57

The cats only heard, over that Niagaran racket, '**TAG!**'

Still the kettle shrieked.

But it had plenty of water in, and this was such a golden lode of an idea Carol chased, like a lucky Klondike miner: on flew her pencil, along line after line.

\*

It was agonising, their inaction, but clearly nobody must go down the track: should whatever had dammed the brook's flow let go, there'd be a far greater deluge than that they could hear.

While the rain kept hissing down, Heather prayed and Sophy hugged to Charlie.

Then Mr Madoc memory-dredged it, old man Griffiths mentioning an underground siphon which had been connected with the mine; and at least, now, their little group could kill time with murmured speculation: what could possibly have blocked the brook, making its waters rediscover that long-abandoned aquifer?

\*

The cats were satisfied: they had kept Carol safe, and this situation surely wouldn't worsen. Now they were finding that kettle most annoying, and came into the kitchen to say–

A mud-saturated Bronny staggered in and, 'Carol, thank goodness you're okay!' slapped a rope on the sink drainer. From the door's threshold she shrilled a procession of notes on a diminutive whistle; then, slamming the rain out, she sobbed against The Snug's steamy din, 'PLEASE BREW THE BLOODY COFFEE!'

\*

All eyes on Mr Madoc.

'"O" is for "Okay"; "S" means "Stay where you are". Therefore, Sophy, your mum and Bronny are fine, but can't be reached – not this way. So let's go back to the stable, where we'll block this track off. When we've found everyone dry clothes, I'll take the Landy to Colliers' Quay: whoever wishes to can walk over to Jill's via the Coal Road, okay? Meanwhile, Missus will get the Coast Path closed: if that blockage above us lets go, Mill Cove will cop it the way Lynmouth did.'

The youngsters knowing from Jill's look that "Lynmouth" was something they should look up, and learn about.

*

Carol boggled.

What had been The Mist Pool steadily disgorged a great brown water-bloom; where once lawns, a foamy gyring lake overflowing the track.

Bronny, now shower-restored, 'I know, I know: as the brook's blocked, there's no telling where all that's coming from. But maybe something geological has given way underground: during the Severn Tunnel's construction, a Great Spring broke in. Certainly looks like that's happened, eh?

'I'll *never* understand it: I scribbled all through the episode, utterly unaware! As for Mogulus's behaviour – for once given the very best of reasons for demanding my attention, what does he choose to do this morning…?'

From his rumbling log basket perch, inscrutable blinks.

'At least,' Bronny stooped for her, 'he and Vincenza are safe.' Some sobby breaths… 'Unlike poor Taggle.' Sofa-slumping, she cuddled the cat closer.

'I'll make more coffee.' *Then try to set down some thoughts about what's happened.*

With regular breaks to go outside and try calling the dog.

*

The rain ceased as Mr Madoc stopped by the kilns.

Climbing that drippy tree-tunnel they confronted a hurtling terrier, in scruffishness so very like Taggle, but this one was all-over orange; though clearly wanting to stop, muddy momentum sledged the wire-haired quadruped projectile pillwards past them at very many miles per hour.

Many seconds later it pantingly reappeared, dirt-brindled and tumbled dizzy, to fall in placidly beside the youngsters as if Sunday strolling.

Over the familiar ridge they went, with Prescelly still cloud-wrapped eastwards and, west, the bay huge-sea'd and sediment-stained…

Sophy suddenly neckprickled, 'It *was* prophetic, that music yesterday!'

Ahead to their right, now, a cra-cra-crashing: tumbling water, pummelling Mill Cove's beach. Each wondered privately, could there be anything of the path down left?

Entering the second field, another roar detected: the land's curve revealed an ugly torrent, thumpily splashed every time turf chunks water-carved from the meadow's edge went slumping in.

Upon this earth-scented destruction the sun began to glimpse.

Sophy sniffed, 'Nothing will ever be the same!'

'But, lass,' Jill tried, 'that's the key to Evolution: try seeing this flood as a kind of test for my garden – meaning that us must just await the results.'

Charlie took Sophy's hand, 'Patiently.'

Heather said, 'This is much more than the brook's flow, even in spate: I reckon we should know before bedtime what the damage is, because the flood will have spent itself before then.'

'Or, put another way,' smiled Jill, 'you lot will refuse to turn in until you've seen what the damage is.'


Many emotions, on their clattering into Drift Cottage's kitchen; before long, though, Bronny was hooting away at Taggle's having turned tangerine. But then, 'Um, has *anyone* heard him bark?'

No.

Charlie chuckled, 'If it's a choice between orange and silent and normal and noisy, we'd better not let the cats decide.'

Sophy snuttered out for the others a word-picture of Mogulus, telephoning the Snowdrop Lane hardware shop in Haverfordwest – the one which Heather had assured her sold *absolutely everything*: 'I need a tin of o-orange d-dog paint; it *must* be weatherproof, and really hardwearing. Wh-What's that...? It's for a t-t-terrier, if that makes a d-difference.'

# CHAPTER 58

Afterwards, what was going to be revealed? Anything recognisable? The three fate-whirled youngsters speculated along the flood's spongy margin.

The last of the storm departing, down shot hot sharp light as if God had slid his sunroof open…

'Jill, JILLY, come and see – and bring your painting gear!'

Sophy inhaled that everso humid jungly glow; 'How about doing *A Primal Scene*?'

'Because,' Heather concurred, 'you can believe that a dinosaur might pop up from that gloop, grab someone, and steamily disappear again, GULP!'

Taggle backed, putting her nearest the water's edge.

'I simply paint what I see, missy; I won't be putting monsters in. Hmm… This'll certainly be done *alla prima* – straight off, no sketching first. It will also be primal, in this sense…'

She'd use colours straight from their tubes, with very little blending needed on the canvas: the turbid water *was* raw sienna; those were chrome green oak canopies with indigo-shadowed trunks; the northwind sky was cobalt. Selecting a brush, 'That's me busy; how about you chaps…?'

'We'll bring the bench round, and set last night and this morning down on paper,' Sophy thought.

'That's a very good idea: record it while your memories are freshest.'

A line each at a time, Heather proposed, off to ask Carol for the writing wherewithal.

Her end of the bench set down, Sophy rubbed her wrists.

Charlie gulped, 'I hurt you earlier, didn't I?'

'It was entirely my fault, your having to hold me so firmly.'

'Sophy, I couldn't have faced life if I'd let you go, and then something really bad had happened.' He sighed profoundly, 'It's already difficult enough, sometimes.'

'Charlie…?'

'I had a younger sister; she had a pony; my parents were out that morning. Maisie said she'd ride round the paddock; I said that was okay. Because it was misty, you see, meaning that her crossing the road to get into the field with the jumps in it wasn't allowed.

'But I sh-shouldn't have acted the bossy big brother: because she was behaving herself I needn't have said anything, but I did; and it obviously made her resentful. To say Maisie was sparky doesn't tell the half of it – and just beyond sparky came prickly.

'I heard her pony cross the yard; a bit later, too late, I realised that the paddock gate hadn't clanged…'

Sophy tried to imagine that horrible truth dawning.

'We'll never know exactly what happened; that must have been a very quiet car, though, 'cos I never heard it.'

'I-It was you who found Maisie?'

'Yes, Sophy. She said, "I'm sorry."'

Sophy hugged, 'The dear sweet girl! Was that all?'

'Such a struggle for her, but she managed to get out, "He saw me!" And I was sure she'd recognised the driver so I stroked her face, saying, "Tell me who it was, and I promise you we'll sort him out;" but, by then, she'd gone. For ages, though, I couldn't believe she had, Sophy; you see, there was no blood.'

She crushed, 'Charlie, *Charlie*! You poor boy!'

'Same as your dad, I'd give absolutely anything to have her back.'

'Yes, Charlie, YES!'

…

'So…? Who was it, Charlie?' *This is a small community, so surely…?*

'The police found no clues; nobody came forward.'

'But your family knew – they know – it was almost certainly someone local: how awful! Somebody you might have dealings with.'

'Nobody, we're sure, who attended Maisie's funeral. There were hundreds, and how my mum and Grandma studied everyone's face… T'wasn't none of them, we couldn't think.'

'Is she buried in Talbenny Haven churchyard?'

He nodded, 'Our family's plot's close to the Gwinear's: that's nice, because Maisie got on so well with Miss G.'

'I've wanted for ages to visit that lady's grave; one day could you, um, introduce me to her and Maisie?'

357

'Gladly, Sophy: she'd have loved to have met you, I know; but, be warned, you might bump into Patsy Flange: her grandma's buried nearby.'

'She often goes there?'

'I'm not surprised you're surprised; but, yes. And, in fact, Mrs Cranston was easily the nicest of that lot.'

'I don't suppose her husband pays his respects regularly.'

'He visits, people say, when he knows he's been bad.'

Sophy's dry chuckle: 'A conscience of sorts, then; never lets it get the upper hand, though.'

Charlie, hesitantly, 'To be fair, Sophy, Patricia… She is much better than him. She's always put flowers on Maisie's grave. I think that actually she had a real soft spot for my sister, from the distance that her family's attitude forced on her.'

'Then there's maybe hope for Patricia Flange.'

'Shouldn't we pray that there is?'


Returning, Heather beamed, 'Writing should chivvy time along: the flood'll seem over sooner.'

Sophy boggled, 'What if it never was, though?'

'A fiction,' her mother firmed, 'you can write another day. Isn't what actually happened enough of a story for you?'

Thus galvanised, the girls started scribbling; meanwhile, however, colours already emerging from under that springy canvas-traversing palette knife mesmerised Charlie: 'May I watch?'

'No,' Jill handed him the palette, 'you mayn't: you can jolly well have a go, yourself.'


The flow lessening, the water retreating.

At a rate which frayingly tested the girls' patience; but it made it a race, for artist and new apprentice, to finish that picture before their subject changed much.

Soon revealed, umpteen cans, bottles, and wrappers which bridge-humptibumping cars had jettisoned over the years; worse, having to stop Sophy from slithering while investigating that gloopy black tidemark, Heather sniffed and then fumed, 'Sump oil!'

Her friend stormed, 'WHY?'

'Because, with the flood, some filthy ignorant sod upstream saw his blooming chance!'

'Or one could say,' Jill murmured to Charlie, 'to make you all three vow that that sort of thing shall stop happening, one day.'

Ever after, when other entertaining disasters had this one come to mind, Dambuster Haroldston.

Nobody was far from the back door but, saucepan in one hand and ladle in the other, to vent the frustration of waiting for the flood to dissipate, Heather bellowed 'COME AND GET IT!' while bonging like a bomb factory fire gong.

At which, from deep in the trees, the sound of a million overturned oil drums – and then a clashing, tumbling seethe as the entirety of whatever had blocked the Mill Brook set sail instanter for the sea, borne along by untold tons of extravasating water.

Cinematic its stereophonic sound, the six of them, the cats, and the dog followed the invisible progress of that immense bombastulation: through the spinney and along the meadow bottoms one, two, three; finally, via a cliff-slope crashtabang, thundering onto the beach below with myriad frapps and bongules – plus, pursuant, a wet avalanche and then its watery echo...

Refreshing Jill's memory of, four-year-old bobble-hatted tomboy, witnessing a thawing fellside waterfall shed "all its every icicles" at once; thus, 'AGAIN, DADDY!'

...

Suddenly, the youngsters were laughing like drains; Carol clapped, urging everyone, 'Wasn't that a superb finale?'

All were with her, then: Sophy bellowed 'BRAVO!'; Bronny and Heather squeed their loudest whistles.

Faintly, southwards, 'ENCORE!' from Mr Madoc and Sabrina.

Heather tugged Sophy and Charlie, 'Let's see what happened – come ON!'

But Bronny bigsistered, 'Not so fast, buster: the brook's banks mightn't be safe.'

'This is already a very late lunch; let's eat now,' Jill insisted, 'and then we'll all go – together, and carefully.'

Entertainment, enough, anyway, without going anywhere: with

the brook unblocked, the lower garden began swirl-quarrelling itself empty like an unplugged bath.

They bowl-slopped the curry and, seizing spoons, piled outdoors to watch while chomping; once on the front lawn, however, the others hung back: surely Jill should look first.

Cautiously across gloop-slobbing grass, she peered over the stone edge into dripping, seeping silence… Then beckoned, everso Englishly, 'It's certainly changed a bit.'

The Mist Pool was now an empty stone chamber, adultly deep; where reeds had mudclumped, a stoopable arch exhaled vapour. Heather boggled, 'That's some bloody tunnel! Explains the huge water-plume, doesn't it?'

Mr Madoc, approaching, 'And the masonry's superb: hats off to the original Mr Gwinear.'

The channel's transformation was even more dramatic: it exited The Mist Pool four feet deep and brick-floored, not one lump of coal in sight. Five yards upstream from where the plank bridge had been – no trace of that, nor the poor old shower hut – a transverse stone sill let into a curved-bottom pit, set into the stone walls on either side of which were iron bearing-blocks…

Charlie and Sophy synchronised, 'There was a water wheel!'

Beyond, where the stream had previously dispersed hidden under asphodel and mares-tail, a near-unbelievable sight: an oblong stone-walled pound which Jill's access track crossed on a low-arched bridge, Pinched Pill's causeway copied in miniature…

'GOOD LORD!' And Jill rushed back indoors.

CHAPTER 59

Returning with a manila envelope, 'The Records Office photos came yesterday. Although the lady had no information at all on *this* picture, I ordered it anyway: we agreed it was jolly interesting, because it gave such a good idea of what the local mines were like…'

The girls chorused, 'But it's *here*!'

'Jill,' Charlie said, 'I can understand you not recognising your own property: it looked so different from this, so overgrown, until this morning. And that's such a cleverly-chosen viewpoint.'

Some enterprising Victorian had hoisted their plate camera into one of the spinney's oak trees.

Only grass grew about The Drift back in the 1870s, and the now thorny rise between it and Jill's paddock had been a bare spoil tip; most strikingly, in those days, there'd been no hedge bank at all. Presumably it had been an equipment store, that wooden shack beside the adit entrance; back then Jill's study and bedroom had served as the mine office, while the Gwinears had lived next door, all squeezed into what were now her dining room, The Snug, and its attic.

An iron-framed water wheel, there'd been; its spokes blurred by the photo's long exposure, the thing appeared to be whizzing. Jill said, 'A weir upstream from the spinney bridge must have held the brook back, to feed water via that tunnel to The Mist Pool...'

'As was,' whispered Heather.

'...and hence stop boards were needed during maintenance work.' The artist now pointed excitedly: 'A breast-shot water wheel, it was; d'you see that its crank drove a series of walking rods, supported on rocking arms? The rods crossed above the track, and then a series of them must've gone deep down inside the adit, because the pump would have been on the lowest level – what rattletrap contraptionry it all made together, I bet! And here's the neatest trick: by draining into the, ahem, ex-Mist Pool, the mine water helped turn the wheel; and, no, Charlie, that wasn't perpetual motion.'

Bronny said, 'How a hundredish years have – I mean *had* – altered everything!'

'Indeed,' Mr Madoc harrumphed, not long arrived back, 'but I've no excuse for forgetting we'd this amongst our papers...'

A large rolled-up something.

He began, not yet revealing its secrets, 'About 1900, the Great Western Railway planned a new route from near Steynton to Talbenny Haven; as well as the usual branch line business, they reckoned on additional traffic of two sorts. They expected Heather's village to expand all along The Sands, resulting in more than a mile of built-up sea front, to become a sort of Weston super Mare for West Wales...'

The faces pulled, then!

'But also, by combining the mines around Pinched Pill into one modern colliery, the Pembrokeshire anthracite trade shouldn't just be revived, they'd reckoned, but greatly expanded. So rich-as-Croesus Lord Cunjic, who owned nearly everything hereabouts then, had The Drift surveyed to assess its potential.

'Fortunately for us, the GWR kept finding more attractive investment ideas; and, after the First World War... Well, the Golden Age was over, wasn't it? He started unrolling, 'This is a copy of Cunjic's plan.'

Carol suggested taking that great scroll to the bench: perhaps it hadn't much monetary value, but it was surely historically important.

They gathered round, fascinated: so much detail!

He finger-tapped, '*There*'s the sluice intercepting the brook; today's flood must have been caused by storm debris heaping against its piers – you'll see soon that only they remain, these days.

'Old Gwinear's miners tunnelled his conduit under *that* spur of land, beyond the hedge; your so-called Mist Pool's just marked as a Header Pound, d'you see? There's the wheel; *those* are the pump rods.

'Now the photo doesn't so clearly show this, but I know other mines did something very similar...' With his pipe stem, 'After turning the wheel, the water poured into a Washery Pound: the women in Jill's picture would have had to wash the duff, or coal dust, from the anthracite before weighing it; they'd have also flushed out the mine's tub wagons after emptying the lump coal out.

'The Washery Pound was divided; after closing one side off using sluice gear, they'd drain it. Then the women climbed down and shovelled the duff into sacks: they could take home so much a week; the rest was sold. Now, even dried, duff was a useless fuel on its own, either choking a fire or pouring straight through the grate unburnt; so, why did those women want it, and why could mines sell the stuff...?'

Charlie knew; for Sophy's sake – she was loving this narrative – he didn't say.

Mr Madoc continued, 'Because Pembrokeshire's poor people had that problem pipped! Duff and culm, that's coal shattered small by underground movement, were mixed with clay and hand-rolled into balls; those were put out in the sun – all those tasks being well suited to young folk, by the way. Dried and hardened, those early sorts of briquette – the Pembrokeshire dialect name is stummin – burnt slowly but pretty much smokelessly, giving a steady heat: ideal for keeping the damp out of earth-walled cottages.'

Heather wowed, 'Pretty tough, all that work, wouldn't you say?'

'No worse,' Sophy suggested, 'than navvies' wives and children producing all the bricks when they were building the canals.'

Jill reminded them, 'And better by far than anything underground, I'm sure.'

Studious Charlie looked up: 'About those iron faceplates on Jill's, um, causeway columns: did the Washery Pound have downstream sluices, too?'

'Well noticed, lad: you've guessed that the water had a last job to do. After the women had shovelled a chamber clear as best they could, it was re-filled and then emptied, Wallop!, through a *bottom-opening* sluice: that swept its floor completely clean. And as the water pumped from the mine was silty, sending a rush down from time to time ensured that the stream's channel never got choked with mud.'

'Sophy admired, 'So well thought out!'

'And with Nature doing all the work,' said Jill, 'this mine never burnt any coal to keep its pump running.'

'Hence,' said Mr Madoc, 'it was one of the last to close.'

Heather frowned, 'But wasn't using horses to carry coal to the quay pretty restricting?'

'Because we knew you'd be interested,' he apologised, 'I think we've previously over-emphasised the packhorse aspect of its story. Naturally, the mines edging the pill concentrated on the sea trade; this drift, in contrast, only ever sent coal down for shipping when the price was right. It mostly sold anthracite directly to farmers, who brought their own carts here; and, of course, for house-to-house sales it was that much closer to Talbenny Haven and Creampot Cove.'

Charlie beamed, 'I'd been wondering why they never built another incline to take this mine's output down to the shore; because The Drift wasn't reliant on the coasting trade, its resorting to packhorse trains when the occasion arose makes sense.'

So mixed, the girl's emotions.

In a relatively short time they'd discovered coal in Jill's stream, worked out how to extract and wash it, and had Hugh help them develop the Anthromatic...

Now, all that fuel had gone – literally tons of it, far more indeed than they'd ever imagined had been there for the winning. But gone also were all traces of mud, and thus the watery saga twisted in their favour: in mere hours Nature had scoured out The Mist Pool, gifting them the very plunging place they'd hoped for.

And, another twist, thanks to the flood they now knew that Gwinear ingenuity had harnessed not just the energy potential of the stream but that of the brook, too; and didn't the ability to pump minewater a century ago imply a contemporary possibility of harnessing that combined flow once more?

Such had been the thrust of their discussions over tea and washing up; but it was time, now, to go as a group and discover what the brook had got up to, down below Drift Cottage.

CHAPTER 60

Considering how much water had rampaged, its anthracite burden excoriating, the brook's course wasn't too scathed in the first meadow. Beside that great glacial boulder in the second, Jill assured them, there'd already been a sizeable swirlpool; this was where they'd seen the bank being badly eroded.

The bottom meadow... Was now a black-tidelined bowl of rust-washed grass, strewn by ripped and buckled corrugated iron sheets, burst haybales, broken branches, and heaps of lesser storm debris.

No coal.

Mr Madoc sighed, 'I'll be gubbered! There's your dam: that's Dai Griffiths' old Dutch Barn, as was; I'd warned him as t'would collapse. Came apart as she toppled into the brook, she must have, and her panels fetched up against the old sluice piers. And, by Christ, didn't they hold some water back? Look how that metal bent when her gave way!'

Sophy wailed, 'What a mess!'

He, mildly, 'Big iron pieces can be collected easily enough; a metal detector will find the rest. Those branches will become lovely logs for the fire; and, as for the ruined hay – Doctor Madoc prescribes a horse rake, some days of drying, then a damned big bonfire.'

'This isn't all the metal, though,' Bronny reasoned. 'Remember that crash as came from the beach?'

Above the culvert, indeed, all the hedgebank foliage had clearly been savaged by hurtling metal.

'Blimey,' Charlie murmured, 'if they hadn't closed the Coast Path to walkers…'

Jill grimmed, 'Drowned, decapitated, or swept out to sea… All three, even.'

The shale-choked culvert of old was gone: a tall water-gushed passage now gaped. Those wellybooted youngsters wanted to explore, but mustn't: heaven knew what – glass, barbed wire, ripped metal – might hide in that leftover stodge aproning its entrance.

They climbed the field gate as a noisy group: 'No worries about meeting nosy hikers today!' And found the Coast Path hideously greasy for many yards: bursting onto it, the floodwave must have far-flung sumpoily spray.

They'd known the culvert's exit as a mere marshy bickering, summer-obscured by brambles; now here projected stout masonry, scoured back to Victorian newness.

Carol boggled, 'It's beautifully built.'

All assumed that the first Gwinear and his masons had again been responsible. Heather–

'No nosing in there!', Bronny ordered. 'Maybe it's suffered arch damage; eh, Mr M?'

'No,' he sighed – knowing she was right, but as eager to explore.

As the iron-laden deluge had driven down the cliffside, everything growing had been slashed back, if not wholly scalped; where once a gravelly path, scoured bedrock.

Well done Bronny for thinking to bring a rope; with it made off to a thorn trunk, she started easing herself down… 'Flaming heck!'

Although it was slithery slow going even with the rope, the girls felt such gratitude that this descent hadn't been wholly obliterated.

Furthermore while ground level growth had been flailed, the lush overhang wasn't harmed; thus, hugely good fortune for them, Mill Cove remained invisible from the Coast Path.

So, now, their first glimpses of it…

A frozen explosion, spread below, of iron sheets and mashed treebits. Sophy phewed, 'No wonder we heard such bongulations!'

Carol sniggered, 'Who would have thought the old barn to have had so much tin in it?'

The crescent of wreckaged strand was bisected by a bedrock-bottomed gully: a veritable wall of water, there'd been, to thus carry that sand overburden off entirely on its way down to the waves. Waves which flummoxed the girls, expecting a sickly brown sea black-edged with coal; for over the reef there troshed and boshed the usual autumn-green aftermath of a summer storm.

Mr Madoc pointed, 'There's likely a strong fetch down the coast, after that northerly blowing so hard for so long: your mud's probably a good mile away already.'

Thankfully the storm hadn't stranded much "ordinary" rubbish, to add to everything the flood had brought down; Taggle, though, quickly snouting out something bulbously yellow nearly hidden by heaped weed, began feverishly digging.

Heavy, metal, bigger than a sweetshop jar…

**FLARE DISTRESS DAYLIGHT (ORANGE SMOKE)**
1) ATTACH LANYARD TO CRAFT
2) REMOVE COVER
3) HOLD OVERBOARD AND DOWNWIND
4) PULL RED RING AND RELEASE FLARE INTO SEA
IGNITION IN 5 SECS
***WARNING***
**IF DEVICE DOES NOT IGNITE DO NOT RETRIEVE**.

Bronny checked: not time-expired, and it had an intact seal; it should be safe to handle, therefore. Knapsacking it, 'I'll cart him home, Jilly; you can tip off your coastguard contact.'

'No need,' the artist breezed. 'He'll be visiting me soon.'

Sophy goggled, '*Really?*'

Hands on hips, 'Because, Little Miss Big Eyes, he won the portrait draw.'

'Then,' Mr M jollied, 'well done him.' *Amazingly well done, seeing as the chap was watchkeeping at Creampot Point while the fête was on yesterday!* He suspected Alice Williams of subterfuge.

Gone burrowing-barmy, the terrier now uncovered a door-sized iron grid; Mr Madoc realised, 'That used to close off the culvert mouth, to stop stock entering the meadow.'

Sophy frowned, 'Entering?'

Charlie explained, 'Cattle used to graze these cliffs: the older Welsh breeds were tough enough.'

'Gosh!'

Pipe lit, Mr Madoc said, 'We must put it somewhere safe. All that land is Druid Pool Farm's; I'll suggest to Ivor Jones that he bolts it back pronto, to keep nosy walkers out of the culvert.'

Jill checked, 'Bolts it back?'

'What's on your mind, my dear?'

'I think it was hinged and padlocked, originally. Miss Gwinear would talk about her grandparents "going down through", meaning coming here.'

'Well, certainly,' he blew blue, 'a laden donkey would rather steadily climb the culvert than struggle steeply up and over the Coast Path.'

'Providing the brook was low,' Bronny cautioned.

Charlie thought hard; then, 'While the sluices still worked, your donkey needn't have ever got wet feet.' Drawing on the sand, 'Suppose you completely drained the Washery Pound, then diverted all the brook's flow down Gwinear's Conduit: for as long as the pound took to refill, no water would reach here.'

Heather, for everyone, 'Well worked out!'

Sophy said, 'An openable gate could be great for beach cleaning: if Mr Jones would agree, we could bring the wagon down through the meadows, then carry rubbish sacks up to it via the culvert.'

Mr M puffed, 'You could do even better! With the route down so clear now, reckon a horse could rope-haul sacks up, loaded on a skid or a sledge.'

Apple eaten, rock-sat Sophy glumly sea-stared.

Jill, nudging alongside, 'Well, sweetheart…?'

'You've lost so much fuel; all top quality anthracite, too!'

'I wasn't depending on it. And, truthfully, it wasn't the prospect of salvaging the stuff which really fired you and Heather up, but devising the scheme and developing the inventions with Hugh – aren't I right? Anyway, consider this: it's better that the coal's gone completely, rather than have other people finding it in the brook beyond my boundary; there'd probably have been squabbles, hmm? Even worse, if folk had started exploring to discover where it came from – well, farewell to our privacy! So let's be satisfied, eh? I still have my garden; you might get a swimming pool.'

'Hmm, it *is* marvellous, the way The Mist Pool was completely cleared; we could have slogged at that for weeks.'

The Jilliest of grins: 'That's true, too.'

*So what did she mean, originally?* 'You can't mean the, um, Washery Pound?'

'Whyever not? Those arches haven't suffered one whit from being buried these hundred years; therefore, I just need new sluices. Enabling,' the artist finger-snapped, 'an earlier idea of yours to come into its own.'

'Um… A clue, please?'

'Segregated flow.'

Such tingly realisation: Sophy leapt up, 'Make the southern half of the Washery Pound always take the stream's flow, and the northern side will keep completely mud-free – perfect for swimming in, therefore!'

'And,' prompted Jill, 'without cold mine water constantly pouring through…'

'The sun could warm it up!' *An enormous private freshwater pool, deep enough for diving in; and no nasty chemicals to bother our eyes.* She hurried away to share the prospect with Charlie and Heather.

Back to Drift Cottage, soon afterwards: into the woodshed with Taggle's smoke flare; then, time for tea and a bun.

Afterwards, implement-armed, the group enspinnied themselves, determined to reach the old Top Sluice. A huge nettle patch in their way readily succumbed, for Jill had whetted Charlie a wicked edge onto the Gwinear scythe: 'That's Sheffield steel, boy – none better!'

Watching the blade tested on wild barley, Sophy comprehended to the biting of her lip those Great War descriptions: of either side's machine guns, swathing young men like corn.

They deliberately didn't clear around The Drift's access gate: let the sleeping Cranston dog lie.

Heather said, 'Reckon that old hedge runs above the conduit; no coincidence, I don't suppose.'

Mr Madoc grinned, 'Even less of a coincidence, perhaps, the conduit's being beneath it.'

'Gubbered if I know which is more logical, and which more Pembrokeshire,' Bronwen muttered.

Of the old sluice and the conduit's portal, when they reached them, Carol observed, 'More scaled-down canal engineering.'

'Aye,' said Mr Madoc, 'a sturdy handsomeness, there is, in all that Cornishman's achievements.'

*And in Charlie Solva*, Sophy thinks, Heather mused.

*

'So much has happened today,' said Carol to Jill as they cooked supper, 'we're in a state of overwhelmed bogglement. How on earth shall we wind the girls down?'

'Might going to tell Slipstream about it all help?'

*

It did; and afterwards, they three took wild flowers and prayers to Arrow's grave; then, Charlie must head home. Back at the farmhouse the girls gladly bathed a gleeful Diana, and helped ready her for bed.

Returned a tad baby-soppy, the two took themselves upstairs unbidden; its scent charmed deep sleep into them, that cot-remembered lotion sweetening each other's skins.

CHAPTER 61

A calm pearl-skied morning: ideal for riding the horses back.

After lunch the youngsters brought Aberdare, and Tracker plus wagon, down to the bottom meadow. Ivor Jones, Mr Madoc, Sabrina, and Kaycee having gathered all the iron sheets, Aberdare, Sophy, and Charlie rope-hauled the beach ones up in clattery batches through the old culvert; meanwhile Heather and Carol used a mine detector (which the airbase mightn't have known it was loaning) to hunt smaller tin fragments.

Warm work for all, after the sun appeared.

As they departed Carol flourished, 'A lovely swimming place, again!'

'Except,' Heather said, 'we must wear gymshoes, from now on.' Because much nasty stuff might still lurk the lagoon: the American girls couldn't do a complete sweep of it for metal until the September low spring tides, and it would take all the seas of winter to smooth-grind any glass.

Might they come back the following afternoon, which was forecasted sunny, Charlie asked; and, had Sophy ever snorkeled…?

*

From his big sack came flippers, masks, and snorkels.

Heather said she wasn't up to swimming underwater again, just yet.

'I know,' Charlie replied; 'but could you lie on… this airbed, and spot stuff for us to dive after? Reckon the visibility's good enough.'

Sophy immediately loved snorkeling; Miss Haroldston, using a well-found bamboo pole, most proficiently pointed out "submarubbish" to the others; and the strumbling bucket – Jill's suggestion – proved an ideal underwater salvage receptacle.

On shore, Jill sketched; Carol, in shorts, from the shallows, studied *The Junk Fishers* at work. Then, with Jill's penknife, rope, and a drifted-in plastic carboy… She was soon wading out: 'This will suspend the strumbler for you.'

Taking its painter rope Heather beamed, 'A subaquatic airship!'

Thanks to Carol's invention they were now a formidable salvage team: and, the more stuff recovered, the slicker their technique became.

Working so hard, Sophy wasn't self-conscious about swimming closely with Charlie; touch-near, in fact, when they together dragged iron pieces shallow-wards for her mother to grab.

So ardently admiring of Sophy's gymnastic grace underwater, the lad couldn't refute Heather's quip; his tribal name would indeed be **Swims Like A Ploughman**: 'Your legs goes as if the sea had furrows, boy!'

Sophy, using Maisie's snorkelling kit: so glad, his sister would have been. Because the girls would certainly have got on, although very different in character – *And what a blessing that is!* Being so unlike Maisie, he believed his mother would cope with him inviting Sophy home…

For ages poor Mam had struggled, hearing warm talk of other people's daughters: too strong, the reminder of her loss. As for seeing girls laughing, and larking… she'd never been to the beach, since. His brother had warned, home on special leave, "Never bring a girl home who's anything like our Maisie, Charlie: you know that Mam couldn't cope." *But I pray that, if Gramps talks first, she'll try with Sophy, for my sake.*

For Maisie's sake, Mrs Solva.


Wisely, they'd worked back across the lagoon from the reef foot: the deepest diving when they'd felt freshest.

By squash time, they'd gathered a deal of debris; Heather then abandoning the airbed to gently elbow the shallows, the others went spashing the lagoon's middle depths, strumbler towed between.

At a quarter past four, 'TEA!'

Proper Swallows and Amazons stuff, Carol had driftwood-brewed in Miss G's black kettle: exceptional, that smoke-edged and ozone-hinted flavour.

Jill said, 'Brilliant work, all; but will that suffice on the salvaging, today? You see, I'd like Charlie and Sophy to hold some poses for me from the reef's far side, so I can proportion my sketch figures.'

They soon set off, taking turns: one swimming on the surface, one doing swoop-downs.

Knowing that intimate archipelago so well, Sophy chose their route; to demonstrate just how proficiently she could snorkel now, she'd do a long, deep swim – and where better than Sun Gully, that bouldered chasm she and Heather had discovered on the Day of the Anthromatic…?

They'd all been observing the Quiet-As-A-Library rule; but an unexpectedly returning Charlie emerged from the lagoon, looking weird below the waist: 'HEATHER – BUCKET, HERE, QUICKLY!'

Sophy momentarily rose beside him, huge in the lower body, then sank again.

Carol started, 'My God! What on earth has bitten the children to make them swell so–?'

A restraining, chuckling, Lancastrian hand: 'Only the sea-coal bug.'

They'd found Sun Gully near choked with anthracite, all sea-polished glossy. Having no other gathering means, the friends had stuffed their costumes to almost-coming-off: what a bumclinky swim back that had been for both! Sophy had indeed so exploited her one-piece's carrying capacity, umpteening handfuls of smoothtickly fuel down its ever tauter front, that on trying to surface just then she'd heard alarming side-seam creaks.

Everyone now back ashore, Jill beamed, 'You've found a fair proportion of the lost coal, it seems, and all now washed beautifully clean; I did wonder why the sea there looked a different colour.'

Heather grinned, 'So *that's* the real reason why you had them swim out!'

Sophy, levelly, 'Um, you do have quite a trip to get fuel, now, AJ.'

'Darling,' Carol tapped, 'maybe that's good. Other people rarely come down here; very few of them swim, never mind bring a mask. But suppose someone did stumble on that coal: firstly, they'd likely gather only a few lumps out of curiosity; more importantly, they couldn't connect it with Jill's place, could they?'

Heather said, 'Local folk know anthracite washes down Pinched Pill; people would think as that swell had swept a load of Black Diamonds from near its mouth, and dumped 'em here.'

Charlie didn't like being a killjoy; however, 'Yes, that's feasible: sand and shingle definitely get shunted up and down the coast by storms. But doesn't that mean the coal out there might easily get moved on?'

Jill approved, 'You're right, Charlie: a change of the sea's mood, and that lot could be gone.'

Sophy gasped the loudest at such nonchalance.

'And,' the artist continued, 'while I'd be disappointed on you youngsters' behalves, d'you know what, I wouldn't be bothered myself. You see, there's people thinking we shouldn't burn coal, oil, or gas: not just because we can use solar energy instead, or because of the smoke and the fumes, *or* because of miners and rigmen risking their lives to get us the stuff…'

Carol, for them all, 'Why, then?'

## Chapter 62

Jill suggested tea refills: 'I've lots to explain.

'After the 1973 Oil Crisis, many governments got really interested in things like solar energy and wave power; also, serious research began into saving fuel and electricity. Miss Gwinear approved, especially from the pollution prevention point of view: less oil demand meant fewer tanker voyages. She bought books about the new thinking on energy as they came out: by quoting up-to-date ideas, she could argue her case most strongly in her letters to the papers, and other correspondence.

'They're inspiring, those books. However the most recent ones, as well as discussing new directions in Energy Studies – that's a university discipline, now – hint at an energy-related problem so big, it could badly harm our planet.'

'Surely not,' Carol sighed, 'as much as nuclear or chemical warfare?'

'Yes, although it does sound benign: it's called the Greenhouse Effect – I'll explain.' Jill drew on the sand, 'Carbon dioxide gas occurs naturally in the Earth's atmosphere; a jolly good thing too, because plant growth depends on the stuff. Also – here that name comes in – carbon dioxide traps solar heat in our atmosphere, just as glass keeps a greenhouse warm. Without it, this planet would be far too cold for any life except tiny organisms. Crucially, it's a very powerful effect: only a few hundred parts per million of that gas in the air maintain our current climate patterns.

'Now since the Industrial Revolution, humans have been pouring carbon dioxide into the air: when you burn coal, oil, or natural gas – the fossil fuels – the carbon component, C, reacts with oxygen, $O_2$... You get heat *plus* carbon dioxide, $CO_2$.

'As you might expect, plants grow better when given extra $CO_2$, but they can't absorb more *ad infinitum*; hence the concentration in the atmosphere has been climbing ever faster as the world population has increased and, at the same time, people's lives have improved. Expected result of that increasing concentration: Earth will become more greenhouse-like; it will get hotter.'

'But surely,' Carol said, 'crops grow faster when the weather's better?'

Jill took a deep breath; 'In some places, plants might thrive; but what if India got much hotter, or the American prairies dried out and couldn't grow wheat? Suppose polar ice melted, making the sea level rise...?' After letting them ponder those prospects a while, 'Some people say that by burning fossil fuels, and thus altering the atmosphere's chemistry, we humans are taking a huge gamble.'

Charlie scratched his head, 'Why haven't we been taught about this?'

'Because Miss Gwinear was well ahead of thousands of university professors around the world, never mind your typical British schoolteacher.'

Heather asked, 'Is anyone disputing this warming theory?'

'Good question; I'm sure someone soon will be. Oil companies won't like anybody saying we shouldn't keep burning ever more of the stuff they sell, will they? And oil companies have a LOT of influence.'

Carol said, 'They're surely much more powerful than tobacco firms – who will fight very dirty, it seems, to discredit lung cancer researchers.'

'This is a bigger, even scarier worry,' said Sophy.

'But your brain can cope,' Jill firmed. 'It managed a Population Explosion discussion, didn't it?'

'So – what could people do?'

'Americans,' Charlie growled, 'could scrap cars which only do ten miles to the gallon.'

Jill said, 'With homes insulated to Swedish standards, we Brits would have tiny heating bills, even if the planet didn't need saving.'

Heather frowned, 'Even if...?'

'Sweetheart, the Earth's atmosphere is, effectively, a mysterious and hugely complex machine. You know my Rubik's Cube…?'

A novel and very clever puzzle toy; you could only un-riddle it by following a set of logic rules.

'…Well, imagine a version with a million squares on each face; what's more, you've no guidance about how to solve this one. If you change the colour of one square on one face, nothing else might happen; or, many other squares might change colour in a random pattern… *Or*, even more confusingly, perhaps nothing would happen for a bit – and then, suddenly, many changes. It looks at the moment as if finding out quite where the Greenhouse Effect might take our atmosphere as carbon dioxide levels rise would be as difficult.'

Charlie, 'But if there are umpteen factors and so very many interconnections, how could you ever, um, write that down as maths?'

Carol patted Jill on the back, 'By programming a computer!'

Heather nodnodded, 'A veryveryVERY powerful one.'

Jill cautioned, 'One much pokier, indeed, than anything running today, even those in secret establishments that one only hears rumours about; but electronic chips keep getting faster, smaller, and cheaper… Every year, there are amazing advances. And, you know, weather forecasters already use very big computers, to which the latest satellites send down huge amounts of geo-data.'

'Hmm,' Sophy hmmed.

Jill understood: 'You're wondering, should I have stayed working as a computer consultant…? Sweetheart, my clients wouldn't have paid me to try and predict the planet's future – no profit in that! And imagine my boss telling his oil company customers that good old Jill Ribblesdale was trying to prove that they were bringing about the Death of Nature!'

Heather fretted, 'But what if they actually *are?*'

'Well, we must hope that humans have some time to take action.'

Carol, 'Such as…?'

'Here's a scenario: scientists who are concerned about $CO_2$ emissions form a consortium: if mankind does nothing, they warn, our planet might on average be two degrees centigrade warmer by, say, 2050 – with all its weather systems fatally mutated: Goodbye, monsoons; Hello, devastating droughts. Now, let's suppose that the world's countries sensibly heed that warning, and together begin a massive project which cuts down on fossil fuel usage, and it proves a success...'

Heather, 'Hurrah!'

Jill, 'Hurrah, indeed. ...But what if, when our grandchildren get to 2050, the increased $CO_2$ concentration – it's bound to rise quite a lot, even with our best efforts – *hasn't* caused the expected temperature rise?'

Charlie said, 'Humans wouldn't have lost out: they'd have developed umpteen super-efficient gizmos, and loads of solar powered stuff.'

'And,' Sophy saw, 'they wouldn't have used up all the fossil fuels, which can't last forever.' She'd dipped into some of those books, herself.

Heather leapt to her feet: 'But people would *also* be okay if the scientists had got it wrong in the *other* direction and, even with fairly modest carbon dioxide increases, the world had warmed noticeably. In that situation, everyone would be *so* grateful they'd taken precautions – otherwise, the planet would be blooming frying!'

Jill nodded, 'Well done, you three, for realising that, because of uncertainties, cutting back on burning carbon is the *only* safe policy.'

'That's pretty encouraging,' Carol proposed, 'seeing how these youngsters' futures could be threatened.'

'But the necessary decisions,' Heather pouted, 'must be made by old fart politicians, who'll all be dead fairly soon! Why should they care?'

Jill grimaced, 'Why even *listen*, if they're oil company shareholders – which most probably are?'

'Or,' Heather growled, 'secretly supported by the oil companies, which they probably also are?'

Charlie thought... 'A supercomputer's needed to predict how much the earth might heat up by; but, as to what would happen if the atmospheric temperature *did* go up by one, two, or three degrees – you'd surely need *another* supercomputer, for modelling how everything on the planet would respond to more heat: how much ice would melt, and so forth. So how could you ever...?'

Jill reasoned, 'They're one and the same problem, actually. For example, if the American prairies did dry out, the moisture locked up in their soil would evaporate, altering the very weather system which caused the drought – et voilà, we have what's called a feedback mechanism.'

Sophy murmured, 'If there'll be one of those, there'll be flipping billions.'

The artist beamed, 'Well done! You now understand what an *enormous* experiment the human race is embarking on, golloping so much fossil fuel.'

Carol snapped her fingers; 'So – you three United Nations supremos have had your briefing from my technical expert; I now want to know what international actions you'll be recommending.'

'Get computers to start crunching numbers.' ... 'Order bigger, better ones.' ... 'Research energy efficiency really hard.' ... 'Work out how people can be persuaded not to do fuely things.' ... 'Ask an expert in addiction.'

This last from Heather; asked what she'd meant, 'Fossil fuels are like drugs which haven't been properly tested: we get kicks out of consuming them, and they *seem* fairly harmless; but in the long term we might end up dead, or living incredibly miserably.'

Sophy, gravely, 'And so would everybody else, too, whether they'd been using those drugs or not.'

How that remark fuelled Charlie's admiration: it mirrored how he saw his own species: *So selfishly flawed, we are.*


# Chapter 63

In thoughtful mood, all, they'd changed for going home.

Sophy, before starting up the slope, 'Mummy, you are writing *real* fiction, aren't you? Not imaginary stuff, with wizards and such?'

'It's "real" fiction – inevitably, I might say, as you haven't liked magical stories for a long while.'

Sophy rallied her friends, 'Heather, Charlie, can't it seem cheating to escape trouble by casting spells, or flashing a pendant? I prefer characters getting out of fixes the way I'd have to.'

'By thinking things out,' Charlie agreed, 'and having your mates help you.'

'Including animal mates,' Heather reminded them. 'Although, actually, I don't mind a little luck splashed into a tale provided the, um, benefiter deserves it; i.e., the likes of Patsy Flange get the bad sort!'

'It was bad luck,' Charlie posited, 'her being born who she was. Anyway, Sophy, your point is…?'

'Mum's story characters might learn about this Earth overheating business, plus the Population Crisis.'

Carol chin-stroked, 'And…?'

Staring out to sea, 'And possibly not much more: just enough said on the page, I was thinking, for the reader to know that those heroes and heroines wouldn't forget: so, whatever they ended up doing as grown-ups, that awareness would always, um…'

'Influence their thinking?'

'And their actions, too, Charlie: everything comes back to Miss G's "Doing's better than praying", doesn't it?'

'Along with "Do As You Would Be Done By", yes.'

Heather's eyes now horizoned infinity… 'I've had my Eve Eats The Apple moment, this afternoon. You see, for some time I have been imagining a life inspired by Miss Gwinear's last years: if not going into business with Dad, then certainly doing something at least connected with solar energy; plus cleaning beaches, of course, and maybe being a bit protesty with letters, sometimes, so that ships do gradually behave better… Anyway, I had thought that I could do everything like that from a quiet and very natural sort of, um, nest, deep in the countryside – but now I know that that wouldn't be enough.

'We all know that naked's really nice – not just for swimming, but for gardening, too; or painting, or getting on with anything where you've good privacy. But aspiring to be a nut-brown hippy living hidden behind a thick hedge in my own little Eden, trying to forget the world outside… it isn't on now, because I've been given The Knowledge – that information of Jill's about how we're all threatening the whole blooming world. So, obviously, anyone who loves Nature must get out, and get around, to spread the word: they *must* begin widely campaigning to try and change people's ways – especially of course the ways of profligate parasites like Patsy F and all her huge-houses, Range-Rovering, overseas-holidaying mates, who'd need a heckish lot of persuading.'

Charlie whistled, 'Good luck, girl!'

Within nearby deep shadows a bitter grimace whispered, 'Over my dead body!'

# Chapter 64

Up through the meadows: Charlie and Sophy well weighed down with bagged rubbish, Heather plus snorkel sack, Carol and Jill dead-tigering a now ponderous coal-filled carboy.

Jill had explained that, once out of the ground, anthracite slowly but unavoidably oxidises into carbon dioxide: therefore, for all that one was concerned about fossil fuels, one might as well bring home what one could of the sea-won stuff for burning, and stash the rest for fetching another time.

While the ladies had been filling that carboy with black nuggets, the beach-scavenging youngsters had wondered what in the bocage behind them had disturbed so many birds: surely not Mogulus, that far from his usual mouse-hunting grounds.

From the late-arrived post Jill eagered out a letter franked PEMBROKESHIRE COUNTY RECORDS: 'Has Hugh's cousin dug out more old pictures…?'

Out fell a faint photocopy of something foxed, and a compliments slip: 'It says, *"Dear Ms Ribblesdale, my colleague found this while doing research for someone else relating to your particular corner of Pembrokeshire. Your Drift Cottage deeds should strictly speaking include a counter-copy of it; however, such documents can get mislaid. If so, you might like to get a decent photo facsimile done of the original to display in your house: an interesting curiosity for visitors. On the other hand, perhaps you fancy grinding your own corn!"* Hmm; I don't get that last remark.'

Heather peered at the spider-waltzed lines transiting that fuzzy sheet: 'Perfectly clear, I don't think, either!'

Jill flipped the form… 'Aha! *"In case you're unsure, these are the Milling Rights for the old Norchard Mill. The original Mr Gwinear had to buy them off Lord Cunjic, so he could divert the brook to drive what is referred to as a Water Engine, intended for draining a mine. This was presumably pretty close to your property; unfortunately we hold very few coal records here, so you'll have go bushwhacking to find out if any traces of old workings remain thereabouts."* Well,' she exhaled, 'isn't that fascinating?'

Heather finger-snapped, 'Dad noticed that some ashlar blocks in the channel were secondhand: Old-Old-*Old* Mr Gwinear must have re-used stone from Norchard Mill to build his Water Engine… And, hey, isn't that a great way to describe the thing?'

Jill resumed, 'She ends, *"Interestingly, the Milling Rights weren't ever assigned to the mine, but granted in perpetuity to the Gwinears; thus I assume they've now passed to you."* Gosh!' Feeling very tingly, she looked up: 'If – and that's probably a big "if" – it's still valid, I needn't worry any more about collecting anthracite from Mill Cove.'

Sophy ventured, 'Because you could build a watermill, and grind corn, and use the profits from selling your flour to buy firewood?'

Charlie knew: 'Because, theoretically, Jilly can legally generate her own hydropower – and no gubber can stop her!'


## CHAPTER 65

A working telephone, again!

Fitfully slept because of that Milling Rights document, Jill badly wanted its status verified. After breakfast she called Mr Prendergast's practice; luckily, a cancelled appointment meant he could see her that afternoon.

Carol said, 'I'll come, and explore around town some more; as it's forecast warm, will you girls stay here?'

Coal-diving that morning, Heather reckoned, and sunbathing after lunch; Sophy nodded.

\*

'Didn't they work hard down at Mill Cove?' Several barrow trips, it had taken, to get all the sacks of anthracite home.

'Aye; but I don't reckon they'll sunbathe, the way they said they would; my money's on them baking a cake.'

'On such a hot day?'

Jill nodded; 'I've my reasons for saying.' Bumble fired fast; she dashboard-patted, 'Much happier since Arnold replaced the points and plugs, and so forth.'

Carol conceded, 'A Morris Traveller's good for round here: you get a better view.'

'Crucially, she can transport many pictures; plus, I've an idea for

380

location work: with this old bus parked head to wind, if I latch the rear doors open and stretch polythene between them – bingo, a painting shelter!

'Then start experimenting soon, Jilly: if you're going to emulate those Newlyn painters, whom you so admire, by working outdoors all year round, you need that method perfected before Autumn.'

*

'It'll be hot, making cakes,' Sophy sighed.

'Aha, well…'

'But you put out some ingredients, plus the kitchen scales!'

'Only as a decoy, Watson: I knew that they knew we wouldn't want to sun-loll all afternoon, so I had to drop a hint about what else we'd be up to. However…' Unpocketing a tape measure, Heather gesticulated gardenwards: 'Jilly's keen to generate pollution-free electricity but, even given that she owns the milling rights, a whacking great waterwheel might raise objections from the ruddy planning busybodies – and, made from wood or steel, it'd cost a packet. So, she needs to consult the hydro turbine people who advertise in Dad's energy magazine; and, as they'll need to know the technical details of her situation, the Water Engine remains need surveying: I thought we'd do her a surprise favour.'

'Lovely idea! I'll get my squared paper pad.'

*

Exiting the lane, Jill must brake hard for a humptibumping cyclist – one far too haughty to wave thank-you.

'My,' Carol murmured, 'what a charmer!'

'There goes the legendary Patsy Flange, to my amazement: normally Mama's posh motor wafts Modom everehwhah.'

'The ex-enemy, hopefully, if Heather's giving up showjumping…?'

'I shouldn't be so sure about–'

Twisting around, 'Well, the girl's evidently off to garden for somebody – there's a sickle strapped on her carrier… Oh; but she's turned down your lane.'

'As there's scant chance of her going gardening for *me*,' Jill chuckled, 'I reckon the girl's just after honeysuckle for her grandma's grave, and poor little Maisie Solva's: folk do reckon it's the sweetest, as grows along there.'

*

Perfect flying conditions as they smoothed down the Irish Sea, gently losing height. Below, ships veed symmetrical wakes, dot yachts sundawdled, and trawlers trailed white gull clouds.

She hummed beautifully evenly; and her new six-bladed propellers were theirs to keep, now they'd tested them in the cold, and in heat, both at her ultimate altitude, and right down on the deck. Meanwhile inside those nacelles purred more puissant turbines: countless trials they'd conducted on them, too, in so many different theatres of operation…

…But, at last, it was back to normal patrol duties for this crew.

\*

Patricia slashed at the gate's nettles: she *must* get in, *must* gain knowledge; *I* must *know my facts, so I can persuade him to exploit the place…*

*DAMNATION!* Nasty plants choked all the track beyond, and she was already puffed…

Then, *Eureka!* The dog Taggle being struck dumb, she could take Tracker without the alarm being raised; that great horse would barge this undergrowth like a tank. And so what if Clever Heather and Slow Flea hadn't gone swimming, and they spotted her…? Let them wonder, even fret over, what she was about: *If Grandfather agrees to my plan, they'll soon have damned good reason to worry!*

\*

Ochre being a permanent dye, a nickname now taunted Taggle: the trademark of a famous orangeade, it was even chalked on his kennel. Bronny'd said, 'Well at least it's fizzy, like you!'

He hadn't barked once since the flood, because of feeling so foolish: if he'd obeyed the girl and shut up, they'd have *both* heard that water coming; also, it was his barky overpulling on that rope which had hurtled him into its path.

After the County Show, there was always a lull; but, this afternoon, he was suffering *deadly* ennui: the day's tuition over, Bronwen was deckchair-flopped outside the office with Daphne…

…Studying the UCCA handbook of British university courses.

*Utterly inert − which is no damned use to me!* He humphed girlwards again, once more got ignored.

Then, the dog heard unexpected noises off: *I wonder who that is?* Having to know, away he crept.

\*

Getting the tack was easy: when Taggle came investigating, she knew exactly where his I'd-do-anything-for-one-of-those biscuits were kept.

As expected, bored Tracker came along obligingly: this was novel for him, not heading down the lane but hushly ambling across the spinney floor.

Patricia, dodging branches, thought, *Heavens, isn't he tall?* Nervous-making, too, because you knew he'd so much power. *So why's Slow Flea never afraid, riding him?*

*

Robert Hoaten had the afternoon off.

He'd collected his niece Jess from her morning riding lesson; they'd enjoyed a picnic lunch by the brook – she so proud of her new riding gear, she'd insisted on keeping it on. They'd soon head back to his cottage to change, and pick up swimming things; first, though, to visit Mother's grave.

Jolly blooming boiling in her riding hat and boots, 'If you don't mind, Uncle…?', she flopped on a newish and therefore lichen-free tombstone.

'Okay, Jess!'

Knowing it wasn't a plaything, she surely only *pretended* to press buttons on his work radio, which he'd left in her charge.

…So very hot, that polished granite slab: unusually, this little live wire shallowly drifted off.

Only shallowly, though: on hearing heavy footsteps she immediately sprang upright, 'Hello!'

But this wasn't typically fast-marching Uncle; it was someone slower, much bigger, and a lot older. Who peered at her oddly, almost accusingly: 'It's you!'

*Silly Billy! Who else would I be?* 'Yes. And it's *you!*' Nasty Patricia Flange's nasty grandpa.

Very worriedly, 'Why are you here?'

'I was riding; then he came for me. I've been asleep for… I'm not sure how long for, actually. Perhaps *ages.*' Then, to make it clear to this always-grumpy man that she wasn't doing anything wrong, 'Here is *exactly* where I'm supposed to be.'

Dropping to his knees, 'Is He here?'

'Of course! He's very close, but you can't see him. I'm sure you soon will, though.'

Amazingly red, his face now: 'Maisie, can you forgive me?'

*I'm not Maisie, so how can I?* 'No.' But that was a funny coincidence: this was the grave of Maisie Somebody, she'd half-noticed earlier.

Apparently through tears, although Heaven knew why because this was man was famously hard-hearted, 'Can He help me?'

*He's a coastguard; you obviously need a doctor.* 'I don't think so, but I'll get him…'

*

Biscuits – there had been a lot – all crunched, plus every equally essential remnant crumb, *Why did that plummy girl want to ride Tracker…?*

*

He saw through his eye-screwing pain a tall sun-surrounded human shape: 'JESUS!'

'Nigel Cranston?' Robert, reading the meaning of that furnacey complexion, and the man's expression, had shooed Jess a score of yards away: she shouldn't witness this.

'I killed Maisie Solva – there, I've confessed it, and I feel so much better. Now what happens?'

Picking up the VHF, Coastguard Hoaten was astonished to see that it was already switched on and, apparently, locked to Creampot Point's frequency. Stooping to hold the set close to the old man's mouth, deepening his voice but deadening its tone, pressing **TRANSMIT**, 'Confess, Nigel Cranston: *how* did you kill Maisie Solva?'

'Had a few lunchtime drinks; was coming home slowly; suddenly a pony was in front of me, in the mist. Didn't see the girl at first, because she was on its other side, opening the gate. Hardly grazed the animal, actually; but, I realised afterwards, it had lunged sideways to dodge my wing, and knocked her over: the child's head must have hit the steel post.'

'And…?' *How can the old bastard not show ANY emotion?*

'She was unconscious – so I thought. So I thought, she's not a witness; and the horse couldn't talk, could it? So…'

Before shakingly incandescent Robert Hoaten could strike the fellow, or strangle him, Frank Llangwm's voice was skrakking at Strength 5 all about the graveyard: 'ROB, BOY, WE HEARD ALL THAT

So sweatily he answered, 'Oh, bless you for that, mate! I'm in Talbenny Haven churchyard – and you'd better have an ambulance on its way here, before you tip off the coppers.'

*

*This is not right!* Tracker's gate gaped open; the big horse wasn't there.

He sniffed; aye, she'd been here, her and her fancy scent; and there went Tracker's spoor. He cocked an ear; and heard noises, far across the spinney. *Is there a connection?* Rather than race straight back for Bronwen, surely better to find out...

*

Good progress, by tea break time: maybe they'd get all the measuring done, *and* knock a cake up.

'So,' Sophy speedgulped, 'let's crack on!'

They were just back at it when the 'phone bell started clangalanging: 'I'd better answer it,' Heather sprinted, ''cos it might be Mum.'

Sophy stilled a moment, tingly all over.

*

Reaching the gate, Patsy realised what Tracker's height made possible... Having hopped down for the sickle, she saddle-stood and swiped: *Not so thundering easy now, planning those nice days out for Heather and Sophy, or inviting your Save-The-Whale friends to supper!* Dismounting, she dragged a storm-felled branch over and dropped it on the fallen cable end; loving the nasty pun, *So nobody will connect that, ahem, accident with me!*

*

Enter a certain terrier, normal noisiness restored.

Bronny sighed, 'I get the message, Tag: you've got your bark back. I'm truly pleased for you; although if you've discovered you've an off switch, I'd love to know where it is.'

'REFF, REFF, REFF, REFF, **REFF!**'

'...Oh, ALL RIGHT!' She efforted from her deckchair, 'Let's celebrate, with tea and BICCIES!'

*

Heather pelted back, 'Blow me if it didn't go dead before–'

As Patsy Flange kneed and kicked a baulking Tracker up beside The Drift, Sophy was shouting, 'Patricia, you mustn't go up there!'

385

So snootily hurled back, 'Get stuffed, Slow Flea: this is our family's land!' Trying her damnedest to nudge the horse forward, but he was having none of it.

Heather murmured, 'And the silly bitch doesn't think to wonder why.'

Sophy tried, 'Patricia, LISTEN! You're almost above the coal mine.'

Jeered back, 'I'm bidding it farewell. Because,' swivelling her crop like a Boche machine gun, 'all this is going: trees, hedges, everything… And then, BOOM! – GOODBYE HILLSIDE!'

Sophy, spine gone icy, 'What does she…?'

Patricia was really getting into her stride: 'You can forget your odd bucket of coal, and those piddling watermill rights: we're dynamiting this whole place to gubbery, blowing it all up for roadstone. And, yeahh, I tell you what, we'll treat your artyfarty friend to a nice new nameboard: Quarry Cottage! And, by God, she'd better like dust, because–'

He'd had enough: jumping his rump and dropping his neck, Tracker flung Patsy off forwards.

Seeing the posh girl sprawled base-over-apex in the grass, Heather said something blisteringly rude; smirking Sophy agreed with the sentiment, at least.

La Flange got up, red-blazing; brandishing her crop, she evidently intended to do something really ill-advised–

Sophy screamed, 'PATRICIA, **NO!**'

The horse went to spring away but, with a gigantic rumble from beneath, he was suddenly plunged forward – because both his front legs had disappeared into the ground.

*

Under Gramps's ancient monument of a van, Charlie cursed the sump plug: with each oil change, undoing it got harder. Before hefting the spanner, he checked either side: were those timbers propping the body securely…?

'Here goes!' He applied pressure steadily; gradually, the rusty crud surrendered its grip…

Donk! It finally dropped into the tin bowl, with gleamyblack liquid arcing after.

'Phew!' But then, 'What the…?'

A crescendo of creaks and groans had him scrabbling quickly out from under – but nothing was visibly amiss. Then, though, CRATABASH!, Aberdare's gate instantly became firewood, and the huge horse neared on the lad grumbling, pawing dirt, shaking his head.

*

Tracker, struggling, sank lower; Patsy dropped the crop and stumbled over to calm him.

'Good grief,' Heather bittered, 'she has some compassion.'

Shaking, Sophy sniffed, 'So must we.' Cupping hands, 'Patricia, you must GET RIGHT AWAY from there: can't you can see it ISN'T SAFE? We'll 'phone the stable, and the vet, and they'll–'

The girl turned a white face: 'You can't, because I just cut your 'phone line.'

Heather flamed, 'You did WHAT, you FU–?'

Another rumble, a smaller one; and, a few paces from where the poor earth-trapped horse sprawled, Patsy Flange disappeared feet-first into the ground.

# CHAPTER 66

'Heather, WHAT DO WE DO?'

'First see what's happened to Patsy?'

'Or go for help? There's always someone at the stables.'

'Sophy, your Mum's left her car keys here; you haven't ever tried driving, have you?'

'No; but I've an idea: come on…!'

*

Once tea was brewing, Tag normally just stared silently at the biccy tin; today he stayed in the yard, barking loonily. She stormed outside, 'WHAT IS IT?'

He fell silent…

Three short; three long; three short.

*

'We'll hornblow every five minutes?'

'Okay!' Flare settled onto the lawn, Heather gingerly unscrewed, as the instructions said to… 'If a 'plane comes, whoever's nearest pulls *this*, okay? Now, can you run round to The Drift?'

'I'm ducking through the culvert, 'cos it'll be faster; meanwhile, get me some rope. I'll try lowering a loop to Patsy: if I can't help her climb out, at least she shouldn't fall any further.'

*

Bumble was that hot, the glovebox could have baked a cake.

Jill said, 'Open all her windows, Carol; meanwhile, I'll nip for ice creams, to celebrate Mr P sounding so encouraging.'

As they enjoyed their treats, 'Today's impressions of Haverfordwest…?'

'Some lovely architecture, at the top of the town; and they all must have been really prosperous churches, once.'

'One of the wealthiest mediæval ports in Wales, this was.'

'Hmm; the Cotswold wool towns have grand churches from that era.'

'Anything else to report?'

'I dropped in to thank that Records Office lady for you; and I was curious, anyway, to know who'd enquired about The Drift.'

Concisely crunching her cornet's remains, 'Go on…'

'Unfortunately, they've confidentiality rules; but,' Carol twinkled, 'I did get a hint: his name rhymes with "pickle".'

Jill frowned, 'I can't think. Jekyll? Bicknall? Tickell…?'

Carol, ice cream finished, thought she'd just–

Suddenly, her friend was aboard and gunning Bumble up like a Formula One: 'In, QUICKLY!'

*

After a tricky hands-and-knees wade-through, Sophy emerged mud-haired to meet a familiar face: 'Taggle's turned up!'

'And, thank God, that's Bron's bike I can hear coming.'

'At least poor Tracker's calmer now.'

'Rope coming over; be so careful, sweetheart!'

'Here I go…'

But the dog barred her, baring growling teeth, while a from-nowhere Mogulus shot past both, scampered up, and plunged into the hole which had swallowed Patsy.

That was Bronny, now: 'Perhaps Tag can sense the ground still shifting, Sophy, and is afraid you'd come to grief too.'

The girl sniffled, 'But how can I–?'

Yowls, echoing from the thicket opposite the ford.

'HEY! That's useful proof for us: Patsy's fallen right into the mine. Bron, pass me some pruning tools through the culvert and–'

'No, Sophes,' Heather countermanded. 'You send us back a rope end, and we'll get Jill's cargo net draped across the hedge, for Bron to climb over.'

Situation no longer feeling helpless, as Sophy set to she called over her shoulder, 'Patsy? Tracker? You'll both be all right!'

*

Hearing heavy fast hooves, Mr Madoc met a lathery Aberdare, led him to the trough, and ensured the lung-burning horse at first drank slowly.

'Mister,' Charlie gasped, 'I honestly dunno why we's here! He literally burst his bloody gate, so I just flung a saddle on and jumped up – seeing as he was obviously off, with me or without.'

'There's trouble at Drift Cottage, boy; Bron's note doesn't say what. And, our thundering 'phone's off again! Go down now, Charlie, can you? And send SOS on the car horn if I'm needed immediately.'

*

The Skipper clicked everybody in: 'Usual approach confirmed, in from the West. We'll kink, I fancy, to give Tracker a little howdydoody.'

From the EO, with a certain intonation, 'Hey, Skip…?'

'Sure, boys, you can ride her in like freight car hobos – but don't forget those safety lines!'

The main bay door's hydraulics rissing it back, snatches of propwash baffed the men as they leaned keenly…

'Sweet Pembrokeshire air again, at last!'

'Do you dig *why* so sweet, today…? The Welsh folks are haymaking – look over there!'

*

Roaring coastwards, cylinder head and half-shafts highly stressed, Jill cursed herself for not realising sooner: 'She meant, rhyming with *a* pickle: in other words, bloody Nigel thundering Cranston – who's up to something, *of course*, and has got Patsy involved!'

As they catseye-hammered another corner, 'Jilly, STEADY ON!'

'It's fine, Carol,' racing change down to third, ''cos M.O.T. Arnold

389

completed his Morris Minor Pembrokeshirisation for me last week: MG carburettor, stiffer shockers, and much fatter radial tyres.'

Grabbing the over-door handle *and* the dash, 'Then perhaps Buzz might be a better nickname, now.'

*

Patsy was alive.

Sophy and Bronny had detected murmurs from the drippy darkness; and had heard, too, irregular gravelly splashes, proving Taggle right about how loose the whole hillside. Plus regular miaows, for Mogulus was – inexplicably – keeping the Flange girl company.

Charlie said, 'We need Mr Madoc.'

Bloodily scratched, the youngsters were well into the bramble-tangled saplings when he arrived.

Quietly they worked, giving Heather over the hedge the best chance of hearing an aircraft approaching; there were murmured just odd reassuring words for that invisible posh girl and the poor blameless horse.

Halting the three momentarily, Mr Madoc sent Taggle ahead into the undergrowth; all listened carefully to how those squeaky yaps sounded.

Bronny said, 'There are echoes, right the way in; the bore isn't completely collapsed.'

'No,' sighed the older; 'but the overburden's so unstable.' Giving her the Land Rover keys, 'While Charlie and I flog on here, you and Sophy fetch ladders and planks from the stable: they'll act as load spreaders, for going in from above. Oh, and bring the bowsaw and sledge hammer: maybe we've to do shoring, too.'

Hearing that concerned Heather, but it pleased her as well: having rubbed blown Aberdare down, she could occupy herself by hoiking out all Jill's planky pieces from the woodshed.

Good old Abbey, who was already doing his bit: hitched where he could see Tracker, he often called encouragingly to his American friend.

*

Gesticulating, 'It's padlocked!', in vain young Sophy tried heaving the gate off its hinges – vainly because they were the bolted, not the pinned, sort.

*Well,* Bronny thought, *this Landy has a front hitch for a reason...*

Low ratio *and* four-wheel-drive selected, she shouted, 'Stand well back, Sophes: the towrope might give!' Instinctively telling the vehicle, 'Easy back, now!', she gingerly reversed...

BADUMPH! The gate and both its rotten posts toppled together: the two girls shoving hard would have sufficed.

Who must, for a moment, lean on that hot bonnet and hoot helplessly with laughter, such was their relief.


Land Rover unloaded, Bronwen had Heather perch atop the hedge as artillery spotter while she from the garden flung over all the boards and—

''PLANE COMING, BRON!'

...**WHOOOOOF!** And that flare was vomiting dayglow orange smoke in steam loco quantities, so densely that its ghastly clouds looked sticky to the touch.

*

Because of cliff rescue exercises near Martin's Haven two coastguards were, unusually for a fine day, manning the Wooltack Point auxiliary lookout.

Immediately pelorus-aligning that garish pall, the men 'phoned a bearing in; unfortunately their colleagues at Creampot Point couldn't see it because of the ridge.

Only when Hugh, dutiful citizen, called from Hasguard where he was working on a roof, did his reported alignment with Roch Castle give a triangulation intersect...

*

As the aircraft appeared over the trees Bronny shouted, 'EVERYONE WAVE!' Then, eyes streaming, 'Help us; oh, **PLEASE HELP US!**'

*

'...That's the Madoc's stable, or somewhere bloody near!'

'Okay; get back on the blower to Wooltack, now – EXERCISE ABANDONED!'

*

The 'plane upped its nose, re-pitched propellers, and, engines hotly vooting, banked over into a very tight climbing turn: crossing the Coal

Road... curving out around Mill Cove... coming back in over Druid Pool Farm... disappearing again behind the spinney...

It reappeared higher; nevertheless Bron could make out some helmet men, frantic by a hatch, and then–

**'JESUS!'**

One of them had fallen out.

## Chapter 67

Horrified eyes watched him fall, not comprehending something detaching, uncoiling...

PHOPP!, a parachute.

Heather, suddenly frantic, 'Bron, WAVE HIM AWAY!'

'*WHAT?*'

'He mustn't land anywhere near the mine, *or* hit Jill's electricity wires!'

After doing a huge arm-beckon skywards, the Swansea girl sprinted for the meadow.

Sunlight struggling through that chemical concoction created a science fiction scene; orange terrier under orange lighting, Taggle fluoresced.

Still hawthorn hacking, Sophy cou-coughed, 'Tracker, we're *so* sorry it's gone weird.'

He seemed unconcerned.

*Or is he too weak to worry, now?*

Thank goodness, the man had spotted Bronny and understood. But Heather, watching him work his cords so hard to steer that way, still felt edgy about the whanging way he pendulumed about.

*

She kept beckoning, though squinting because now his alignment was the sun's, too.

As up there he pivoted a grassy heat-gust she heard, very faintly...

'What's the trouble, honey?'

*

A stone-arched adit entrance; but, 'Don't be fooled,' Mr Madoc warned. 'That masonry won't extend at all far; beyond, it's basically a bare tunnel through badly faulted rock.'

*

Landing at the run, he'd slickly unclicked even before the 'chute had sagged flat. Taking his horribly hot helmet off…

'SAM…! **SAM!**'

Un-hugging her with huge reluctance, he snapped into his radio, 'Down safe, Skipper, over!' Then, hurrying hand-in-hand with his always, his forever girl towards Jill's gate, 'Bronwen Landore, you didn't set off that crazily big flare just to get me home quicker, so…?'

*

Mr Madoc cursed very quietly: torchlight revealed only vapour wraiths. Ordering the youngsters back, 'I'm going a bit further in – but only to look, of course. Even loud noises could be bad news so, Charlie, relay my words to Sophy; and you, girl, will write everything down, hmm?'

She hugged, 'Please, *please* be careful, Grampy Madoc!'

From within, that sentiment echoed: 'Maoh-ohhh!'

## CHAPTER 68

Emergency services including Mines Rescue having been alerted, the 'plane stopped circling and departed.

'Now,' Sam said in the welcome peace, 'a more detailed status check, please.'

Bronny started, 'Patsy's gone dead quiet – um, I mean really quiet. We should assume she's lying in water; even if not, in there's cold enough for hypothermia. Also, loose stuff keeps coming down *and*,' she pointed, 'we can't start helping poor Tracks until she's safe.'

Mr Madoc took over, 'Patricia can't be reached via the adit: the old roof supports have failed. I know we can save the professionals time by getting crawling boards up to that fissure; and *maybe* when we reach it we can advise Patsy's situation to them before they arrive. Those boards'll also get us much closer to Tracker.'

*

Determined from the moment she'd come round to save face by escaping unaided, Patricia Flange had deliberately stayed silent. Grateful for the cat's company and warmth while she'd lain still, she smirked to hear that praise for his doggedly encouraging her; actually, those Mogulus miaows now voiced doubts about her trying to climb out.

But she was managing to, and actually everyone's fretting was *so stupid*: stuff wasn't dropping of its own accord, but only when she dislodged it.

And this wasn't a fissure, but obviously something human-built: an air shaft? *Meaning that Grandfather could get to this mine's coal, despite the entrance having collapsed – and damn anyone else!*

It was slow climbing, inevitably: she ached badly from the fall, and this damp clay was greasy.

*

Sam worked delicately, wearing a tether; Mr Madoc, sat far above, was anchorman. Sophy and Charlie tied the planks onto Sam's rope; Bronny co-ordinated, radio belt-clipped ready in case of a sudden problem. Heather's job, assisting Taggle, was listening at the adit entrance for indications of trouble.

With one spreader now laid sideways below the hole and another above, Sam had Mr Madoc haul the longest metal ladder into position.

Sophy said, 'I should go and take a look.'

Heather agreed, 'She's by far the lightest.'

*

*I'm damned if Slow Flea will be a bloody hero again!* Seeing the ladder pulled across up there, Patricia put a slithery shift on: she MUST reach the top under her own steam, and so what if she sent loose bits showering back down?

*

Knowing from working with Hugh how aluminium creaked, those tensemetal noises didn't bother Sophy as she prepared to shuffle out along, asking Mr Madoc to slightly slacken the tether.

*

Patsy could just hear overimaginative Heather clucking away about that extra splashing below: *Silly bint!*

Then she realised, *Dammit, Slow Flea's on her way across already!*

Scrabbling with now furious determination, she was soon very nearly there.

*

As instructed, Sophy only looked ahead, crossing that void: the others were watching for the ground about her shifting. Only when she'd reached the middle – and had prepared herself for a possibly nasty sight – should she look down.

*

Now, not nice movement beneath Patsy's feet; so, making an ultimate drive upwards…

*

They saw a filthy arm suddenly grab; instantly the ladder turned turtle, pitching Sophy off.

Hearing that horrid choking, Bronny screambellowed to Mr Madoc, 'LET GO, YOU MUST **LET GO**!'

He did; and the child's wildly-kicking feet disappeared.

Momentarily from the hole, muffled squeals…

Then, just the sound of soil tumbling.

## Chapter 69

'SOPHY!' Charlie sprinted up those planks and, oblivious of every-body's shouts of '**DON'T!**', launched himself down the hole after her.

Bronny catted cautiously after him, jabbing buttons: 'MAYDAY…!'

Having retrieved the tip-skewed ladder Sam repositioned it, crept out, and peered, pointing his torch: 'CHARLIE?'

Heather prayed, fists clenched…

The American phewed, 'Hey, everyone: he's fine, and so's Sophy; from what they're saying both're real covered in dirt, though. Patsy's broken her leg, they think – she certainly needs stretchering out.'

Mr Madoc warned, 'You *can't* go hauling her up, Sam: it's TOO RISKY.'

Taking the radio from his beloved Bronny, as Sam began a long discussion a buffling was already sounding from northwards.

Bronny crept a bit closer to Tracker along the lower board: 'It's going to be ruddy noisy, boy: you must be brave!'

With his pained eyes he was, she saw, willing everyone safe deliverance.

Soon a blade-whirling yellow metal belly, strobes aflash, was hovering directly overhead. A helmet man cabled down; he seeing into the hole better than Sam, the two discussed possibilities radio to radio.

*

A blue and white Panda car guarded Mill Lane; as well-scorched brakes were still arriving them, window-leaning Carol roared ahead to the policewoman, 'I'M THE MOTHER!'

Whipping away the traffic cone, 'Carry on, Mrs Flange!'

*

Charlie lashed Patricia onto that stretcher which Sam and the helmet man had patiently fiddled down; wire-hoisted carefully up past the American she was then, without warning, terrifyingly airborne – and, hating flying at the best of times, the girl oh-so profusely peed her jeans, with EVERYBODY watching, and cameras rolling, too.

Soon she lay damply shame-sobbing in a deedahing ambulance; gentle-worded Jill held her pain-clenched hand as – the artist couldn't help smiling inside – they scorched the tarmac *back* to Haverfordwest, *also* because of Patsy Bloody Flange.

*

After rescuing Patsy, the helicopter landed and shut its engines down: firemen who'd bridged the sunken ground with one of their huge ladders and were preparing ropes for the youngsters had demanded quiet.

Both of them were so very well cheered as they ochrely scrambled out, Mogulus head-popping from Sophy's shirt just in time to see Carol Fossway almost crush Charlie Solva flat with admiration. They accepted tea and biscuits but insisted, though filthy, 'We're NOT going ANYWHERE 'til Tracker's been freed!'

The newly-arrived Mines Rescue team made their assessment.

The worst unknown was the possibility of more subsidence, after that flood: might there be a great washed-out void just beneath the surface? If so, men working to free the animal would be risking a sudden fall to an unknown depth, quite possibly with the creature landing on top of them.

First, anyway, to try and prevent Tracker's situation worsening.

They eased planks under his back legs: now they shouldn't sink in, when taking extra weight; and any way the team could envisage of extricating his forelegs would inevitably tip his body backwards.

When the Mines men suggested using the helicopter to lift the horse, Charlie and Sophy objected: the low-hovering Sea King's blade-beat had sent soil and pebbles showering; and much splashing, they'd heard, from deeper within. 'Also,' said Charlie, 'I believe the ground was shifting nearby.'

Sophy didn't care how expert, these men: 'I *know* it was: the cat's look said so.'

'MAO-WOW!', Mogulus concurred, for Sophy's sake just as worried about the horse.

Their leader pacified, 'We're all for heeding animals: many a time pit ponies have saved–'

'Then you need to know,' Bronny butted, 'that Aberdare's having a bloody funny spell. He's been tied up in Jill's garden all afternoon, quite placid, in sight of Tracker, until…'

'Well?'

'Just now he bust his tether, lay down, and began rolling from one side to the other, then back again. He's not itchy, 'cos he isn't wriggling with his feet in the air; and, anycase, that sort of carry-on is pretty ruddy unusual for such a heavy horse, eh, Mr Madoc?'

From just behind whom, a grumble; and there stood the selfsame horse – having found his way round via the spinney, and negotiated a track filled with fire engines, Land Rovers, squad cars…

*Where have I seen that particular look of Aberdare's before…?* 'The Sands!'

Charlie frowned, 'What about them, Sophy?'

Eyes fire-bright, 'You remember us freeing that net by unpeeling it? This might sound cranky, but surely Aberdare's suggesting that we extricate Tracker by gently loosening his front legs and then *rolling him over*, d'you see? That can't wrongly bend his spine, *or* make his back legs sink!'

'Hey, yes,' a fireman conceded, 'because as the slope's already canting him over, gravity would be working with us.'

'Mind,' a Mines man's cautioning finger rose, 'we don't want the poor gubber rolling out unchecked, or he could go a-tumbling down, and–'

Through thick tobacco smoke Mr Madoc spoke: 'We'll build a hay bale crash mat for the boy to fetch against. And Aberdare shall do the pulling: it's his idea, isn't it, and that one's his best mate, so he'll understand exactly what to do – and when and how to make his moves, too.'

'And I'll go close up beside Tracker to keep him company all the while, okay…?'

Carson Lightfoot.

# In case you were wondering...

That 1980 holiday was my first visit to Drift Cottage; now, it is my home. Indeed I am writing these words sitting at the very same kitchen table where I breakfasted those many years ago – always tingling with anticipation whether I chatted with Jilly, sang to Puss, or bantered plans with Heather. Pinned to my cardigan, a tortoiseshell cat enamel brooch; around my neck, a fine chain of Welsh gold with a heart-shaped anthracite pendant.

A Drift Cottage no longer jet-buzzed, for the airbase closed long ago.

Those postcards with their delightful sketches certainly did inspire Mummy; that autumn Jilly sent us copies of her best photographs, and each evoked more memories from me. When Mum and I came down to Pembrokeshire subsequently, she was able to gain much extra knowledge from conversations with Heather, and Bronny, and our many friends – partly because once too much time has elapsed for a child to be punished for a transgression, they are prepared to talk about it freely! My mother was also able to explore this beautiful coastline and understand the important part it played in what transpired – and, being one of them, to start feeling the strong loyalty it secures from those who fall in love with it.

Mummy wrote loads of notes, we were all aware of that; but then other things and other people – especially my stepfather, stepsister, adopted sister, and half-brothers – came to occupy her time, and she had to set the book idea aside... permanently, it seemed.

Three summers ago, however, Mummy learned about word processing while collaborating on a Women's Institute local history project. Such was her enthusiasm, for her birthday Charlie and I bought her a desktop computer, on which she could write up her own research notes: how delighted she was – and how impressed our children were!

I wish I had known that the following winter she had dusted off the old photo albums, got her notebooks down from the attic, and planned *Sophy's Adventures with Tracker*, a "more realistic" adaptation of the original story concept, in quite some detail, even writing various scenes in full. Sadly, she never got round to showing me the resulting document and asking if I'd check it before she wrote any more; plainly, though, from the accompanying notes which I found after she died, that is what she'd intended to do "very soon".

No: Fate did not allow dear Mum enough time on our beautiful Earth to complete this project. Or many others, either: she always had too much to do – but then, don't we all?

Heth and Bron having helped fill the gaps in Mummy's story, I had planned to complete it – but when the moment came, I couldn't bear to make any changes to the words she had written, for fear of diluting that spiritual voice within: her manuscript was, as it were, perfectly incomplete.

But so many people said, quite rightly, that it had been such an amazing episode in our young lives, that "Summer Break", that we who had been there should set the story down for others to enjoy; so – what to do?

While wonderful Alice Williams had gone long before, I knew that she had inspired many writers; one local author in particular came to mind, and he it is who has created this book, this novel indeed, which is not based on Mummy's story idea at all. It is, rather, the result of him listening at length to Charlie and we three girls-as-were spiritedly reminiscing about the many remarkable events which occurred during that now distant summer, and then contriving a distillation.

I like to think that Mummy and Alice would approve of *A Summer Break* as wholeheartedly as do I – for all that Chris's choice of writing voice at first surprised me.

The past is the past: one could never have brought this story up to date. For had mobile phones, computers, and so forth existed in those long-ago days, the outcomes of many incidents would have been so different – indeed, nothing would have happened in the same way.

It shouldn't matter to anyone that this is a tale from more than a generation ago, provided that its characters seem real, and the reader can believe in how the people and animals – especially the people and the horses – get on with each other. True, what is written can't exactly describe how things actually were: particularly, we never knew what any animal was thinking; but I can't imagine anyone getting closer, necessarily using much imagination, to the feeling of being there at the time, sharing those experiences with other so sentient creatures. I state this confidently because they were many, the fireside evenings that my sisters, Charlie, and I spent reliving that special summer, while Chris's pencil and paper quietly listened – and, all about us, those dear horses and Mogulus, Taggle, and Vincenza looked down from their portraits, each so silently wise…

…And all continuously checking, we jointly had the feeling – not so much that we'd got all our facts right, but that we'd *told the story* as best we could!

Portraits, by the way, signed "Ribblesdale" but painted by a certain Jill Hoaten.


To those of you who feel that the tale doesn't go far enough, and that you **must** know more about what happened to Chris's characters – well, one of my earlier sentences has told you quite a lot, and my signature tells you some more…

What's more, Chris is now working on another Pembrokeshire-based story – thus allowing me to hand the narrative bâton to somebody you've briefly met in this one. Of course I may not say who they are, so you shall just have to speculate; nevertheless, rest assured that you haven't heard the last of quite a few of us!

In the meantime, you should know that dear Hannah recovered completely; also, I'd better tell you that learning what her grandfather had done transformed Patricia Flange instantaneously: she so utterly rejected his credo that, ever since, it's been the honest truth that you couldn't meet a nicer person…

Who used some of her inheritance from Nigel Cranston to pay for Tracker to be flown home, and was there alongside Carson Lightfoot to witness that moment of infinite joy when Listens Well and his horse were reunited…

Patsy, who is still in the United States as I write – and will soon be celebrating thirty-two years of marriage to Carson!


If you know the county of Pembrokeshire, I hope that the setting of this story seemed correct and felt brightly, wildly, and earthily familiar; if you haven't visited our beautiful part of the world – and met its proud and rugged inhabitants – perhaps you will be inspired to.

Do come down to walk, cycle, swim, or sail – and however you go about, quietly for Nature's sake, be sure to EXPLORE! Here's hoping that you will make new friends, cats and dogs included: we are an affable lot, on the whole, and good companionship is priceless.

Last of all, to be sure you remember: if you either love riding or you think you might like riding and are game to try it, may you meet and get to know here horses as trustworthy, helpful, and deeply caring as were Tracker, Aberdare, Arrow, Lamorna, and Slipstream – and, RIDING SAFELY, may you embark on your own so memorable adventures.

With my very, very best wishes,

S. S.

*The End*

Born in Oxfordshire, brought up in Gloucestershire, Christopher Jessop graduated from University College Swansea (as it then was) in 1980.

His home is in Pembrokeshire, just a short walk from the Saint Brides Bay coastline.

Chris contends that Living By The Sea is a full-time occupation, considering that his surroundings inspire his fiction writing, his poetry, his art, and his work promoting renewable energy; were he forced to confess a hobby, he would plump for beachcombing.

You are very welcome to visit the website

www.asummerbreak.co.uk

Via it you can get in touch with Christopher Jessop, the author of

### *A Summer Break*

He welcomes questions or comments from
individuals or reading groups.

In the website's Gallery section you will find some of the illustrations
Chris created for this book, and examples of his photographs, paintings
and drawings…

Please note: Chris doesn't believe in posting regular reports describing
how he is getting on with his writing: creating good fiction is a slow and
painstaking procedure, and time spent updating website entries is time
lost to the true creative process – i.e. the Pencil & Paper Department!

0 800 887766 AA

GU1 6BL
Auto check
Unit 8-10.